PRISONER OF LOVE

Cole parted the curtains. Gwin was lying on her side, a sheet pulled up, revealing only the slim straps of a chemise. Her long-lashed eyes glimmered mischievously. "What are you going to do now? Search me for weapons?"

Cole took the handcuffs from his pocket.

She jerked back. "Hey! What's this? Where do you think I'm going to go in my underclothes?"

"I shudder to think."

"I can't believe this! How am I supposed to sleep all tied up?"

Her sheet had slipped down, baring cleavage. That was all his imagination needed. He gritted his teeth and tried counting to ten silently.

"Fresh and utterly delightful . . . The humor and tender emotion weaving the characters and the story together will touch readers' hearts."

—Kari Sutherland

A Touch of Camelot

⚐ DONNA GROVE ⚑

HarperPaperbacks
A Division of HarperCollinsPublishers

If you purchased this book without a cover, you should be aware that this book is stolen property. It was reported as "unsold and destroyed" to the publisher and neither the author nor the publisher has received any payment for this "stripped book."

This is a work of fiction. The characters, incidents, and dialogues are products of the author's imagination and are not to be construed as real. Any resemblance to actual events or persons, living or dead, is entirely coincidental.

HarperPaperbacks   *A Division of* HarperCollins*Publishers*
10 East 53rd Street, New York, N.Y. 10022

Copyright © 1994 by Donna Grove
All rights reserved. No part of this book may be used or reproduced in any manner whatsoever without written permission of the publisher, except in the case of brief quotations embodied in critical articles and reviews. For information address HarperCollins*Publishers*, 10 East 53rd Street, New York, N.Y. 10022.

Cover illustration by Jacqueline Goldstein

First printing: September 1994

Printed in the United States of America

HarperPaperbacks, HarperMonogram, and colophon are trademarks of HarperCollins*Publishers*

❖ 10 9 8 7 6 5 4 3 2 1

To my husband, who continues to put up with me,
and my sons, who know what it is to lose
their mother to a computer.

Prologue

Abilene, Kansas, June 1871

"Ladies and gents, are you bothered by the rheumatism? Consumption? Night sweats? Cold feet? Are you haunted by headaches? Back pains? A sick and nervous stomach? I have in my hand the answer to your prayers!"

The gentleman on the makeshift stage was dressed all in white. His hair, as white as his suit, was swept back into a pompadour. He stood in relief against the side of a tall wagon, upon which was painted in bright red calligraphic letters: *Professor Throckmorton's Restorative Cordial and Blood Renovator.*

Cole Shepherd might have been only sixteen years old and from a backwater Kansas town nobody had ever heard of, but he sure wasn't stupid. He had already pegged the "professor" as a fast-talking charlatan. Still, the fellow was a prime example of the consummate showman, and until a few moments ago, even Cole hadn't been able to tear his eyes from the stage.

At this particular moment, however, Cole's undivided attention was reserved for an adolescent boy standing no more than three yards away in the crowd. Like the scores of rapt listeners around him, the kid now appeared to be listening to the pitchman onstage, but only seconds before...

Cole would have given just about anything to get those last thirty seconds back. After all, it might have been one of the most important moments in his entire life, but it had happened so fast, Cole wasn't even sure he could trust his own eyes.

The kid just stood there, innocent as a newborn babe, his hands tucked idly into the pockets of an oversized duster. A dark blue engineer's cap was pulled low on his head, hiding the color of his hair, but Cole judged his height and weight and guessed him to be a scrawny thirteen.

"... and so, it is only by the grace of God and Professor Throckmorton's Restorative Cordial and Blood Renovator that my own lovely wife, Emmaline, stands glowing and healthy before you today!"

Cole's gaze was drawn back to the stage. The "professor" wasn't lying about one thing, anyway. The lovely Emmaline Throckmorton was certainly that and more. Her complexion was pale and flawless, her lips full, her eyes clear, shining emeralds, but it wasn't even this exceptional face that captured the attention of both males and females alike. It was her hair, hair the color of a flaming summer sunset and tamed only by a demure black ribbon cinched at the crown of her head. That hair cascaded in a thick waterfall of curls almost to her waist.

Earlier, she had charmed the crowd with a singing voice as sweet as that of the legendary Jenny Lind. Then she had amazed them all with a daring exhibition of pistol marksmanship, neatly flicking the ashes from a cigar Throckmorton held clenched between his teeth at the opposite end of the stage.

Now, Cole tore his eyes from the woman and glanced back at the kid, who was . . . gone. Cole whipped his dark head around, scanning the crowd anxiously. Damn! Now, where the devil . . . ?

Cole felt a light, persistent tapping on his knee and looked down to see a redheaded boy in knickerbockers, not more than three or four years of age. "It's fwee," he said solemnly, proffering a pamphlet.

Cole took the pamphlet, noting briefly that its front featured a lithograph of the "professor" displaying a bottle of his miracle elixir. It was just as he was slipping the pamphlet into his shirt pocket that he caught sight of that familiar engineer's cap peeking in and out of the throng just ahead.

Cole pushed past a matronly woman and a few cowboys, shadowing the boy's movements. When he reached the edge of the group, he stopped, his eyes glued to the kid, who was once again in full view. His heart began to pound as the kid sidled along the outer perimeter of the crowd, mingling into its fringes with studied expertise.

Then it happened again.

The kid stumbled up against a well-dressed gentleman. His hand snaked out. Smooth as silk, slick and quick as sin, it dipped in and out of the man's side coat pocket. There was a flash of gold just before the kid's fist vanished once again into his own coat pocket. The gentleman who had just been fleeced turned to glare at the boy, who proceeded to mutter a humble apology. This time there was no room for doubt. Cole was witnessing a bona fide pickpocket right in the act!

Cole's sense of justice was inflamed. His long-suppressed appetite for adventure was kindled. He could feel his muscles tensing, his heart gearing up for double duty.

Back in his hometown of Beaver Creek, Cole's father, a general merchant by trade, was also that small settlement's only peace officer. Unfortunately, it was rare that he was called upon to draw his gun. Except for an occasional saloon brawl, sleepy Beaver Creek was probably the most crime-free settlement west of the Mississippi.

This was just fine and dandy for most of the town's residents, but for Cole, who, when not pursuing his studies or working in his father's store, could unerringly be found with his nose buried in the latest issue of *Police Gazette*, this rather dull state of affairs had always proved to be a disappointment. This was because, for as long as he could remember, Cole had wanted nothing more than to become a Pinkerton detective.

" . . . and I could recount dozens, no, hundreds, ladies and gents, *hundreds*, of equally astounding testimonials, but *seeing is believing!*"

The pickpocket now turned his head to the right, scanning the crowd to make sure he wasn't being observed, then to the left, and it was then that his eyes met with Cole's incredulous gaze. An understanding, total and complete, struck between them like a lightning bolt. The boy knew he had been discovered, but, to Cole's grudging admiration, he didn't panic. He just turned very casually and started to stroll away.

"For today only, I am offering two bottles for the low, low price of one! Try it for yourself and *feel* the results!"

The boy moved faster, weaving through the milling crowd, up Texas Street toward the center of town. In another few seconds, he would be out of sight and home free. Cole set out after him.

The main street, lined with wooden false-fronts and two-story brick buildings, bustled with out-of-towners. Cole pushed through the foot traffic, all of which seemed to be moving against him. The boy, who was much smaller and narrower in the shoulders than Cole, was having an easier time negotiating the human obstacle course.

Strains of tinny piano music fell on Cole's ears as he passed the swinging batwing doors of a dance hall, but he barely heard it. He had been overtaken with a sudden, exhilarating vision of himself apprehending the criminal singlehandedly, his name on the front page of the *Abilene Chronicle*, Allan Pinkerton wiring his pa from Chicago: "Whenever that young man of yours is ready, you send him to me. He's Pinkerton material!"

Knowing that he was never going to catch the little pilferer if he kept to the boardwalk, Cole sidestepped and skirted along the edges of the street. The boy, however, chose this moment to fling an apprehensive glance over his shoulder. Seeing that Cole was gaining steadily, he jumped down off the boardwalk and broke into a run.

"Hey, you! Wait!" Cole cried out, frustrated.

Dirt flew out in divots from beneath the kid's boots as he rounded the corner of a livery and shot into the narrow alley that separated it from the bathhouse next door.

Cole picked up his own pace, rounding the same corner in time to catch sight of the kid's coattails disappearing around the back of the bathhouse. Cole knew he was bigger and faster than the boy. As long as he didn't lose the trail, it was only a matter of time until he caught up with him.

Cole emerged out into an open backyard to see the boy darting toward the cattle pens at the edge of town. By the time he closed the distance between them, the kid was already scrambling up over one of the stock pen fences. Inside the pen, hundreds of longhorns milled about aimlessly, shoulder to shoulder, hoof to hoof. The air was pungent, a mildly offensive combination of cowhides and manure.

Got you now, you little crook, Cole thought eagerly, gripping the top slat of the fence and pulling himself up.

From his new vantage point, Cole could see the busy staging area where cattle cars lined up on the tracks. Some men poked cows single file up a ramp to fill one of the cars, but they were much too far away to even notice the drama that was being played out between Cole and his pickpocket. The kid was negotiating a thready route toward the opposite end of the pen, scuttling sideways between bawling cattle.

Cole dropped to his feet and started clearing a clumsy path of his own. "Hey, kid! Give it up!"

The boy didn't even look around but continued pushing through the dense bovine forest, nearing the far end. Cole felt his bootheel sink into what could only be a hefty cow patty and gritted his teeth. Enough was enough. This scenario was rapidly boiling down to a matter of personal pride. If he couldn't catch one lousy pickpocket, what business had he aspiring to the future rank of Pinkerton operative?

The kid reached the opposite fence and scaled it easily, fleeing in the direction of still more cattle pens behind the train depot. Cole cleared the fence seconds later and dashed after his escaping little thief with inflamed determination. Although they garnered a few stares from some amused cowpunchers as they streaked past the depot, none were apparently curious enough to follow.

The kid was climbing the fence of another pen, this one temporarily empty, and Cole grinned to himself. *Ha! I've got him for sure now!* He scaled the fence and hit the ground running, now only seconds behind his half-pint nemesis. Close, closer.

The split tails of the black linen duster flapped in the wind as the kid tried in vain to pull ahead. Cole could hear his labored breathing and the sounds of his boots thudding dirt.

The kid reached the corner of the pen and whirled around, his arms raised as if prepared to take a stand and fight. But that was ridiculous. Cole was nearly twice his size.

Cole skidded to a stop, breathing hard. Only a water trough separated them now. "Let's have the watch. I saw you take it."

The kid didn't answer. He threw a quick look around, apparently trying to figure a way out of his predicament. But he was cornered. And knew it. He faced Cole again, panting.

"Come on," Cole said, taking a step in his direction. "Just give it up and come with me. I won't hurt you."

The kid's voice was high and bright, like a small child's. "Why don'tcha come on and get it?" Then he darted to the right, and Cole started after him.

By the time Cole realized it was a feint, he was already three steps gone. The kid broke off and went left instead, moving for the fence.

"No you don't, damn it!" Cole yelled, swiveling wildly back to the left. He leaped in a desperate attempt to pull the kid down before he could get to the fence, but the feat was badly mistimed. His shins slammed into the side of the water trough.

With a cry of bone-shattering pain, Cole catapulted forward, missing the kid by a good foot and knocking the heavy trough over onto its side. Gallons of water sloshed out. He just missed gashing his forehead on a corner of the trough as he went down with it, soaking himself in a sea of mud and water.

A TOUCH OF CAMELOT

By now the kid had reached the fence and was getting away. Cole glared at those dusty boots. They were just barely out of reach, climbing first one slat, then the next. Cole scrambled to his feet and lunged, reaching out just in time to snag the kid's pant leg.

Like a tiger scenting blood, he felt victory tantalizingly close. He held on tight, refusing to let go even as the boy kicked back at his face. *"Give it up!"* Cole yelled, *"Give it up now, and it'll go easier on you!"*

Kicking out again, the kid narrowly missed Cole's cheekbone. Cole ducked his head and yanked hard, bringing the boy down on top of him. They collapsed together into the slick mud, Cole landing on his back as he wrapped triumphant arms around his captive's middle.

The boy wasn't that strong, but he sure did have a lot of spunk. Cole fought to keep a grip as his new catch kicked and squealed, flailing like an upended beetle trying to right itself.

The contents of the kid's pockets spilled out over the ground: an astonishing collection of coins, bills, watches, and playing cards. Many of those cards scattered merrily to the prairie wind as the two of them continued to grapple, splattered from head to toe with mud. Cole howled a curse as he felt teeth sink into the flesh of his forearm, but he didn't let go.

He rolled over instead, yanking his arm free and flipping his adversary onto his back. They had already lost their hats in the scuffle, and Cole saw thick, carrot-red curls fashioned into a crude bowl cut. It looked soft and glossy, and it was just about the time Cole thought he had never seen hair quite like that on a boy that his palm swiped across the kid's chest and he stopped dead to discover that he wasn't wrestling with a boy at all!

Cole's jaw unhinged and he froze. They both froze, their eyes locked. "Oh my God," Cole gasped.

Cole had never felt a girl's breast. He had dreamed about it a few times, and of course, he had contemplated it quite a lot in his spare time. There were a few girls in Beaver Creek who probably wouldn't have minded if Cole came courting, but none of them were exactly the type that a fellow would rightly consider grabbing at. Besides, marriage was the last thing on Cole's mind. A Pinkerton operative didn't have time for a wife and a homestead. No, Cole had finally been forced to reach the gloomy conclusion that breasts were not likely to play any large part in his foreseeable future.

But now his moment had arrived! And he wasn't quite sure what to do about it. His hand, though, had taken on a life of its own and refused to budge. *Get your hand off her bosom, Cole!* his conscience screamed. *Give it up now, and it'll go easier on you!*

He forced his mouth open again, his tongue thick as tar. "You're a girl—"

Whatever hit him hit him from behind, and hit him hard. Bright pain exploded behind his eyes. Stunned, Cole dropped to the ground, now only vaguely aware of the boy—*the girl*—he reminded himself dazedly—*the breast*—wiggling out from under his limp right arm. Then he heard disembodied voices hovering somewhere above as the ground seemed to swell and slant beneath him.

"You didn't have to hit him so hard, Clell! What if you really hurt him?"

"Aww, he'll wake up with a goose egg, that's all. Besides, I had to hit him. It looked like he was gonna try something."

"He wasn't gonna try anything! I'd have gotten away!"

There was a burst of male laughter. "Oh sure, Gwinnie!"

"Shut up, Clell! It isn't funny!"

"Come on, get your stuff, and let's get out of here. Silas is gonna have a fit. We'll have to get you out of town right away. Damn! And the pickings were so good! Suckers around every corner!"

The voices faded. Cole, who was still so stunned he couldn't seem to move or even force his eyes open, continued to lie helpless. His head thrummed hot and painful. It felt wet. He hoped it was mud but was pretty sure it was blood. *Gonna die right here,* he thought miserably. Pinkerton material indeed.

Part One

1

San Francisco, California, June 1879

"Brothers and sisters! Do you believe?"

The assent of the crowd rose like the swell of a cresting wave. "We believe! Yes! Yes! We belieeeve!"

It was hot and stuffy inside the old circus tent. Tonight, it was packed full of believers and curiosity-seekers alike. Brother Christian put on a show that might have convinced Old Scratch himself to turn over a new leaf. Sister Guinevere Pierce, daughter of God, knelt sweating and uncomfortable at the head of a line formed before the raised stage, her hands clasped in prayer below her chin.

"I say, brothers and sisters, *do you believe?*"

The crowd was emphatic. *"Yes! Yes! Lord yes! We believe! We belieeeve!"* There were moans and shouts, stomps and whistles, and even some weeping coming from the crowded back rows.

"Remember Matthew eight! Jesus' words to the woman from Capernaum. 'Your faith has made you well!'"

Arthur, Gwin's eleven-year-old brother, stood next to her, looking convincingly pitiful in an old pair of patched, high-waisted denim overalls and teetering on homemade crutches. He nudged her shoulder and whispered between clenched teeth, "That's from chapter *nine*, not *eight!*"

Gwin winced. Arthur was right. Silas was misquoting again. The crowd, of course, either failed to notice or didn't mind. Such was the phenomenal hold Silas Pierce wielded over his audiences. He was a gifted speaker, a man who perhaps had never quite grown up himself. Even as a child, Gwin had known what it was about Silas Pierce that so enticed his listeners. When he was onstage, he didn't just pretend to believe, he *believed*, and that unwavering faith seemed to emanate from his very pores. It scattered into the crowd and caught like sparks on a dry prairie.

Silas had been misquoting all evening, which was uncommonly sloppy of him. He was distracted. Only part of him was believing, and Gwin knew instinctively that something was wrong.

Earlier this afternoon, he had disappeared into the city, returning to camp only in the nick of time to don his black broadcloth suit and emerge onto the platform. This was not like him. He always took a few minutes to prepare himself mentally for an appearance. This was his way, and it, unlike the products he sold—be it miracle elixirs, hair tonics, magic pills, or salvation—had never changed.

Tonight he had gone on without any preparation whatsoever, and Gwin found this unnerving. After all, this might have been the largest gathering they had ever played to. San Francisco was a big town, and Brother Christian was beginning to get a big reputation. No longer did they have to hustle to attract new followers; new followers were ready and waiting in each town they came to. Gwin and Clell now traveled only two days ahead of the rest of the group, posting signs on telegraph poles to advertise Brother Christian's Sinbusting Tent Revival. This was all it took. The crowds came out. And the money poured in.

Silas's deep voice resonated throughout the tent. "Your faith will heal you! Brothers and sisters, *do you believe?*"

As the crowd screamed and moaned its undying faith, Gwin waited patiently for her cue. There were times when she wondered what it might have been like to be raised in a normal family, to have lived in a house rather than in the back of a rambling medicine wagon. She wondered what it would have been like to be raised by normal parents with respectable occupations.

Her stepfather, Silas, and her late mother, Emmaline, had preferred to call themselves entertainers. Gwin thought that the euphemism might have been stretching it a bit. Even among those unorthodox members of society known as show people, Gwin was aware that her parents had been, well, rather unique.

She tried not to brood too much over the past. She only wondered about such things during her most quiet and sentimental moments, and she never would have spoken of them aloud. She loved Silas. He had raised her the best way he knew how, and, rascal or not, he was, in every sense of the word that meant anything to the heart, her father.

Besides, she figured that in many ways she was really quite lucky. At the ripe old age of twenty-two, she might not have learned much about cooking or sewing or hosting a tea party, but she could read and write and articulate well enough to impersonate a gentle-born lady. More importantly, she could run a scam, pick a lock, shoot a bull's-eye, and blind-shuffle a deck of cards. Those were skills that were not easy to come by in conventional society; skills that a practical young woman such as herself knew how to put to good use.

Silas now addressed her, breaking into her thoughts. "Speak your name, little sister!"

Gwin looked up to meet her stepfather's ice-blue gaze, the peculiar coloring she had inherited, although not exactly from him. Otherwise, no soul would have guessed that they were related. The blazing red of her hair, the pale cast of her complexion, the shape of her nose and her mouth she had taken from her mother, Emmaline.

"My name is Susannah! My brother and I have come all the way from Laramie!" Gwin's voice was convincingly tremulous.

"You've traveled to this place to be one with the Lord God Jehovah! I can see that, my sister! Do you believe?"

Gwin nodded vehemently. "I believe, Brother Christian!"

Silas lifted his dark head. His blond hair was now dyed midnight-black, but it was beginning to thin on top. Indeed, these days he sported a rapidly expanding patch of scalp that not even Professor Throckmorton's Incredible Hair Tonic seemed able to cure. Silas closed his eyes and touched his forehead as if listening to the exhortations of angels. The crowd hushed.

"But it is not you who is to be healed this night, is it, Sister Susannah?" Silas opened his eyes and, fixing his fevered gaze upon Arthur, cupped the child's face in one big hand. "It is this young man, lame and hurting, who has come to be healed by God this night! Glory hallelujah! Do you believe, little brother? Do you *believe?*"

Arthur bobbed his head. "Oh yes! I sure do, Brother Christian! I really do!"

Silas motioned to Clell Martin, who stood near the rear of the stage next to a pair of ex–dance-hall girls, twins named Molly and Lolly. They had joined the troupe as gospel singers only two months before. "Bring me my Bible, Brother Jonathan! Quickly! I feel the spirit of the Lord upon me!"

When Clell joined their group, he had been an orphan, picked up by Silas in the streets of Kansas City. That was almost fifteen years ago. Since then, he had grown into a tall, handsome young man, and now, as he crossed the stage, dressed all in black, his golden hair gleamed in the light of the lamps that were strung around the perimeter of the stage.

As Clell passed the dog-eared Bible to Silas's outstretched palm, Silas's deep orator's voice rang out, mangling yet another verse from the Book of Matthew. Gwin rolled her eyes. Much more of that, and they would be dodging tomatoes before this night was over. What was *wrong* with him?

Sweat beaded on Silas's forehead as he proceeded to thrust the Bible over Arthur's head. With his free hand, he capped the boy's red hair, his long fingers splayed. "Join with me now, brothers and sisters! It is only through your faith and belief in God that He will work His miracles through us here tonight!"

Silas raised his hand from Arthur's head and presented an open palm to Gwin. "Give me your hand, Sister Susannah!"

Gwin raised her head, and, with her fingers spread wide, lifted her hand to join with Silas's. It was only for a brief second that her own deformity flashed visible. The thin web of skin that joined the lower third of her ring and smallest fingers was almost translucent when held up to the light.

"Remember the words of the Lord Jesus! *All is well! Your faith will heal you! Brothers and sisters, do you belieeeve?*"

The crowd was bellowing and shrieking, crying and bouncing to their feet. *"We believe! We belieeeve!"*

"Believe, little brother, that God will give you the strength to walk again! I say, walk again! Waaalk again!"

It was Arthur's cue. His face stretched into a grimace of pain as he cast away one crutch. The crowd *oooooohed*. He teetered precariously, then cast away the second crutch. The crowd *ahhhhhhed*. He pitched sideways, catching himself against Gwin's shoulder. A woman in the front row shrieked and promptly fainted, overcome with either spiritual ecstasy or heatstroke.

Arthur took one trembling step forward. He took another few steps and fell into Brother Christian's waiting arms. The crowd erupted.

Gwin jumped to her feet, tears now streaming down her face. "My brother walks again!" But her well-rehearsed line was immediately lost, drowned out by the clamor of the crowd.

Gwin stood quietly beneath the moonlit sky, her arms folded as she surveyed the twinkling hills of San Francisco in the distance below. Molly and Lolly had brought the service to a rousing conclusion by leading the congregation through all four verses of "Stand Up, Stand Up for Jesus." Obviously, Gwin's premonitions of disaster had been ill-founded. The show was over and this was their last night in town. What could go wrong now?

After the show, Gwin, Arthur, and a man named Wilson had filed from the overheated tent right along with the rest of the animated crowd. But, unlike the others, they circled back about a half a mile into the outlying hills to wait until the camp was completely deserted.

Arthur, who was always wound up tighter than a watch spring after a triumphant performance, was playing true to form. His child's voice rose high to spike the clear night air as he paced back and forth excitedly behind her. "Our revels now are ended! These our actors, as I foretold you, were all spirits and are melted into air, into thin air!"

Wilson appeared by Gwin's side, taking a slow draw on his crumpled cigarette. "What is the matter with that boy?"

Silas had discovered Wilson working in a carnival sideshow. The man with the "melting face" was horribly disfigured from burns he had suffered as a child. These days, Wilson elicited mingled gasps of horror and pity as he edged his way, with the use of a cane, through the gathered crowds. No one ever doubted his claim to blindness, and when, thanks to Brother Christian, he "saw the light" again, he never failed to usher a whole new flock of believers into the fold. Gwin truly liked Wilson and felt sorry that most people were unable to overlook the dreadful scarring of his face in order to get to know the man beneath.

"He must have read it in one of our mother's books," Gwin replied to his question. "Arthur remembers everything he reads."

"Everything? He remembers *everything*?"

"Pretty near."

Arthur stopped to squint up at them from beneath the brim of an old engineer's cap, a battered hand-me-down from Gwin's own childhood. "Shakespeare. *The Tempest*, Act Four."

Gwin swatted him on the arm. "Stop showing off."

Wilson nudged the boy. "Shakespeare, huh? You know, I seen that *Macbeth* once in a playhouse in New York City."

A TOUCH OF CAMELOT 23

"Really?" Now it was Arthur's turn to be impressed. "You've been to New York City, Wilson? When was that?"

As Wilson proceeded to enthrall Arthur with stories of faraway New York City, Gwin watched her little brother's wide-open face, trying to ride out the sudden wave of affection that threatened to engulf her. While it was true she tried not to brood over her own past, she wished things were different for Arthur. Her little brother was bright. No, he was more than just bright, he was truly special, and he deserved better than to be raised in a family of nomadic sharpers. He deserved to be in school where his special talents would be recognized and nurtured. He deserved to be raised in a proper home. Gwin knew this, but there was little she could do about it. She couldn't very well take Arthur away from Silas, could she? Losing his only son would hurt him too much.

Gwin tried to push down these melancholy thoughts. "Why don't we start back?"

Not bothering to wait for an answer, she started down the hill toward the billowing circus tent. Behind her, Arthur began to badger poor Wilson with more questions about New York.

Gwin wasn't listening. She was thinking that maybe later, when they knocked off in Kansas City for the winter, she would take some of her earnings and hop a train back to San Francisco.

There was a good chance that her natural father had settled in California many years ago, before she was born, and now, because of certain remarks Silas had recently let slip to Arthur, Gwin believed her father might still be living here.

Silas knew more than he was letting on. Gwin was convinced of that much, at least. Getting him to talk about it, though, that was going to be a problem. The whole subject was still painful and awkward for the both of them. Nevertheless, Gwin was determined to get at the truth, and if her real father *was* still here in San Francisco, she was just as determined to find him.

When they reached the deserted back end of the tent, they could hear muffled voices and see shadows moving inside. These manifestations were Silas, Clell, Molly, and Lolly at work packing up the props.

The thought of Clell working side by side with Molly and Lolly brought a frown to Gwin's face. She wasn't blind. She had seen Clell eyeing up the twin dance-hall girls. Worse yet, she had seen *them* eyeing *him* up. Soon, he would probably pick one or the other.

Gwin tried to shake off this thought. Clell had already asked her to marry him and she had refused. She had even let him kiss her a few times, but each time she had felt nothing. Gwin wasn't sure what she was supposed to feel when a man kissed her, but she was fairly certain she should feel *something*. Her own girlish dreams told her that much.

"Now, who in the dickens do you suppose that is?"

Startled by Wilson's sudden question, Gwin looked up to see a man on horseback emerging into the circle of lantern light that surrounded the old circus tent. He was big, very big, that much was plain, but his broad-brimmed hat was pulled low over his forehead, discouraging any view of his features. He was well dressed, an expensive knee-length coat stretched over massive shoulders.

Gwin looked at Wilson. "We'll have to stay out of sight until he leaves."

Wilson nodded, and, together, they stepped back into the shadows around the side of the tent. Gwin peeked around the corner just as the stranger was dismounting. She still couldn't make out his face.

"What's he want?" A loud whisper. This was Arthur.

"Shhhhh!" Gwin pulled back around the corner of the tent and motioned for him to hush up.

"I'm gonna go see what he wants!" Before Gwin could catch Arthur's sleeve, he scurried off to the back end of the tent. She knew he was going to sneak a peek through one of the loose flaps.

"Darn that kid."

"Don't worry. He'll be all right," Wilson said. "He handles himself better than any kid I ever saw."

Well, that was right enough, she supposed. Gwin edged along the side of the tent, her ears pricked to catch the conversation that was passing within.

"Are you Brother Christian?"

The man's voice was rumbling and deep, his tone flat and emotionless. Gwin saw the length of Silas's shadow against the faded canvas, elongating and shortening, as he moved to face the stranger. "That I am. And you, sir, are?"

"Who I am doesn't matter. Is this your whole group?"

Gwin heard Clell's voice, challenging. "I'm sorry, sir, but if you aren't going to identify yourself and state your—"

"Silas Pierce?"

Frozen silence. Gwin sensed trouble. No one outside of their troupe ever used Silas's real name.

Silas's tone was wary. "So it's trouble you've come for."

"I've come to deliver a message to Silas Pierce."

"Well then, deliver it and be—No! Wait!"

A deafening shot rang out. Gwin jerked back as Silas, blown clean off his feet, flew back against the side of the tent not five feet from where she stood. She gaped, horrified, as he slumped to the ground, leaving behind a darkening snail trail that soaked through the thick canvas.

"Silas!" Clell cried in a stunned voice. Then the shotgun roared again.

There were screams, earsplitting, terrified screams, as Molly and Lolly tried to make a break for it. Then, three more shots, each punctuated by the meticulous scratch-click of the lever-action as it ejected spent shells. The screaming stopped, followed by a preternatural silence.

Wilson's fingers dug into Gwin's elbow. He spun her around, whispering, "Let's get out of here!"

"We can't just leave them!"

"He's after everyone, you hear? All of us!"

The meaning of his words sizzled into her brain. "Oh, my God, where's Arthur?"

Inside the tent, the big man's voice boomed. "Hey, you! Kid! What are you doing?"

Gwin snapped out of her lethargy, spinning on her heels and heading to the rear of the tent. She spotted her little brother, frozen, still down on his knees just as she heard the man inside the tent reloading.

Gwin snagged the shoulder strap of Arthur's faded overalls, yanking him off balance. He reeled back, his arms flung out, his face white. He was unexpectedly heavy, and Gwin went down with him.

The shotgun roared, and a huge, jagged hole blew open the side of the tent. Gwin rolled onto her side and pulled at Arthur's arm, screaming. "Get up! *Get up!*"

Gwin felt strong hands hook under her arms. She was suddenly on her feet, Arthur along with her. Wilson whirled them around to face the darkened hills and shoved. *"Run!"*

He didn't have to say it twice. Gwin's legs started moving, and she ran like she had never run before, dragging her little brother behind her. She looked back only once to see the gunman cursing as he struggled to push through the tangled tent flap.

Wilson gasped and wheezed as he pounded along at their heels. Gwin remembered that he had once mentioned to her that his lungs had been damaged in that fire long ago. But what could she do?

The campsite was far behind, their only light a three-quarter moon. Arthur pulled ahead of Gwin, picking up speed. She prayed that none of them would misstep into a gully.

Another gunshot. Gwin's heart skittered in her chest, anticipating the horrific sensation of being hit. The steady thud of Wilson's bootfalls began to fade, but she could still hear him back there, wheezing as if his lungs were collapsing. It was only then that she realized very real tears were streaming down her cheeks.

Another shot, and she heard Wilson go down with an awful strangled cry and a heavy thump. Gwin stumbled, nearly crashing headlong to the ground, but her legs miraculously kept moving.

"Run, Arthur!" she screamed. "Don't look back!"

And so they ran, Arthur and Guinevere, children of God, panting and terrified, into the dark California night.

2

Pinkerton's National Detective Agency, Chicago
July 10, 1879

Cole rose from his seat and started pacing, working up a healthy case of nervous tension as he continued to cool his heels in the outer office of the assistant superintendent.

The secretary, Mrs. Avery, a gray-haired, slightly built widow with patient blue eyes, looked up from her desk with a sympathetic smile. "Would you like a glass of water while you're waiting, Mr. Shepherd?"

"No, thank you. I'm fine."

"I'm sorry he's taking so long."

Cole forced a smile. "It's not a problem. I'm fine."

Mrs. Avery smiled back—a sweet, understanding smile, one that nursed fevers in the night, wiped runny noses, and kissed skinned knees; a motherly smile that reminded young boys to wear their coats on cold autumn days, to comb their hair before leaving the house, and to carry an umbrella when it looked like rain.

This expression was not unfamiliar to Cole. When older women looked at him in just this way, he always vowed anew to grow a beard. Cole knew his youth had something to do with it but was sure his clean-shaven appearance only aggravated the problem.

He looked away from Mrs. Avery's soulful, blinking eyes and resumed pacing. His nervousness was not caused by the idea of meeting with his superior, Fritz Landis. He had known the man for over nine months, and if anyone was his mentor here at the Agency, it would have to be Fritz. No, his nervousness was caused by what he hoped would be the subject of their meeting.

From the very first day he had crossed the threshold of the Chicago office, passing beneath that watchful Eye and the now-famous slogan, "We Never Sleep," Cole, only two years out of college, had been an eager student of the trade. After all, hadn't it always been his fondest dream to join the elite Pinkerton's National Detective Agency?

Cole had worked doggedly these past nine months, shadowing older, more experienced operatives, learning their methods and practices. He had helped track thieves, some petty, some grand, and the week before last, he had even been in on the arrest of an international forger. And now his time had come.

Fritz had sent for him, and Cole knew that this time there would be no senior operative to supervise his performance. From now on, Cole would be on his own.

The door to the office swung open. The Agency bookkeeper, a harried, wiry man with a balding pate, emerged, a thick sheaf of expense reports clutched to his thin chest.

Fritz Landis appeared in the open doorway after him. He was a tall man, lately in danger of becoming stout as well. Today, as always, he was nattily dressed, his gray frock coat unbuttoned, revealing the choker-collared white shirt he always wore beneath. His tie was still knotted as cleanly as it had undoubtedly been when he had first come in this morning.

Fritz addressed the departing bookkeeper. "I should have an answer for you by next week at the latest."

"Yes, Mr. Landis." The bookkeeper gave Mrs. Avery a curt parting nod before scurrying around the corner to his own office.

Fritz smiled at Cole. "Come in, come in." He held the door open as Cole passed into the utilitarian office, then closed it firmly behind them as he proceeded to his desk.

He motioned casually for Cole to take a seat. "I hope you've had enough time to rest up since your last assignment."

Cole tried to smile as he settled his rangy frame into the chair that faced Fritz's desk, but the effort came off stiff. His stomach was still feeling a little queasy, the result of butterflies that had no business fluttering about the digestive tract of a full-fledged Pinkerton operative. "You have something for me?"

Fritz began rifling through an impressive stack of

paperwork. "Yes, I do. Now, where was that thing? Oh, yes, here it is. Take a look."

Fritz handed Cole a wrinkled handbill. Now dry and brittle, it looked as if it had weathered more than a few nights of soggy weather. Cole peered at the wording, still discernible despite the fact that the colors had faded and most of the inks had run together.

Brother Christian's Sinbusting Tent Revival.

Two nights only! The public is invited to witness the faith-healing prophet at work! Hear the Word of the Lord! Seek Redemption and Salvation!

Cole tapped the handbill with one finger. "Hey, I've heard of this fellow. Didn't he claim to have healed some woman blinded in a stagecoach accident?"

Fritz raised a bushy eyebrow. "What do you think?"

Cole tossed the handbill down on Fritz's desk. "I think it's all a lot of hogwash."

"I happen to agree with you, but a lot of people believe in this stuff. Brother Christian was raking in a bundle."

"A flimflam man?"

"A flimflam man by the name of Silas Pierce. He's gone by a lot of other names, too." Fritz pulled a file from the desk. He flipped it open, reached into his coat pocket for his spectacles, and set them on his nose. "Ah yes, Silas Pierce, alias Wilbur Jacks, horse trader; alias Franklin Singleton, lightning rod salesman; alias Grenville Charlesworth, English earl; alias Malcolm Throckmorton, snake oil salesman."

Cole frowned. *Throckmorton?* The name sounded familiar, but nothing else jogged loose in his memory. He shrugged it off, thinking it might come to him later. Fritz closed the file with a sigh. "There are probably more, of course. That's just the few we have on record."

"The man has had a long and varied career," Cole commented.

"A career that ended quite abruptly a few weeks ago just outside of San Francisco."

"Arrested?"

Fritz's reply was blunt. "Murdered."

Cole sat forward. "What happened?"

"It was following one of his tent revivals. The man was shot point-blank with a Winchester shotgun. Not a pretty sight."

Cole nodded slowly. "Pretty thorough. I guess someone didn't like what he was peddling this time."

"Unfortunately, that's not all. Four other members of his group were murdered just as brutally. A longtime companion named Clell Martin, another named John Wilson, and two sisters identified as Molly and Lolly Mehegan, from Dodge City."

"Damn." Cole felt a little sick. "Two women?"

Fritz removed his spectacles. "A ghastly crime by all accounts."

"But why?"

"Money, we assume. That night's offering was missing."

"It's hard to understand, isn't it? Killing all those people for money?"

"Brutality for brutality's sake is never understandable, but it exists nonetheless." Fritz leaned forward, flattening both palms on his desk top. "But we're getting away from the subject, and that is your assignment."

"Which is?"

"There were two eyewitnesses to the murders in San Francisco. Pierce's eleven-year-old son, Arthur, and his daughter, a young lady named . . ." Fritz reached for the file again, flipping it open to squint at its handwritten contents. "Let's see, that was a young lady named . . . Jenny? No, that's not it. Gwen, I believe." He began to mutter as he patted his coat pockets for his spectacles. "Now, where the devil did I put those—?"

"Gwen? As in, short for Gwendolyn?" Cole prompted, eager to get on with it.

Fritz grunted and gave up on locating his misplaced eyeglasses. "I would assume so."

"Hmmm. Do they have any suspects in custody?"

"Yes, they have one who was set for trial, but Miss Pierce and her brother fled California the day before they were to testify. The district attorney has succeeded in having the trial postponed temporarily, but they can't wait forever. Since Miss Pierce and her brother openly defied a court order to appear, it looks like they have no intentions of returning voluntarily. That's where the Agency comes in."

"Are we to locate them?"

"No longer necessary. Kansas is your home state, isn't it? Do you know of a small town called Caldwell?"

Cole thought for a moment. "A little cow town right along the southern border?"

"That's the one. Miss Pierce and her young brother have been detained by the town constable, and he's quite eager to claim the reward that's been offered for recovering them. At any rate, your first solo assignment is to escort them to San Francisco without, uh, misplacing them along the way."

"What? Wait a minute, Fritz. I thought this was going to be a real assignment. This sounds more like playing governess."

Fritz laughed. "Don't underestimate your charges, Cole. A week ago, they were picked up for horse-stealing by the authorities in Garden City only to slip away from them before we could even get one of our operatives down there."

Cole snorted derisively. "That doesn't say much for the authorities in Garden City, does it?"

"Just remember, Cole, Gwendolyn and Arthur were raised at the knee of one of the slickest confidence artists in the Midwest. They've learned to survive by their wits, and so far they've done a pretty darn good job of it."

"There's one thing I don't understand."

"What's that?"

"I assume we've confirmed all this with the San Francisco authorities and that there's a subpoena for their appearance."

"Right." Fritz clasped his hands over his ample middle.

"It doesn't make sense that these two wouldn't want to testify. Their father was murdered in cold blood. The others were presumably close friends. You'd think they'd want to see this killer brought to justice."

"You'd think so."

"So, what's going on, Fritz?"

The older man threw up both hands as if at a loss to understand the workings of the criminal mind. "Who knows? Most likely they're afraid."

"But you said the killer is behind bars."

"Maybe they don't expect it to stay that way. Maybe they're just averse to cooperating with the authorities. They've been well trained since the cradle to avoid the law."

Cole shook his head. "It just doesn't sound *right.*"

"Far be it from me to tell you not to follow your own instincts when you're out in the field, but just remember, these two will lie to you faster and slicker than you can blink an eye. Don't let your guard down."

Cole sighed. "Who's the client?"

"A millionaire from San Francisco named Phineas Taylor. He's running for mayor."

"So, what's he got to do with the murder of a con man?"

"The man accused of the murders is a bandit named Ricardo Cortez. Without the testimony of the young lady and the boy, there's not enough evidence to convict him. Mr. Taylor feels it will be an outrage if Cortez is set free."

"And he's willing to pay for it?" Cole asked doubtfully. "Very noble of him."

Fritz smiled in cynical agreement. "I don't doubt that it will help him look good politically." Closing the file, he pushed back from his desk, preparing to stand. "Well, there you have it, Cole. This assignment shouldn't keep you tied up more than ten days at the most. Do you want it?"

"Do I want it?" Cole echoed, feeling as if Fritz had just casually offered to throw the brakes of a speeding locomotive. What was Cole supposed to say? Was he to speak the truth? *You know, this wasn't exactly what I had in mind when I signed on with the Agency.* Was he supposed to ask Fritz why they had trained him with their best men for nine months if all they were going to do was assign him to escort duty?

No, that wasn't what he was supposed to say. What he was supposed to say was yes. *Yes, I'll take the damned assignment. This one and every one after it, because, sooner or later, after I've proven myself to you, I'll finally get something I can sink my teeth into. Sooner or later, I'll get to do what I've wanted to do all my life, real detective work.*

Cole rose to his feet. "I'll take it, Fritz, but count on my being back very soon. By then, I hope you'll come up with something a bit more challenging."

Fritz chuckled good-naturedly. "Not every job well done makes the newspapers, Cole, but rest assured they never go unnoticed at the home office." He picked the *Brother Christian/Silas Pierce* file from his desk and offered it to Cole. "All the information and necessary paperwork is here."

"Ten days," Cole stated firmly, taking the file and turning to leave.

His hand was already on the doorknob when Fritz's parting comment reached his ears. "Good luck, Cole. I have a feeling you're going to need it."

Caldwell, Kansas, July 11

Temporary Deputy Hollis McGee was beginning to think he could use a stiff shot of rye whiskey about now. Constable Mears had promised Hollis a part of the reward money if only he would sit guard over the girl and her kid brother for a few hours. Nothing to it, he had said. How much trouble could they be? Like most bad ideas, it had sounded like a good one at the time.

"Deputy McGee! Are you listening to me out there?"

Hollis felt the muscles in the back of his neck bunching into a knot. He renewed for probably the tenth time in the last hour his solemn vow to remain a bachelor for life. He suspected marriage would be a lot like this—like being stuck in a box with one of them yippy little Chihuahua dogs.

"So, Deputy McGee, how many cards do you want?" The kid blinked at him from across the desk, his huge blue eyes sparkling like a couple of brand-new pennies.

Now, the kid, he was another story. Good as gold. Sweet as a stick of horehound candy. And sharp as a tack, too. He was a pretty fair poker player, especially for such a little squirt.

Before Hollis could reply, his ears were assaulted anew by the banshee in the back room. "It is hot as Hades in this stinking cell, and I am sweating like a pig in a barnyard! I demand that I be permitted to bathe!"

"Jeez damn!" Hollis slapped his cards onto the desk. "Don't she *ever* plug it up?"

"She's been in a bad mood ever since we got here."

"Sheee-it! Ya can say *that* again!"

"Did you *hear* me, Deputy McGee? *Deputy McGee!*"

"Keep yer petticoats on back there! I heard ya! And ya know I cain't let ya out fer no bath! Mrs. Henry will see to yer woman-needs when she gets back from visitin' the Widow Palmer!"

"This is an outrage! Just exactly what crime am I supposed to be charged with, anyway? I haven't heard a word about that!"

Hollis focused on the dingy mirror that hung on the wall to the right of the constable's desk. The mirror, situated strategically between a brewery calendar and a collection of WANTED posters, afforded Hollis an unobstructed view of the jail cell in the back room. The girl was busy pacing its short length, back and forth, back and forth, like a restless tiger in its cage. She was a pretty little thing, but a fellow sure forgot that soon enough. As soon as she opened her mouth, to be precise.

"The way I hear it, Miz Pierce, you done got yerself caught a-stealin' long johns off the mayor's wash line! Ain't that a fact?"

She threw both hands up as she paced. "Oh, pooh! How was I supposed to know they belonged to the mayor?"

"Well, that's no never mind to me!" Hollis retorted. "All I know is you two must be important to *someone* cause they got one of them Pinkerton fellas comin' to get ya, and there's a hundred dollar reeward out on yer heads!"

She stopped pacing and clutched the cell bars. "I don't know anything about any reward money! There must be some mistake!"

Hollis chortled gleefully. "Well, I'm fixin' to spend *my* share of that mistake down at Moreland's Saloon as soon as—"

"This is the sorriest excuse for a jail that it has ever been my misfortune to encounter!"

"Well, Miz Pierce, I am so sorry, but the princess cell is plumb full up at the moment! What do ya 'spect me to do?"

She just glowered at him in reply.

Hollis returned his attention to the kid. "Now, where were we, little fella?"

"This cot is filthy! I probably have fleas, and you people won't even let me take a bath!"

Hollis gritted his teeth. "Miz Pierce, you got a basin of water, a sponge, and a cake of soap back there! Why don't ya put it to good use and wash out that big mouth of yours?"

"Well! I beg your pardon!"

"My pardon? You got it, Miz Pierce! Just shut yer yap and let us get back to our game!"

"Fine and dandy! I'll make do with what I got, but you just be sure to keep your eyes to yourself out there, Deputy McGee!"

Hollis picked up his playing cards. Now, what did she mean by that? He tilted his head to peer up at the mirror. She had her foot up on the bunk and looked to be wrestling to get her shoe off. He reckoned next time he rounded the corner, he would have to watch out for one of those pointy little shoes to come flying out at him from between the cell bars.

The kid drummed stubby fingers on the desk. "Deputy McGee, how many cards do you want?"

"Two." Hollis slapped down a pair of cards, then hawked and sent a sleek jet of tobacco juice straight into the spittoon at his feet. It was nearly empty and made a delightful little *ting!* Hollis loved that little *ting!* He prided himself on his marksmanship.

Hollis glanced up at the mirror casually, then back down to the cards in his hand. Then he almost fell out of his chair. He jerked his eyes back up to the mirror, not quite sure of what he had just seen. His eyes bulged. She was unbuttoning her dress! Surely, she wasn't going to . . . ? Surely, she wouldn't! *Would she?*

Hollis tore his eyes from the mirror, feeling a hot blush creep up his neck. He took the two cards the kid offered from the deck and threw in a matchstick to bet. As the kid mulled over the cards in his hand, Hollis snuck a peek at the mirror. Her dress was off, revealing some flimsy cotton doohickey-thing she wore beneath. Sunlight filtered into the cell through the bars of a small window above the cot. When she turned sideways, ever so slightly, Hollis thought he could *almost* see through the doohickey-thing.

"Deputy McGee?"

He jumped, startled. "What's that?"

"I raised you one. It's your turn."

Hollis swallowed hard, trying to concentrate on his hand. Constable Mears had never said what Hollis should do under these particular circumstances.

Should he march on back there and tell her to cut it out?

What if Constable Mears returned to find his prisoner stripped down to her whites? Would Hollis be in trouble? Then another thought occurred to him, a thought that darn near starched his shorts. What if she went even farther than her whites? What if she stripped down till she was *buck naked?*

Hollis couldn't help it. His eyes flew back to the mirror. She was stepping out of her petticoat! Jeez damn! The guys down at Moreland's Saloon were never going to believe this!

The kid sighed. "Are you in or out, Deputy McGee?"

Hollis threw in two matchsticks. "Call and raise one," he said hoarsely, loosening his collar. He was starting to sweat. Was it getting hot in here? Jeez damn!

The kid threw down his hand. "I'm out!"

Hollis took his winnings and started to gather up the cards, trying to be inconspicuous as he observed her in the mirror. She was in the process of removing her stockings. He caught a brief flash of a smooth, white, shapely calf.

The boy cleared his throat. "Deputy McGee?"

"Hmmmmm?" Hollis kept one eye on the mirror as he shuffled. She had a bare foot perched up on the bunk again and was busy swishing the water in the basin with one hand, making soapsuds.

"Deputy, I got to go to the outhouse."

Hollis dealt the cards. He barely noticed as first one, then another, missed the desk and fluttered to the floor. She was rolling up one leg of her drawers, revealing a knee.

"Deputy? I said, I got to go to the outhouse."

Hollis tore his eyes from the tantalizing vision in the mirror to glare at the kid peevishly. "What? *Now?*"

"Yes, *now!*" the boy insisted, fumbling in his seat.

"Well, can't ya just *hold it?*"

The kid jumped up from his stool, looking cross. "Why do I need to hold it?"

Hollis threw a desperate glance at the mirror. Her head was thrown back, her eyes closed. She was squeezing the sponge against the hollow of her neck. Hollis's mouth dropped open slightly as a rush of water ran down her chest, soaking the front of her undergarments.

Hollis flapped one hand at the kid. "Well, go on then!"

"You're not going to go with me?"

"Hell, no!" Hollis barked, then, realizing he had raised his voice, he calmed himself and ripped his eyes away from the mirror. "Uh, I mean, I can trust ya, right? Ya ain't goin' nowhere without yer sister, right?"

The kid cocked his head, appearing to ponder this point before he grinned. "That *is* right! Good thinking, Deputy! I'll be right back!"

Hollis shooed the kid away and spat his whole wad of chew at the spittoon, not caring that he completely missed his target. He returned his full attention to the mirror. "Good boy! Ya take yer time now, ya hear?"

The kid slammed the door on his way out. Hollis barely noticed. She was loosening the ribbon tie on her doohickey! Whoa doggies! And to think that

44   DONNA GROVE

Constable Mears was going to actually pay him when this was all over! Hollis could hardly believe his luck.

"Deputy McGee?"

The elated deputy didn't have much time to think about the fact that he had not heard the door open again *before* the kid called his name. He only had time to think, *Back already? That kid must go faster than a jackrabbit*, because it was just about then that his own personal show curtain fell with a crash. And everything went dark.

Cole emerged from the alley between a bank and a dry goods store. The constable's office was located just across the main street thoroughfare, a modest wooden structure, sandwiched like a second thought between two red brick buildings. Cole was crossing the dusty street when he saw the door open and two figures step out into the sun-drenched afternoon. A woman and a boy. They both wore hats that shaded their faces; hers a frowsy sunbonnet, his a navy blue engineer's cap.

Cole stepped up onto the boardwalk and stopped, squinting at the pair curiously. A woman and a boy. Cole cocked his head to one side and spoke aloud, "Nah, it couldn't be."

He watched with growing interest as they set off at a brisk pace in his direction. To Cole, they now took on the impression of two scurrying mice, two scurrying, escaping, *guilty* mice. The woman's head was down and so was the boy's. Neither of them looked up in time to keep from barreling into Cole,

A TOUCH OF CAMELOT   45

who stood like a statue in the middle of the boardwalk.

"Oooh!" The woman smacked right into him and stumbled backward, tripping over her skirt hem and landing with an indelicate thump onto her behind.

Cole bent to give her a hand and found himself staring into two of the roundest, palest blue eyes he had ever seen in his life. Her cheekbones were high and tinged with color, her mouth perfectly shaped, her lips a dusky rose. The wisps of hair that peeked out from that ridiculous sunbonnet were the blinding color of match flame.

It was Gwendolyn Pierce, all right. She fit her file description perfectly, except for one small thing: It hadn't mentioned how incredibly pretty she was. It hit Cole like a slap in the face.

"Are you all right, ma'am?" he asked.

She didn't take his hand. She just stared up at him, her mouth hanging open like a barn door.

Cole looked deep into those long-lashed, nearly transparent blue eyes and felt, for one dazzling, disorienting moment, that he knew her. Then the odd feeling passed as quickly as it had come. "Uh, I said, are you all right? Can I help you up?"

"Yes, I'm all right."

Her brother danced from one foot to the other excitedly. "She's all right! Come on! Get up, Gwinnie!"

Gwendolyn Pierce continued to stare at Cole as if she were seeing the ghost of a dead lover. He wondered guiltily if she hadn't knocked a rafter or two loose in their collision. She finally took his hand. It felt unexpectedly small and delicate, not at all like the hand of a criminal. Then she was on her feet, brushing off her skirt with quick, nervous strokes. "I'm sorry, we were in a hurry to . . . to get home."

"I'll bet you were."

The kid grabbed his sister's arm and tugged. "Come on, Gwinnie! We gotta get home! We gotta get home right now!"

They started moving away.

Cole debated how much of a head start he should give them. They had obviously put a lot of effort into this little escape of theirs. "You sure you're all right?" he called out.

The girl threw a last, rattled glance over her shoulder. "Fine! Just fine!"

Then the mice were scurrying once more, this time across the busy street. Cole observed as they just missed being run down by a passing buckboard. How very inconspicuous.

He turned briefly to squint at the closed door of the constable's office. Everything appeared quite peaceful, but Cole guessed that if he were to enter that office, he would probably encounter one spitting-mad peace officer. According to his agency's report, the deputy they'd left behind in Garden City had been found gagged, hog-tied, and locked up securely inside his own jail cell—a position not likely to win him much respect throughout the community.

Cole caught one last glimpse of the Pierces before they vanished into the alley from which he had just emerged. He grinned, then sprinted across the street and headed back into the alley after them.

He emerged in a yard that opened onto the flat prairie

beyond. Except for the two escapees and one lone stallion tethered by the rear of a dry goods store, it was deserted. This was the perfect opportunity for a heist.

Cole approached as Gwendolyn boosted her young brother into the saddle. This had to be one of those golden moments in law enforcement he'd always heard about. He just wondered if anyone back at the Chicago office was going to believe him when he turned in his final report. "Uh, ma'am?"

She jumped and whirled, one hand at her throat. "Oh, my heavens! It's *you!*"

He offered a smile to put her at ease. "Is there something I can help you with? You look a little put out."

"Put out? Why, no! You just startled me! Do you make a habit of sneaking up on people from behind like that?"

Cole looked down at her, noting with more than passing interest that although she was petitely built, she appeared to be quite nicely endowed up top. He thought that perhaps this assignment wasn't going to be so dull, after all.

"As a matter of fact," he replied, "I do like sneaking up on people from behind. You'd be surprised at what I catch some of them doing."

She placed one hand on each hip and glared, openly irritated at his visual inspection. Then, turning her back, she gathered up her skirts. "As I said, we're in a hurry."

She insinuated one small foot into the stirrup. As she swung up onto the stallion behind her brother, Cole couldn't help noticing that she also had a pair of mighty fine legs to go with the rest of her.

Cole took hold of the reins, pointedly delaying their departure. "Uh, ma'am? There's just one more thing."

"What's that?"

With his free hand, Cole reached into his coat pocket and pulled out a pair of gleaming silver handcuffs. "That horse you're stealing? It's mine."

3

Topeka Train Station, Topeka, Kansas

The spacious dining hall teemed with midwestern society in all of its varied shapes and sizes. There were businessmen in expensive suits, ladies in fine traveling clothes, drummers, cowboys, farmers, children, and emigrants. They dashed about willy-nilly, casting hurried glances at their pocket watches, hailing busy waitresses and waiters, waving and bellowing and embracing in fond farewells.

Gwin was seated on a stool next to Cole Shepherd and Arthur at the bar in the serving area. She had barely touched the food on her plate. She was too busy studying Cole Shepherd's handsome profile as he finished his own lunch. Having measured him from top to toe, she was entranced by the lines and angles of his princely face despite her efforts to be objective. *Lancelot.* Gwin had recognized him immediately. How could she not? Hadn't he lived in her dreams for as long as she could remember?

Cole stabbed a piece of beefsteak with his fork and turned unexpectedly to capture her gaze before she could look away. He gave her an infuriating grin, an expression she was growing quite familiar with. "What's the matter, Miss Pierce? Do I have gravy on my chin?"

Gwin folded her arms and scowled. "No. Why do you ask? Do you normally dribble at meals?"

He shrugged as he turned back to his plate. "It's just that you've been staring at me ever since we sat down. Either I've got gravy on my chin or you've fallen in love with me."

Before Gwin could open her mouth to retort, the blare of a train's whistle cut the air. She heard the rhythmic *chufa-chufa* of a locomotive's steam engines as it pulled into the depot and turned her head in time to see the Union Pacific Express come to a squealing halt in front of the open dining hall. The number on the side of its hulking engine read 840. This was the train that, if Cole Shepherd continued to have his way, would carry the three of them most of the way to San Francisco. This was the train that, if Gwin had *her* way, would pull out of the station without them.

"You've barely touched your lunch, Miss Pierce."

Cole Shepherd wore an expression so insufferably patronizing, Gwin felt an immediate urge to ball up her fist and punch him right in the nose. Instead, she gave him a chilly smile. "If I wanted motherly advice, I'd ask for it, Shepherd."

"Well, Miss Pierce, you might be sorry later. We won't be getting off the train again until the dinner hour. You should take a lesson from your little brother here."

Arthur was perched on a stool to Shepherd's immediate right. As usual, he was shoveling food into his mouth as fast as he could swallow. It mattered not to Arthur's growing-boy stomach what sort of dire situation they might be in. He could always eat.

Gwin looked back at Shepherd to find those intelligent, tawny brown eyes settled on her. It was unnerving. Gwin avoided his gaze by picking up her fork and playing with her eggs. Cole Shepherd had her at a crippling disadvantage, even if he didn't know it. How could she think straight when she was constantly confronted with those eyes, that *face?*

She supposed she could blame some of it on Emmaline. While she might have been a less-than-perfect mother, she was one humdinger of a storyteller. Even before Gwin had started to talk, Emmaline had begun to regale her daughter with dazzling bedtime stories; stories of kings and queens, princes and princesses, sorcerers, dragons, and white knights. Among Emmaline's favorites had been the King Arthur legends. She had told them to her young daughter so many times that it was no wonder Gwin's childhood dreams had begun to revolve around the fantasy.

Over the years, the characters in these recurring dreams had taken on familiar faces and personalities. Gwin was always her own namesake, of course, that lady of all ladies, Queen Guinevere. Merlin soon came to resemble Silas. King Arthur as a child inevitably took on the precocious, shining personality of her baby brother. And as for the evil, scheming Morgan le Fay? Why, who else had been better equipped to take on that part than Emmaline?

It was Sir Lancelot, however, the greatest of all the knights of the Round Table, who had continued to remain faceless for so many years. The valorous, mysterious knight had rescued her from captivity or death how many times? Fifty? A hundred? And afterward, he would drop to one knee by her feet, kiss her hand, and profess his undying love, only to ride off into the sunset on his trusty white steed. After all, what had Gwin as a child known of passion and star-crossed love?

Gwin could not remember exactly when it had been that she had stood as Guinevere on her palace balcony in Camelot, overlooking a jousting tournament on the field below. She could not remember exactly when it had been that her White Knight, victorious in battle, had finally removed his helmet and turned to gaze up at her. It had been then, she was sure, that his face had finally been revealed, and that face had been proud and intelligent and handsome and strong. Indeed, it had been nothing short of masculine perfection. What's more, he resembled no one that Gwin had ever known. That face had been her most perfect creation, the fairest and gentlest and bravest of knights; her lover, her fantasy, her deepest of darkest secrets. He was hers and hers alone. *Until yesterday.*

It was yesterday that her fantasy had come crashing

down around her ears. It was yesterday that she had discovered that her knight in shining armor walked in the flesh. Her dream lover had turned out to be, of all the loathsome, vile things walking and crawling upon this earth, a *Pinkerton man*. Sometimes life could be so cruel.

Gwin observed him out of the corner of her eye. His hair, she thought, was the color of coffee with an added dash of cream. It was neat and clean and so thick it practically begged to be touched. When he rose to full height, he topped a lean six feet, and his chest and shoulders were broad enough to capture the attention of any woman with two eyes in her head. He was beautiful. Gwin couldn't think of any other word that fit.

Frowning at the direction of her spoony musings, she set down her fork and threw a quick glance around the dining hall. In this confused melee, it wouldn't be very difficult to slip away from Cole Shepherd. The problem was Arthur. Shepherd was keeping an eagle's eye on him. He was apparently smart enough to realize Gwin wasn't about to try anything that would entail leaving her brother behind. And so what Gwin needed was a distraction.

Shepherd was busily scratching out figures in a tally book he kept tucked into the pocket of his sack coat. Having seen him at this task a number of times since leaving Caldwell, Gwin was suddenly overcome with curiosity.

"What is it you're doing there, Shepherd? Jotting down fond reminiscences of our trip?"

He smiled absently but didn't look up. "Keeping

track of expenses, Miss Pierce. I suggest you finish whatever it is you want from your plate. We'll be leaving in ten minutes."

Ten minutes. That didn't give her much time. Gwin was running out of ideas. She had already tried flattery and flirtation, and neither had gotten a rise out of him. Unfortunately, Cole Shepherd was a tougher nut to crack than the gullible deputies in Caldwell and Garden City. Gwin thought that even if she had the nerve to strip down to the quick and parade naked before his eyes, his only reaction would be to raise one faintly disapproving eyebrow: *"Miss Pierce, you're liable to catch your death of cold. Now, stop all this nonsense and get dressed."* She was beginning to wonder if he was even human.

"You wouldn't have any objections to a lady freshening up before boarding, would you, Shepherd?"

He looked up from the tally book, his pencil poised over the paper. "You have five minutes, Miss Pierce. If you aren't back in five minutes, I'll be coming after you."

Gwin gathered her skirt and slid off the stool, clutching her reticule primly. "Your lack of trust is most disappointing."

She didn't give him a chance to reply as she made her way into the crowd. As she crossed the vast dining hall, she glanced back only once to see that he had swiveled around on his stool to track her. His face was expressionless as he tucked his tally book back into his coat pocket, affording only a fleeting glimpse of the Colt revolver holstered at his hip. Oh, he was a suspicious one, all right.

Gwin sent him a smile and a wave before continuing to push through the crowd to the convenience rooms where a line of hot, restless women had formed. Gwin took her place behind a hook-nosed old woman clutching a Bible to her chest and fanning herself with a temperance pamphlet entitled, "Demon Rum: Scourge of Mankind."

After a moment, she rose up on her toes to see that Shepherd had finally turned his back to her and appeared to be conversing with Arthur. Good. She scanned a nearby crowd of travelers to size up the pool of possibilities and immediately picked out a well-dressed, gray-haired gentleman.

Shifting his cane from one hand to the other, he pulled a gold watch from his vest pocket. Gwin caught the lilting tones of a deep southern accent as he replied to the inquiry of a passerby. "It is now exactly eleven thirty-eight, suh!"

Perfect. Gwin checked Shepherd's position once more before starting in the man's direction. When she was close enough, she brushed up against him, dropping her reticule to the floor.

"Oh!" She wrung her hands and slipped into her best Dixie accent. "I declare to goodness! I am at my wits' end!"

The gentleman whirled and bent immediately to retrieve her bag. "My pardon, ma'am! Allow me!"

Gwin gushed and fluttered. "I am most grateful to you, sir! I can tell by your impeccable manners and elegant appearance that you are a true southern gentleman!"

The man's full gray mustache twitched modestly as

he removed his top hat and swept into a gracious bow. "Indeed I am! Colonel Samuel T. Smythe at your service, ma'am!"

"You wouldn't be boarding the eight forty, would you, Colonel?"

"I would indeed, ma'am!"

Gwin raised a hand to her bosom. "It is such a comfort to know that, sir!"

"Is there a problem, ma'am?"

"Well, I . . ." Gwin twisted the strings of her reticule and forced a tear that proceeded to slide down her cheek quite convincingly. "I do hate to trouble you with my problems, Colonel, but, you see, I am traveling alone to San Francisco with my young brother." She brushed away the tear with the back of her hand.

"Yes? Please, go on!" Colonel Smythe's brow wrinkled as he fumbled for a handkerchief. He finally produced one from his coat pocket and offered it to her with a flourish. "Is there any way in which I can be of service?"

"It's just that there's this gentleman—well, no, I'd hardly call him a gentleman."

"Has someone been accosting you, ma'am?"

Gwin dabbed at her eyes. "Why, I declare! You are a mind reader! How could you know?"

"It is apparent by your manner, ma'am, that you are in dire straits!"

"That I am, sir. There's this man who has been forcing his company upon me and my brother ever since we arrived at the station! I have tried, Colonel Smythe, to be polite, but it seems that he has mistaken good manners for something more. I've asked him to leave us alone. Do you think I should speak with the management?"

Colonel Smythe's face suffused pink with chivalrous indignation. He brandished his cane threateningly. "Why, this is unconscionable! These damn Yankees! Where is he? Perhaps I shall have a word or two with this rogue myself!"

"It's that man seated by the—" She stopped in midsentence. There was Arthur, in plain sight, his back to her as he finished off his second helping of beefsteak and fried eggs, but the stool next to him was empty.

"Which man did you say, ma'am?"

"I . . . I . . ." Gwin stammered, thrown off keel. Where was Shepherd? He had been there only a second ago. She started to get a bad feeling in the pit of her stomach.

She felt a hand close around her elbow from behind. It was a firm grip, an authoritative, possessive grip. Gwin stiffened. His presence, his unmistakably masculine person, towered over her from behind.

"Has this young lady been bothering you, sir?"

Gwin twisted around to glare up at Shepherd, but his attention was currently fixed on Colonel Smythe. Except for that unrelenting grip he had on her arm, he was completely ignoring her, talking over her head as if she were an errant child.

Smythe sputtered, confused. "Bothering me? Why, certainly not! How could such a lovely young lady be bothering me?"

"Well, you see, I thought for a moment I'd lost her." He offered his free right hand to the confused gentleman. "Cole Shepherd, Pinkerton's Detective Agency, Chicago."

Smythe stared at Cole, his expression growing more discombobulated by the second.

"It seems," Cole continued, "that Miss Pierce occasionally suffers from the effects of an overactive imagination, if you get my meaning. Her family has arranged for her to be treated at one of the finest sanitariums on the West Coast, and I'm afraid it's my job to see that she gets there without any mishaps."

"Oh, I see." Smythe cleared his throat, his face turning the color of a blooming tea rose. Obviously embarrassed that he had been taken in by some kind of raving lunatic, he looked Gwin over like a piece of moldy bread.

"Come, Miss Pierce, we wouldn't want to miss our train, would we?"

Gwin was disgusted as Shepherd proceeded to guide her back through the crowd toward the bar where Arthur was still busy stuffing his mouth. If her brother weren't such a glutton, she thought, he would have made a break for it while he'd had the chance.

Shepherd stopped suddenly, pulling her around to look at him. Gwin squinted, distinctly uncomfortable at being so suddenly confronted once again by *that face*. Cole Shepherd didn't only *resemble* Lancelot, Cole Shepherd *was* Lancelot, and Gwin, who could be accused of being whimsical only in her dreams, had a hunch. She had a hunch that she hadn't created Lancelot out of thin air after all. She had a hunch that she had met him somewhere before. And she knew she wouldn't be able to rest until she had figured out where.

A TOUCH OF CAMELOT

His tone of voice was infuriatingly smug. "I expected better from you, Miss Pierce. It looks like I'm not going to be able to trust you."

Gwin was growing annoyed with his self-satisfied attitude. *Sanitarium, indeed.* Well, he hadn't seen anything yet. It was a long way from Topeka to San Francisco, and she had absolutely no intention of returning to California. Sooner or later, she would get the best of this particular Pinkerton man.

Gwin tilted her chin and replied, in the coolest tone of voice she could muster, "We have four more days to California, Shepherd. Might I suggest you hold on to your hat?"

At least they had managed to board the train without making a scene. Cole figured he should probably be grateful for even small favors when it came to the lovely but troublesome Miss Pierce. He was beginning to feel more like a mischievous child's governess than ever.

Arthur was clearly more excited than his older sister over the prospect of long-distance travel by rail. He bounced up and down on the plushly upholstered seat, changing subjects faster than hell could scorch a feather. "Gee whillikins! We're riding in a real Pullman car! Do you think they serve dinners on this train? Gee whillikins! I'll have steak if they do! Hey, Mr. Shepherd, can we open the window? Heeeeey!" His big blue eyes rounded ominously. "You think we'll have a *wreck?*"

His huge, delighted grin made it quite clear that he

could not fathom anything more truly exciting than an honest-to-goodness train wreck, the kind that made *Harper's Weekly*.

"No, Arthur, I do not think we'll have a wreck," Cole said with a sigh.

As the boy turned to concentrate his exceedingly short attention span upon prying open his window, Cole's gaze was inevitably drawn back to Miss Pierce. Her wrists rested on the small table that separated the facing seats of their compartment. Those dainty, nimble fingers were busy squaring, cutting, and riffle-shuffling a deck of playing cards.

He caught a flash of something that snagged his attention and reached out impulsively to still her hands. "What's that?"

She transferred the deck to her right hand and splayed the fingers of her left, displaying a bizarre, almost imperceptible, webbing of skin between her smallest finger and ring finger. Cole had never seen anything like it in his life.

"What's the matter, Shepherd? Do imperfections bother you?"

He tore his eyes from the odd disfigurement and met her slightly hostile gaze. "No, of course not."

She slipped her wrist from Cole's grasp and returned to shuffling her cards. "I was born with it."

Cole threw a glance at Arthur, who had finally succeeded in opening his window and was back to fidgeting restlessly in his seat. Arthur's hands, both displayed clearly as he drummed his fingers on the tabletop, were normal. It was apparent that he hadn't inherited the same trait as his sister. Cole made a mental note to add this peculiar physical characteristic to Miss Pierce's file when he returned to Chicago.

She hummed to herself, clearly unconcerned with Cole's scrutiny as she continued to manipulate the deck with astonishing finesse. She shuffled, squared the deck, then drew the ace of spades from the top. Replacing it, she picked up the deck in her left hand and rapidly dealt from the top: a six, a jack, a ten, and . . . the ace of spades.

"You actually carry a deck with you?" Cole asked.

She carefully replaced the ace of spades once again facedown on top. "Always."

Arthur piped up brightly. "That's her lucky deck!"

"That's her marked deck, you mean."

"Why, Shepherd," she said, looking at him askance as she dealt rapidly once again: jack, six, jack, ace of spades. "Are you insinuating that I would cheat?"

"Yes, Miss Pierce."

She scooped up the dealt cards and replaced them in the deck. She laid the ace of spades facedown on top, set the deck on the table, and squared it up neatly with both hands. "Well, normally I would take offense, but seeing as how you're cursed with an unusually suspicious nature, I'll overlook it."

The afternoon sun spilled through open venetian blinds, casting flickering bars of light across her exquisite features as the train picked up speed. To the naked eye, Cole thought, she certainly appeared harmless enough. She was conservatively dressed, a white, high-necked jacket blouse tucked into the tiny waist of a brown, no-nonsense skirt. Her only apparent concession to fashion, a small porkpie hat, nested atop dazzling red hair pulled back into a thick braided coil at the nape of her neck. Seated as closely as he was to her now, he kept catching subtle, but distinctly distracting, whiffs of feminine perfume. Lilac, he guessed.

Ever since foiling her escape yesterday, Cole had been wrestling with the nagging, elusive feeling that he had met her somewhere before, but of course that had to be his imagination. He would never forget that face.

"So, what's your game, Shepherd?" she piped up suddenly. "Poker? Three-card monte?"

Cole glanced down just in time to see her cut the deck three times, square up, then casually flip over the top card. Ace of spades. *Of course.*

"I don't have a game, Miss Pierce."

Those dazzling blue eyes turned on Cole full force. "Everyone has a game, Shepherd."

Cole folded the Topeka newspaper on his lap and rested his head back against the soft bolster seat. "I don't play games unless the odds are in my favor."

"Or unless an assignment demands it of you. Am I right?"

Cole closed his eyes wearily. "That's right."

She stage-whispered to her brother. "In other words, he's a skinflint."

Cole let the insult pass unnoticed. Having picked up its best speed by now, the train traveled over straight, flat track. The constancy of motion and the steady *clickety-clack* of the wheels began to seduce him into sleep.

"Well, we don't have to play for money, Shepherd."

He cracked one eye open grudgingly. She wore a cunning smile. *That lovely mouth.* It was just too darned bad she was a crook, too darned bad that those incredibly kissable lips were so adept at lying. "What would you have us wager, Miss Pierce?"

"Oh, I don't know." She tapped the corner of the deck on the table, pretending to think, then she batted her lashes at him invitingly. "How about, if you draw the winning card, my brother and I promise to behave ourselves for the rest of the trip?"

"And if you draw the winning card?"

"We get off at the next stop."

"Not a likely scenario, Miss Pierce."

She sniffed and turned away. "You know, over the span of four long days, Shepherd, you're likely to 'Miss Pierce' me to death."

Cole straightened up in his seat again with a sigh. It was clear she was not going to let him have any peace. "Would you prefer I call you Gwendolyn, then?"

Arthur interrupted. "Her name's not Gwendolyn!"

"Really?" Cole was surprised. "That's the name in your file at the Agency."

"Your precious file is wrong, Shepherd."

"Her name is Guinevere!" Arthur said.

"Guinevere?" Cole raised an eyebrow. "Like in— "

"Yes," she said.

Arthur's enthusiasm was not quelled by his sister's annoyance. On the contrary, he appeared quite delighted. "She was named after Queen Guinevere of Camelot!"

Guinevere sank down in her seat and scowled out

the window. Cole winked at her brother. "Then you, young master, must be none other than King Arthur himself!"

The boy beamed, his freckles standing out like pinpoints on his impish face. "You bet!" He scooted to the edge of his seat and plunged one grubby hand deep into the side pocket of his high-waisted overalls. "And this," he announced, proudly displaying a ratty-looking slingshot, "is Excalibur!"

"I thought Excalibur was a sword."

"Well, you thought wrong, Mr. Shepherd!"

Cole couldn't help but like this kid. He was bright, naturally ingenuous—something of a miracle considering his shady family background—and he had a good sense of humor. "Ah, I see. Well, I'm honored to be in such royal company."

Guinevere whipped her head around. "Could we just dispense with all this nonsense and get down to business?"

"We don't have any business to get down to, Guinevere," Cole said.

"No one calls me that. My name is Gwin, period. Maybe our mother believed in fairy tales, but I certainly don't."

Cole appraised her. "No? You mean, you don't believe in 'once upon a time'?"

"No."

"Not princesses in white towers, not knights in shining armor?"

"Certainly not," she said.

"Not even happy endings?"

"Especially not those, Shepherd."

"As you wish, your ladyship."

"My brother has a big mouth. I suppose now we're going to have to put up with your feeble attempts at humor all the way to San Francisco." She threw Cole a shrewd look. "That is, if we make it that far."

"Oh, we'll make it that far, all right," Cole assured her.

She didn't answer him. Cole looked over in time to catch Arthur's abrupt change in demeanor. He was biting his lip and blinking expectantly at his sister, all traces of good humor now vanished from his freckled countenance.

"What's the matter?" Cole asked.

The boy didn't look away from his sister, who pointedly ignored him from across the narrow table. "Gwinnie? Why don't you tell him?"

She shook her head, her gaze fixed on the featureless prairie that passed outside the train window. "He wouldn't believe us anyway, Arthur, so just save your breath."

Arthur turned back to Cole. "You're not such a bad guy, are you, Mr. Shepherd?"

"I suppose that depends on who you talk to about it, Arthur."

The kid forced a weak smile, but it rapidly disintegrated into another worried frown. "If you take us back to San Francisco, Mr. Shepherd, they're going to try to kill us, just like they did the others."

"What do you mean, 'they'?"

"I mean—"

Gwin reached across the table to grasp her brother's wrist. "Shut up, Arthur."

The boy gave her a pleading look, then continued. "I mean, the ones who killed Silas and the others."

"I thought there was just one man," Cole said.

Gwin released her brother and sat back. "There *was* just one man."

"And you both saw him."

"No. Arthur saw him. I didn't get a good look at his face, but I'd sure recognize that voice again if I heard it."

"Well, together, you can both still identify him. You can testify at his trial, and that'll be the end of it. He won't be able to hurt you or anyone else again."

Gwin shook her head. "It's not that simple, Shepherd. The man they arrested is not the same man who killed Silas."

Arthur nodded soberly to confirm his sister's words. Gwin, who was now biting her nails, avoided eye contact. "And did you tell this to the authorities?" Cole asked.

Indignant anger sparked Gwin's eyes. "Of course we told them! That's when the trouble started!"

"Wait a minute. Back up. What trouble?"

Arthur pushed up in his seat. "I told them, Mr. Shepherd! I told them that the fella they had in jail wasn't the one who shot them! I saw the man who shot them, Mr. Shepherd, and he was a giant! Big as Goliath himself! Swear to God, Mr. Shepherd! I saw that giant's face!"

Cole eyed Arthur dubiously. A giant? Wasn't Arthur a little old to be making up silly stories about giants? Cole looked back at Gwin. "I don't understand."

"Well, understand *this*, Pinkerton man, they told him to look harder and to think about it. They said maybe he would change his mind. And when he didn't, they said, 'Look, kid, it was dark that night, wasn't it? How can you be sure of anything you saw?' And then, when he *still* wouldn't change his mind, this one particular detective, he took me aside and said to me real quiet so nobody else would hear, 'You better talk to your little brother, miss, because things might start to go hard on the two of you if your story doesn't begin to make more sense.'"

"Are you saying they were trying to force him to make a false identification?"

Gwin folded her arms neatly. "Aren't you smart? No wonder you work for a famous detective agency."

"What you're telling me doesn't make any sense, Gwin."

"It didn't make much sense to us either, but we got the message loud and clear. Either we identified Cortez as the killer or we were going to be considered suspects ourselves."

"Well, that's not all that unusual. I'm not saying you had anything to do with it, mind you. I'm just saying that as the only two survivors, it's only normal procedure for them to include you in their list of suspects."

She rolled her eyes. "That makes about as much sense as two turkeys strutting up to the chopping block on Thanksgiving day. Who do you think reported the murders in the first place?"

Arthur interjected eagerly. "It was after I told them they had the wrong man that they tried to kill us!"

Cole held up one hand. "Who is this 'they' you're referring to?"

"We don't know," Gwin replied. "Someone took a potshot at us outside our hotel. Two nights later, someone tried to break into our room. That was enough for me. If we stuck around much longer, we were going to end up either in jail or dead."

Cole studied Gwin's face. There was no indication there that she was lying, but then again, lying was her vocation, her specialty, wasn't it?

Doubtful, he looked away only to catch the eye of an attractive blonde sitting in the next compartment. She smiled at him prettily, and he had the passing thought that she looked a lot like Cynthia.

Cole had always prided himself on his ability to size people up, but he had soon discovered, fresh out of college and newly inducted into the New York City Police Department, that when it came to women, he had a hell of a lot to learn.

He had met Cynthia, and had soon, like a fool, grown incapable of thinking with anything but that which riseth below his belt. For six long months he had fancied himself in love with Cynthia Ferguson. He had been so bowled over by that pretty, lying face, he had even managed to overlook the small fact that she was married. Hell, she hadn't just been married, she had been married to a Tammany Hall–backed city councilman. In allowing himself to get involved with Cynthia, Cole had taken a chance on destroying his entire career before it could even get started. And for what?

I love you, Cole. I love how you touch me, Cole.

Make love to me, Cole. He had believed her. Perhaps he should have been a little suspicious of the fact that the prim and proper Cynthia Ferguson had shown him a few tricks in bed that he had never even imagined before. Then he had gotten word that his father was ill, and he had taken a leave of absence to travel back to Kansas. His father had died a week later, leaving him alone in the world. Except for Cynthia, of course. Cole hadn't given much of a damn about his career at that point. He had returned to New York planning to ask Cynthia to leave her husband and marry him. Instead, he returned to find that he had been quickly and effortlessly replaced in Cynthia's affections. And her bed. *Women.* He had learned a hard lesson about women. They smiled when they lied.

Cole looked back now at Guinevere Pierce. She wasn't smiling. As a matter of fact, her small chin was tilted up, challenging him. Cole challenged her back, not bothering to disguise the doubt that edged his voice. "And so that's why you ran? That's why you don't want to go back to San Francisco?"

"When someone shoots at me, I don't stop to ask questions, I just run."

"Gwin, you're asking me to believe that the San Francisco Police Department has conspired to convict an innocent man and to murder you and your brother, and even you can't offer up one good reason why."

Gwin held Cole's gaze as she addressed her brother. "See, Arthur? I told you he wouldn't believe us. They all stick together like glue."

Cole didn't bother to refute her statement.

After a long, tense moment, she picked up her deck of playing cards and resumed shuffling. Her tone of voice turned breezy and cool as she changed the subject. "So, Shepherd, from what I've seen so far, you don't smoke or drink or swear. Now you tell me that you don't gamble, either. What is it that you *do* do?"

Arthur tucked his magic slingshot back into his pocket. He kicked the table leg and eyed Cole solemnly from beneath the lowered brim of his cap. *Thump. Thump. Thump.*

Cole settled back and closed his eyes, trying to ignore that dull, steady, *accusatory* sound. All at once he felt very tired. "What I do, Miss Pierce, is my job. I do my job, that's all."

She didn't answer, and Cole didn't bother to open his eyes for a long time. He listened to Guinevere Pierce shuffle her cards and thought about the ridiculous story she and her brother had just tried to foist on him. What was their angle? Were they hoping to gain pity? Did they think that Cole would actually let them go free before they got to San Francisco? Crazy. They had to be crazy as loons if they thought he was going to buy into some farfetched con story about murder conspiracies.

4

San Francisco, California

"Mr. Ringo here tells me that our two little pigeons have boarded the eight forty Express. They're due to arrive in San Francisco in less than a week."

Sidney Pierce, better known these days as Phineas Taylor, stood facing the tall polished glass window behind his desk, his back deliberately turned to his two guests. The view of San Francisco from Nob Hill was breathtaking, but Sidney wasn't feeling very appreciative at the moment. He was a man in a hole, a deep hole, a hole that included obsequious servants, massive bank accounts, and an elegant mansion, but a hole nevertheless. It was a hole he had eagerly helped dig for himself, and he saw little chance of clawing his way out of it at this late date.

He turned to face the man who had just spoken, his

longtime business associate and lawyer, Jasper Barnes, whose squat, thick body was mashed into an upholstered chair facing Sidney's desk. The little man puffed on a fat Havana cigar and smiled up at Sidney. Jasper Barnes always smiled. He smiled when he was happy. He smiled when he was nervous. He even smiled when he was angry. That smile, that face, even by the most generous of hearts, could only be described as ugly, but the brain that hummed inside that misshapen skull had something akin to financial genius.

"I still don't agree with how you've handled this. When they left town, that should have been the end of it," Sidney said.

Jasper's eyes gleamed in their sockets like a pair of obsidian marbles, indicating to Sidney that the particular smile he wore at this moment was not one that boded good tidings. "But they could always come back, and *that* is a loose end we cannot afford to leave untied."

Sidney rued the day he had ever gotten involved with Jasper, but it was a little late for regrets. Sidney had been playing the Big Game for quite some time now. He had been born to play the Big Game. It was one of the reasons he probably would have left his brother, Silas, in the long run anyway. Silas had never thought big enough. He had never looked beyond tomorrow. Silas, unlike his ambitious younger brother, had been incapable of playing the Big Game.

It was only a few years after Sidney had struck out on his own for the West Coast that he had been drawn to Virginia City. It was there that he had met Jasper Barnes, and they had hit it off right away, each seeing in the other a missing key to future success. Indeed, Jasper had recognized and articulated Sidney's special talents almost immediately: *"There's something about you, Sidney, something rare and divine. Without even being aware of it, people smell it on you. They're attracted to you. They want to follow you. You've got charisma. We can use that, Sidney. We can use that in a big way."* Jasper had used the right word to capture Sidney's attention. *Big.*

Sidney hadn't realized then what high stakes the Big Game entailed. The Big Game was business. Politics. The cards were dealt: money, power, favors, graft, bribery, corruption, vice, even murder. Sidney had learned to close his eyes to the last.

He pressed both palms down on the gleaming surface of his mahogany desk and leaned forward. "This is not a loose end we're talking about, Jasper. This is my niece and nephew. They're family. Can't you understand that?"

"I understand that they're the offspring of a brother you despised and a woman who spurned you." Jasper jabbed his cigar at Sidney. "You told me that story yourself, remember?"

Oh, yes, Sidney remembered. He remembered all too well that night in New Orleans when he had discovered his brother, Silas, and the woman he loved in a passionate embrace. The sight had cut into his gut like the cold blade of a hatchet. Some men would have drawn a pistol in jealous rage, but Sidney was not one of them. He had chosen instead to turn his back, to cut them out of his life forever. He had caught the first ship headed for California.

Sidney looked down at his hands, hands that had, without him even noticing until now, grown old. The tiny web of skin between his little finger and ring finger had been a part of him since birth. For years, he had looked through it, barely even realizing it was there. Now, the thin membrane flared before his eyes, reminding him that his own father had been afflicted with the same deformity.

Family and blood, blood and family. How often had Sidney's father drilled it into both of his sons' heads? Family was all-important. You never betray family. But Sidney had severed the last of his family ties when he had left Silas in New Orleans. Now, because he had not been able to foresee Jasper's knee-jerk reaction to a bad situation, Sidney felt indirectly responsible for his own brother's murder.

Jasper cut into his glum thoughts. "Enough with the guilt, Sidney. Your brother tried to blackmail you. He deserved the fate that was dealt him."

"I told you at the time I would take care of it. You didn't have to panic and have him killed."

"If he had exposed your past, you would have been ruined, both in business and politics," Jasper pointed out calmly. "We all would have suffered because of it."

"It was a mistake," Sidney insisted.

"Well, that's all water over the dam. Now, we have Mr. Ringo here to consider. He's been compromised. After so many years of faithful service, are we to just leave him to twist in the breeze?"

Sidney observed the subject of Jasper's inquiry, the third party in the room who had remained characteristically silent. Mr. Ringo was perusing the various pieces of medieval weaponry mounted on the wall opposite Sidney's desk. While they were only a small part of Sidney's ever-expanding collection, they were some of the more rare and valuable pieces, and Sidney winced as the big man reached up to disengage a silver seventeenth-century mace from its wall rack.

Normally, Sidney would have requested that his guest refrain from fondling his collection, but the laconic Mr. Ringo was not a man he liked to risk offending. The man was huge. When he rose to full height, he measured an impressive six and a half feet tall. With hands the size of dinner plates and arms as thick as stovepipes, it was easy to imagine Mr. Ringo snapping a man's neck single-handedly. At the moment, he was gripping the mace, flexing his fingers, and swinging it gently through the air to test its weight and balance.

Jasper blew a perfect smoke ring. "The boy saw his face. That is a loose end that cannot be left untied, Sidney. And it's not only Mr. Ringo's security that's on the line, it's our own also. There are people who know of Mr. Ringo's associations with us. We cannot risk the possibility of him being indicted on murder charges."

Sidney forced a smile and turned his palms up innocently. "But it won't ever come to that, Jasper! Don't you see? The boy doesn't want to testify! He ran away with his sister!"

"The boy's father was blown to kingdom come before his eyes. Even if he's too frightened to testify now, who's to say his feelings won't change on the subject as he grows older? Mr. Ringo was only following orders. It's just not fair to him or to any of us to leave those loose ends untied. If one of us goes down, we all go down. Certainly you can understand that."

Sidney glanced uneasily at Alphonse Ringo. The big man had just been following orders. Jasper's orders. Mr. Ringo's loyalty to Jasper was as certain and immovable as a mountain. Many years ago, Jasper had, by means of legal chicanery, rescued Ringo from the hangman's noose. The ever-grateful giant had trailed Jasper like the world's biggest lapdog ever since.

Stifling a shudder, Sidney turned and fixed his attention on the lavish oil painting which hung over the marble fireplace. That painting, titled *The Final Parting of Guinevere and Lancelot*, featured the two tortured figures holding hands and weeping over the death of King Arthur. He had commissioned the painting over ten years ago. The face of Guinevere had been inspired by a faded daguerreotype he still kept in a desk drawer next to an old Calvary Colt revolver, a picture that he perhaps should have burned a long time ago. He doubted, though, especially now, as his eye traveled over the compelling lines of her face, that even burning that picture would have purged the memory of her from his heart. *Emmaline.*

With great effort, Sidney took a deep breath. "I told you from the beginning that I could handle my brother, but you didn't listen. Then things started to go wrong, didn't they? There were witnesses left behind. You saw fit to use my name to hire the Pinkertons to find them, and now—"

"And now they're found, aren't they?"

"Yes," Sidney allowed. "And now that they are, I'm asking you again to let me handle this problem in my own way."

Jasper ground out his cigar in the freestanding silver ashtray by his elbow. "Sidney, the Round Table has met on the subject. It's already too late."

The Round Table. Sidney had once coined the term in jest and Jasper had pounced upon it eagerly. The Round Table, in this instance, had nothing to do with kings or knights or anything even remotely connected with honor. It was a group of wealthy, unscrupulous men who were growing more powerful and influential with each passing day. They spent their days manipulating mining stocks, their evenings frequenting fancy receptions, and their weekends basking on country estates. The men who made up the Round Table had "friends" all over; in the police department, the local judiciary, and City Hall. Now they had their own serious candidate for the mayor's office, none other than Phineas Taylor, of course.

That candidate narrowed his eyes at Jasper. "What do you mean, it's already too late? They're not even scheduled to arrive for another four days."

"One of our people has been dispatched and will be boarding the eight forty connection at Promontory."

Sidney felt a surge of helpless frustration rise in his chest. "You can't just go ahead and do this without discussing it with me!"

"Can't we?" Jasper was smiling again, his eyes growing cold.

"This is my family we're talking about! My *family!*"

"You're too emotionally involved to be objective. We'll handle it."

Rising from his chair, Jasper Barnes barely touched five and a half feet in height. The top of Mr. Ringo's black bowler hat, by contrast, just missed brushing the ceiling. If Sidney hadn't been so thoroughly disgusted at this moment, he might have found the sight of the two men standing side by side quite comical.

"I suggest," Jasper offered with a wink, "that you practice your speech for tomorrow's campaign rally." As he turned to leave, he plucked up his cane, which had been hooked neatly over the arm of his chair. "And by all means, try to get some rest, Sidney. You're not looking well at all."

After one full day of "luxurious" travel via the Union Pacific Railroad, Cole was beginning to think he just wasn't built for modern travel. His legs were too long, for one thing. No matter how he tried to situate himself in their cramped compartment, it seemed he couldn't remain comfortable for any longer than five minutes at a time.

Cole was also beginning to think he wasn't built to be spending so much time with Guinevere Pierce. Maybe it had been too long since he had been with a woman. How else to explain the fact that he was becoming so distracted with her very femaleness in such constant proximity?

When they had disembarked for dinner, Cole had only picked at the bland train station food on his plate, and this despite the fact that he had worked up a good appetite. The trouble was, the appetite he had worked up sitting next to Gwin on the train hadn't been for food.

Throughout the rushed meal, Arthur had kept up a steady stream of excited chatter and eager questions about Cole's experiences in New York City. Nevertheless, Cole had found his attention wandering, his gaze repeatedly drawn back to the boy's sister, from her lovely face to the gentle curve of her rounded bosom to the slender lines of her waist. He had found himself pondering the burning question of whether or not she wore a corset beneath that snowy-white jacket blouse, and, after twenty minutes of intensive study, he had finally reached the conclusion that she did not.

Unfortunately, the result of all that mealtime distraction was that he hadn't found time to actually finish the food on his plate. His empty stomach had started gurgling about an hour ago, and, by now, it was sending up hunger pangs sharp enough to put him in a decidedly bad mood.

Cole looked forward to escaping into blissful, dreamless sleep. He was exhausted. The night before, he had spent a restless night on the uneven puncheon floor of the constable's office in Caldwell, not quite trusting their prison security after that afternoon's fiasco. He was ready for a good night's sleep, but there was one thing he had to see to before he could finally close his eyes in good conscience, and that one thing was Guinevere Pierce.

Cole had rearranged their seats into a lower sleeping berth for Arthur and himself, then pulled down the upper berth for Gwin. Safely snuggled in for the night, Arthur snored like a full-grown buffalo.

Cole waited in the narrow aisle for his other charge to situate herself. She huddled behind pulled curtains while Cole marked time, his arms folded stiffly. "Are you decent yet?"

Her voice was coy. "Are you saying that I'm usually indecent?"

"I'm very amused out here, Gwin."

"Good. Maybe it'll take that permanent frown off your face."

Cole reached out to grasp the edge of the berth, steadying himself as the train went into a curve. Sudden turns and bumps were becoming quite a nuisance, occasionally causing embarrassed passengers to stumble into one another as they passed in the aisles. "Will you hurry, please?"

"They do not make women's garments as simple as men's, Shepherd. You'll just have to wait until I . . ." She paused, then exclaimed breathily, "There! Oh, that feels better! It's so awfully hot in here, don't you think?"

Cole had to agree, only it wasn't just the summer heat that was getting him into a sweat. A lot of it had to do with the mental image he was conjuring up of her disrobing behind that flimsy little curtain.

"Here!" Her arm suddenly popped out from between the curtains, offering him a carpetbag.

"What do you want me to do with that?"

"I don't know. Shove it under your berth or something. Just don't lose it. My clothes are in there."

Cole took the bag and bent to slide it beneath the

bottom berth. He straightened, jingling the handcuffs in his coat pocket. "Now, are you decent?"

"Decent as I'll ever get, I suppose."

Cole parted the curtains to find her lying on her side, a sheet pulled up over her chest, revealing the slim shoulder straps of a white chemise. Her head rested on one hand, her long-lashed eyes glimmering mischievously in the flickering overhead lamplight. "What are you going to do now? Search me for weapons?"

Cole studied the delicate line of her jaw, the curve of her lips. Oh, she knew what she was doing to him, all right, and he didn't doubt for a minute she would try to use it. When Fritz Landis had warned him back in Chicago not to let his guard down, Cole had never foreseen this particular danger. He hadn't known then he would be stuck traveling across the country with a sharp-witted, smart-mouthed, pint-sized temptress.

He took the handcuffs from his pocket and reached for her right hand. She jerked back. "Hey! What's this?"

"Just taking precautions, Gwin."

"Where in heck do you think I'm going to go in my underclothes?"

"I shudder to think."

"Are you going to shackle Arthur, too?"

"No. He's sleeping with me. He can't go anywhere without crawling over me, and, I assure you, I'm a very light sleeper."

She rolled over onto her back and covered her face with both hands. "This is outrageous! How am I supposed to sleep all tied up?"

Cole couldn't help noticing that her sheet had slipped down, baring cleavage. That was all his erotic imagination needed. He gritted his teeth, looked up at the paneled ceiling, and tried counting to ten silently. "You won't be tied up. One wrist locked to the berth chain, that's all."

"That's *all?* Why don't *you* try sleeping that way?"

"*I* don't have to try sleeping that way. *I* haven't broken the law lately."

"Which brings us to the subject of charges, Shepherd. No one's actually charged us with anything. What right do you have to kidnap us, shackle us, and drag us halfway across the country in the first place?"

Cole was losing his patience. "If you want charges, we could start with horse-stealing."

"I *didn't* steal your horse!"

"I'm talking about Garden City, Gwin. They sent us a warrant."

She rolled her eyes and snorted. "Oh! Well! If you're going to go try picking hairs off an egg, we could be here all night!"

"All right, Gwin, leaving all egg hairs aside, we could move on to the fact that you and your brother are witnesses in a murder case. Have you ever heard of subpoena powers?"

"Supeena? Sounds like something you'd find on the menu at one of those fancy French restaurants!"

"No, it means you have to appear if the court orders you to, and the court, in this case, has ordered you to."

"But I'll wager it's not the court that's paying you, is it? Who *is* paying you for this, Shepherd?"

"I'm employed by the Agency, Gwin, you know that."

"Who's paying the Agency?"

"I can't divulge that information."

She studied him grimly in the dim light. Her voice grew quiet. "Well, it seems to me that I have a right to know."

Cole held up the cuffs. "Give me your hand."

"No."

"Either you give me your hand or I take it."

She frowned. "All right, but do me one favor."

"What's that?"

She offered him her left hand. "If you have to do it, do this one instead. I always sleep on my left side."

Cole grimaced, exasperated. "What the hell difference does it make which side you sleep on?"

She arched an eyebrow. "You said a bad word, Cole. My opinion of you is slipping. Am I asking so much?"

"All right, all right!" Cole climbed up onto the lower berth and reached across her supine body, trying to find an anchor point for the cuffs. His forearm brushed against the swell of one breast and he jerked back guiltily.

Rattled, he looked down to find Gwin blinking up at him, appearing a little disconcerted herself. She didn't move, however, *or* open her mouth, for which he was extremely grateful. He averted his eyes and leaned over her more carefully this time.

"It sure is a pity that a big strapping fellow like yourself needs handcuffs to control one small, helpless female."

Small, helpless female. Like a black widow spider this one was a small, helpless female. Cole didn't look at her as he pushed and probed at the wood and metalwork. "I think I've handled you just fine up until this point, Gwin."

"If I were you, I wouldn't go tooting my horn just yet."

Cole tested a corner joint by tugging on it a few times. "Oh, I don't know. Caught you twice already, didn't I? What's that come to? Two out of two?"

"Well, you know what they say."

Cole paused to look down at her. It was a mistake. She was as good as lying flat beneath him. Her hair was plaited into a single braid that snaked down over the plump rise of her right breast. Cole would have liked to see what that hair looked like loose and spread out, how it felt to run strands of wild red curls through his fingers. With each breath she took, the rise of her breasts spilled out over the top of her chemise.

He tore his eyes from that arousing sight only to see that she wore a cunning little smile, a come-hither smile if ever there was one. Cole felt a physical stirring down below, a definite danger signal, which he ignored. "No, what is it that they say?" he asked.

"Even a blind pig will find a pea *sometimes.*"

The train suddenly lurched, throwing Cole forward, off balance. He caught himself but not before his groin jammed into the corner of her berth. Pain flashed brightly, then climbed into his lower abdomen and snuggled there, a dull, throbbing ache.

"Ahhhhh!" Cole bent his head and groaned. His

eyes practically crossed behind clenched lids. He felt her hands at his waist, fumbling to catch at the material of his jacket.

"Are you all right?"

She was staring up at him, wide-eyed, puzzled, seemingly innocent. He couldn't quite bring himself to believe she didn't have any idea what had just happened to him, the little vixen.

That jostle, however, painful as it had been, was just what he needed to bring him back to his senses. He removed her hand from his waist. "Yes, I am quite all right." He gripped her left wrist firmly in his right hand. She didn't try to pull away.

"Where did you go to school, Shepherd?"

Cole hesitated, wary at her change in subject. "I went to college in New Jersey. Why?"

She gave him a sweet smile. "Is that where they taught you to handcuff helpless young ladies to their berths?"

"No," he answered firmly, slipping the open cuff over the slim bones of her wrist. It snapped shut with a click. "They teach us that at the Agency." He attached its twin to the wooden joint in the lower corner of her berth and rammed that one home with finality. "It's a special course. They call it *Know Thy Enemy*."

Later, Cole dreamed of dining on one of Guinevere Pierce's sleek, succulent legs. Perhaps that shouldn't have come as much of a surprise. After all, he liked women with nice legs and he had gone to bed hungry.

In the dream, her hair, that magnificent mane of

blazing curls, was loose and flowing, framing her pristine face. It spread wantonly across her pillow. Her eyes were closed in repose, her delectable neck arched just so. Since it was Cole's dream, he knew she wore nothing beneath the blankets that hid her from his ravishing gaze.

He approached the bed and threw the coverlet back to bare one smooth leg. He held one perfectly shaped, naked foot in his hand. She sighed, and her lashes fluttered open. Sky blue sapphires settled on him just as he bent to press his lips to the soft skin of her instep.

Cole's dream banquet began there, at her instep, and proceeded on to the delicate point of her ankle. He nibbled his way slowly up one side of her calf. Her skin was like silk and smelled faintly of lilacs. Her flesh tasted salty on his tongue. Cole let one hand slide up her thigh as he paused to sink his teeth, ever so gently, into the flesh at the inside of her knee—

"Mr. Shepherd!"

She never called him *Mister* Shepherd. How odd that she should start addressing him formally at a time like this.

"Mr. Shepherd! Cole!"

Cole frowned. That wasn't Gwin's voice, it was Arthur's, and Arthur had *no business whatsoever* in this dream.

"Cole! Wake up! You're having some kind of nightmare!"

Cole opened one groggy eye to find, much to his dismay, he wasn't in bed with Guinevere Pierce at all.

He was in bed with her freckle-faced little brother, and that was a most bitter disappointment.

The boy leaned over him, wide-eyed and alert, his hair standing up in sleep spikes. "You sounded like you were dying or something! Are you all right?"

Cole groaned and closed his eye again.

"Mr. Shepherd?"

He was too miserable to answer. Ever since Cynthia, he had more or less sworn off women, and Cole was feeling a little sorry for himself. He couldn't even seem to get any in his dreams anymore.

"Cole? Was it a bad nightmare?"

"Awful."

"I have them sometimes, too. Gwin always gets me awake and asks if I want to talk about it. Sometimes that helps. Do you need to talk about it?"

"No, thank you, Arthur. You've done quite enough already." Cole turned over on his side. "Why don't we go back to—" His right arm was yanked back sharply.

"What? What the . . . ?" He snapped wide awake and tried to pull his arm around again, only to have it come up short. Metal cut into the flesh at his wrist. *"Sonofabitch!"* He rolled onto his back and craned his neck to see that he was securely cuffed to the berth.

"Cole, why are you sleeping with handcuffs on?"

"I am not going to dignify that stupid question with an answer!" Cole sat up abruptly and slammed his forehead into the bottom of the upper berth. "Ouch! Damn it!"

"Uh-oh, did Gwin . . . ?"

Cole finally righted himself. "That bitch of a sister of yours is right! I don't know how she did it, but she did it! Just wait till I get my hands . . . my *hands!*" He yanked again at the cuffs, succeeding only in rattling their traveling bed and enraging himself anew. "Ah, hell!"

"I don't think she escaped or anything, Mr. . . . uh, Cole. I think she was just, uh . . ." Arthur trailed off sheepishly.

"Just what?"

"I think she was just mad at you for something."

Cole muttered under his breath and reached below the bunk to retrieve his coat. "Mad at me for something. Oh, *that's* rich. I'm going to strangle her." He found his coat and rifled through his pockets, searching for the key to the handcuffs.

Arthur's voice was anxious. "You aren't really going to hurt her, are you, Mr. Shepherd?"

Cole, having found his pockets infuriatingly devoid of keys, tossed the garment aside in disgust. "Hurt her? Why would I want to hurt the scheming little wench?"

"She must've palmed your key."

"She's a woman of many talents, your sister. Where's my pants?"

"She isn't so bad once you get to know her. It's just that she doesn't like being bossed around. It gets her fur up, and when her fur's up, she sometimes does things without thinking ahead."

Cole struggled to climb into his wrinkled trousers with the use of only one hand. "Well, she's gotten *my* fur up this time, and she's going to be woefully sorry that she did!" He paused and muttered under his breath, "As soon as I figure a way out of this."

"Gwin will have the key. Don't worry, Mr. Shepherd, she doesn't stay mad long. And I know she'll be real sorry."

"Damn it! I'm going to have to call the conductor!"

"I'm sure she'll be back soon."

Cole would be royally damned if he was going to wait here for her to return and then beg for the key. He thought he would rather dine on rat meat than be forced that low.

"Or . . ."

There was a certain wheedling tone in Arthur's voice that caused Cole to raise his head. "What?"

"If you promise that you won't be too mad at her, I could maybe—"

Cole grabbed Arthur by the top of his collarless nightshirt, dragging him forward and up, nose to nose. "Don't give me any of this 'maybe' hogwash! If you know how to get these damned things open, you'd better do it now, or I'm going to tan your sneaky little backside, understand?"

"I said *maybe*, Cole! I'm not sure I can do it! I need a lock pick!"

"A lock pick?" Cole lowered his voice. "Oh, certainly! Maybe I'll just ask that nice old lady two seats back! She's bound to have an extra one in her traveling bag!"

Arthur shrugged as best he could with Cole's fist still entangled in his nightshirt. "Maybe one of Gwin's hatpins?"

Cole released the boy and bent down to feel around for Gwin's valise. It was, of course, not there. He stood and felt around blindly on the empty upper berth. His fingers snagged on one corner of the bag, and he dragged it down with a thump. Releasing the clasp, he started pulling things out haphazardly. His fingers entangled in a lacy thing, and he held it up briefly to the dim light. A camisole. He tossed it aside, and caught a subtle whiff of lilac. Trying to ignore the scent and the images it conjured up, he burrowed deep down to the bottom of the bag and immediately pricked his finger on a pin. He drew it out and gave it to Arthur. "This had better work."

The boy inserted the pin into the locking mechanism. "I'll try my best, Cole. I haven't done it in a long time."

"Don't you need more light for this?" Cole asked.

"Not light, just quiet."

Cole tried to see what the kid was doing. "Did you learn this trick from your charming sister?"

"No, I learned it from a fellow by the name of Fuzzy Garrison who traveled with us a while back."

Cole waited in silence, struggling to remain patient as Arthur continued to pick and probe for another five minutes. Finally, there was an almost imperceptible click.

"Yessiree bob!" Arthur's head flew up, his eyes alight. Cole was pleasantly surprised to feel the cuff open and slide from his wrist.

"Arthur!" Cole grasped his skinny shoulders, fighting an urge to hug him. "You're a pint-sized miracle worker!"

Arthur beamed, clearly pleased with the compliment. "Well, we men, we gotta stick together, right?"

Cole clapped him on the back in comradely fashion.

"You betcha, kiddo! You betcha!" He reached for his shirt, which was slung over the bottom of their bunk.

"Cole?"

Cole finished buttoning his shirt and jerked on his boots, contemplating what form his revenge on Guinevere Pierce should take. "What?"

"You're not mad anymore, right? I mean, you aren't gonna *hurt* her, right?"

Cole didn't answer for a moment. He located his coat and shrugged one arm into the sleeve. "Hurt her?" He reached out and plucked the hatpin from Arthur's hand. "I'll take that. Thank you." He dropped it into his pocket.

"You just stay put, Arthur," Cole said, snatching his gun belt and rising to his feet. "I'm not going to hurt her, but I *am* going to find her, and when I do . . ." The rest of his sentence was lost. He was already halfway down the sleeping car's narrow aisle.

5

Saloon Car

Gwin peered coolly over a full house to size up the gentleman seated across from her at the small table. The cards were marked. She knew it. He knew it. This was a cat-and-mouse game, only Gwin wasn't sure yet who was going to end up being the cat and who was going to end up being the mouse. All she knew for sure was that she had to earn a few dollars before skipping the Union Pacific Express 840. She was tired of stealing horses.

With two fingers, she slid a pair of chips into the growing pot in the center of the small table. Her own small pile of chips represented the sum total of her accumulated wealth in this world, an engraved silver pocket watch Emmaline had once given Silas. She had already shaken off the small twinge of guilt that had arisen at staking her only remaining family heirloom in order to earn traveling money. After all, if anyone would have understood her reasoning, it would have been Silas.

Gwin smiled, hoping she appeared more confident than she felt. "I'll call and raise you one, Mr. Monroe."

He was grinning, but this expression, she knew, had nothing to do with what he presumably held in his hand. He was in his mid-thirties, a flashy dresser with a closely trimmed mustache and slick black hair parted down the middle. He had very dark, very discerning eyes that kept focusing with disturbing regularity on Gwin's bosom. Gwin, who had long ago learned the advantages of engaging in a bit of innocent flirtation for a good cause, didn't mind as long as he kept his hands to himself.

She reached for her brandy snifter, raising her gaze just in time to see the door to the saloon car yawn open. She bit her lip as Cole Shepherd's rangy form filled the doorway. Drat! Gwin still had the key to those handcuffs snuggled deep in her skirt pocket. How the devil had he escaped so quickly?

As her eyes locked with Cole's, Gwin's stomach did a flip-flop. Even from where she sat, she saw the storm brewing, and for the first time since lifting the key from his coat pocket, she began to have second thoughts about her impulsive actions. Cole wasn't just mad, he was *furious*.

Gwin gulped a mouthful of brandy. "Uh-oh."

Mr. Monroe, who was settled back into his seat puffing on his cigar contemplatively, looked up. "Is something wrong, Miss Pierce?"

Heads turned as Cole crossed the length of the saloon car. Edging his jacket back with his forearm, he rested one hand on his gun belt as he addressed the man seated across from Gwin. "The lady is through for this evening, sir. She's coming with me."

Mr. Monroe plucked the smoking cigar from between his teeth. "And who are you? Her husband?"

"The lady is traveling in my custody."

"Is that right? Well, maybe she's ready to change *custodies*."

"Look, I don't want any trouble here, mister, but I *am* leaving with the lady, whether you like it or not."

"Seems to me that the little lady here should be the one to make that decision."

Gwin glanced from Shepherd to Monroe and back to Shepherd again. Stuck between Monroe's clearly lecherous intentions and Shepherd's clearly murderous ones, she was beginning to think that she might have gotten herself into something of a pickle.

Cole's voice was low, straining patience. "In this case, sir, the lady does not have a choice. She's coming with me."

For what seemed like the longest time, the two men proceeded to stare each other down. Gwin could see that they were getting ready to engage in the sort of male posturing that more often than not ended up with one or the other of them bleeding facedown all over the carpet. The small, all-male crowd in the saloon car had grown ominously quiet. Gwin shifted in her seat uneasily and set down her glass, hoping to break the tension. "Uh, gentlemen?"

Unfortunately, neither of them paid any attention to her.

Monroe puffed on his cigar and blew out a frothy smoke ring. His voice was thick as syrup. "Why don't you run along, son? The lady is in the middle of a game right now and doesn't wish to be disturbed."

Cole finally turned to Gwin. "Is that right?"

Gwin looked up at him apprehensively. Her original intention had been to teach him a lesson for treating her so high-handedly. Cuffing him to his own berth had just been a bit of last-minute inspiration. Tit for tat, as the saying went, but, oh dear, it certainly appeared he was turning out to be quite a poor sport.

Gwin didn't see how quibbling with him at this point was going to improve her situation, and so, after a moment of awkward silence, she laid down her cards. "I'm terribly sorry, Mr. Monroe, but I must have lost track of the time. It's dreadfully late."

Before she could even start to rise, she felt Cole's fingers wrap around her elbow, practically hoisting her to her feet. He addressed Mr. Monroe. "Does the lady owe you any money?"

Monroe's dark eyes held Cole's for another tense second before flicking to Gwin's expectant face, assessing. "The lady and I are even," he said finally, reaching out to nudge Silas's gleaming silver watch across the table toward her. "I believe this belongs to you?"

"I'm so sorry we had to cut our game short, Mr. Monroe," Gwin said hastily, taking the watch and slipping it back into the pocket of her skirt. "Perhaps another time."

Before she could continue, Cole gave her elbow a jerk. Gwin found herself being steered purposefully toward the rear of the saloon car. Every eye in the place followed their progress, but Gwin was hardly aware of it. This wasn't the way back to their sleeping coach. Where was he taking her?

"Hey! Ouch! Not so hard!" Gwin struggled against his manhandling once they were outside in the narrow vestibule. She raised her voice to be heard over the deafening clatter of the locomotive's wheels. "Where are we going?"

"In here!" Cole pulled the door to the next car open, and, shoving her inside ahead of him, swung it closed with a smack behind them.

Gwin squinted in the murky light. Only one overhead lamp illuminated the car and that one was turned low. This was not surprising, since very few people chose to frequent the baggage car in the middle of the night. On either side of them, piled high, were crates and steamer trunks, valises and satchels, and even one odd-shaped, pillowslip-covered item that might have been a birdcage.

She shifted her attention to Cole as he backed her up against the wall by the door. "What are we doing in here?"

Cole's grip on her arm tightened, causing her to wince. His gaze was fixed determinedly on the wall just over her head. "If it's at all humanly possible, just shut up a minute, Gwin. I'm trying to keep from murdering you."

Gwin opened her mouth, then thought better of it. She eyed Cole's rigid jaw above her and waited, acutely aware of their physical proximity.

"Well," she said after a few minutes, slipping gingerly from his grasp and massaging her arm, "are you ever going to speak to me again, or are we just going to stand here all night while you decide how to dispose of my body?"

"A seemingly small, but very significant part of the plan, disposal of the body."

She thought maybe he had calmed down a bit, judging by the subdued tone of his voice. At least, she hoped so. She tried to sound bright. "Well, I must say I'm impressed. It didn't take you long to find me."

"No thanks to you."

"Where's your sense of humor?"

"I must have left it shackled to my berth. You know, I feel like I could just about strangle you right now."

"But you aren't going to, are you?"

There was a silence, during which Gwin had to reconsider her original impression of Cole Shepherd's basically nonviolent personality. She thought that his voice, when he finally did reply, was distinctly threatening. "Don't ever try to pull a stunt like that again."

She steeled herself. "You didn't need to lock me up like some kind of horse thief!"

"You *are* a horse thief, Gwin."

"All right, you may have a small point there, but what did you expect me to do? Get down on my hands and knees and thank you for it?"

"What you did was just plain stupid. You could've gotten yourself into trouble."

"I can take care of myself just fine."

"Sure, Gwin, you'll be just fine until you run into the wrong man."

"Wrong man? What are you talking about?"

"Just what the hell did you think you were doing with a guy like that?"

Gwin narrowed her eyes, distinctly annoyed by the tone of his voice. "A guy like *what?*"

"You know what I'm talking about! He didn't look like the type of guy who would exactly take well to being fleeced by a cardsharp!"

Disgusted, Gwin squirmed out from between him and the wall. She didn't get more than three steps before her shins barked into the side of a protruding steamer trunk. She swung around only to find that he had followed her and had her cornered again. "I am not a cardsharp, Cole Shepherd!"

"Like hell you're not! What do you call it?"

"What I *do,* Mister Pinkerton man, is an *art!*"

He snorted. "An *art?*"

"That's right! It's the art of card manipulation! And in case you didn't know it, it takes years and years of practice to master!"

"It's the art of cheating!" His voice rose. "That's goddamn well what it is!"

"Think whatever you want! This game wasn't high stakes, anyway! Just a few dollars, and Mr. Monroe could well afford it!"

Cole's tone turned coldly sarcastic. "You may be right. I reckon by the way he was looking at you, it wasn't the card game he was interested in, anyway."

"What's *that* supposed to mean?"

"Just exactly how were you planning on paying Mr. Monroe if you lost?"

Gwin blinked at him, taken aback. What was he insinuating? It took her a moment to recover from her surprise. "I beg your pardon?"

Cole's handsome mouth curved into a grim smile. "What were you betting, Miss Pierce?"

"A watch."

His brows climbed dubiously. "A watch?"

"A pocket watch!"

"That's *it*?"

"Of course that's it! What else do I have to wager?" Gwin demanded indignantly.

"What else, indeed?"

Gwin glared up at him, simmering at his male arrogance. "If you have something to say, Shepherd, why don't you just *say* it?"

"Say it?" His tone was mockingly innocent. "I'm not *saying* anything. I'm merely asking a question. It's obvious Mr. Monroe isn't the kind of man to be satisfied with a good-night kiss at the end of the evening."

"Is it?" Gwin shot back. "You know, it seems to me that you have little room to talk about *ungentlemanly* intentions."

"What?"

"I've seen you looking at me, too, Shepherd, and those aren't exactly saintly intentions I read on your face."

Gwin saw by his shocked expression that she had hit him right between the eyes with the truth. She had seen him looking. She had felt his eyes on her any number of times since they had boarded the train at

Topeka, and she had felt a little of what he was feeling, too, even if it utterly galled her to admit it. How could she not feel something?

For years, she had dreamed of this man, this stranger who wasn't really a stranger at all, kissing her and touching her in places that brought a blush to her cheeks to even think about. She still couldn't get over the feeling that she knew him from somewhere, but the answer continued to elude her. It would dance near the surface of her consciousness, then, like a wily fish, dart away and dive deep before she could grasp it.

Cole's expression rapidly changed from one of shock to one of anger. "How you may *imagine* I look at you is irrelevant. I have a job to do, and that job is to get you and your brother to San Francisco."

"And that's just what you intend to do, isn't it? Despite what we told you this afternoon? Despite the fact that you might be delivering us into the hands of people who want to see us dead?"

"Don't string me along. I'm not one of your marks, Gwin."

"I'm not lying to you, Cole. You've got to believe me. I wouldn't lie to you."

"Do I look like I was born yesterday?"

Gwin shifted her weight from one foot to the other. "All right, all right, I *would* lie to you, but I'm not lying about *this*."

"What do you expect me to do?"

Gwin peered up at him, her voice softening, beseeching. "Just, please, let us go."

The train rounded a sudden curve, catching them

both by surprise. Cole stumbled forward, capturing her around the waist just in time to keep her from flipping back over a trunk. She clutched at the lapels of his coat, her heart thumping. A hot blush rose to her cheeks, as much due to her near fall as to their sudden physical contact.

The wheels of the locomotive were once again on firm, straight track, but he still held her. Gwin felt the unyielding firmness of his chest press against the fullest part of her breasts. It was an unexpectedly welcome, sweet pressure, and Gwin became aware all at once of an embarrassing glow of heat beginning to rise from low in her belly.

His head was bent close to hers, and she thought, for a dazzling instant, that he might kiss her. She tilted her head back, feeling his breath on her cheek as her eyes traced the straight line of his nose, the angle of his jaw, the shadow of his hair where it brushed the nape of his neck.

She knew in her right-thinking mind that he was her enemy, that they were at cross purposes here in the real world, but now, at this moment, it was just the two of them here in the dark, alone; and at this moment, it didn't matter who they were outside of this place and time. She *wanted* him to kiss her, just once, because then she would know for sure if it was really him, Lancelot. . . .

"Stop pushing up against me, Gwin. It's not going to work." His voice was strained and uneven, thoroughly unconvincing. Gwin could still feel the heat of his hands, the strength of his fingers, wrapped snugly around her waist.

She swallowed hard, and, with no small difficulty, forced her mouth open to speak. "*You're* the one pushing, Shepherd. *You* stop it."

He let go of her, stepping back in one abrupt move, and Gwin almost lost her balance. The moment had irrevocably passed. He didn't say anything, and it was quite an awkward span of time before Gwin managed to recover her voice.

"I meant what I said, Shepherd. I'm not lying about what happened in San Francisco. I don't care if you believe me or not. I'm not going to let you take us back there."

But even as the words formed on her lips, Gwin was struck by the novel realization that she *did* care whether he believed her.

"Well, Gwin, that's just too bad, because I'm not going to let you stop me."

The remainder of Gwin's first night aboard the Union Pacific Express passed restlessly, and her morning wasn't going much better. She sat forward in her seat and craned her neck, trying to see past Arthur's head to the rear of the car where a long line had formed by the ladies' washroom. It hadn't budged an inch in the last ten minutes. She sat back and shifted the carpetbag on her lap from one knee to the other. Along with her bag, she clutched a new cake of soap wrapped in a clean towel, the latter two items purchased by Shepherd this morning from the newsboy.

He had also bought a new deck of cards. At the

moment, he was using his tally book to keep a running score of the rummy game he and Arthur had been engaged in since this morning. Arthur was, of course, trouncing all over Cole.

Knowing Shepherd's suspicious turn of mind, Gwin thought he probably suspected Arthur of cheating. But that wasn't the case. Arthur didn't need to cheat. Gwin wondered how long it was going to take this clever Pinkerton detective to figure out that Arthur memorized every card as it was discarded, that he could accurately recalculate his odds of obtaining any given combination at each new turn, and from that information retailor his strategy accordingly.

Cole grinned as he pulled a card from the deck, then promptly laid out three sixes. Despite the fact that he couldn't have gotten much more sleep than Gwin had, he seemed in good spirits. "Oh, yes!" he exclaimed. "Perfect!"

Gwin turned back to the window, idly biting at her nails. They were in Colorado now. The flat, featureless prairies of Kansas were left behind. The lay of the land was taking on an almost desertlike character, but Gwin's restless mind could not focus on appreciating the change in scenery.

Gwin stopped biting her nails and rested her head back against the cushion of the seat. How could she expect Cole to understand anything of her life? To him, everything was right or wrong, black or white, good or bad. Appearances were all. Why, last night he had come very close to accusing her of trying to seduce Mr. Monroe for money. And that had hurt, maybe more than she was willing to admit, even to herself. She might be a liar and a thief, but she certainly wasn't a . . .

Gwin closed her eyes. Perhaps it had stung all the more because she had tried for so many years to convince herself that she wasn't like her late mother. Gwin could remember the night she had discovered the bitter truth about Emmaline. Perhaps it had been obvious before then, but Gwin had still been a child, capable of seeing Emmaline only through a daughter's eyes, eyes blinded by love and adoration.

Emmaline Pierce had been breathtakingly beautiful, with rich, flame red curls and flashing emerald green eyes. Her singing voice had been ambrosia to the ear and she'd had a flair for telling stories that Gwin had never seen matched. Even if her mother had always been a trifle irresponsible, it had never really mattered to Gwin. She was daring and buoyant and fun to be around. She was happy most of the time—in the beginning—before Arthur had been born. By then, it must have become apparent that she was growing older and her life with Silas was not going the way of fairy tales. That was when she had really started to change. Gwin remembered it well.

That winter their home had been a drafty, two-room flat above a dance-hall saloon in Kansas City. Gwin was eleven. Silas was out late as usual, earning the bulk of their precarious livelihood in the wee hours of the morning.

At the sound of Emmaline's approach on the creaking floorboards outside her room, Gwin quickly

A TOUCH OF CAMELOT

doused the stubby candle on the nightstand and slipped beneath her blankets to feign sleep. It wasn't terribly difficult to fool her mother, who was lately preoccupied with her own concerns. Indeed, laboring under the strain of caring for a new baby and with her singing career at a complete standstill, Emmaline had not been acting at all like herself. Gwin was not surprised, then, that her mother failed to notice the lingering aroma of burning wax in the darkened room this night.

As soon as Emmaline laid the sleeping baby Arthur in his fleece-lined cradle and slipped from the room, Gwin was up like a shot, striking yet another match to the candle. From beneath her blankets, she withdrew a well-worn deck of playing cards. For weeks, she had been practicing the one-handed shift, a feat that the smugly superior Clell had informed her was practically impossible for a female to master.

"A woman's hands are generally too small," he had calmly explained one day, displaying the deck in his left hand, then deftly releasing the lower half to fall into his palm. "And it takes a certain dexterity that a woman could never hope to master as well as a man."

Gwin had watched solemnly as he had extended his second and third fingers so that the upper portion of the deck passed the upturned side of the lower portion before dropping down neatly beneath to square the deck once again. It was done in the blink of an eye.

Clell handed the cards back to her, grinning as he turned to walk away with an affected male swagger.

"Why, if you pull that one off, Gwinnie, I'll eat my hat!"

"I'll do it, all right," Gwin had muttered at his departing back. "And when the time comes, *I'll* darn well pick the hat!"

And so it was that on that particular night, by candlelight and at ten past one in the morning, Gwin still struggled to master the one-handed shift with the grim determination of a law student studying for final exams. And she was finally getting close, so close.

She was just releasing the lower portion of the deck with her thumb to fall into her palm, avidly picturing Clell Martin sprinkling salt on the brim of a huge sombrero, when she heard it. A woman's laughter coming from the alley directly below her open window.

This was not unusual in itself. She usually kept her window cracked open, even on cold nights, preferring fresh air, even frigid fresh air, to the stale tobacco smoke and kerosene fumes that usually permeated the building. Since they were located in a less reputable section of town, an occasional giggle from the alley below was hardly out of the ordinary.

This particular woman's laugh, however—a familiar sparkling titter—caught Gwin's ear and froze her fingers on the deck. It was Emmaline. And she wasn't alone. Gwin caught the unmistakably deep murmur of a man's voice.

Gwin climbed out of bed. What was her mother doing outside at this hour? She tiptoed over to the window, pushing the curtain back to peer outside. The air pouring in was icy, biting at Gwin's thin body through her flannel nightdress, but she didn't shy away from it. A distant street lamp illuminated the narrow alley just enough for Gwin to make out two figures below, her mother and a tall man she didn't recognize. Their words came out in little gray puffs that swirled and evaporated above their heads.

Emmaline's voice was eager. "Did you—"

"Yes," the man said. "I spoke with Gallagher and he's interested. The singer he has now is nothing better than a drunk, and he's looking to get rid of her as soon as possible."

"Oh, Frank! That's wonderful news!" Emmaline threw her arms around the man's neck. "When would I start?"

"Soon. Next week." Gwin could see that the man's hands settled comfortably around her mother's waist—too comfortably, as if they had been there before.

"Next week? Oh dear! I'll have to wean the baby by then. Oh dear, I've been trying, but—"

"Gallagher doesn't care much about weaning babes, Emmaline, honey." The man pressed his lips to her neck.

"Oh well, what he doesn't know won't hurt him. Besides, if I can wean Arthur, Gwinnie will be happy to take care of him. She fawns all over him as it is."

"Fine then, it's settled. That is, as long as your husband doesn't make a fuss."

"He wouldn't dare. He knows I'd leave him." Emmaline threw her head back, giving the strange man free access to her neck. Even from where Gwin stood, her feet seeming to grow roots into the cold plank floor, she saw that her mother's eyes were closed. If they hadn't been, Emmaline Pierce might have glimpsed her own daughter gazing down at her in numb disbelief.

"Oh, Frank, how can I ever thank you?"

The man lifted his head and Gwin caught the flash of a wicked grin. "I can think of a few ways, honey. More than a few. It's been a long time for you and me, too long."

"Too long, yes, but we can't," Emmaline said. "I have to get back."

"Your husband's not coming back for hours."

"No, but the baby will wake and want to be fed again. I swear, the child eats like a horse."

"Then we'll get reacquainted right here." The man slid Emmaline's woolen cloak down from one shoulder to nibble eagerly at bared flesh.

"Here?" Emmaline sounded mildly surprised. "Now?"

The man laughed as he pushed her back up against the wall. Alarmed, Gwin's heart started to pound. The playing cards slipped from her fingers, scattering unnoticed to the floor by her bare feet. She opened her mouth to scream for help, to shout down at the man who was attacking her mother, but her mouth clamped shut again as she saw her mother's arms wind tight around the man's neck.

Emmaline was giggling like a schoolgirl at a cotillion. "Oh, Frank! Frank! We can't! Not here!"

"We damn well can try, honey! Lift your skirts and belly up to the bar!"

Gwin dropped the curtain and scrambled back into

bed, yanking the blankets up to her chin and pulling the pillow around to cover her face. She could still hear her mother's giggles, faded and far away, mingling unintelligibly with the muffled laughter and melodeon music that always drifted up from the dance hall below.

I hate her, Gwin had thought fiercely, hot tears stinging at the corners of her eyes. *I hate her, I hate her, I hate her—*

"Ooooh yes! Lady Luck is smiling on me now!"

It was Cole Shepherd's voice that shattered Gwin's reverie, snapping her back to the here and now. She opened her eyes, fighting a lingering sense of time disorientation.

The landscape moving by outside her train window had changed little from a few moments ago, and Cole and Arthur were still embroiled in their rummy game. Judging by his latest outcry, Gwin thought Cole must be under the mistaken impression that he had a snowball's chance in hell of winning this hand.

Gwin sat up in her seat and strained to see back to the rear of the coach. The line to the ladies' washroom looked even longer. Disappointed, she slumped back with a sigh. This was only their second day on board, and already she was sick to death of dust and smoke and cinders. What she really needed to soothe her raw nerves was a hot bubble bath. Unfortunately, a bath was out of the question. The best she could hope for was a rushed toilette in the washroom of this cramped rail coach.

"You might as well give it up now, Arthur, my boy! It'll go easier on you!"

Gwin froze. *What was that? What had Cole said?* Her heart was suddenly thumping in her chest, *pitter-pat, pitter-pat, pitter-pat,* keeping a heady beat with the metallic click of the locomotive's wheels on the tracks beneath them.

"Give it up! Give it up now and it'll go easier on you!"

Gwin's mouth dropped open. She remembered where it was she had met him before.

6

"Good Lord!"

Gwin didn't even realize she had spoken aloud until Cole glanced at her. "What's the matter, Gwin? Not feeling so good? Doesn't sneaking around at all hours of the night agree with you?"

Gwin swallowed hard, unable to formulate even a weak retort to this baiting question. Luckily, Cole was too involved in the game to notice her stupefied expression or the fact that she didn't reply.

Abilene. The memory, the one that had been eluding her all this time, finally broke the surface. It swam up swiftly from the deep and burst into sunlight so bright it was blinding.

Gwin remembered it vividly; she didn't just see it in her mind, she could feel it, smell it, the underlying stench of cowflesh, the dust, the summer heat rising up from the dry prairie. She even thought she could hear Silas pitching his miracle elixir from somewhere in the distance. Oh, she had run like the dickens from Cole Shepherd, had tried her darnedest to shake him, but he had refused to be shaken. She remembered wondering why in tarnation this fella was so hell-bent on bringing her down when it hadn't even been his watch she'd filched in the first place.

She had gotten two fairly good looks at his face—first when she had spotted him eyeing her in the crowd and then when he had cornered her for the last time in the stockpen—but it wasn't until he had pulled her down from the fence and flipped her over onto her back that it had really hit her. She had been trapped beneath him, staring deep into his shocked brown eyes, when, despite the mud splotches on his nose and cheeks, she had thought to herself, *Sure as eggs are eggs, he has to be just about the handsomest boy I've ever seen in my life!*

"What's the matter, Gwin? You look like you just swallowed a beetle."

Gwin jumped. "What? A b-beetle?"

For a moment, it appeared as if Cole were going to say something, but he didn't. He just gave her a slightly bemused look, then turned back to his game.

Thank heavens. Gwin didn't know if she was capable of carrying on any kind of coherent conversation with him right now. She had to get her bearings. She rose to her feet, clutching her valise and towel to her stomach, feeling a little light-headed. She thought maybe she'd had just about all the *remembering* she could take for one day, thank you.

"Could you let me through?" she said breathlessly. "I'm going back."

Cole rose to his feet to let her past. "Remember, Miss Pierce, five minutes."

His tone was such that if Gwin had had her wits about her, she would have contemplated turning right around and smacking him over the head with her bag. But her wits seemed to be nowhere in the immediate vicinity. Without looking back, she edged her way along the center aisle of the moving rail car.

Cole watched Gwin's behind as she made her way toward the ladies' washroom.

"You're still mad at her, aren't you?"

Cole was too distracted to answer. The alluring memory of Gwin's lush feminine curves pressed up against him in the baggage car was still uncomfortably fresh and immediate.

Arthur raised his voice. "I said, you're still mad at her from last night, aren't you?"

Gwin's posterior passed out of sight as another passenger stepped out into the aisle behind her. Disappointed, Cole looked back at Arthur. "Why do you say that?"

"The way you're looking at her."

Cole tried not to smile. "How am I looking at her?"

"Real hard-like."

Smart-aleck kid. It was difficult, but Cole managed to keep his expression serious. "Well, I have to keep an eye on her, Arthur. Your sister has already demonstrated that she can't be trusted."

A companionable silence settled over them as Cole picked a card from the deck and calmly laid out three aces. Gwin's scent, lilacs, still hung in the air to haunt Cole's concentration. Even when she wasn't sitting beside him, her presence lingered on in his consciousness.

Arthur pulled a card and gave Cole a sneaky little smile. His own expression fell as Arthur laid off an ace, a three, three nines, and a discard, the remainder of his hand.

"I can't believe it!" Cole threw down his cards in disgust.

"Add thirty-six to my score. That gives me sixty-one."

Cole pulled out his tally book. That had to be the fourth or fifth time the kid had done it—calculated his points and added them to the running total before Cole even had a chance to put pencil to paper. The kid was bright, real bright. And Cole was beginning to think this was only a very small sample of Arthur's capabilities.

Cole jotted down the score, sixty-one to a dismal twenty-two in this, their sixth straight game. Arthur had won four out of five so far and seemed well on his way to yet another victory.

Now that Gwin was out of earshot for a few minutes, Cole decided to try a little experiment to confirm the suspicions he harbored about the little ragamuffin perched so innocently across from him.

He flipped the page of his tally book and scratched out a random arithmetic problem. "Arthur, I'll bet you a nickel that I can figure the answer to an addition problem before you can. Are you up to it?"

A TOUCH OF CAMELOT

Arthur scooted forward in his seat. "You got yourself a bet!"

"What's four hundred sixty-three plus two hundred ninety-six plus six hundred eighteen plus eighty-nine?"

Arthur's forehead didn't even wrinkle. Cole barely got a chance to carry the first two. "One thousand four hundred sixty-six!"

Even though he knew Arthur's answer was correct, Cole finished the problem. "Okay, you just earned yourself a nickel. Let's try multiplication. Are you ready?"

"Double or nothing?"

Cole stifled a smile. "All right. Ready? This is going to be a hard one."

"That's what you think." Arthur clasped his hands on the table and furrowed his pale brow in a scholarly manner. "Go."

"Twenty-six times forty-two times sixteen times nine."

Cole watched Arthur's face. There was no sign that the kid was calculating; no screwing up of the face, no biting of the lip, no squinting eyes, certainly no sweating. His stubby kid fingers drummed the table, staccato-quick, then his mouth opened and the answer dropped out. "One hundred fifty-seven thousand, two hundred forty-eight."

Cole worked out the problem, then looked up at Arthur's grinning, wise-acre face. He couldn't disguise his amazement. "I guess I owe you at the next whistle-stop."

Arthur beamed, clearly pleased with his own performance and Cole's reaction to it. "Easiest money I ever stole!"

Cole closed the tally book and tucked it into his coat pocket. "So, Arthur, where did you go to school?"

"I never went to school. We moved around too much."

"Who taught you to read and write and figure, then?"

Arthur pulled out his slingshot, raised it to eye level, and pulled the strap back, back, back. "Emmaline was a schoolteacher before she took up singing. She taught me some, but Gwinnie taught me mostly. That is, until I got smarter than her." He released the strap. *Snap!*

"Who's Emmaline?"

"She was my ma."

Cole dealt them each ten cards. It struck him as odd that the kid referred to his parents by their Christian names. But then again, he came from a background that was nothing if not slightly eccentric. "Gwin's been looking out for you for a long time, hasn't she, Arthur?"

Arthur tucked the slingshot back into his pocket and reached for his cards. "Gwinnie acts like a mother hen. She still checks behind my ears and like that. She's got what they call maternal instinct."

"That's probably because she's so much older than you."

"Well, our ma was always real busy with her own stuff."

Cole drew from the deck and discarded. "What was your mother like, Arthur?"

"Oh, she was great fun. She could sing like a nightingale, and, gee whillikins, could she ever tell a story!"

"It sounds like she was very special."

"She could shoot the ashes off a burning cigar at twelve paces! How many ladies do you know who can do that?"

"Not too many."

Arthur looked down at his cards, his grin fading. "You bet yer boots."

Cole watched the boy rearrange the cards in his hand. "Did your mother pass away?"

"Yeah. A coupla years ago." He threw down a card and picked Cole's from the discard pile.

"And Silas, was he real busy too?"

"Sure, but he still played with us and stuff. He always treated Gwinnie like his own kid, even after—" Arthur stopped, clearly troubled.

"After what?"

"It's a long story."

Cole picked a six, laid down a trio of the same, and threw an ace. "We've got time."

Arthur stared at his cards, but Cole could tell he wasn't thinking much about the game. "Well, a little while before she died, Emmaline left us in Dodge City. She had a terrible fight with Silas and told him Gwinnie wasn't his real kid. That hurt his feelings pretty bad, I think. And the way she told him was kind of mean, right before leaving like that."

"You mean, Gwin wasn't Silas's natural daughter?"

Arthur nibbled at his lower lip. "Well, see, Gwinnie explained it to me. It all happened a long time ago in New Orleans before Silas and Emmaline got married. Emmaline was with Sidney then."

"Sidney?"

"Silas's brother."

Cole wasn't sure he was understanding Arthur correctly. If the boy was saying what Cole *thought* he was saying . . . "You mean, Gwin's father was actually Silas's brother?"

Arthur nodded, drawing a card and laying off a six on Cole's original trio. "Emmaline and Sidney must have, uh, you know, done the thing to get a baby, but before Gwinnie could be born, Sidney and Silas had a really big fight. Sidney got so mad he left on his own for California."

"What ever happened to him?"

Arthur shrugged, still staring hard at his cards. "I don't know. No one ever heard from him again."

Arthur was quiet as Cole drew from the deck and discarded, then said, "Cole?"

"What?"

Arthur's face was pink and his eyes bulged slightly, as if he were about to part with the hefty breakfast he had consumed earlier.

Cole straightened, alarmed. "What, Arthur? What's wrong?"

The kid swallowed so hard, Cole heard the gulp over the noisy clatter of the locomotive's wheels. "Could you answer me a question?"

"I can try."

"Well, did you ever do the thing . . . you know, with a girl?"

Cole was taken aback by the nature of Arthur's question. He debated whether or not to lie, then, seeing the strained, earnest expression on the boy's face, decided against it. "Well, yes, Arthur, I have."

Arthur's face went from pink to deep scarlet, but he forged ahead nevertheless. "Did she get a baby?"

"No, Arthur, she did *not* get a baby."

"Well, why not?"

Cole shifted positions in his own seat, feeling distinctly uncomfortable with this line of questioning. "Because not every act has that outcome. It only happens sometimes."

The boy contemplated this. About the time Cole began to hope that maybe the subject would be dropped, Arthur cleared his throat. "How do you know when it'll happen?"

Why had Arthur picked him to deliver the birds and bees sermon? Cole glanced toward the rear of the car. Gwin was still waiting her turn in line. He caught her eye easily even though there were over a dozen other passengers moving around in the fifteen feet that separated them. She was watching him, looking guilty as original sin, and Cole couldn't help wondering what was going on behind those beguiling blue eyes. Was she planning another escape?

With more reluctance than he liked to admit, Cole returned his attention to Arthur. Gwin was the boy's only family now, and she was a woman. Cole had to sympathize with Arthur's position. The kid was at an age where he was growing naturally curious about sexual matters, and this entailed some questions no boy could rightly be expected to ask his own sister.

Cole laid his cards facedown on the table. "You don't know for sure when it'll happen, Arthur, but there are certain precautions that can be taken to lessen the odds. You understand about odds, don't you?"

"Yeah. Like in cards and roulette, right?"

"Like in cards and roulette. Exactly."

"What precautions?"

"Well, that's a complicated question to answer, Arthur. There are a few different methods. One has to do with timing."

The boy seemed to accept this and moved on. "Well, did you do the thing with more than one girl?"

"Why do you want to know?"

"Well, what I want to know is, well, you're supposed to love her, right? Did you love her?"

Cole sighed, his gaze drawn once again toward Gwin, who was still in line outside the ladies' washroom. There had been a few women in Cole's past, most of them fleeting, impulsive affairs of the moment, but only one where the word love had even crossed his mind.

"Well," he said, "I thought I did, Arthur, but it turned out I was wrong."

"Like Silas."

Cole wrested his gaze from Gwin to look back at Arthur curiously. "Like Silas?"

"Yeah. He loved Emmaline but he was wrong. She loved Sidney. He was her Sir Lancelot."

"He was her *what?*"

"Sidney was her one and only true love, her Sir Lancelot. That's what she told Silas the night she left."

This Emmaline must have been some woman, Cole thought. Time enough to spout fairy tales but too busy to check behind her own son's ears. "I'm sorry, Arthur. That must have hurt him pretty bad. And you too, huh?"

Arthur shrugged. "Nah. She said she'd come back for me. And she would've, too, except she died before she had a chance. Whose turn is it?"

But Cole could see his eyes watering and starting to redden around the edges. He picked up his own cards and discreetly looked away. "It's your turn, kid. And, by the way, what was that score again?"

There was only a slight hesitation before Arthur answered. "Sixty-one to twenty-two. You don't have a prayer."

Gwin watched Cole through veiled lashes as he finished setting up their sleeping berths. Ever since the handcuff incident, he had been sticking to her like a tick, and it was getting on her nerves.

"I have to use the convenience room," she said.

Cole's jaw tensed as he continued to spread a bed linen on the upper berth. "You just used the convenience room."

"I have to use it again."

"What's it going to be this time? Fainting in the aisle or crying out 'Fire' again in an effort to create a state of all-out pandemonium?" He fixed her with a look that could have melted lead.

She managed to muster up an innocent expression in reply to this reference to their last dinner stop. "I thought I smelled smoke."

He bent down very slowly until they were nose to

nose. Her eyes started to cross, and she jerked her head back a notch to focus better. His murderous expression didn't improve any with distance. "In a train station," he said, enunciating each syllable, "you *thought* you smelled smoke. How unusual. How alarming."

She had finally succeeded in wearing those cool Pinkerton nerves down to a frazzle. She could now, in good conscience, call it a day. "Really," she said, "this mood of yours is positively horrid. Perhaps you need to get some sleep or something."

"Perhaps I do." He straightened, towering over her like a disapproving redwood.

"So, what'll it be tonight?" she inquired breezily. "Are you going to tie me up again?"

The hint of a smile tugged at the corners of that exasperatingly handsome mouth, his first in many, many hours, and Gwin's guard immediately flew up.

"Not tonight, your ladyship. Tonight we're going to do things a little differently."

Cole bent to tap Arthur, who was busy playing solitaire on the lower berth. "You're up top tonight."

"Really? You mean it?" Arthur quickly gathered up his playing cards and scrambled up onto the second berth. "This is gonna be fun!"

Gwin wrinkled her nose. "You mean I'm going to be stuck sleeping with him?"

"Not quite." Cole pointed to the lower berth. "You're down here."

"Oh, well, that doesn't sound so bad." Gwin tossed her valise onto the berth and started to bend down, then straightened abruptly at a sudden thought.

Surely, he wouldn't dare! Gwin's cheeks flushed.

She sputtered like an old water pump. "Oh, no! You can't! You wouldn't! That would b-be . . ."

"You've got two minutes to get undressed and do whatever it is you do before getting yourself all the way under those sheets. Then I'm coming in. Ready or not."

Gwin recovered her senses and squared her shoulders. "This is highly irregular, Shepherd!"

Cole narrowed his eyes dangerously. "*You* are highly irregular, Gwin."

Gwin searched his face for any sign that he might be bluffing. There was none. His unblinking brown eyes were clearly focused, his jaw firmly set. "But what about my reputation?"

"What reputation?"

"You know what I'm talking about!"

"Well, if you weren't such an all-fired pain in the—" He caught himself, closed his eyes, took a deep breath, then opened his eyes and began again in a calmer tone of voice. "You proved to me last night that you cannot be trusted sleeping alone. Fine. Tonight we sleep together. Now, thanks to you, I'm just about dead on my feet, so shut up and get your delectable little bottom in there before I put it in there for you." He pulled out his pocket watch. "Your two minutes starts now."

"I can't believe you're doing this! What are people going to think?"

"If anybody asks, we'll tell them we're married. We sure as hell act like it. One minute, forty-eight seconds."

Gwin's mind worked furiously. He was bluffing. He had to be. After all, Cole was not the kind of man who would stoop to such embarrassing, improper levels just to teach her a lesson, would he? *Would he?* Gwin scrutinized his grim face. Of course he was bluffing! Well, Gwin was an expert at short card games. She could bluff with the best of them!

"Oh, I see what you're doing. You're still mad about last night, so you're just trying to get a rise out of me. Well, the joke's over. You've had your laugh."

"One minute, thirty-six seconds."

Gwin bit her lower lip.

"I'd get moving if I were you."

Gwin decided he was, indeed, serious. And what had he said? *One minute, thirty-six seconds?* She moved, and pretty quickly too, ducking barely in time to keep from smacking her forehead into the edge of the upper berth. "Oh, this is an outrage!"

She went in headfirst on all fours, posterior presented toward the aisle, and was suddenly struck, too late to do anything about it, by the fear that Cole might just see fit to help her in with the toe of his boot.

She scrambled around quickly, still crouching on all fours, and yanked the curtains closed behind her. She blinked in the sudden darkness, listening to the abbreviated conversation above.

Arthur's awestruck voice. "Holy crow! Hey, Cole, are you really gonna—"

"Go to sleep!" Cole snapped irritably.

Arthur clammed up, apparently deciding not to push the point. Gwin heard the upper berth creak as her brother settled in for the night. She knew that, despite his nosiness, he would undoubtedly be asleep as soon as his pointy little head hit the pillow. He was going to be no help to her at all.

"One minute, fifteen seconds!"

"Oh, be quiet out there, you . . ." She couldn't think of a word vile enough to hang on him, so she let it drop, rolling onto her back and bringing one knee up to hurriedly unlace a shoe.

He's just trying to rattle you, she lectured herself sternly, pulling off her shoe, throwing it down, and starting to unlace the other. *Don't let him get to you. Stay strong. Stay calm. So what if the two of you are going to be sleeping together? Sleeping is sleeping. This is stick-in-the-mud Cole Shepherd we're talking about. It isn't as if anything's actually going to* happen *here.*

Gwin tried to control the hot blush that burned from her cheeks to her ears. Good heavens! It had to be at least a hundred twenty degrees in here with the curtains drawn!

She sat up, smacking her forehead into the upper berth, swearing profusely as she unbuttoned her blouse with unsteady fingers to shrug it from her shoulders.

"Fifty-eight seconds!"

"Unchivalrous bastard," Gwin mumbled, bending her head and rising up on her knees to unhook the back of her skirt. She sat down again and rolled onto her stomach, pushing the skirt down over her hips and wiggling it the rest of the way down to her ankles. He had some nerve! She would make him pay for subjecting her to this indignity! In spades! And soon!

"Twenty-five seconds!"

Gwin yanked pins from her hair with both hands to set curls tumbling free past her shoulders. Stripped down to her chemise, pantalets, and stockings, she grappled around in the dark for her discarded clothing. Gathering up her skirt and blouse, she heedlessly crammed them, along with a handful of hairpins, into her valise, snapping it closed with an angry oath.

"Five seconds and counting, Gwin."

"You just stay right where you are, Shepherd, or I swear, I'll scream, you despicable worm, you . . . you . . ."

She batted aside the curtain, remembering at the last second to grab one side up to her bosom as she stuffed her shoes and her valise beneath the berth.

Cole's jacket was off, slung over one arm, and his shirt was already unbuttoned, hanging open, allowing just a glimpse of smooth, bare, bronze chest. Gwin's mouth suddenly went as dry as if she had swallowed a cupful of chicken feathers.

Luckily, he spoke first. "Your time is up."

7

Cole sat on the edge of their makeshift travel bed, bending down to pull off his boots. Gwin inched backward, plastering her body against the far side of the berth in an effort to put as much distance between them as possible. She tried to slide undetected beneath the coverlet.

Cole ignored all of these various contortions as he shed his gun belt and started unbuttoning his trousers.

Gwin's mouth fell open in horror. "Good heavens! You're not actually going to take them *off*, are you?"

"Gwin, it's hot enough to fry an egg. Now, what do you *think*?"

Gwin groaned, slipping all the way under the coverlet and pulling it up to her chin. Cole stripped down to his drawers and socks, then stowed his gun belt and clothing beneath the berth.

Gwin was grateful that it was dark. What little she

could see, the outline of his broad shoulders and chest, was unsettling enough.

Apparently oblivious to Gwin's anxiety, Cole collapsed onto his back with a weary sigh, the berth creaking precariously beneath his weight as he settled in for the night.

Gwin lay stiff and very still, feeling suddenly smaller than she had ever felt in her life. She had stopped growing at sixteen, permanently stalled at an annoyingly petite five feet three inches in height. She had learned early on how to deal with people taller than she, and Cole's towering height was no exception. She had grown used to tilting her head up to meet his gaze, and she wasn't at all intimidated by him. *Lying* next to him, however, seemed to be an altogether different matter. He suddenly seemed so *big.*

Angry with herself, she turned over and was doubly horrified to find her breasts smashed up against his arm and her nose poking his shoulder. "For Pete's sake!" she cried, shooting up, thumping her head on the upper berth. "Ouch!"

"You'll want to watch out for that," Cole offered calmly.

This comment only infuriated her all the more. "You're taking up the whole bed! I can't even move!"

He chuckled in the dark. "Well, how much room do you need? Arthur and I managed just fine last night, and you two are about the same size, aren't you?"

"I happen to be two inches taller than he is!"

Cole yawned. "Really? Have you checked *lately?*"

"Ooooh!" Exasperated, Gwin buried her face in her hands. "I'm never going to get any sleep!"

"All right, all right, it's cramped quarters, I'll admit, but there is a way this can work if you'll cooperate for a change."

"How?"

"Lie down on your left side." Cole tugged on her arm, pulling her down next to him. "You do prefer to sleep on your left, isn't that what you told me?"

Gwin eased down as instructed, turning her back to him warily. His arm settled comfortably around her waist as he snuggled against her from behind.

"See? Just like a couple of spoons," he said, yawning like a big, lazy cat into the back of her head.

Gwin could barely concentrate on his words. She was having too much trouble sifting through an assortment of queerly familiar stirrings in the pit of her stomach. She had felt those stirrings before, but only in her dreams. Dreams of *him*.

She could feel the entire length of his masculine body, so strong and firm and surprisingly warm. *This is what it's like to be with a man,* she thought, relishing the sensation despite herself. Had she imagined anything like it even in her dreams?

He spoke then, his weary voice stabbing the darkness. "You're stiffer than a pine needle. Why don't you relax? You're perfectly safe. I'm so beat, I probably couldn't rise to the occasion even if you begged me."

Gwin felt a hot blush sweep over her from head to toe—a combination of indignant embarrassment at the suggestive nature of his comment and the horrifying certainty that he had just read her mind. Disconcerted, she muttered, "I thought you Pinkerton men were supposed to be so virtuous. I can't believe you're compromising a lady like this."

"You are not being compromised. If I were compromising you, you wouldn't have the time to be lying here jabbering about it."

"Well, I can't help wondering what your lady friend back home would have to say about this."

There was a pause. "What lady friend?"

"Well, I just assumed you had one," Gwin ventured cautiously, unable to deny to herself that she was fishing.

"Well, that's not the case."

"Oh." She let a significant silence pass before she could no longer resist asking, "Well, why not?"

"Why not?" he echoed, seemingly astounded by the audacity of her question.

"Yes, why not?"

"None of your business why not."

A moment passed as Gwin listened to the ever-present *clickety-clack* of the iron horse's wheels and Arthur's gurgling snores coming from overhead. Finally, she spoke up. "Sorry. I didn't realize it was such a sore subject."

"It's not a sore subject. I just don't have the time for it right now, that's all."

"Oh. How much time does it take?"

He sighed. "I'm very busy with my job, Gwin."

"Is that all?" Gwin asked. "In case you haven't noticed, there are plenty of marriage-minded women who are willing to wait around for their men."

"Are there?"

"Certainly. The shrinking violets, the sweet, empty-headed types." Gwin had no idea why she felt so compelled to pursue this subject. "You know the types I'm talking about."

"Ah, yes," Cole replied dryly. "The types who don't steal horses, you mean."

"Hmmm. Well, I suppose so."

"You know," Cole continued, pushing up onto one elbow to look down at her in the dark, "it's just too bad you're not going to be around when I get back to Chicago. To help point out these types for me, I mean."

Gwin couldn't help noticing that his hand came to rest rather intimately across the soft expanse of her abdomen, and he didn't sound nearly as sleepy as he had only minutes ago. "Well, you don't have to go back to Chicago to find them," she said. "They're all over. Take that flirty little blonde in the compartment across the aisle, for example."

Cole hesitated a moment before inquiring too innocently, "What flirty little blonde is that?"

"Oh, please," Gwin said, disgusted. "I'm talking about the one who's been making cow eyes at you ever since Topeka. Like you haven't noticed, like you haven't been egging her on all along, grinning at her, small-talking with her every chance you get."

Cole started to laugh.

"What's so funny?"

"You're jealous, my dear."

"That's ridiculous."

"That's why you tripped her in the aisle this afternoon when we were boarding at Limon. I didn't realize it at the time, but there it was. Female spite rearing its ugly head."

"I did *not* trip her in the aisle!"

"How presumptuous of me. That must have been somebody else's foot attached to your ankle."

Gwin folded her arms stiffly. "You are so conceited, Shepherd."

He didn't answer right away. Instead, he settled once again on his side, his hand resting comfortably on her belly. Gwin stiffened slightly when his long fingers began to spread slowly, experimentally, as if measuring the width of her abdomen.

He spoke in a low whisper. "Didn't your mother ever teach you that nice girls don't lie?"

Gwin tried to ignore his physical nearness and the confusing emotions it stirred within her. Somewhere along the way, he had managed to turn the tables. All the fun was suddenly gone from their verbal sparring, leaving only a thick tension hanging in the air between them. She was beginning to get the feeling that Cole Shepherd was not nearly as harmless as she had assumed him to be. No, not harmless at all.

Hesitant to move lest his hand wander into even more dangerous territory, Gwin struggled to keep her voice unaffected. "My mother taught me two things, Shepherd. How to shoot straight and deal crooked."

"She must have been an interesting woman, your mother."

"Most men apparently thought so."

Cole's long fingers spread again, spanning her abdomen, pressing gently as if testing bread dough.

"Was she a cardsharp even before she hitched up with Silas Pierce?"

Gwin sucked in a deep breath as his fingers slid slowly around to play idly at the side of her waist. "My mother was a schoolteacher, the youngest daughter of a Methodist minister."

"That's a far cry from dealing crooked cards, isn't it?"

Gwin closed her eyes, not answering. His thumb drew lazy circles along the side of her rib cage, sending out little ripples of pleasure that were becoming more and more difficult to ignore. She grew both apprehensive and eager at the thought of his hand sliding up a little farther, just a little farther, to finally touch her breast. What would happen then? Would they stop talking? *It's your dream, Gwin. What happens next in your dream?*

She didn't know for sure. A kiss. A caress. Whispered words of love. Her dreams had always ended there, for even her dreaming mind could not imagine what she had never experienced in her waking life. She could not know what it felt like to be made love to by a man. She could only suspect that it started out something like this, awash in a sea of overlapping physical and emotional sensations, needing and wanting to touch, to draw closer and closer until two became one.

Gwin's eyes flew open. *Good heavens! What was she doing?* His fingers massaged her lazily through the thin material of her chemise, and they *were* moving up!

"Cole! Your hand!"

His fingers stilled. "What about it?"

"It was moving!"

"Was it?"

"You know darned well it was! I thought you said I was perfectly safe with you!"

"Did I say that? *Perfectly* safe?"

"Yes."

Gwin detected no sign of contrition in his reply. As a matter of fact, without even being able to see his face, she got the unsettling impression that he knew exactly what he was doing and what effect it had on her.

"And you call yourself a gentleman," Gwin muttered. She turned and burrowed her head deep into her pillow, trying to force her swirling emotions back into check. His arm wrapped snugly around her waist again, and only part of her was thankful that his hand seemed better behaved this time.

"In the interest of safety, perhaps we could both use a little distraction," Cole suggested into her ear. "Tell me more about your mother."

Gwin swallowed hard. "Like what?"

"Like, what makes the youngest daughter of a Methodist minister turn to cardsharping and confidence games?"

"I don't know," Gwin said, grateful for the opportunity to turn her attention to something else, even if it was Emmaline. "She always had an ambition to sing, to become rich and famous. She used to dream of living in New York City."

"And so where did Silas Pierce fit in?"

"Well, she met Silas when he and his brother got

jobs at a skinning house in New Orleans. Emmaline was already working there, singing a few nights a week, dealing faro the rest of the time."

"So they met in a gambling house? How romantic."

"For Silas it was. He fell in love with her right away, but it was his brother she was interested in. Sidney wasn't like Silas. He was younger and more ambitious. He had big ideas of his own. He wasn't the type to consider settling down and marrying a woman just because they were . . ." Gwin faltered, searching for a delicate euphemism.

Cole finished for her. "Involved?"

"Yes. Involved is as good a word as any."

"Sidney was your father."

Gwin turned her head to eye him shrewdly. "You knew?"

"Arthur told me."

Gwin turned back and sighed. "What a big mouth."

"He didn't mean any harm."

"Oh, I know. It shook him up too, I guess. Emmaline never said it in so many words until three years ago, on the night she left Silas. She dropped that cannonball, then walked out of our lives to be with some rich cattleman in Dodge City."

Gwin paused, remembering that awful night. After overhearing her parents' last argument, Gwin had followed her mother from the hotel, demanding that she admit it was an awful, hateful lie. But, instead, Gwin had found herself listening in stunned disbelief as her mother recounted the whole story.

Emmaline knew that if she told Sidney of her pregnancy, he was just as likely to skip town as to marry her. Instead of taking her chances with the truth, she decided to force his hand. By purposely leading Silas on and arranging for Sidney to discover them in a compromising situation, she succeeded in pitting brother against brother. Only things didn't work out as she had hoped. Sidney had been jealous, all right, furious, as a matter of fact, but he hadn't stuck around to fight for her. He chose instead to storm out of their lives for good. A classic case of a con gone bad.

"Arthur told me she passed away," Cole said, breaking into Gwin's thoughts.

"Yes. We found out about it six months later when Silas went back for her. She was singing in a saloon and got caught in the cross fire when two drunken cowboys drew on each other. It was a stupid accident. A stupid, laughable accident."

"Tragic, if you ask me," Cole said.

A lump suddenly formed in Gwin's throat. "Hopeless. A hopeless, meaningless end to a hopeless, meaningless life."

"Not so meaningless," Cole offered. "She had you and Arthur. And not so hopeless, either. She named her children after kings and queens."

"She lived in a dreamworld."

"There's nothing wrong with having dreams, Gwin. It gives us something to strive for. Sometimes they even come true."

Dreams. Her mother had been nothing but dreams. *Reach out,* Emmaline had so often told her daughter when Gwin had still been young and blindly adoring of her beautiful mother, *close your eyes and reach out. Wiggle your fingers, Gwinnie, and imagine that you can touch Camelot.*

In his own peculiar way, Silas had been a dreamer, too. Hadn't he gone on for years pretending everything was just fine between him and Emmaline? Gwin had grown up watching both of her parents fail to touch Camelot, so, as far as she was concerned, dreams had only one place in life, and that place was sleep.

Gwin attempted to inject a lighter note into the conversation. "And so, what is your dream, Cole Shepherd?"

"I suppose my dream is to be doing exactly the kind of work I'm doing right now."

Gwin had to smile at this. "What *work?* Sleeping next to a strange girl in a cramped berth on an express train?"

"Well," he replied, "I never actually expected it to be so . . ."

"So what, Shepherd?"

"Never mind." He tightened his hold around her waist and squeezed gently. "In the interest of safety, I think we'd both better get some sleep."

San Francisco

It was past midnight. A new day. Sidney Pierce rose from his bed, being careful not to disturb the woman as she slept. He plucked his silk robe from the carved mahogany headboard and slipped it on. Silently, he crossed the darkened master chamber, his bare feet scuffing the plush nap of the imported Persian carpet.

Jasper's dispassionate voice continued to echo in his mind: *"The Round Table has met on the subject. It's already too late."*

He frowned as he turned the silver knobs of the double doors that led out onto the balcony. *Too late.* But was it? Really?

Sidney inhaled the salty night air and felt inside his pocket for the cigar he had decided to forgo earlier in the evening. It was still there.

"One of our people has been dispatched and will be boarding the eight forty connection at Promontory."

Sidney wet the tip of his cigar and struck a match on the stone balustrade. It flared, bathing his face in ghostly orange light as he lit the cigar. He shook out the match and tilted his blond head back, exhaling in a long sigh.

Today, Sidney thought, surveying the clear, glistening night sky. *It will happen sometime today.* By tomorrow, it would be all over. And then what? Sidney raised the cigar to his mouth contemplatively. *Return to business as usual.*

Below him, the echo of a distant gunshot rent the air. The unintelligible lyrics of a sailor's drunken song wafted on the night breeze. Sidney found it delightfully ironic that from up here on Nob Hill, among the Victorian palaces of the silver kings and San Francisco's wealthiest nabobs, the raucous late-night revelry of this town's most depraved neighborhoods should be so clearly audible.

But there was a time, many years ago, when he had called the Barbary Coast home. Fresh off the boat and with a Herculean chip on his shoulder, he had gravitated to that section of town like steel to a magnet. Bartlett Alley, Dupont Alley, Bull Run, Deadman's Alley, Murder Point. Those were lost years, dark years, during which he had nearly allowed his own festering bitterness to devour him alive.

A part of him still yearned to return to those days of misspent youth, to start over with a blank slate, to hustle those filthy streets down by the old Bella Union. In those days, he'd had nothing to depend on for survival but his own wits.

Control. He finally put his finger on part of what had been bothering him ever since Silas had shown up unexpectedly on his doorstep weeks ago. *Somewhere along the way, I've lost control.*

But you can get it back, an inner voice whispered. *Maybe it's not too late, not if you send a telegram to the Pinkerton operative that's with them. You might be able to save Silas's children.* Sidney's mouth curved into a mirthless smile. No doubt he would also end up getting himself killed for his trouble. His unscrupulous associates had little patience for those who stepped out of line.

Looking out over the darkened courtyard below, he thought back to the days when he and Silas had roped for McDaggert's skinning house in New Orleans. Sidney had frequented the saloons and hotels, Silas the railroad stations, and between the two of them, not a night had gone by that they hadn't befriended some poor hapless out-of-town gent with the express purpose of inviting him to come play at their club.

Sidney chuckled aloud at the memory. Oh, how that sucker's eyes would nearly pop from their sockets at the sight of Emmaline dealing from behind the faro table, ivory flesh swelling over a scooped neckline of scarlet satin, diamond droplets flashing at her ears, flaming red hair spilling over bare shoulders in shining, luxuriant waves.

"Place your bets, gentlemen," she would purr, her green eyes glittering like precious gems in the lamplight.

"Is she available?" the sucker would inevitably intone in a hushed, awed whisper.

"Only to whet your appetite," Sidney would reply with a conspiratorial wink. "Later, I'll take you to a little place around the corner where the ladies are most discreet."

But, of course, there would be no later for that poor sucker. By the end of the night, he would have been sent on his way, dazed and dispirited, his pockets turned inside out.

Those had been good times, the best of times now that Sidney had the perspective of many years to look back upon, but he had been too young and too impatient to see it then. He had always been looking ahead to the next conquest. *"California,"* he had urged Silas time and again. "The West Coast is the New World now, and we have the opportunity to be in on the start of it!" But Silas hadn't listened, or hadn't wanted to listen. "We're doing fine where we are, Sidney. Why rock the boat?"

Why rock the boat indeed? That was precisely what was keeping Sidney awake this night. He was forty-six years old, too old to be rocking the boat, too young to be giving up the ghost. He still had quite a few years ahead of him, and if the election went as they all hoped, those years promised to offer up many new and exciting challenges.

Well, I have it, Emmaline. Camelot. Right here in the palm of my hand. And you want to know the truth? It's not anything like we thought it would be.

"Can't sleep?"

Sidney turned to see Jasmine leaning languidly in the doorway, her green eyes luminous in the moonlight. Her thick red curls, disheveled from sleep, tumbled, layer upon layer, over her shoulders and down her back to her waist. She wore a sheer black peignoir of Turkish silk.

"I didn't mean to wake you," Sidney said, turning his back, stabbing out the cigar, and flicking it out onto the flagstone walk that ran along the outer perimeter of the courtyard below. The gardener would take care of it in the morning.

"Oh, certainly you did, love," Jasmine returned in a husky voice, approaching him. "You always mean to wake me."

Her talented fingers brushed lightly over Sidney's shoulder blades, trailing down to play idly with the sash of his robe. "You are so solemn this evening, love. Can I help?" She tugged gently at the sash, pulling it free. "Is it that woman?"

"What *woman?*"

Jasmine's fingertips played down the column of his flat belly. "The woman in the paintings. The one who looks like me."

Sidney took a deep breath, feeling the first stirrings of physical arousal. "The woman in the paintings is dead."

"Ahhhhhh, how tragic." Jasmine pressed the swell of full breasts up against him from behind. "Is that why you never married?"

"Is that what I pay you for?" Sidney inquired tightly. "To ask questions?"

"No, this is what you pay me for." Jasmine laughed as her hands started to play lower . . . still lower.

Sidney allowed Jasmine's talented ministrations to nudge all troubling thoughts from his mind.

"Do you want me to leave?" she inquired teasingly.

Sidney reached back to wrap one hand around the nape of her neck, forcing her to him, entangling his fingers in the rich thickness of her hair as he lowered his mouth to hers. "No," he whispered, "I don't want you to leave. Tonight you stay. Tonight you stay until morning."

8

Central Pacific Express 420

Their third day on the line was tedious and exhausting. Late in the afternoon, they switched from the Union Pacific to the Central Pacific line at Promontory, Utah. Before that, at Ogden, they had lost many of the tourists in their coach to another connecting line that ran to Salt Lake City.

Since then, they had taken on far fewer passengers than they had lost, and so their new coach, a Silver Palace, although not as luxurious as the Pullman they had traveled in since Topeka, was much less crowded. This suited Gwin just fine, especially since one of the passengers they had lost was that annoying blond tart across the aisle.

As Gwin bent to retrieve her soap, towel, and toothbrush, Cole and Arthur set about rearranging their seats and pulling down the upper berth for the night. Cole was in relatively good spirits, no doubt because Gwin had done nothing in particular to antagonize him all day. She wondered if he had reconsidered their sleeping arrangements. Part of her hoped he had. Part of her hoped he hadn't.

Arthur unfolded their bed linens. "Hey, Cole! I'm not tired at all! You want to play a couple more games of rummy?"

Cole pushed down on the upper berth, testing its sturdiness, then stepped back, brushing his hands together. When he finally looked down at Arthur, Gwin noticed a lock of hair fall over his forehead. She fought a ridiculous urge to brush it out of his eyes with her fingers.

"Arthur, if we were playing for stakes, I'd already owe you my life savings and my firstborn son." His words were stern, but his tone was good-natured.

Arthur's face lit up like a chandelier as he beamed adoringly up at Cole. If Gwin hadn't known better, she'd think her little brother was witnessing the Second Coming.

"I have to use the convenience," Gwin interrupted, displaying her wrapped towel as if in proof.

Cole had removed his coat earlier, and he hadn't shaved since yesterday. Hatless and with his sleeves rolled carelessly to his elbows, he looked considerably less starched than he had when they first started out together from Caldwell, Kansas. It was clear that the long trip had begun to wear on him as much as it had on Gwin.

Has it been only three days? Gwin was losing her

sense of time. She felt as if she had known Cole Shepherd a good deal longer than that. Spending every minute of every day with a person would tend to distort anyone's sense of acquaintance—and that was not even to mention sleeping in the same bed together. Then again, she *had* known him for quite a long time—ever since that day in Abilene—in her dreams, at least, if not in reality.

"What is it about you women, anyway? Is there ever a time when you *don't* have to use the convenience?"

"Well, what is it about you men? Is there ever a time when you *do?*"

He raked a hand through his disheveled hair, clearing away the stray lock that Gwin had felt the urge to interfere with earlier. He took on the expression of a man who is truly baffled by female physiology. "You know, I never met a woman who—"

Gwin averted her eyes and started to push past him in the aisle. "Well, I never met a man like you either, Shepherd."

When he failed to budge an inch to let her through, she looked up to find those handsome lips curving into just about the heart-meltingest smile she had ever witnessed in her life. And that included her dreams.

"Five minutes, Miss Pierce."

Gwin felt something low in her belly go soft and fluttery. With great effort, she squared her shoulders. "Don't wait up for me." She pushed by him without waiting for a reply.

Having finally grown accustomed to the constant rocking motion beneath her feet, Gwin threaded her way down the narrow aisle with little difficulty. She worried that Arthur was getting too attached to Cole. And that was not good at all.

She supposed that after losing Silas and Clell so suddenly and violently, it was natural for Arthur to latch onto an older male figure, but just because it was natural didn't mean it was good. Cole Shepherd would soon be out of their lives forever, and then what? Gwin was Arthur's sister, sometimes even acting the part of his mother, but she could never make up for the lack of a father, could she?

Gwin passed a well-dressed Chinese gentleman in the aisle, their bodies brushing up against each other so intimately that in any other environment it would have probably been considered scandalous. Gwin was used to it by now.

Without a word, the Chinese, who was not much taller than Gwin, tipped his black bowler and smiled pleasantly. She caught a whiff of something peculiar, something that reminded her of a doctor's office. Funny. A Chinese riding first class was not unheard of, but it certainly was unusual enough to catch her notice. She glanced over her shoulder briefly to see the sleek, braided pigtail that swung at his back. Dressed as he was, in a pinstriped frock coat and matching trousers, it was an odd sight, that pigtail.

Gratified to see that the ladies' washroom was vacant, Gwin pulled the door open and locked it behind her, savoring these few precious moments of privacy in a coach full of passengers.

She pumped some cool water into the marble washbasin, wet the cake of soap, and worked up a lather. She washed her face and neck and peered into the mirror over the washbowl. Her hair was frazzled from the heat, standing up in crazed curlicues around her face. Her eyes looked positively haunted, such were the gargantuan shadows that lurked beneath them from lack of sleep.

Her first night's sleep aboard the Union Pacific Express had been short, thanks to her unsuccessful foray into the male confines of the saloon car, and last night, well, she had slept fitfully, at best, not at all used to sharing her bed with a man. She had awakened frequently during the night, thinking foggily that she had to be dreaming his strong arm encircling her so intimately from behind. And she had come wide awake quite early this morning, not with her back to him, but with her cheek resting snugly on his warm, breathing chest, her legs carelessly entangled with his.

Gwin reached into the pocket of her skirt and withdrew a bottle of lilac-scented toilet water. She dabbed some on each wrist and behind her ears.

It was time she admitted to herself that maybe Arthur wasn't the only one becoming attached to Cole Shepherd. The truth was, ever since boarding their train at Topeka, Gwin had been stalling. She had put off making her escape, telling herself that she had plenty of time to come up with a workable plan. Well, her time was running out.

She pointed a finger, lecturing her own reflection. "Wise up, Gwin. Kick that Pinkerton man out of your dreams for good. Tomorrow, you and Arthur set sail on your own course."

She had made up her mind. Today she had examined the train's schedule and decided that Reno was the place to jump ship. Virginia City was close by. It was a gambling town, and if there was one thing Gwin knew how to do, it was raise stake money in a gambling town.

Kansas City, Missouri, was her goal. Silas had a bank account there. After fleeing San Francisco, Gwin had wasted no time in pointing them in that direction, however, their money had run out in Colorado. Crossing into Kansas on foot, they had begged rides from passing farmers, but that hadn't been enough. It was then that Gwin had sailed into her ill-fated career as a horse thief. That rash act had landed them behind bars in Garden City. They had managed to escape once only to be picked up again in Caldwell. Sometimes, when bad luck hit, it hit like a ton of bricks.

But that was about to change. Gwin was determined to get them to Missouri. She knew enough not to expect too much concerning Silas's banked funds, but she hoped there would be enough to help get her and Arthur established somewhere, preferably somewhere in the East, because that's where the best schools were.

Gwin tried to put all of this out of her mind as she saw to the rest of her personal needs. Sometimes it wasn't wise to look too far ahead. A good night's sleep was what she needed. She had to be well rested and sharp tomorrow morning when they pulled into Reno.

She threw one last doleful glance at her reflection before unlocking the door. A part of her—the part she considered weak and sentimental—was sorry to be leaving Cole behind. After all, it wasn't every day that a girl stumbled across her very own Sir Lancelot.

Clutching her folded towel and perfume bottle, Gwin started back to her berth. She was still thinking about Cole Shepherd's heart-stopping smile when she felt a slight jostle from behind.

She didn't even have time to turn around. An arm encircled her waist, pinning her arms. A damp, foul-smelling cloth covered her nose and mouth. Gwin let out a muffled cry as her panicked eyes swept the coach, but Cole was nowhere in sight. As a matter of fact, *no one* was in sight. Only green baize curtains, dozens of them, pulled tight for the night. *This can't be happening,* she thought crazily. *I'm being suffocated in the middle of a rail coach full of witnesses!* It was unbelievable! But unbelievable or not, it was true.

Gwin's struggle was swift and silent. She tried to turn her head, to wrest her face away from that cloying smell, but the hand clamped down even harder, forcing her head back until she thought her neck might snap. Her lungs filled with choking fumes. Her strength drained and her mind fuzzed. Black fingers wiggled before her eyes as she felt control of her own body slip away.

Less than one minute had passed since Gwin had stepped out of the ladies' washroom. She slumped, her head rolling to one side, her eyelids fluttering closed. Just before she passed out of this world, she thought vaguely that it was a shame . . . a sad, sad shame she would never get the chance to really know him. *Lancelot.*

9

She was taking too long.

Cole poked his head out from between the sleeping curtains. The aisle was deserted. He muttered to himself, "She wouldn't dare." But, of course, he knew very well that she would.

He reached for his shirt, berating himself for even stripping it off in the first place. How stupid of him to think she would actually make this easy! How stupid to believe that maybe she was as exhausted as he was and would cooperate for a change!

"What's the matter, Cole?"

Cole was so annoyed, he couldn't even bring himself to look Arthur in the face.

"What are you doing?" the boy persisted.

"I have a feeling your sister is up to her old tricks again."

Arthur, who was undressing for sleep, stopped, his

thumb hooked in the shoulder strap of his overalls. "She wouldn't, Cole. I just know she wouldn't. She's probably just back there fooling with her hair. You know how girls are."

Cole ignored Arthur's cajoling as he pulled on his boots. He reached for his gun belt, thought better of it, and instead extracted the Colt .45 from its holster.

Arthur's voice rose to a horrified squeal. "What are you going to do with *that?*"

Cole slipped the Colt into the pocket of his jacket and pointed a stern finger at Arthur as he rose to leave. "Don't you move! Understand?"

Arthur's eyes were big. He gulped and nodded, looking, at that moment, very small and very young. Cole felt a jab of compassion, sudden and strong, almost overwhelming, and his tone softened. "Just stay where you are, and I'll see about dragging your sister back here. By her *hair* if necessary."

Arthur offered him a tremulous smile, apparently relieved to know that Cole did not intend to shoot Gwin. Not *tonight,* anyway.

Cole had to turn sideways to avoid disturbing the solid row of sleeping curtains that lined either side of the aisle, but it didn't hamper his progress. He was utterly exasperated with that woman and intended to find her quickly.

He reached the ladies' washroom and was about to rap on the door when something crackled beneath his heel. He looked down to see Gwin's towel, but it was the shattered perfume bottle that caught his undivided attention. He stooped to examine the discarded items. The towel was damp. She must have come back here, washed up, dropped everything, and made a run for it.

Cole frowned. Even for Gwin, the idea seemed a bit farfetched. He stared at the towel and the fragrant glass shards in his hand and started to get a bad feeling in his gut. As impossible as it seemed, it appeared as if Gwin had vanished into thin air.

Arthur sat cross-legged in the berth, his shoulders slumped and his head bent. Cole's parting words—*"Don't you move!"*—still rang in his ears, and it wasn't only because Arthur was still much more child than adult that he was loath to disobey. He liked Cole. As a matter of fact, he liked Cole a lot, and there was a part of him that yearned desperately for Cole to like him back.

"Don't you move!"

Arthur didn't move. He missed Silas. Sometimes he missed Silas so bad, he had to bite his knuckles at night to keep from crying himself to sleep. He missed Clell, too. Clell had been the one who had picked Excalibur from among the odds and ends in the wagon of a street peddler in Salina, Kansas. Clell had even shown Arthur how to shoot it so that the rocks he used for ammunition didn't go all kerflooey in crazy directions.

Arthur was plenty old and smart enough to realize that Cole Shepherd wasn't Silas in any way, shape, or form. Cole wasn't anything like Clell, either, but Arthur liked him anyway. Yesterday, when Arthur had finally worked up his nerve to ask Cole a "man"

A TOUCH OF CAMELOT

question, Cole hadn't patronized him with silly platitudes about cabbage patches and storks. Cole hadn't treated him like a stupid little kid.

Arthur was sure going to miss Cole. During their dinner stop, Gwinnie had signaled him. A subtle, unobtrusive gesture, imperceptible to anyone who didn't know what to look for. With the knuckles of her forefinger and middle finger, she had casually brushed beneath her chin before picking up her fork to eat. Arthur had seen it immediately, of course. He had been trained since birth to recognize that signal, a disguised gesture of recognition from one sharper to another.

A few minutes later, when Cole had been distracted briefly by the waiter, Arthur had known to look at Gwinnie for more information. She had made a shadow-bird with her hands and had mouthed one word: *Tomorrow*. And Arthur knew what that meant. It meant that sometime tomorrow they were going to fly the coop. Arthur was to keep sharp and watch for her lead. And *this* time, Arthur knew she was going to pull it off.

So now Arthur was torn. Something didn't seem right, but Cole had told him to stay put. Even though Arthur was learning to respect Cole's sense about life and things, the fact remained that Cole didn't know Gwinnie like Arthur knew Gwinnie. What was more, he didn't have any way of knowing that she planned to escape sometime *tomorrow,* not tonight. She had no reason at all to be giving him the slip now. And that's what was troubling Arthur. Something had happened to Gwinnie.

The more he thought about it, the more anxious he became. Arthur tried to block out the inner voice that urged him to move despite Cole's warning. *Something has happened to Gwinnie, something has happened to Gwinnie!* Arthur couldn't stand it. With one hand, he pushed the sleeping curtain aside and set one bare foot out into the carpeted aisle.

Cole was getting a bad feeling, all right. A bad feeling, but a familiar one, a creeping, indefinable warning signal he privately referred to as the spider on his neck. Once, on the darkened streets of New York City, as a new foot patrolman, Cole had strolled into an alley, unwittingly interrupting a robbery in progress in an adjoining jewelry store. That spider-on-the-neck feeling had caused him to whirl around just in time to avoid having his skull shattered by a swinging baseball bat.

Pushing his way through the third sleeping coach with no luck, Cole thought about the two most important lessons he had learned during his brief career in law enforcement: Never let your guard down, and *never* ignore the spider on your neck.

He thought about the man in the saloon car with Gwin the other night. What was his name? Monroe. He was a slick, flashy gambler who was used to getting his way with women. No doubt he had been bitterly disappointed when Cole had thwarted his amorous plans. *So disappointed that he would kidnap her? So disappointed that he would try to force himself on her?* Cole tried to shut out an infuriating mental picture of Monroe tearing at Gwin's clothes.

"Damn you, Gwin Pierce," he swore under his breath as he picked up his pace. He was headed for the day coach where the train's few night owls might still be socializing. He actually hoped to find her there. He actually hoped to catch her in the act of hustling up a card game, but the spider tickling the hairs on the back of his neck already hinted at something very different. Its insidious voice whispered: *You won't find her there. Something's happened to her, Cole. Something baaaaad.*

A needle-nosed old woman in a puffy nightcap suddenly thrust her face from between a set of curtains, stopping him in his tracks. "Good heavens! Is there a fire? All this activity in the middle of the night!"

Cole tried to remain patient as she struggled unsuccessfully to settle a pair of spectacles onto the skinny bump of her nose. "Excuse me, but I'm looking for someone. A pretty redhead?"

The woman's face wrinkled into a disdainful frown. "Oh, *her!* Yes, I've seen *her,* all right! Drunk as a lord and dead to the world!"

"What?"

"Disgraceful! That's what it is! Demon rum! Public debauchery! The whole world's going to hell in a hand basket!"

"I don't understand, ma'am. Could you explain?"

Growing impatient with both her uncooperative spectacles and Cole's exasperating thickheadedness, she gave up on the eyeglasses and pointed a sharp finger toward the rear of the car. "They went that way! That nice Chinese gentleman was helping her back to her seat! Why, it was disgraceful! You could smell it all over her! Demon rum!"

Cole was totally confused. Chinese gentleman? Gwin passed out and smelling of liquor? It didn't make sense. "Thank you, ma'am, you've been a tremendous help."

"To hell in a hand basket, I say! Disgraceful!"

Cole was already crossing into the narrow vestibule that connected the last sleeper coach to a day coach behind it. Gwin had not been drinking, there was no reason for her to be passed out, and the Chinese gentleman the lady had referred to was obviously not helping her back to her seat.

When Cole stepped into the next coach, any last vestige of hope abruptly dissolved. It was deserted. Gwin wasn't here. Neither was Monroe. And neither was the Chinese man the old woman had referred to.

He kept moving, his gaze fixed with growing trepidation on the rear door of the day coach. Behind it were two baggage cars and a caboose. No matter how hard he racked his brain, Cole could not think of one honorable reason why a male passenger would take an unconscious young woman into an empty baggage car at this late hour. Not one. And that's why, as he left the day coach behind and moved into the narrow vestibule connecting it to baggage, he pulled the Colt from his coat pocket.

10

Cole hesitated at the door to the baggage car, his fingers tightening on the doorknob. Through the door window, he saw them, and what he saw confirmed all the fears that had nagged at the back of his mind since discovering Gwin's shattered perfume bottle. It was not Monroe, but the Chinese man.

He was on his knees, leaning over Gwin's sprawled, unconscious form. Cole's stomach lurched at the sight of her lying so deathly still. He swallowed a growing knot of panic. *Keep your wits about you, Shepherd.*

He twisted the knob only to discover that the door had been locked from the other side. The man's dark head jerked up at the first rattle, and Cole knew he had to move fast. He stepped back and kicked, the heel of his boot landing squarely against the wood just above the doorknob. Luckily, the flimsy connecting door had not been made to withstand such punishment. It splintered and flew back on its hinges, cracking into the wall behind it.

All of this took less than five seconds, but it was plenty of time for the other man to react. Still on his haunches, he pulled Gwin's limp body up and around to front him like a shield. The lamplight caught and glittered on a sliver of steel at her throat—a stiletto poised at her jugular. Her eyes were closed, and she still didn't move. Cole couldn't even tell if she was breathing.

His eyes flicked back to the Chinese man's face. They recognized each other in that instant, the way one professional recognizes another. This was no coolie imported from the Orient as cheap labor for the railroads. This man had been imported for a very different reason.

When he spoke, Cole was jarred by the hint of a British accent. "I am surprised by your timeliness, Mr. Shepherd, but, then again, they say if you want a job done right, call in the Pinkertons, is that not correct?"

The man's familiarity with Cole and his employer confirmed his initial impression that this man's presence was no matter of chance. Cole's grip on the Colt didn't falter, even though his palms were beginning to sweat. The floor of the baggage car rocked gently beneath his feet as he eyed down sights trained on the other man's forehead.

The man spoke again, reading Cole's thoughts. "I would not consider it if I were you, Mr. Shepherd. There is a chance that you will hit your mark, but, then again, there is a chance you will miss. On a mov-

A TOUCH OF CAMELOT 159

ing train such as this, it could mean an early demise for our Miss Pierce."

Cole took one measured step forward.

"Do not come any closer. I will kill her if you do."

Cole tried to read the man's face, but those Oriental features remained implacable, hopelessly inscrutable to Cole's Occidental eye. "Who are you? What do you want?"

"I want you to drop your weapon to the floor and kick it to me, Mr. Shepherd. Otherwise, Miss Pierce will suffer the prick of my blade."

What the man had said earlier was true. The cars were rocking only slightly at this moment. Cole might be able to adjust his aim to compensate for it, but what if they took a turn or hit a rough piece of track? He didn't think he could live with himself if he hurt Gwin. And, inscrutable or not, Cole believed this man when he said he would slice her throat. He had no choice but to believe him. To do otherwise would be reckless. Cole knew he had to give up his gun. He also had to close the distance between them.

The other man raised his voice. *"Now,* Mr. Shepherd!"

Cole dropped the Colt and kicked it as instructed—but he kicked it back with his heel rather than forward where his adversary could reach out for it. He took another step forward in the process.

The man's dark features screwed up angrily. "That was a mistake!"

His grip on the stiletto tightened, its tip pricking the white skin of Gwin's throat, drawing blood. Cole's stomach muscles tightened convulsively as he watched a shiny scarlet thread creep down her neck to disappear behind the curve of one shoulder. She didn't even flinch. What had he done to her? Why didn't she wake up?

Cole heard a sound from behind.

"Gwinnie! What's the matter with Gwinnie?"

It was Arthur.

I told him to stay put! Cole almost lost his composure out of sheer, unadulterated frustration. Now he had *two* of them to worry about!

The man's gaze faltered at Arthur's untimely interruption. Those dark eyes flicked behind Cole for just a fraction of a second. Then the train lurched into a curve, and Cole saw the man's grip on the stiletto momentarily slacken. The point dropped away from Gwin's jugular.

Recognizing an opportunity, Cole sprang forward, crashing into Gwin and her captor. All three of them went sprawling onto the floor. Cole heard Gwin moan before she curled up and rolled out of harm's way. He didn't have time to notice much else.

Cole blocked his adversary's arm just in time to avoid being blinded by the sharp point of the stiletto. Grasping the man's wrist, he slammed it back down to the floor. The stiletto clattered free.

The next instant was a blur. Cole didn't know whether it was instinct or premonition that told him to move. While he had been dealing with the threat of the knife, the other man had apparently managed to pull a derringer with his free hand. Cole lunged to the right, but not quite fast enough. He felt the heat of the bullet as it passed into the flesh of his left shoulder.

A TOUCH OF CAMELOT

The pain that was sure to follow didn't immediately register. What registered was the humbling thought that if he hadn't moved, that bullet would have drilled straight through his frantically pumping heart.

Arthur knelt by his sister, crying out and slapping at her wrists. Good. If they were going to get out of here, they were going to have to do it under their own steam.

The man rolled out from under Cole and sprang to his feet, the double-barreled derringer rising to level at Cole's face.

Cole scrambled to his own feet at the same time, throwing a desperate, clumsy punch that knocked his adversary off balance. The derringer's second bullet plugged a new hole somewhere in the paneled ceiling before the gun flew free from the man's hand.

Cole's wiry opponent recovered quickly, dropping into a crouch. Then he moved, lightning quick, catching Cole by surprise. Before Cole could duck, he was assaulted by a sharp, shockingly forceful blow to the neck.

Cole stumbled back into a stack of luggage, toppling some pieces over his head. One oblong parcel bounced off his shoulder and fell to the floor with a jarring *clang!* followed by an angry rustling of wings. "Demon rum! Demon rum! Squawk!"

Cole regained his footing, clenched his fists, and waited for an opening to strike back at his circling, dancing opponent. When he saw it, he angled in for a blind right cross that connected squarely with the bridge of the smaller man's nose.

"Cole!"

He jerked around and saw Arthur waving his Colt, the one he had been forced to surrender. Arthur tossed it. Cole followed its graceful arc with his eyes, reaching up to snatch it in midair. He missed.

The revolver clattered to the floor and slid, spinning out of reach.

Cole was distracted for only the briefest of seconds, but it was enough. The kick came out of nowhere. It made solid, jarring contact with Cole's jaw. He reeled back into the wall of the baggage car, his senses gone awry. *He did that with his . . . foot?* This dazed thought, the only one he seemed capable of putting in order, bounced off the inside walls of his head like a rubber ball. Then he was down.

Arthur was terrified. If it had only been himself in danger, he would have run long ago, but Cole was in trouble, and Gwinnie . . . something was terribly wrong with Gwinnie!

Stupid! I should have shot at that horrible man myself! Arthur thought as he watched the revolver sail through the air and miss its mark. Unlike the rest of his sharpshooting family, however, Arthur had never taken much of an interest in learning how to use firearms. Except for his trusty slingshot, Arthur doubted he could aim well enough to hit the broad side of a barn, much less a moving human target.

He dropped to his knees by his sister, who was finally starting to come around. Her eyelids fluttered open. She groaned, gripping both sides of her head and trying to sit up.

A TOUCH OF CAMELOT

"Gwinnie!" Arthur grabbed her forearms, struggling mightily to pull her to her feet. "Gwinnie! We've got to get out of here!"

Arthur heard a crash, and he turned, still on his knees. His eyes widened in horror. Cole was down, and he looked down to stay. The Chinese man was scrambling to reload his gun.

Arthur turned and tugged at his sister's arms frantically. Hot tears spilled down his cheeks as his voice rose to a panicked scream. "Gwinnie! *Gwinnieeee!*"

Arthur heard a small sound behind him, a soft *click*, then, "She'll come around, young man, but not in time to save you or herself."

Arthur stood, his arms falling limp to his sides. He felt suddenly unreal, like he was in a dream, a very very bad dream at that.

Gwinnie moaned, but the sound faded away in Arthur's ears. He realized dimly that he wasn't crying anymore, which was good. He wasn't, after all, a baby. If he was going to get shot, the least he could do was take it like a man. He thought about Silas and Clell, about Emmaline, and thought that if he was really going to die right now, at least he wasn't going to be alone up there in heaven, was he?

He stared down the twin muzzles aimed at his chest. *It's a little gun,* he thought to himself dazedly, *a little gun like that probably doesn't even hurt much.*

Cole had no idea whether two seconds or ten had passed when reality started to creep, on all slogging fours, back to him. His head ached, his vision was blurred, the floor beneath him seemed to slant forward at a dizzy rate as he raised his head. He saw his gun, only two feet away, and he strained to focus on it as he inched forward on his belly.

Miraculously, on his first try, his fingers closed tight and perfect around its ivory grip. Rolling onto his side, he focused on the gunman whose back loomed above him not five feet away.

The man was speaking, but the words were lost on Cole. He raised the barrel of his Colt at the precise moment his adversary raised the derringer. Cole cocked the hammer and called out hoarsely, "Hey!"

Startled, the man whirled, his nose bloodied, his black eyes rounding in their sockets. Cole squeezed the trigger. The man's mouth contorted in surprise, and it wasn't any wonder. It looked like a cigar had burned a hole straight through the center point of his pin-striped vest. A dark wetness bloomed. He was dead before he hit the ground.

Cole didn't move for a full ten seconds after he had fired. He was a little surprised too. He had never killed anyone before.

Gwin cried out, "Arthur! Are you all right?"

Cole turned his head just as she tried to rise to her feet. Still groggy and unsteady, she tripped over the hem of her skirt and collapsed onto hands and knees. Arthur stood frozen, staring blankly at the inert body of the man who had been about to kill him.

The parrot in its cage screeched. "Demon rum! Demon rum! Squawk!" Wings flapped indignantly as the cage slowly rolled toward the rear of the car. The train was taking a steep incline.

Exhausted and fighting shock, Cole rolled onto his back, the fingers that clutched the revolver so tightly slackening to a limp grasp. His wounded shoulder throbbed with a vengeance that promised to grow worse. He groaned. What exactly had just happened here?

Cole pulled himself to a sitting position and rested his back against a stack of trunks by the door. By now, Gwin was cupping Arthur's face in her hands, shouting at him sternly, trying to snap him out of his shock. *How many people has that poor kid seen die in the past month?* Cole's mind started to play back over the farfetched conspiracy tale Gwin and Arthur had spun on their first day out of Topeka. Somehow, it didn't seem quite so farfetched anymore.

Bits and pieces fell into place in Cole's mind like a jigsaw puzzle, hinting at a picture far bigger than he had imagined. The fact that the gunman happened to be an Oriental fit quite nicely. Most of the Chinese population that had migrated to America were now settled in one place: San Francisco, California. The very town they were bound for. The very town Gwin and Arthur had fled in fear of their lives.

Arthur started to come around, and Gwin caught him up in a fierce embrace. The boy didn't attempt to fight this overtly maternal show of affection. On the contrary. Arthur's arms moved hesitantly to encircle his sister's waist, his stubby fingers clutching at the loosened folds of her blouse. Something wrenched in Cole's stomach at the sight of them, something as painful in its own way as the brutal throbbing in his shoulder.

He closed his eyes to the paralyzing thought that if he had allowed just one more minute to go by before deciding to go after Gwin . . . He could not allow himself to dwell on the awful possibility of what might have been. The question he was forced to ponder now was, where did they go from here?

11

"*Demon rum! Demon rum!* Going to hell in a hand basket! That's right! Squawk!"

That bird might be on to something, Cole thought wryly, *but if it doesn't shut up soon, I'm going to shoot it.* He sat on the floor of the baggage car, his back up against a stack of trunks and assorted pieces of luggage, his legs sprawled listlessly in front of him. The ache in his wounded arm was growing teeth.

Arthur had thoughtfully righted the parrot's cage. It was no longer shrouded in its original pillowslip, which was already torn up into strips to bandage Cole's arm. The parrot was making so much racket, however, Cole thought that he would gladly sacrifice his bandaging if it would just afford them some peace and quiet.

"I think it's stopped bleeding."

Gwin knelt beside him, working at applying the

makeshift bandage to his wound. Her hair was a mess, half up, half down, frazzled out all over in crazy curls and squiggles. Dirt streaked her worried forehead, her skirt was wrinkled, her blouse yanked free from the waist of her skirt. At this moment, there was absolutely no doubt in Cole's mind: He had never seen a more beautiful woman in his life.

He groaned and closed his eyes. His arm hurt and he ached all over. He was, however, appropriately thankful to be alive. If the gunman had had his way, all three of them would be knocking at heaven's gates about now.

"You saved our lives, Shepherd, mine and Arthur's, and I suppose I should thank you for that."

Cole didn't open his eyes. Right now, all he wanted, more than anything else in the world, was to go to sleep. "Just doing my job, your ladyship."

There was a long pause, then, "I think as soon as you get that bullet out, you're going to be all right, Shepherd."

"I think so, too. Hurts like hell, though."

Another pause, a long one, so long, in fact, Cole was obliged to open his eyes to see if she was still there. She was busy folding his bloodstained coat on her lap.

As if sensing his scrutiny, she looked up sharply. "What are you staring at?"

He answered truthfully. "You."

A flood of color rose to her cheeks. She pressed her lips together and dropped her gaze. After a minute, she cleared her throat. "What if there are more?"

"More what?" he asked, although he knew perfectly well what she meant.

"More of *them*," she said, inclining her head in the dead man's direction. "I never saw him before in my life. How do we know there aren't more of them on this train right this minute?"

"Look, I seriously doubt—"

Anger flashed in her eyes. "Well, you *doubted* when we told you they tried to kill us in San Francisco, too, and look where that got us!"

Arthur, who had been poking his fingers through the bars of the parrot cage behind her, rose to his feet and turned around to face them. "Yeah, but he doesn't doubt us now, Gwinnie! Do you, Cole? You don't doubt us now, isn't that right?"

Before Cole could even open his mouth, Gwin challenged him. "But your assignment still hasn't changed, has it?"

Cole's gaze clashed with hers. "Well, the circumstances sure have! As soon as we reach the next whistle-stop, I'll wire the Agency and inform them that—"

Gwin shot to her feet, hugging Cole's jacket to her chest. "That is exactly what you will *not* do, Cole Shepherd! I won't allow my brother's life to be endangered one more minute!"

She started to pace anxiously. From the moment she had regained consciousness, she had remained calm, too calm, and Cole knew that by now it was all starting to sink in. If he didn't handle this right, she was going to panic and try to run. He tried to keep his voice reasonable. "But we didn't know the situation before this, Gwin. Now we do. We can handle it differently."

"Handle it differently?" She stopped pacing. "Oh,

we'll handle it differently, all right! I was handling it just fine until you got involved! We might have ended up in the hoosegow a couple of times, but at least no one was trying to kill us!"

"Gwin—"

"We can't, we just can't!" She paced again, agitated, muttering to herself.

"Gwin, listen to me."

She stopped pacing, her back to him. She didn't turn around.

"You've got to listen to me. We can figure out what to do next if you just give us some time."

She didn't move. Arthur wasn't moving either. He was staring at his sister's rigid back, his eyes two big blinking question marks.

Cole shifted positions and winced silently. Sweet mercy, his arm felt like it was on fire. "You're just upset right now, and that's understandable, but you can't let it cloud your judgment. *Think,* Gwin. There's no need to do anything stupid."

"Think . . ."

She fumbled with his coat, twisting and wrinkling it beyond recognition before turning to face him. There was no sound but the rhythmic *clickety-clack* of the iron horse's wheels beating the tracks beneath their car.

Arthur broke the silence. "What are we going to do?"

The question hung in the air as she crossed the baggage car to Cole's side. She knelt in front of him and searched his face.

"What's the matter, Gwin? Is something wrong?"

She wore an odd, dreamlike expression, and Cole had to wonder if she hadn't finally gone off the deep end, because her next words made absolutely no sense at all.

"For so many years, all I knew was your face."

Cole shook his head, baffled. "What?"

She closed her eyes and whispered softly, as if reciting from memory, "'She knew naught but his handsome face. It was when her fair knight returned to her in the garden that the queen first asked him his true name.'"

Before Cole could ask what she was talking about, Gwin leaned forward. He felt her lips touch his, gentle and warm as sun-kissed rose petals. It was fleeting and chaste and incredibly compelling. For a second, he even forgot the agony in his arm. He caught a heady whiff of lilacs and raised his hand to bury his fingertips in her hair. It felt soft and thick, heavenly. Before he really had a chance to absorb what was happening, she pulled back. He stared at her, shocked and speechless.

Her eyes were still closed. "Oh, my love," she whispered, "I am all yours."

Cole knew for sure that he had heard her right *that* time, but the words she had just uttered didn't make any sense, did they? "Gwin, what's . . . ?"

Her eyes opened. They were shining in the dim light. Her pale skin was radiant. Cole thought for a moment that there might be tears brimming in her eyes.

"I'm sorry, Cole."

A handcuff slipped over his wrist before he could

react. If it hadn't been his bad arm, he could have easily yanked it away before she had a chance to anchor the other end to the metal lock of the sturdy trunk behind him.

"Hey! What are you doing?"

She rose to her feet and jumped back, dropping his jacket to the floor. He caught a flash of silver as she tucked a key into her skirt pocket. "The bleeding's stopped, so you'll be all right if you don't try to struggle," she said, spitting out the words hurriedly. "The conductor will be through here on his rounds soon, and—"

Frustrated, Cole tried to stand. The trunk, which he would have sworn was packed full of nothing less than pure lead, didn't budge an inch. He only succeeded in jarring his injured shoulder. "Gwin, don't do this!"

But she was already moving away from him, pulling up her skirt in handfuls, tucking the hem into her waistband. He saw before she turned her face away that she really was crying. She looked almost comical with her skirt all bunched up around her waist, revealing the stark white pantalets that clad her slim legs beneath it, but he didn't have much time to pay attention to that. He knew now what she was planning to do, and there was nothing funny about it. She was planning to jump the train!

She snagged Arthur by the arm and swung him around, pointing him toward the door, toward the open observation deck that sided the day coach ahead of them. "Let's go!"

Arthur hesitated for just a second, then reached

into his pocket. He pulled out his treasured slingshot and tossed it to the floor next to Cole. "Here, take care of this for me, will you?"

Desperate, Cole tried to reason with him. "Arthur, you don't have to—"

But the kid wasn't open to argument. He was sticking with his sister, crazy or not, stupid or not, reckless or not. Without another look back, he vanished through the open doorway.

Cole strained at the cuffs, ignoring the razor-sharp teeth that gnashed through his damaged shoulder. "Damn it, Gwin! Please don't do this!"

She turned to look back at him, her fingers clutching at the splintered archway as she blinked back tears. "I'm sorry. I have to. Why can't you understand?"

"This isn't the way! Just stay, and together we can . . ." But the plea died in his throat.

"Good-bye, Cole."

And then she was gone.

Part Two

12

The Virginia Range Mountains, Nevada

Cole figured he must have eaten something so horribly disagreeable before going to bed that it was now fighting its way out somewhere within his digestive system. The result, of course, was a long night of bad dreams. He was in his own narrow bed in his own neat-as-a-pin second-floor apartment on Madison Street in Chicago. If he listened hard enough, he could hear the clip-clop of the horses' hooves passing along the cobblestone street below and the familiar call of early-morning street vendors. If he opened his eyes, there, flanking his bed, would be an oak dresser. Atop the dresser, inside two oval brass frames, would be the faded daguerreotypes of his parents, the father he had idolized and the mother he had never had the chance to know.

If it was Thursday, Mrs. Chalmers, the housekeeper who came in once a week to tidy up and take care of his laundry, would soon be knocking at the door. A heavyset woman, Mrs. Chalmers would wheeze like a set of hearth bellows as she squeezed her way through the open archway, laden with a basketful of baked goods.

In terms of housekeeping, Mrs. Chalmers didn't have much of a job when it came to looking after Cole's apartment. Cole always picked up after himself. Perhaps it was because Mrs. Chalmers was not kept busy enough that she had taken to concerning herself with Cole's state of bachelorhood. Or maybe it was just because she had seen all six of her sons safely to the altar and had nobody else to pick on. "You go on out and find yourself a nice girl to marry, Mr. Shepherd," she'd advise in a high, wheezing voice. "There are plenty of nice young ladies who would jump at the chance to snag themselves a fine young buck like you!"

Cole smiled to himself. Perhaps Mrs. Chalmers was right. Maybe it was time he thought about finding himself a nice girl to settle down with, a nice, sweet, young—

"Damn it all to hell! I can't budge him! He must weigh two hundred fifty pounds! I swear, if he up and dies on us, I'm gonna just leave him here for the birds!"

Not two-fifty, dear heart, one-ninety last time I checked. And even as he corrected her exaggeration of his weight, Cole was forced to confront the gloomy possibility that he might not be the victim of bad dreaming after all. When he forced his eyes open, he saw that he was not in his cozy little apartment overlooking Madison Street. It was dark, he was face-down on the ground, and he was cold.

"Gwinnie! He's waking up! He's waking up!"

There was dirt in his mouth and his arm felt like someone had driven a railroad spike through it. He thought he felt someone pulling on his left leg, and he made a mental note: Remind her never to take up nursing.

The leg-pulling stopped just before Guinevere Pierce's pale, dirt-streaked face swooped down into his narrow line of vision. "You're bleeding all over the place, and you're too blasted heavy for us to move you! Are you all right?"

Cole spat out some dirt. "Sure I'm all right. I'm just dandy, Gwin."

He closed his eyes again, perhaps in a last-ditch effort to convince himself that this was all a dream. It had to be. If it wasn't, and he really was on his first assignment, it certainly wasn't going very well, was it?

Fritz Landis's words came back to him with stunning clarity: *"Your first solo assignment is to escort them from Caldwell to San Francisco without misplacing them along the way."*

It had sounded simple. Insultingly simple. Fritz had neglected to mention, however, how incredibly lovely Guinevere Pierce was, how she had a way of getting under his skin that made him want to choke her one minute and pull her into his arms the next. There had been no mention about the kid, about how

Cole might find himself growing attached to the redheaded ragamuffin who carried a cheap slingshot named Excalibur. There had been, come to think of it, no mention either of Oriental assassins, gunshot wounds, or jumping trains that were moving at close to twenty-five miles per hour across rocky, desertlike terrain. Just a simple assignment. Simple.

The memory of his own escape now came back to him. He had wasted a good two or three minutes swearing at the top of his lungs and struggling with the handcuffs, trying to drag that trunk full of lead across the floor of the car—a worthy cause, certainly. Then he had frittered away more time trying to devise a way to reach the call rope to signal the conductor—another physical impossibility. It was at that point he had begun to pity himself, vividly picturing his entire career going the way of raw sewage. Finally, he had remembered the hatpin Arthur had used the night Gwin had cuffed Cole to his berth. Cole had taken that hatpin from Arthur, and, if he remembered correctly, he had dropped it into his coat pocket.

Gwin might have confiscated the key from his pocket, but she couldn't have known about the hatpin, could she? She had dropped his coat on the floor within easy reach, and Cole snatched it up eagerly.

Picking the handcuff lock had seemed to take forever, and he had been tempted more than once to just throw in the towel, but he had sweated it out. After all, a Pinkerton man never gives up. Isn't that what he had always believed?

By the time Cole had finally freed himself from those wretched cuffs, he figured he was fifteen minutes ahead of Gwin and Arthur on the line. Since it was night, he hoped that they would be sticking close to the tracks. If he headed east on foot, he had a good chance of running into them. And with that last thought in mind, he flung all caution to the wind and jumped the Central Pacific Express 420.

He didn't remember much after that. Whatever he had banged his head into upon landing had been made of much sterner stuff than his poor, aching skull.

"Cole! Can you sit up? Are you all right?" There was an exasperated feminine squeal. "I think he's gone out again! What are we going to do now?"

Cole groaned and rolled over onto his back. His arm sent up a flare of pain. "I believe you mentioned leaving me for the birds," he mumbled.

He felt her hands on him then, smoothing his hair back, cupping his face. Actually, it felt kind of nice. "Cole Shepherd! Open your eyes, damn it!"

"I can't. If I open my eyes now I'll find myself somewhere in Nevada with a mangled arm, a dented head, and two crazy people who will not rest until they've destroyed my career and left me for the birds. However, if I continue to keep my eyes closed, the dream will eventually end. When I finally do wake up, I'll be back in Chicago in my own bed, and—"

"Good heavens! He's delirious! Arthur, come here! We've got to slap him awake!"

Cole glared up at her. "If I have to take one more slap, bump, dent, kick, punch, or bullet tonight, I will be forced to retaliate."

Gwin reached behind his shoulder, grunting as she

tried to pull him into a sitting position. "Can you walk?"

He winced as a sharp new pain bolted from the back of his head straight through to his forehead. "You should've known I'd catch up with you, Miss Pierce. I always do."

She muttered something he couldn't quite make out.

Arthur dropped to his knees beside them. "You didn't catch up with us, Cole, we caught up with you!" His voice was bright and Cole risked another stab of pain to focus on the kid's beaming face. "I told her you were no quitter!"

"Come on, Cole. Help me."

Cole hooked one arm around Gwin's neck and pushed the rest of the way up to a sitting position. His head throbbed, but it was still attached to his neck and seemed to be pointing in the right direction. That was good. He surveyed the landscape. They were in the mountains, the eastern side of the Virginia Range. On the other side would be Reno, Carson City, Virginia City. There were a few trees, tall, standing silhouettes against a starry, moonlit sky, but most of what he could make out were rocks—rocks, dirt, scrubby grass, and prickly bushes.

"How did you get loose from those handcuffs so fast, anyway?" Gwin asked.

"That's for me to know and you to find out, little lady. You're not the only one with a few tricks up your sleeve."

Arthur crooned, "Oh, I bet I know how!"

Cole gave him a warning look. "And you'll keep it

to yourself. There are some things we men have to stick together on, am I right?"

"You bet yer boots!"

"Can you walk?" Gwin asked again.

Cole moved his legs, bending and straightening them out with gratifying ease. "It looks like it. As a matter of fact, these might be the only fully functioning parts of my body right now." He raised his head to meet her gaze, and at the sight of her, still luscious even in her disarray, he fought back a loopy grin. He thought that there just might be one other part besides his legs that was still fully functioning.

"All right," she said, rising to her feet. "Let's go. We've got a lot of walking to do. Hopefully, we'll be able to beg a ride when we get closer to civilization."

Cole stood slowly, mindful of the pain in his head, which stayed thankfully quiet, and the pain in his arm, which wasn't behaving itself nearly so well. "Any particular destination in mind, Miss Pierce?"

"Virginia City."

"Why Virginia City?"

"Because I know some people there, and—"

Cole eyed her suspiciously. "And what?"

She turned her head, deliberately avoiding eye contact. "And because I know how I can earn some money."

Cole wondered what she meant by that, but he decided not to ask. Not yet, anyway. "Fair enough. So, Virginia City it is. And then what?"

"And then we part ways, Shepherd. If you weren't bleeding like a stuck pig and looking sorrier than a stray mutt, we wouldn't have stopped for you in the first place. In case you've forgotten, it's you we were trying to get away from, remember?"

"Oh, I remember, all right. But, like you said, we've got a mighty long walk ahead of us, and a lot of things could change between now and then."

She picked up her bedraggled skirt as daintily as if she were the Queen of England. "Oh, I doubt that, Shepherd. I doubt that in a very big way. Now, let's get cracking. We don't have all night."

13

Judging by the position of the Big Dipper relative to the North Star, Cole guessed that it was almost two in the morning when they finally collapsed beneath a clump of spindly pines.

"My feet hurt!" Arthur complained.

Cole didn't doubt it. The ground was rough and rocky, the grass stiff and dry. He hunkered down next to the boy, ignoring his own discomfort. "Let's see."

Arthur winced as Cole examined the soles of his bare feet. A full moon cast just enough light to see by, but Cole would have known just by feeling them that they were cracked and tender. He pulled a handkerchief from his coat pocket and wiped away some of the dirt. "We'll have to get these taken care of when we get to Virginia City."

Arthur slipped his foot from Cole's grasp and crawled a short distance away to lie down on his side, his hands tucked neatly beneath his cheek, his eyes already closed. "All I wanna do is sleep."

"Me too, kiddo."

"My poor feet!" Gwin chimed in miserably. She had already plunked herself down onto the ground, one knee bent and twisted sideways as she worked feverishly at removing her shoes.

How ladylike, he thought to himself with amusement.

She finally pulled one shoe off, almost losing her balance and tumbling flat onto her back. She flung it aside to massage her foot, then set to work on its twin.

"You'd better be sure to check those before you slip your pretty toes back into them in the morning."

This caught her attention. "What?"

"Scorpions."

"*What?*"

Cole doubted that scorpions were indigenous to this particular section of Nevada, but at the moment, he was too weak to fight the childish pigtail-pulling part of him that had caused him to blurt this out in the first place. "You heard me," he said, grimacing at a sudden flare of pain as he slipped his wounded arm from his coat. "Scorpions. The place is crawling with them."

She catapulted to her feet and jerked her head around to scrutinize the ground. "It is?"

"No doubt about it, Miss Pierce," Cole said, removing his gun from his pocket and rolling his all-but-ruined coat into a makeshift pillow.

"Aren't they poisonous?"

"Deadly." Cole tucked the coat-pillow beneath his head and closed his eyes, thankful that the pain in his shoulder was dropping back to a dull, throbbing ache. A lengthy silence intervened, filled only by the shrill machinations of busy nocturnal insects and Arthur's soft, gurgling snores. Gwin moved about nearby, the folds of her skirt rustling as she circled, picking around stealthily in the moonlight.

Right on cue, she piped up again. "I don't see any."

"Well, of course you don't *see* any. What do you think they are, stupid?"

Her voice rose about a half dozen decibels. "Well, they're animals, for Pete's sake! Of course they're stupid!"

Cole sighed much like a man trying to explain Euclidean geometry to a six-year-old. "Gwin, they don't go after moving prey. They would stay hidden until we were asleep."

"They would?" Her voice softened. "Oh dear."

"Put it out of your mind," Cole said after a satisfying moment of apprehensive silence. "There's nothing we can do about it anyway. Get some sleep."

"Horrible, crawly little monsters. How can we sleep knowing they're just waiting for us to—"

"Well, if it'll make you feel better, you can sleep right next to me, Guinevere, my sweet. That way, if we go, we go together."

"What?"

Cole offered her a crooked grin. "What are you looking at me like that for? You were the one who kissed me, remember?"

She was clearly mortified that he had even dared to bring the subject up. "Well, that's just because I figured I'd never see you again, you lout! How was I supposed to know I'd be tripping over your wretched body less than an hour later?"

"Ah, well, I guess we were just meant to be together, Miss Pierce."

"Oh! You are so conceited! Just the most arrogant man I've ever met in my entire life!"

"Suit yourself."

There was a hesitation, two slow beats, then, "You *were* lying, right? There aren't any scorpions, right?"

He didn't answer.

"Cole Shepherd! You tell me the truth! There aren't any scorpions around here, are there?"

"Gwin, you should know by now that I never lie."

After a moment, Cole heard her approach and kneel by his side. He looked up to see that her hair hung in loose, curling tendrils about her face, her forehead was streaked with dirt, and her clothes were a wrinkled, misshapen disaster. He found her incredibly desirable this way, disarmed, disheveled, *uncivilized*. And he was perilously close to doing something about it. His self-control was slipping, and that was not good at all. He decided he must be delirious— delirious from shock, delirious from pain, delirious from loss of blood, certainly delirious from lack of sleep.

Cole had visited a brothel only once in his life, on his eighteenth birthday, for the express purpose of shedding his virginity. The experience had never lingered as a particularly pleasant memory, but now he was seriously reconsidering his aversion to the whole idea. Perhaps it was just what he needed to clear his head. It was painfully obvious that he needed to do something. His distraction with Gwin was interfering with his job.

Gwin spoke. "I'm only doing this because, otherwise, I'll never get any sleep."

"What's the matter? Don't you trust me?" Cole asked. "We slept together last night and nothing dire befell you."

Gwin just gave him a long, lingering, suspicious look, a look Cole devoured, thinking she was absolutely, unequivocally *right* to be suspicious. She finally moved to lie next to him, her head coming to rest at the crook of his good shoulder. Cole's arm looped comfortably around her neck, his fingertips hanging perilously close to her right breast.

Oh, this is delicious! This is just what you've been angling for from the beginning, his nasty, chuckling self whispered.

Don't think about it, his conscience interrupted sternly. He lay still as she continued to settle in, getting comfortable. "See?" he said, clearing his throat guiltily, "I don't even bite."

But he *did* want to bite. He would especially like to start with her earlobe, then work his way down to the spot where her neck met her shoulder.

She let out a soft, beguiling little sigh. It was a small sound, a woman-sound. The kind of sound a woman made after she had been made love to *thoroughly,* and Cole decided right then and there that the wisest thing to do would be to change the subject. "Gwin, I want you to tell me about San Francisco."

Her tone was predictably hostile. "As I recall, we

already did tell you about San Francisco, and you chose not to believe us, remember?"

Cole absorbed this stoically. After all, he deserved it. "You told me what happened after the murders. Why don't you start from the beginning this time?"

"Why? Didn't you get all the facts from your precious Agency file?"

"The official version, certainly, but as we all know, *Gwendolyn,* sometimes the file can be wrong."

"It's not going to help, you know. I've gone over it a hundred times, and I still can't make any sense out of it."

"Humor me. How long were you in San Francisco before it happened?"

"Less than a week. Clell and I always traveled a few days ahead of the rest of the group to post signs for the revival."

Cole listened closely to her tale as it unfolded: five days in San Francisco for Gwin and Clell Martin, three for the doomed Silas Pierce and the rest of his group.

Gwin related the details of that final night in a grim, controlled voice: the tent revival that had gone well despite her premonitions of disaster; the interval afterward when she and Arthur and a man named Wilson had waited in the dark hills for the camp to empty; and, finally, the horrifying events that had ensued upon their return. Her description of the killer was infuriatingly vague. *Big. Well-dressed. Deep voice.* Not much to go on. Arthur was the only true eyewitness, and, bright or not, he had seen the killer through the traumatized eyes of a child.

"You know, it was Wilson who brought me back to

my senses. If it hadn't been for him, I mean, he saved our lives, Cole. We ran as fast as we could. We all ran, but Wilson couldn't keep up."

Cole felt her start to tremble, and he hastened to stop her. "That's enough." His fingers stroked her hair as his mind worked over the facts. "You never saw the man's face, but you said you would recognize his voice. Are you sure you never heard that voice before?"

"I'm sure."

"And Arthur, he saw the man's face, but he didn't recognize him from anywhere, either."

Her reply was edged with bitterness. "Well, whoever he was, he had a hell of grudge against Silas."

"Not necessarily."

"What?"

"He said it himself," Cole explained. "He had a message to deliver. This man wasn't just a killer. He was a delivery boy, hired help, just like I suspect our friend the Chinaman was. There's more here than meets the eye."

"I wish there was something I could have done to stop it! I just keep thinking that if only—"

"Wait a minute," Cole interrupted, suddenly alert. "You said Silas went into town that day. What kind of business did he have in San Francisco?"

"I don't know."

"You told me you'd never been to San Francisco before. Was that true of Silas, too?"

Gwin hesitated. "I think so. No, wait a minute, I *know* so. Before we got to California he mentioned that he was finally going to see it for himself, Sidney's land of milk and honey."

"Sidney's land of milk and honey?"

"Do you think whatever Silas was doing in town that afternoon had anything to do with what happened?"

Cole paused before answering. "Maybe. Maybe not." But he thought to himself, *maybe.*

"Well, none of it matters anyway," Gwin said heatedly. "They've got the wrong man waiting for trial, and I'd bet my bottom dollar they'll have him convicted for it. No one really cares who the real killer is."

"Don't you?"

"What kind of question is that? Of course I do!"

"Then why are you so intent on running? You and Arthur are the only eyewitnesses. Without you—"

She cut in passionately. "Running, you call it? Well, I don't call it running; I call it surviving! I won't put my brother's life in jeopardy! Not for Silas's memory, not for my own personal sense of justice, and certainly not to further your career!"

Cole bristled at her insinuation. "My career has nothing to do with this."

"Are you so sure?"

"Yes."

The entire length of her body stiffened against him. "Are you still going to try to take us to San Francisco? Because if you are, I'm going to fight you on it. You know that, don't you?"

"Yes, I know that," Cole replied, growing more and more annoyed with her combative attitude. Why did she still insist on casting him as the villain?

"You don't understand. You just think I'm being obstinate," Gwin said.

"No, I don't think you're being obstinate."

"You think I don't care! You think I'm afraid to go back there, don't you?"

Afraid? That thought had never crossed his mind. Guinevere Pierce didn't seem much afraid of anything as far as he could tell. "No, Gwin, I *don't* think you're afraid."

She didn't seem to hear him. "Well, maybe I am a little afraid, but I wouldn't let that stop me. Silas raised me and I loved him very much. And Clell—" Her voice caught, and she bent her head. Cole suspected she might be fighting off tears, and he suddenly regretted upsetting her in the first place.

She pressed on, her face still averted. "Clell was very important to me, too. I'd give anything to find the real murderer, to find out why it happened, to make some kind of sense out of that awful night."

On impulse, Cole reached out with one finger to lift her chin. His wounded shoulder protested the movement by sending up a warning flare of pain, which he ignored. "I told you," he said gently, "I understand."

"It's Arthur," she persisted. "It's not right to—"

"Stop. Just who are you trying to convince?"

Cole was almost relieved to see a familiar glint of defiance light her eye. "Nobody! I do what I need to do!"

"And I told you, I can understand that. If he was mine, I'd feel exactly the same way."

"You would?"

Cole nodded, half-smiling, letting his finger run up along the curve of her cheek. "I would."

Gwin studied his face, her expression relaxing, her

long-lashed eyes slowly losing focus. He recognized that expression. It was the same expression she had worn the moment before she had kissed him in the baggage car, the moment before she had uttered those nonsensical words. *"Oh, my love, I am all yours."*

At that moment, Cole's ever-analytical mind switched gears.

The case was forgotten. His job was forgotten. He was assaulted by a series of fleeting images—that brief glimpse of her white-stockinged calves as she had mounted his stallion that very first day in Caldwell, the curving shape of full, rose-red lips when she smiled, the vibrant color of her hair when the sun played tricks through the open venetian blinds of the train window. He remembered the jolting, electric sensation of her body suddenly pressed up against his as they had argued in the baggage car of the Pacific Union 840 and how she had felt lying nestled in his arms just last night.

He was delirious, all right. How else to explain the fact that he suddenly found himself kissing Guinevere Pierce? She didn't open her mouth right away, but he was patient, kissing it open, nudging her lips with his tongue. A tiny sound escaped her throat as her mouth finally parted beneath his, and Cole took it as an invitation, unabashedly tasting the essence of her. She jerked back slightly when they touched, as if shocked by the intimacy of contact.

Was it possible that . . . ? Cole hesitated for just a second before casting his doubts aside. Gwin was certainly no innocent. Hadn't she been flirting with that slimy character, Monroe? There was little doubt in

Cole's mind how that night would have ended if he hadn't interrupted them.

He kissed her again, this time parting her lips with little difficulty, and *this* time she didn't pull back. She wrapped her arms around his neck and kissed him back just as fervently, their tongues mating and mingling sensuously. Oh, no, Cole thought to himself, she was no stranger to a man's kisses. She tasted sweet, sweet as a fresh-picked strawberry.

Ignoring the yammering pain in his left arm, he eased her down next to him and shifted position to run his fingers down along the curve of her tiny waist, gently coaxing her hips until they drew flush against his own. He allowed his free hand to roam back up over the swell of her breast.

He was right to guess that his legs weren't the only fully functioning parts of his body. As the two of them melded together, as he basked in the pleasurable sensations of Gwin's soft feminine curves meshing against him, he grew hard and full and aching for release.

Gwin made no move to discourage him as he worked at undoing the buttons of her blouse, bending his head to kiss her neck, to bury his face in her hair. Her hip gently nudged him, making his ache grow pleasantly worse. He groaned into her neck and thought that when a woman moved like that, there was no doubt she knew what she was doing.

He pushed aside her blouse, his hand sliding over a smooth cotton camisole to finally close over the soft, pliable flesh of her breast. Cole thought dazedly that there was nothing else on earth quite like it—the feel of a woman's breast. He glided his palm lightly, in small circles, over the tip and felt it come alive beneath his touch. She let out a soft, warm breath and, again, arched her hips against him. Sweet mercy! Cole was amazed that he didn't lose control right then and there.

He rained little kisses down the length of her neck, tasting damp, salty flesh, working his way hungrily to the gentle rise of her breast. She whispered through her teeth, "Cole, we shouldn't." But her fingers were entangling in his hair, pulling him to her.

Cole knew enough about a woman's body to tell what she did and didn't want, and Gwin's body told him that she was as hungry as he. Cole ignored her feeble protests, hearing only the soft, shallow sound of her breath catching as he cupped his hand beneath her breast and lifted it, lowering his mouth to its tip. She shuddered, crying out in a frantic whisper, "We can't. My brother . . ."

Cole moved up to reclaim her mouth, very soon stifling all protests down to a series of weakening moans. He pulled her against him full length, cradling his growing hardness in the soft flesh of her belly. He slid one hand down along the line of her waist, circling back around, unhooking her skirt.

It had been a long time for him, *too* long, much too long since Cynthia. No man could be expected to wait so long. All it would take was a few precious seconds buried deep inside the welcoming moist warmth of her.

He whispered against her parted lips, his quickened breath mingling with hers. "He's asleep. We can be quiet or we can move back behind the trees. He won't know."

She stiffened and turned her head, gasping in a ragged whisper, "No!"

The agonized confusion in her cry was just startling enough to finally penetrate his consciousness. He let go of her, raising his hand to cup her chin, feeling a sudden necessity to see into her eyes. Those eyes, however, were closed tight, denying him the answers he sought to find there.

He kissed her once more, gently, slowly, regretfully. "You're right. Of course you're right."

"If Arthur woke up and—"

"You're right, Gwin. Absolutely . . . correct."

Gwin struggled with her skirt, reaching up with trembling hands to button her blouse. This was for the best, Cole reminded himself, swallowing a knot in his throat.

"Come here," he whispered when she moved to lie back down. He slipped his good arm around her shoulders, pulling her up snug against him, glad that she didn't try to pull away. "I'm sorry."

"It's all right."

He shifted positions to get comfortable, even though he knew it was useless. The pain in his shoulder was returning, throbbing dull and hot at the very surface of his consciousness. He wasn't cold anymore. He was warm. Too warm. He suspected that the beads of sweat breaking on his brow were not all due to misspent passion, either. *Fever*, he thought, closing his eyes wearily. The tiny slug of lead embedded in his flesh had already started to poison his body.

He opened his eyes and offered up a few more empty words. "I guess I lost my bearings. It won't happen again."

Gwin buried her face against his chest with a shaky sigh. "I guess I did, too. We're tired, that's all. It makes people do stupid things."

"Oh, yes," Cole agreed, "stupid things." His breathing was finally slowing, his heart rate falling back to something approximating normal. He just wished that his third fully functioning body part would also get the message that the show was over.

"I'm sorry," he said again, feeling miserable, stumbling over his words like a fool. "I'm sorry, Gwin, I just . . . I don't know what's the matter with me. It won't happen again."

"It's all right."

But it *wasn't* all right. Cole stared up at an enormous night sky where a blanket of stars, millions of them, winked down at him. The crickets chirped, Arthur snored, and Gwin continued to lie unnaturally still as he pondered the enormity of his professional misconduct.

Gwin didn't bother to say anything else. Neither did he. Except for Cole's fingers, which continued to stroke her hair, they both lay very still. After a bit, he sensed a slackening of tension about her shoulders. Her chin drooped low on his chest, and he heard her breathing revert to the soft, rhythmic cadence of slumber. It wasn't until much later, when the first peach-colored rays of dawn were straining over the mountainous horizon, that Cole was finally able to surrender to a fitful sleep of his own.

14

Virginia City, Nevada

"*Yep. You got a* real nasty infection there, son, but it's my best guess you're going to live anyway."

Dr. Julian Price, a skinny old codger, bald except for a fringe of closely cropped gray hair that ringed his head just above the ears, wiped his bloodied hands on a towel. He was surveying Cole Shepherd's battered body, a body that was still sweating bullets on his examining table.

"Oh, you poor thing!" Mrs. Price, as stout as her husband was thin, made a series of sympathetic clucking sounds as she dipped a cloth into a washbowl and wrung it out to dab gently at Cole's forehead.

The doctor peered at Gwin from over a pair of gleaming spectacles. "You hear that? Sometime soon,

I reckon this young man will be walking out of here intact." His wizened face cracked into a teasing smile. He winked and thumped the nub of his wooden leg against the floor for added effect. "And that's more than you can say for his doctor, ain't it now?"

With the clumsy reflexes of one rising from the depths of a deep sleep, Gwin blinked and focused, realizing that the doctor was trying to put her at ease. It was also then that she realized she was gripping the edge of her chair so tightly that her hands were beginning to cramp. She relaxed her grip and smiled weakly.

Gwin hadn't been to Virginia City in almost two years, but not that much had changed. She had nosed out the elderly doctor's house like a pup returning to its home. The unassuming two-story white frame structure stood looking out on E Street just exactly as it had two years ago.

Gwin had been glad to see that Mrs. Price still maintained the colorful flower boxes that adorned her homey front porch. Petunias, marigolds, violets, and geraniums burst forth from their planters in tiny explosions of bright, cheery color. The house, much like the garrulous couple who owned it, oozed a come-on-in-and-set-a-spell hospitality that seemed oddly out of place in this fast-moving, oftentimes hard-hearted boomtown known as the Queen of the Comstock Lode.

Upon turning the corner of E Street this afternoon, after traveling many miles in the back of an old prospector's wagon, Gwin had been almost moved to tears at the welcome sight of Mrs. Price's flower boxes. She recalled dragging Clell up those very same porch steps two years ago, threatening to never speak to him again if he didn't act like a man and get that bum tooth of his taken care of.

No, nothing much had changed here, Gwin thought sadly. But things had certainly changed for her, hadn't they? Today, she was sitting in the same chair she had sat in over two years ago after poor Clell had submitted himself to the sure cure for a toothache. But poor Clell was dead now, and in his place lay another young man.

Today, after their straggly trio had arrived on the Price's doorstep, Cole had insisted that the doctor take a look first at Arthur's tender feet. Gwin had excused herself to wash up, and by the time she had gotten back, Arthur was already in the Prices' cozy parlor, his bare feet bandaged and propped up on a tasseled hassock. Gwin left him there, contentedly munching on a plateful of gingersnaps and thumbing through a medical book.

Gwin had gone back into the examining room, where the doctor was cutting off what remained of Cole's bloodstained shirt. Even from where she hovered in the open doorway, Gwin had seen the angry red swelling around the entry wound, and her heart had caught in her throat.

"Sorry, but this is going to hurt like the devil, son," Doc Price had warned Cole as he had set to serious work on his shoulder, using a probe and a nasty-looking, sharp-toothed metal extractor to remove the bullet. Two years ago, Gwin had stood stoically by Clell's side, holding his hand and calmly encouraging him.

This was entirely different. Today, Gwin had been forced to sink into the nearest chair, not trusting her wobbling legs after catching sight of that first sickening rush of bright red blood.

She wondered dazedly why she hadn't just elected to wait in the other room. Even though Cole hadn't cried out from the pain, Gwin figured she had probably started gripping the edge of her seat just about then. She had even feared for a moment that she was going to faint dead away, landing like a child's rag doll on the polished hardwood floor of the good doctor's office.

Now, it was all over. And thank God for that. Mrs. Price helped Cole over to one of two cots that were set up in a room behind the examining area. His eyelids were already starting to droop. The laudanum was taking effect. That was good. He needed to sleep.

As the doctor turned to wash his hands of Cole's blood, Gwin rose shakily to her feet. "He *is* going to be all right, isn't he?" she asked in a hushed voice.

The doctor dried his hands on a clean towel. "Right as rain, young lady. All he needs is some rest and some time to recuperate. Don't worry. He's young and plenty strong. He'll be back on his feet soon enough."

Gwin nodded and followed Mrs. Price and Cole into the adjoining room. She gazed down at him as he stretched out on his back, bare-chested, his long legs sprawling the full length of the cot. *My God, he's exquisite,* she thought dreamily, admiring the broad expanse of his chest and the smooth, curving line of sinewy muscle in his arms. *He looks like one of those classical Greek sculptures.* She continued to survey the impressive physical length of him, suddenly feeling as if all the air were being squeezed from her lungs. *He looks the way you always dreamed he would look,* a little voice whispered in her head.

"And how's that young man of yours doing?"

Caught off guard by the doctor's casual inquiry, Gwin looked up to see him limping out of his examining room behind her, his wooden leg thumping the floor. "My . . . my young man?"

"The one with the bad tooth! I'm surprised to see there's no ring on your finger, young lady! I'm not usually wrong about such things, and judging by the way he was looking at you . . ."

Gwin's eyes fell once again on Cole's reposing figure. "Oh, you mean Clell." Cole's steady, languid gaze settled on her, and she hesitated, stumbling over her words. "He was . . . I mean, he wasn't my young man. I mean . . ."

Doc Price chuckled. "Oh, so it was *that* way, was it? Poor fella! Take it from me, and I'm a doctor, young lady. He had it bad for you. But then again, I guess a pretty thing like you has left more than one broken heart in her wake!"

Gwin didn't answer. Her gaze lingered on Cole's hands, unusually fine-looking hands for a man, long fingers, neatly trimmed nails. Those hands were slack and empty at the moment, one slung across his flat midsection, the other resting at his side, but they hadn't been so slack and empty last night, had they?

He touched me, she thought, the memory of it rising in a hot flush to color her cheeks. Oh, and how he had touched her! She had tried not to think about it, but with so many hours of traveling, she'd had little else to dwell upon.

Why? she had asked herself over and over. *Why did I let him touch me like that, kiss me like that?* She was painfully aware of what had almost happened between them, and even more painfully aware of the fact that, had he been just a little bit more persistent, she would have given herself to him. She didn't just suspect this possibility, she *knew* it. And there it was—the plain and naked truth. Gwin Pierce, the girl who for years had privately vilified her own mother for her loose morals, had been ready to surrender herself to a man she had known for less than a week! This was not a truth about herself she cared to examine too closely in the harsh, glaring light of day.

She turned away abruptly, covering her face with her hands, pressing down on her eyelids until brightly colored flowers bloomed in the dark. "If you're sure he's going to be all right, then I guess I've got some things to do," she said.

"Things? What things?" Mrs. Price sounded horrified. "You, young lady, have rest to do, that's what!"

Gwin let her hands fall back to her sides. "There will be time for that later. I've got a lot to do."

"Well, I never heard such stuff and nonsense! There's an extra bed just waiting for you in our daughter's old room upstairs! Julian! Talk some sense into her!"

"Lil," the doctor admonished wearily, "if I were any good at talking sense into people, my business would not be nearly as brisk as it is."

Gwin gave the doctor a weak but grateful smile.

A TOUCH OF CAMELOT 205

"Just take care of Mr. Shepherd for me and make sure he doesn't try to—"

Before she could finish, she saw out of the corner of her eye that Cole was already pushing up onto one elbow. "Gwin, wait."

Mrs. Price frowned at this, her second rebellious patient, and promptly pulled his elbow out from under him.

"Achhhh!" Cole fell back onto the cot with a heavy thump.

"That'll teach you," Mrs. Price said sternly.

"Don't mess with her, son," the doctor warned, "she can be a bear when her Florence Nightingale instincts are up."

It was clear to Gwin that Mrs. Price had the situation under control, and so she moved to leave. "It might be late before I get back."

"Gwin! Damn it!"

She hesitated and turned back.

He raised his hand and beckoned her closer. "Where do you think you're going?" His words were starting to slur.

Gwin knelt by his side, satisfied that he was in no shape to thwart her plans. She spoke close to his ear, whispering so that the Prices wouldn't catch her words. "I'm going to get us some money. Arthur needs shoes. And we both need a new set of clothes, in case you haven't noticed."

He shook his head. "No. I can get money. Just wait."

Gwin fought the urge to reach out and smooth the hair from his damp forehead. She tried to sound firm. "I'll be back." She rose to her feet.

"Don't . . ." His fingers brushed feebly across the folds of her skirt, missing purchase.

"Don't what?"

He was losing his battle with the painkilling drug that was invading his system. His eyelids were already fluttering closed. "Don't . . . don't do anything I wouldn't do," he mumbled.

And then, she was relieved to see, he was finally, blessedly asleep.

San Francisco

"Ah, yes! Few of life's pleasures can surpass a truly delectable repast!" Jasper exclaimed, sipping the burgundy that sparkled in his crystal wineglass. His squat, rotund figure was settled at the end of a long, lace-covered mahogany table in the main dining room. He set down his wineglass and promptly changed the subject. "You've heard from the Pinkerton Agency?"

From his seat at the opposite end of the table, Sidney looked up. The ever-present, behemoth Alphonse Ringo sat to Jasper's right, midway between them, ominously silent, as always, and apparently oblivious to the dinner conversation that went on around him.

"How did you know?" Sidney asked back, trying to mask his irritation.

Jasper chuckled. The sound was annoying, like an old man cracking his knuckles. "The walls have ears."

The walls have ears. Sidney picked up his soup spoon and tasted from his bowl of chicken giblet soup. He had fired and hired every member of his household staff three or four times over in an attempt to purge it of Round Table spies, and *still* Jasper managed to have his "ears." "Yes," Sidney replied, "I did receive an answer to my telegram this morning."

"And?" Jasper prodded, dipping his spoon into his bowl.

"Their operative has not reported in for over twenty-four hours, and they found—"

Jasper finished for him. "They found a dead man in the baggage car of the four twenty when it pulled into Wadsworth." He made a disgusting noise as he slurped some broth.

Sidney stopped, his spoon poised over his soup bowl. "Why are you bothering to ask if you already know the answer?"

Jasper grinned. "Just comparing notes, Sidney. It's always good policy to compare notes, isn't that right, Mr. Ringo?"

The laconic bodyguard shifted in his seat, causing it to creak precariously. "Unequivocally, Mr. Barnes."

Jasper's black eyes danced. "Yes, unequivocally. Helps to forestall any errors that may crop up due to miscommunication."

Sidney looked at Jasper, expressionless. "There was no sign of the girl or her brother."

"Yes, it does appear that they've managed to slip away, and at the expense of one of our finest employees, I'm sorry to say. No doubt the Pinkerton man had something to do with that. In retrospect, it might not have been the best thing to involve that agency. It served its purpose well enough in locating them and keeping track of their whereabouts, but this operative of theirs seems to have taken his obligation of protecting them a bit too seriously."

Sidney fought a smile. "I told you it was a mistake to bring them back here. And trying to take care of them en route was overeager and sloppy. Perhaps it's for the best that they've escaped. They'll be on the run. I predict that our troubles are over."

"Oh, I don't know." Jasper set down his spoon and picked at his teeth. "This Pinkerton man who takes his obligations so seriously just might deliver our pigeons yet."

"I told you, his Agency hasn't heard from him. That in itself is highly unusual. Either he's dead or sulking somewhere because he let a woman and a child get away from him."

"It's never wise to assume."

Sidney looked at the gilt-framed painting on the wall above Jasper's balding head. It was one of Sidney's favorites, *First Kiss*. Lancelot and Guinevere indulged in their first indiscretion beneath the watchful eye of Galehot. In the distance, three ladies huddled beneath a tree in the garden.

"Sidney! Did you hear what I said?"

Sidney promptly snapped out of his reverie. "You were saying it's not wise to assume."

Jasper let out an exasperated sigh. "Sometimes I get the feeling that one of these days you will just fly away despite all of this!" With one arm, he made a grand sweeping motion, clearly indicating the trappings of material wealth.

Sidney's lips crooked into a dry smile. "Why, whatever would make you think such a thing?"

"It's the way you moon over those paintings of yours, as if you would like nothing better than to dive into them, to fling yourself once and for all out of time and place!"

"Don't we all feel that way from time to time, Jasper? Isn't that only human? To dream?"

"Well, I'm sure I wouldn't know. All I do know is that you have everything you've ever wanted in the here and now, Sidney, and you didn't do it alone."

"I'm well aware of that, Jasper."

"Why, if it weren't for the Round Table, we would not be on the verge of taking City Hall!"

We? Sidney thought cynically.

"Why, if it weren't for the Round Table, you would not have been able to build this—"

Ringo cleared his throat.

"What's that?" Jasper whipped his head around. "Finished with your first course already, Mr. Ringo?"

The blond giant nodded as he lifted his napkin to his lips, dabbing at them so daintily that it struck Sidney as ludicrous. "Fine grub," he muttered in his broad bass voice.

"Fine grub indeed!" Jasper broke into a fat grin and raised his wineglass in a hearty toast. "What is the name of that new cook of yours again, Sidney?"

"Mrs. Wilson."

"Ah yes! A veritable treasure, this Mrs. Wilson! Pray tell, what is the entrée for this evening?"

"Broiled oysters, salad, and cheese," Sidney answered, allowing his mind to wander again.

He felt a certain perverse exhilaration over the fact that the Pierces had miraculously escaped the assassin sent to end their lives aboard the Central Pacific Express. They had, in essence, thwarted the all-powerful Round Table. Sidney just hoped that they had also managed to escape the Pinkerton operative assigned to bring them back to San Francisco. He hoped they were well on their way east and far away from here, because if they weren't . . .

His eyes rose surreptitiously to *First Kiss*, to Emmaline's enraptured, ever-youthful face. *I hope you're watching over your children, my love. There's only so much I can do for them in the here and now.*

"Excuse me, sir."

Frederick, his newly hired butler and the servant Sidney now most suspected of Round Table spying, appeared in the open archway of the cavernous dining room. "Will you be requiring your second course?"

Sidney gave the tall, rake-thin man a perfunctory nod. "Yes, Frederick, thank you. I believe we'll be looking forward to the second course momentarily."

15

Virginia City

In the back room behind Dr. Price's examining area, Cole raked a hand through hair still damp from his bath. He reached for the coat lying at the foot of the cot where he had spent most of the past two days on his back. He was feeling much better, physically, anyway.

He slipped his arms into his new coat, a brown, single-breasted alpaca. It was almost identical to the one that had been ruined two nights ago on the train. He shrugged his shoulders and flexed his arms, wincing slightly at the protesting ache from his healing wound. "Where did your sister learn to shop for men's clothing?" he asked Arthur, who was perched on a three-legged stool by the narrow bed.

Arthur grinned. "Does it fit?" The boy still wore

his faded red undershirt and overalls, both of which were growing riper by the minute. Gwin had bought a new set of clothing for her brother, too, but he had shown no interest in actually trying them on.

"It fits like a glove," Cole said, surprised that Gwin had managed to choose a full set of clothes that fit him so perfectly without either his measurements or his physical presence.

Arthur folded his arms and grinned. "Oh, Gwinnie's got a lot of hidden talents. Don't you ever doubt it."

"Oh, I never doubted it, Arthur. I never doubted it for a minute."

During the time that Cole had been laid up, Gwin had been out earning money. God only knew what *that* meant. At first, he had assumed she was probably hustling up card games. That idea hadn't exactly set well with him, but now his imagination was conjuring up even more troubling possibilities.

Somehow, in a short span of time, Gwin had managed to earn enough money to buy all three of them new clothes and pay Dr. Price for his medical services. And now, she was determined that the three of them go out for a fancy dinner. That all added up to a pretty penny, a *very* pretty penny for a young woman to earn in less than two full days.

Cole frowned. He was beginning to wonder if Gwin had been up to a little more than just cardsharping. He pictured the scene he had stumbled upon in the saloon car: Gwin sitting across from that slimy gambler, Monroe, smiling coyly as she slid a couple of poker chips into the pot. He was imagining her voice, soft, silky, and enticing, *"I'll call you and raise you one, Mr. Monroe."* And him, that gutter slime, ogling her figure, grinning like a hungry fox as he slid his own chips to the center of the table. *And by the way, Gwin, just how were you planning on paying up if you'd lost to Mr. Monroe?*

"Cole? What's the matter?"

"What?" Cole turned to Arthur, who wore an expression of mild alarm.

"What's the matter? Is your arm hurting?"

"No." Cole glanced down and realized his fists were clenched. He flexed his fingers stiffly. "No, it's fine. I'm fine. I was just thinking of, uh, nothing. Never mind." He bent to gather up his old clothes.

Why do you care how she earned the money?

Because I'm wearing the clothes she bought with that money. Dirty money is dirty money. If she was—

If she was what? If she was prostituting herself to buy these clothes for you, you're too good to wear them?

Cole's grip tightened on his shirt. Lofty, high-minded reasoning, that. And a trifle illogical, too. Hadn't he been thinking just the other night that maybe he needed to pay a visit to one of those girls himself?

"What are you going to do with your old clothes?" Arthur asked. "Burn them?"

Cole examined the torn, bloodstained shirt in his hand. "That wouldn't be a bad idea."

A sudden thought struck him, and he reached down to scoop up his ruined coat from the cot. "That reminds me," he said, shoving his hand deep into one of the inside pockets. "This wouldn't happen to belong to you, would it?" He extracted Arthur's slingshot, holding it up by its strap.

"Excalibur!" The boy leapt to his feet and snatched it from Cole. "You remembered Excalibur!"

"You told me to take care of it for you, didn't you?"

"Thanks, Cole! I thought with all that happened, you'd forgotten it on the train!"

Gwin's voice interrupted their exchange. "And better that he should have! When are you going to give up that old thing?"

Cole looked up to see her standing in the open archway, and something in his chest constricted. She was stunning. She wore a bright turquoise silk dress that only heightened the dazzling blue of her eyes. Her cheeks were flushed bright with color, her blazing hair pulled back at the sides and swept up into an elegant chignon. The neckline of her dress was a low-cut square, revealing enough swelling, pale flesh to rivet any red-blooded man's attention. His eyes stuck there before they rose again to meet her expectant gaze. She was waiting for him to say something, but his mouth had gone unaccountably dry. Luckily, Arthur said it for him.

"Gee whillikins, Gwinnie! You sure do look pretty!"

Gwin disengaged her gaze from Cole's long enough to frown at her little brother. "And what are you doing still in those old clothes? Didn't I tell you to—"

"I did take a bath! I really did! Didn't I, Cole?"

Gwin turned back to Cole. "Why didn't you make him change those old stinking clothes? Do I have to see to everything?"

Cole cleared his throat, still having some difficulty recovering his vocabulary. "Well, I, uh . . ."

Gwin threw up her hands. "Men!" She crossed the room and scooped up a pile of folded clothes from a night table: a white shirt, a brown coat, matching trousers, socks, and fresh underdrawers. She shoved the thick bundle beneath Arthur's wrinkled nose. "Now!"

"Ah, jeez, Gwinnie!"

"Now!" she repeated, the expression on her face clearly brooking no tolerance for argument.

Arthur donned a tragic expression and craned his neck to look around her stiff shoulder at Cole.

"Don't look at me." Cole shrugged in reply to his unspoken request for a second opinion.

"I thought we men were supposed to stick together," he accused, accepting the bundle from Gwin reluctantly.

"Only on some things, kiddo."

Gwin folded her arms and tapped her foot.

Arthur's shoulders slumped. "Ah, jeez! These are sissy clothes!"

"You can change in the upstairs bedroom!" Gwin added as Arthur disappeared around the corner.

When he was gone, Gwin turned back to face Cole. Immediately, he found his eyes drawn back to the plunging neckline of that dress. *That dress!* The bodice hugged her tight to the hips where a ruffled overskirt draped back into a short train behind her. Sweet mercy.

"Well?" she asked, interrupting his thoughts.

"Where did you get the money for all of this?"

"None of your business."

Cole tried to read her eyes. Blue ice. Nothing there. Inside Cole's head, Monroe turned to rest one elbow on the back of his chair, wearing a lazy smile. *"Why don't you run along, son? The lady is in the middle of a game right now and doesn't want to be disturbed."*

"Does that mean you have something to hide?" Cole asked, an irrational knot of anger tightening in his stomach.

"Of course not. I just don't like your tone of voice."

Cole clasped his hands behind his back and looked down at his feet, struggling to remain calm. "All right, your ladyship," he said, raising his head again. "How about this? *Please* would you mind telling me how you managed to get your hands on so much money in such a short time?"

"Now you're being condescending."

"How much do you have left?"

Gwin drew in a deep breath, clutching her gloves and reticule tight, hugging them to her stomach. "None of your business."

"What's in the bag?"

"Nothing."

Cole took a step toward her. "What's in the bag, Gwin?"

She took a step back. "Personal things. *Woman things.*"

"Don't lie to me. Let me see what's in there."

"No."

Cole reached for the reticule. Gwin jumped back. "Hey!"

"How much do you have in there? Ten? Twenty? A hundred?"

"I have enough for dinner, but—"

Cole held out his hand, wiggling his fingers expectantly. "Well, then, you shouldn't mind if I have a look, right?"

Gwin didn't move to oblige, so Cole wrapped his fingers around the bag and tugged. Gwin tugged back. Trying to disengage that blue silk bag from her stubborn fingers was like trying to pry fresh meat from an alligator's jaws, but Cole finally won their little tug-of-war.

Gwin bent to retrieve white silk gloves that had fluttered to the floor in their scuffle. "You almost tore it! Do you have any idea how much I paid for that thing?"

"Oh, I have an idea, all right!" Cole shot back, loosening the drawstring. He dumped the contents out onto a night table. A handful of silver and gold coins spilled out, two double eagles among them, a small perfume bottle, a silver pocket watch, a comb, a lace-edged handkerchief, and . . . Cole reached out and picked up three walnut shells and a small round object. He dropped the shells and held the tiny ball up to the light to examine it more closely. It looked like a cherry pit.

"What . . . ?" he began, trailing off. Then it hit him. "Shell games?" he asked, his eyes shifting to her distinctly guilty face. "You were running *shell games?*"

Gwin jerked on first one glove, then the other. "Well, I didn't know where to get my hands on a decent deck of cards on such short notice."

Cole started to laugh. He laughed so hard, he doubled over. "You've got to be joking! That's the oldest scam on earth!"

"Well, I don't see what's so funny about it! It bought us each a nice set of clothes, and it's going to put food in our mouths tonight!"

"Shell games!" Cole was hardly able to get the words out. For the last two days, Gwin had been out running shell games, for Christ's sake! He was so relieved, he didn't have the heart to be angry.

"Cole Shepherd, stop laughing! What's the matter with you?"

"Thimble-riggers!" Cole managed to get out between guffaws. "That's what we used to call you people! I'm surprised there's still people around who'll fall for those old tricks!"

Gwin sniffed. "Well, there's a sucker born every minute! Besides, how stupid do you think I am? I let them win often enough."

"I'll bet!" Cole straightened, miming a fisherman casting his pole. "Just enough to reel them suckers in!"

"Oh! You think you're so darned smart! I'll just bet you would never fall for it, right?"

"Oh, I don't know." Cole chuckled, finally regaining some control over himself. "Maybe if the girl running the game looked like you, even I might be tempted to—"

Gwin cocked her head. "Tempted to *what*, Shepherd?"

On impulse, Cole closed the distance between them and gripped each of her shoulders, pulling her up against him. The subtle fragrance of spring-fresh lilacs assaulted his senses. "Just tempted, Gwin. Just *tempted*," he replied wickedly, smiling down at her shocked expression. "By the way, did I happen to mention that you look—"

Arthur's whining voice shattered the moment. "Ah, jeez! These pants are so stiff, I can hardly bend my legs, Gwinnie!"

Startled, Gwin pulled away and whirled to face her brother, who sulked in the open doorway. Cole took a discreet step back. Arthur was apparently too distracted by his own miserable situation to notice his sister's embarrassment.

She recovered smoothly. "Now, that's more like it!"

Arthur scowled. "I don't want to go to any stupid old restaurant anyway! Why can't we stay here for dinner like we did last night?"

"Don't you dare complain, young man!" Snatching a comb from the night table, she marched over to his side and started running it through his hair.

"Hey! Ouch! Owwwwch! Stop it, Gwinnie!"

She ignored his protests, concentrating instead on plastering his hair back from his forehead. "Looks like you need a haircut, too, but we'll just have to take care of that tomorrow. Tonight we're going to order us up a fine meal and enjoy ourselves. I think we deserve it after what we've been through. Then—"

Cole interrupted pointedly. "And then we need to talk."

Gwin continued as if she hadn't heard him. "Then we need to figure a way to earn some more money. What I have now isn't going to get us very far."

"Just how far were you planning to go?" Cole asked.

Gwin bent to button the open collar of Arthur's shirt. "That is none of your business, Shepherd."

Arthur grimaced. "Ah, jeez, Gwinnie! You're gagging me!"

"I can get money," Cole said, "I tried to tell you that before. I can wire the Agency."

Gwin folded down Arthur's starched collar, then turned briskly to cross the room. The elaborate ruffles of her evening gown wish-whooshed as she moved. "It's too late for that today."

Cole approached her from behind and touched her shoulder. "Tomorrow, then. I can wire the Agency first thing in the morning."

Gwin whirled around. "No! Not first thing in the morning! Not *ever!* You can't wire the Agency! Don't you understand?"

"No. Why don't you explain it to me?"

"Your precious Agency is what got us into trouble in the first place! Who do you think was behind that last attempt on our lives? Who else knew what train we were going to be on?"

"What are you trying to say? That someone at the Agency is in on this conspiracy?"

"Well, it sure does look like it, doesn't it?"

"That's preposterous."

"Not so preposterous! Think about it!"

Cole eyed her stiff figure pensively. Oh, he knew that from her point of view, it probably did appear that someone at the Agency was actually in on this mysterious conspiracy. Cole, however, knew that the idea wasn't only preposterous, it was virtually impossible. Even though this was not what the Agency would consider a high-priority or secret assignment, Cole knew that the general rules of protocol concerning confidential communications would nevertheless be followed. Only Fritz, his secretary, Mrs. Avery, and the old man himself, Allan Pinkerton, would be privy to any of Cole's telegraphed reports. The integrity of all these people was above reproach. Cole's theory was that the Agency was most likely being used as a conduit for information. Unless Cole were to inform him any differently, there would be no reason for Fritz to withhold information from the client who had hired them. *There,* most likely, was the leak.

"All right." Cole knew it would do no good to reason with Gwin. "I'll put off wiring the Agency for a while, but we'll have to find a way of supporting ourselves in the meantime."

Gwin picked up a walnut shell and carefully replaced it back in her reticule. "As I was saying, there are a lot of gambling halls in this town, and after dinner, we can use what stake money we have left to—"

"Whoa! Hold it right there, Gwin. Gambling? That's your big bright idea? Doesn't that amount to little more than leaving our fate in the hands of Lady Luck?"

"Oooh, not necessarily." She used one cupped hand to sweep the coins on the night table into her open reticule.

"Oh, no, you don't," Cole said firmly. "I'll go along with you on not wiring the Agency, but I will not abide anything dishonest. No stealing, no lying, no cheating."

"Oh, for Pete's sake, Shepherd! Sometimes you are such a nitpicker! Doesn't it get tiring? Dragging that halo around with you everywhere you go?"

Cole smiled. "No stealing, no lying, no—"

"All right! I heard you!" Gwin interrupted. "I already figured you'd feel that way about it, so I came up with an idea."

"An idea?"

Gwin flashed him a winsome smile. "Twenty-one."

"Twenty-one what?"

"The game. Have you ever played the game, Shepherd?"

"Sure I've played the game."

"Then you know it's darn near impossible for the players to cheat, right?"

Cole smirked. "Right. But if you're not planning on cheating, Gwin, my lovely, how can you be so sure we'll come out ahead and not lose our, excuse the expression, shirts instead?"

"Oh, I just have this *feeling*." She turned around slowly to focus on her little brother, who was busy prying two fingers into the opening at his collar and twisting his neck.

Cole followed her gaze. A silence fell over the room and Arthur looked up guiltily. "What? What are you two staring at? Do I look that stupid?"

"Oh, you don't look stupid at all, little brother," Gwin intoned sweetly.

It was then that Gwin's questionable strategy dawned on Cole. "You mean you're going to have Arthur . . . ?"

Gwin crossed the room and patted her brother's arm affectionately. "Arthur, dear, you're going to learn a new game tonight. Cole and I are going to explain it to you over dinner."

"Oh, this will never work," Cole protested. "Never in a million years. A kid in a gambling hall? Even if they let him play, there's still no guarantee—"

"But you and I will be doing the playing, Cole! Can't you see it?" Gwin's blue eyes sparkled like polished sapphires as she warmed to her subject. She clasped her hands together rapturously, crossing the room to stand before him. "It's just too perfect! We won't win every turn, of course, but if we keep our heads and play the odds, we can't lose over the long run. And it isn't even cheating. Even you have to admit that, don't you?"

Cole felt himself being swayed. After all, what could it hurt to humor her? "Well, I don't know."

"Cole, my darling. My handsome, suspicious Pinkerton man!" She smiled coyly, fingering the open lapel of his coat, batting her long lashes in an exaggerated fashion. "Just trust me, and I'll show you a night on the town that you'll never forget."

16

Cole stepped out onto the boardwalk and breathed in the crisp night air, a pleasant contrast to the smoke-filled gambling hall. He couldn't help smiling to himself. He had decided to trust Guinevere Pierce, and even *he* had to admit, they had done pretty darned well.

Arthur tugged at his sleeve. "What's taking her so long?"

"She's cashing in her chips, Arthur," Cole answered, "and she's got a whole lot of chips to cash in."

Unimpressed, Arthur yawned and leaned up against a nearby post, his arms folded, his eyelids hovering at half-mast. Cole sympathized with him. It was late for a kid his age to be up.

Soon after leaving Doc Price's house, the three of them had dined at an outrageously expensive restaurant on C Street. Cole had been surprised to find himself relaxing and thoroughly enjoying himself. It was by unspoken agreement that they had left their prior differences outside the door. No one had mentioned San Francisco, the Agency, or the attempt on their lives.

A pair of well-dressed, cigar-chomping men pushed through the frosted glass door of the gambling hall, and Gwin slipped out after them, appearing at Cole's side, swinging her reticule. "Ready to go?"

Cole nodded to Arthur, who appeared to be dozing. "We might have to carry him back."

Gwin poked her brother's shoulder playfully. "Come on! It's time to go!"

Arthur's eyes flew open, and he straightened. "Best news I've had all night."

They ambled down the boardwalk. After a moment of companionable silence, Gwin turned to look up at Cole, her lovely blue eyes shining. "Cole Shepherd, bucking the tiger! If I hadn't seen it for myself, I wouldn't believe it!"

Cole smiled tolerantly at this, a teasing reference to the fact that he had tried his hand at the faro table. "Just don't go passing it around," he replied amiably.

"You liked it, didn't you? Admit it." Gwin stepped in front of him, cutting him off. "You liked it."

"Sure I liked it. Everyone likes it when they're winning. It's when they start losing—"

"There you go again!"

"Sorry, I guess it's just my nature." Cole shoved his hands into his pockets and started forward again. "A penny saved is a penny earned and all that."

Gwin linked her arm with Cole's, matching his

pace. "We made a good team tonight. You, me, and Arthur. You have to admit that."

Cole was about to reply when he suddenly realized they had neglected to turn onto E Street. "Hey, we missed our turn."

"Oh, no, we didn't."

Cole didn't miss the sly note in her voice. "What do you mean?"

She squeezed his arm. "Don't you think we've imposed on the Prices long enough?"

"Well, yes, but—"

"I mean, we've got plenty of money now."

"Wait a minute." Cole stopped.

"Hey! What are we stopping for?" This was Arthur, turning and backtracking to stand before them.

Cole ignored him. "What are you saying?"

"I'm saying," Gwin said, disengaging her arm from his and placing a hand on one hip, "we can afford to put ourselves up in a nice hotel for the night, and then—"

"And then?"

Gwin threw up both hands, exasperated. "And then! And then! And then! Honestly, Shepherd, can't you ever do anything without planning two weeks ahead?"

Cole considered this seriously for a moment. "Well, I suppose I could if there were a valid enough reason."

"Ahhhhh!" Gwin rolled her eyes and turned on her heel, heading briskly up the street.

"Wait a minute! Slow down!" Cole trotted along behind her starched back, ignoring the amused glances they drew from other late-night pedestrians. "If you want to stay at a hotel, that's fine, but shouldn't we tell the Prices?"

"I already told them."

"You already told them? Hey!" Cole called out as she deliberately picked up her pace.

He came to a stop in the middle of the walk and nudged the brim of his derby back with one finger. She'd already told them? Plucky little wench, wasn't she? But, then again, she had been raised to be plucky.

Earlier, at the restaurant, Gwin and Arthur had amused Cole with tales of their past exploits and scrapes with the law.

"Remember that time in Texas when those fellas almost strung poor Silas up?" Arthur had asked this question around a hearty mouthful of boiled potatoes.

"What happened?" Cole shifted his gaze across the elegant table to Gwin. Her pale blue eyes were shining and clear, her face radiant and animated with relaxed good humor. Her hair glowed a soft, burnished hue in the candlelight.

She took a discreet sip of champagne before replying, "Well, they must have gotten a bad batch of hair tonic. Under normal circumstances, it was harmless, but—"

"It turned their heads blue!" Arthur said. "Holy crow! Were those fellas mad!"

"Well, it was more like a light shade of violet." Gwin set her champagne glass on the table delicately. "I still don't understand what all the fuss was about. I'm sure it would have worn off in a couple of days."

Cole barely managed to stifle a grin behind his napkin.

Gwin waved a hand dismissively. "That's no matter. We were traveling through west Texas. It was the kind of town where the marshal also happens to be the mayor as well as the judge, and whoever is leaning up against the bar that day is drafted for jury duty."

"I've heard of places like that. So, how did Silas get out of that one?"

"Well, luckily, Emmaline and Clell saw trouble coming. Clell rode on ahead to the next town to hire someone to impersonate a *federal* marshal."

Cole laughed. "You can't be serious!"

Gwin continued, "That big old federal marshal rode right on up to the local lawman's office to inform the irate citizenry that Silas was wanted in Tarrant County on federal charges and that there was a generous reward for his return. After taking down every blue-headed man's name and promising to wire the reward money, he finally got Silas released."

Cole shook his head. "And they actually fell for that?"

Gwin raised her champagne glass, her eyes sparkling mischievously. "The bigger the lie . . ."

One story had inevitably led to another, each more outrageous than the last. Cole had laughed until his stomach ached. By the time they had left the restaurant, he felt as if he had finally gotten a small glimpse of the wily Silas Pierce through the eyes of his adoring children.

But now, as Cole stood watching Gwin stride down the street ahead, it wasn't Silas Pierce he was thinking about; it was Clell Martin. Tonight, Cole had studied Gwin's expressions whenever she had spoken of him, and in her eyes he had seen a wrenching mixture of affection and sorrow. He remembered Doc Price's casual inquiry the day they arrived in Virginia City.

"And how's that young man of yours doing?"

"My young man?" Cole remembered the look on Gwin's face. Surprise. Guilt.

"The one with the bad tooth! I'm surprised to see there's no ring on your finger, young lady! I'm not usually wrong about such things, and judging by the way he was looking at you . . ."

And Gwin, the consummate actress, had been so shaken by the mere mention of Clell Martin that she had stumbled over her words. *"Oh, you mean Clell. He was . . . I mean, he wasn't my young man. I mean . . ."*

What she had meant to say was, he was dead. He had died before having the chance to slip a ring on her finger. Cole was certain that there had been more between Gwin and Clell Martin than just friendship, and this new certainty brought with it a stab of something like jealousy.

She's your assignment, not your woman, Cole. Whether or not she and Clell Martin were lovers shouldn't matter to you one way or another. But it did. Somehow it did, and Cole was forced to admit to himself that Guinevere Pierce had come to mean much more to him than just the personification of his first solo assignment for the Pinkerton Agency.

Cole eyed Gwin's determined figure disappearing down the street. She hadn't even glanced back to see if they were coming. Not once.

"Awww, what's the matter with her?" Arthur whined piteously. "All I wanna do is go to bed!"

"And you will go to bed, Arthur, my boy," Cole said. "Just as soon as I figure out what that addlepated sister of yours has up her sleeve. Let's go."

Less than thirty minutes later, Cole was lighting the gas jet of a sparkling chandelier.

Gwin, who had followed Cole and Arthur into their lavish hotel room, let out a sigh. The furnishings—two four-poster beds, a dresser, a small writing desk complete with hotel stationery and pens, even the elaborately carved hat rack behind the open door—were all made of a deep, rich walnut. The wallpaper above redwood-paneled wainscoting featured an ornate green and gold scrollwork design.

Gwin was awestruck. "It's beautiful, isn't it? Just like something out of Camelot." The soles of her dainty court shoes whispered over plush carpeting as she crossed the room. She bent to run her fingertips over one of the downturned bedspreads.

"Hmmmmm, yes." Cole set the long-handled wand he had used to light the chandelier on the writing desk. "And it costs like something only a king could afford, too."

"It's worth it," Gwin said. "Sometimes you have to live for the moment."

"If you say so. Now me, I like to plan ahead."

Even under normal circumstances, Gwin thought Cole one of the handsomest men she had ever met, but tonight he was enough to take any woman's breath away. Dressed in his crisp new suit of clothes with a striped ascot tie cinched at his collar and his brown derby set back at a jaunty angle on his dark head, Cole Shepherd cut an uncommonly dashing figure.

Arthur, who was long beyond caring much about his surroundings as long as they included a place to sleep, scrambled up on one of the beds. He started yanking at his collar and pulling off his jacket. "Goooood night!"

Gwin started for the open doorway. "Well, it's late. I guess I'd better go find my own room."

"Wait. I'll walk you."

She acted as if she hadn't heard. Throughout the evening, Cole had been trying subtly, but persistently, to get her alone to talk. She had managed to stave him off until now.

"Wait a minute!"

She almost made it out the door before Cole caught up to her, snagging her by the elbow and spinning her around. "Gwin, I said I'll walk you to your room. Besides, there's something I want to talk to you about."

"Can't it wait until morning?"

"You've been avoiding me all night."

"Let go!"

"There are things we have to discuss."

Arthur interrupted. "If you two are going to start arguing again—"

Gwin glared at Arthur impatiently. "We're *not* going to start arguing again! Go to sleep!"

"Oh, yes we are," Cole said.

"Come on, Shepherd. We're all tired."

"How am I supposed to get any sleep if you two are yelling at each other?" Arthur asked.

"Don't worry, you go on to bed while I make sure

your sister gets to her room safe and sound." Cole held Gwin's elbow and steered her out through the open door, closing it firmly behind them.

Once outside, he still didn't let go of her as he led her down the deserted hallway to her room. Cole stopped and turned her to face him. "All right, Gwin, you've been trying to put me off all night. What are you so afraid of?"

Gwin avoided his gaze. "I wanted this night to be . . ."

He waited for her to go on, then prodded. "To be what?"

"Never mind. I just wanted it to go smoothly, that's all."

"And it did."

"Yes."

He paused. "What are your plans?"

"Plans?" Gwin tried to sound innocent and fell far short of her mark. "What plans?"

Cole pulled her closer and slipped two fingers beneath her chin, forcing her to look at him. Gwin suddenly felt dizzy, as if all the champagne she'd drunk this evening had finally caught up with her. His voice was low and pressing, barely above a whisper. "You're planning on running away, aren't you? That's what tonight was all about, wasn't it? That's why you wanted it to go smoothly? Because it's your way of saying good-bye?"

"You're imagining things."

Cole's hand slipped behind her neck, warm and strong, pulling her still closer. "Am I?"

Gwin raised her free hand to press against his

chest. Her intention was to push him away, but instead, her hand just rested there, her fingers spreading out over the smooth material of his coat, then closing together again. The scent of his shaving soap mingled with the faint aroma of bourbon, and she smiled to herself, thinking that tonight was the first time she had seen him take a drink of anything stronger than whistle-stop coffee.

"Gwin?"

She blinked up at him and was surprised to see such a serious expression on his face. "What?"

"I'm half-afraid I'll wake up tomorrow and you'll be gone."

Gwin couldn't bring herself to answer. She had thought of slipping away in the night. It was inevitable that they must part ways. That was why she had wanted this night to go perfectly. This was the last night she would have with him. She didn't want it to be marred by pointless bickering. Tomorrow, they had to face the hard choices. Cole had his career in Chicago to go back to. She and Arthur had a future in the East.

Cole studied her face. "I'm right, aren't I?"

"No."

"Gwin." The hand that gripped her elbow moved down to her waist. He bent his head and Gwin caught her breath as his lips brushed lightly over hers. His arm encircled her waist, tightening, pulling her flush up against him, and Gwin tilted her head to accept his kiss. *Champagne bubbles,* she thought giddily, her arms sliding up to lock around his neck, *nobody ever told me they could actually cause your feet to leave the floor.*

The sound of keys jingling at the end of the hall startled them, shattering the moment. Mortified, Gwin jumped back as a portly gentleman in a black top hat approached, thumping his cane on the carpet. He grinned, his eyes glittering impishly. "Had a winning night, then, hey?" he inquired in passing.

Gwin felt her cheeks grow warm as the man stopped outside a door down the hall, inserted his key, then threw them a rakish wink before sweeping inside and closing the door behind him.

Cole muttered, "Bad timing."

Gwin frowned up at him. "How embarrassing!"

"Oh, it was nothing. Just a kiss, Gwin. It's not like it hasn't happened in this town before."

Just a kiss? She glowered. "Well, excuse me if I can't be as casual about it as you seem to be!"

"Look, I'm sorry. I didn't mean to—" He stopped and corrected himself wearily. "I mean, yes, I meant to kiss you, but we've still got to talk about this."

"Not here, Cole. We're out in the hallway."

"Fine. We'll continue this in private." He held out one hand. "Do you have your room key?"

Gwin drew herself to full height proudly. "I am quite capable of opening my own door."

Cole sighed, his patience clearly stretched. "Do you think that just this once you could do as I ask without putting up an argument?"

Gwin pulled out her room key and slapped it into his open palm.

"Thank you." Cole jammed the key into the lock, turned it, then shoved the door open with one hand. "After you, your ladyship."

Moonlight filtered through lacy summer curtains at one window, illuminating the room just enough that she was able to make her way to a night table by a large canopy bed.

"I'll light the chandelier," Cole said.

"Don't bother. There's a lamp right here," Gwin answered, locating a box of matches, then carefully lighting the wick, shooing away a puff of smoke with one hand.

"Nice," Cole commented, closing the door behind him.

Gwin dropped her reticule on the night table and looked around, pulling off her gloves, tossing them down. The room was luxurious, just as beautiful as Arthur and Cole's, but she was growing too nervous to appreciate it.

The thick, quilted coverlet on the canopy bed had been turned down for the night, baring a set of immaculate white sheets. Her eye lingered there a moment too long before she turned to face Cole, who still stood by the door, taking in their surroundings.

He kissed me. She thought about that kiss and about the others before it, the impassioned embraces they had shared beneath the stars. She had been kissed before, but never, *ever* like that.

Cole finished his idle perusal of the room and caught her gaze. He didn't say anything; nor did he look away, and Gwin shivered slightly, as if fighting off a chill. But she wasn't cold at all. She was growing warm, *too* warm. Good sense told her it was time to leave Cole Shepherd behind, to forget that he ever existed and get on with her life, but good sense had little to say about the warm feeling that blossomed inside of her when he kissed her.

Last night, sleeping alone in a bed that had once belonged to the Prices' eldest daughter, Gwin had dreamed of Lancelot for the first time since meeting him in the flesh. In the dream, he had stolen into her bedchamber in the night. He had taken her in his arms and kissed her senseless. He had undressed her lovingly and placed her upon the bed. In the dream, there followed caresses and whispered words of love, but it had ended there, as always, and Gwin had awakened abruptly, feeling an unsatisfied ache in her body as well as her heart. She had remained awake for the better of part of an hour after that, tossing and turning, frustrated and confused.

Gwin abruptly averted her eyes from Cole's steady, silent gaze, afraid that he would see the shocking truth in her eyes: She was ready to finish this dream, once and for all.

After a moment, she heard him moving around, and she looked up to see that he had already doffed his hat and was hanging it on a carved walnut hat rack next to the door. He started to slip out of his coat but stopped after catching the anxious look on her face. "It's a little warm. Do you mind?"

Gwin licked her dry lips and cleared her throat, but the word still came out sounding like a hoarse croak. "No."

He took off his coat and hung it up neatly next to his derby. "I suppose you know what it is I want to talk to you about."

"I think so." Gwin silently cursed her stomach,

which had suddenly turned into a butter churner. What was the matter with her?

Cole spoke. "All I want you to do is hear me out."

"Fine."

"I want you to go to San Francisco with me."

This was *exactly* what Gwin had been trying to avoid all evening. If they really were going to just talk, they were inevitably going to argue. Perhaps dreams were not meant to come true after all. She took a deep breath, steeling her resolve. "I can't do that."

"If we work together, I think maybe we can find out who killed Silas and the others. Don't you think it's at least worth a try?"

Gwin sat on the bed, kicked off the dainty court shoes that matched her evening dress, then bent to peel off her stockings. "Why do you even give a damn?"

"What?"

Gwin brushed the soles of her feet back and forth lightly over the soft, thick carpet, trying to appear unconcerned. "Is it because all of this won't look good for you when you go back to the Agency?"

His tone held a note of carefully controlled anger. "Because it won't *look* good?"

Gwin's rational-thinking mind knew that she had to goad him. It was her only hope of getting at the truth. "Letting a woman and a boy slip away from you wouldn't look very good on your record, would it?"

"No, I suppose not."

"It would be an easy scam, you know. Convincing us to return to San Francisco to help you uncover the true killer, then delivering us straight into the hands of the police."

The look on his face cut through her like a knife. The mere five feet that separated them might have been the depth and breadth of the Pacific Ocean for all the good it did them. "You think I'd do that after what we've been through?" he asked.

"Well, I don't know, Shepherd. I haven't gotten this far by placing my trust in strangers."

"No, I reckon not, but I thought that by now maybe we'd gotten to know each other a little better than that."

Gwin felt her resolve wavering. "It hasn't been so long."

"No, not so long," Cole agreed, his voice softening. "It just seems that way."

Gwin's heart fluttered. Looking at him now, she felt an intense longing rise up from the pit of her stomach, very sudden and very strong. She struggled to push it down as she crossed the room to the walnut dressing table. She stared into its large oval mirror, seeing nothing. "You still haven't answered my question. Why do you care? Why bother risking your neck to try to solve the murder of some no-account like Silas?"

"I'm not going to deny that solving this case would look good for me at the Agency, but that's not all of it. Why do you think I got into this kind of work in the first place?"

"I don't know, Cole. You tell me."

She sensed his approach. "Look, I don't care who the victims are. No one should get away with cold-blooded murder. No one. It's not right."

"No, it's not right," Gwin agreed, subdued.

Cole now stood directly behind her. "And that's exactly what's going to happen if someone doesn't try to do something about it."

Gwin felt her determination crumbling like the walls of Jericho. "And that someone is you?"

"No, that someone is us."

Her problem, she knew, was that she wanted to believe him. She wanted to trust him. "But what about Arthur? He's just a child. It's not right to put him in danger."

Cole gripped her shoulders from behind, his fingers so warm and strong, they seemed to burn straight through the fabric of her dress to brand her skin. "I won't let anything happen to you or Arthur. I promise."

"How can you make a promise like that?"

"When I took this assignment, you and Arthur became my responsibility. That hasn't changed." His hold on her tightened. "You want to find out who killed Silas, don't you? You want to see him pay for it, don't you?"

"Yes, of course I do, but—"

"You're safe for now, Gwin. For today, that is. Maybe even tomorrow and the day after that. But what about later? No matter where you go, how long are you going to feel safe? You don't have any idea of who or what you're up against. Do you want to go on running forever?"

Gwin looked at him in the mirror. "Running?"

"As far as the rest of the world is concerned, you and Arthur fell off the face of the earth when you jumped that train. No one will know you're back in

San Francisco. No one but me. I'll wire the Agency that I lost you, that I'm pursuing some leads on my own before returning to Chicago."

Gwin felt the last remnants of her anger and suspicion drain away to a useless trickle. He wasn't lying to her. She didn't need to see the truth in his eyes to know it. He was too honorable for that; too honorable, even, to try to force her to return to San Francisco with him, which he could do if he wanted. Even setting his damnable "supeena" powers aside, there was still that pesky horse-stealing warrant for her in Garden City. And they both knew it.

"Just think about it," he urged, one of his hands leaving her shoulder, traveling lightly up the side of her neck to touch her hair. Tingles of delight raced down Gwin's spine. "Think about it, won't you?"

"Yes." She felt a little faint. "I'll think about it." But how could she think straight under such circumstances? She was, slowly but surely, losing herself to him. She thought it might have started the very first day she had laid eyes on him in Caldwell, Kansas.

"You have beautiful hair, Gwin," he said softly, pulling one hairpin from her elaborate coiffure and dropping it to the surface of the dressing table.

Gwin didn't move, couldn't move.

Another hairpin slipped from her hair. Then another. Then another and another, until a thick mass of curls tumbled past her shoulders and down her back. Cole took a handful of it and lifted it to his lips. "God, you're so lovely. You would tempt a saint, you know that?"

He took her by the shoulders and turned her

around slowly to face him. Gwin closed her eyes as his lips brushed her forehead, his breath warm and tantalizing on her skin. She flattened both palms against the smooth linen material of his shirt. He was warm and firm, and she marveled at the feel of his heart beating strong beneath her fingertips. He was *real*.

He kissed her temple, then her eyelids. Gwin tilted her face up as his lips slanted down her cheek to press at the corner of her mouth. Then his hands slipped down to close possessively at her waist, and he spoke. "If you want me to leave, you'd better tell me now."

Gwin's fingers slid up to play over broad shoulders. She felt the thick bandaging beneath his shirt and was reminded of how he had risked his life to save her and Arthur. "No, I don't want you to leave."

He pushed her hair from one shoulder, bending his head to kiss her neck. Gwin shivered as his lips moved up, up, up, where she felt his teeth nip gently at her earlobe. He whispered, "I want to make love to you."

He lifted his head. With both hands, he cupped her upturned face, his thumbs resting at the corners of her mouth. "And you want it, too."

17

"Say it," he urged.

Feeling as weak and pliable beneath his touch as a day-old infant, Gwin locked her arms around his neck. "Yes."

"No excuses," he said, one hand slipping down and back around to deftly slip open the tiny buttons of her dress.

"No excuses." Her heart started to pound at the finality of these words. It was time to push the hard, cruel reality of their circumstances from her mind.

She met his seeking mouth, opening herself to him, her tongue finding his to mate in a slow, searching kiss that seemed to last a sweet eternity. Cole finally pulled away, pushing the sleeves of her dress down over her arms to her waist, then pressing warm lips to a bared shoulder.

She was only vaguely aware that he was undressing

her, unbuttoning the waistband of her petticoat, loosening the ties to her corset. With barely a tug or a pull, the corset fell away from her body, dropping to the carpet by their feet. He kissed her again, her dress seeming to melt off of her as he urged it down over her hips to collapse into a puffy cloud of satin and crepe around her ankles.

His hands rested on her hips for a moment, kneading gently as he spoke against her lips. "I've wanted you ever since the first day I saw you."

Gwin marveled at his touch, at the tingling sensations spreading like tentacles to warm even the tips of her extremities. She had felt these stirrings before, on board the train the night they had shared a berth and the night they had spent together beneath the mountain stars. And, of course, she had felt them countless times in her own dreams—just before waking up flushed and scattered and eminently abashed at herself.

She was slightly abashed now as Cole pulled away from her, his hands moving artfully up over her rib cage to close over each breast, molding them gently with his palms through the filmy material of her chemise. *Don't think,* a tiny voice urged in her mind. *Just let him . . . let him . . .* Gwin caught her breath and closed her eyes as his thumbs played over each crest, circling and teasing until she thought she wouldn't be able to bear any more.

Cole's hands finally slipped back down, his thumbs hooking into the waist of her camisole, starting to ease it up. Hesitantly, Gwin lifted her arms as he slid it up and off of her, the garment fluttering to the floor.

She stood mutely before him, naked from the waist up beneath a man's gaze for the first time in her life. Her cheeks flushed hot as his eyes seemed to drink her in—very slowly, agonizingly so—from the top of her head down to her satin-buried ankles. *If there is indeed a God in heaven,* she thought, shivering slightly, *the lamp will flicker and burn out. Now.*

But the lamp did not burn out.

He reached for her, sweeping her off her feet and carrying her over to the bed where he lowered her gently to sheets that felt heavenly cool and soft beneath her. He turned the lamp down to a soft, flickering glow, then sat to remove his boots. Gwin studied his masculine silhouette when he rose to full height to dispense with the rest of his clothing. As he shrugged off his shirt, the bandaging at his shoulder seemed to glow stark-white against the dark.

Then he was settling down beside her, naked, the bedsprings creaking beneath his weight. His hand settled at her waist, and she felt the sole of his foot slowly ride up the length of her calf.

Curious, she allowed her fingertips to roam tentatively over the broad expanse of his chest. She delighted in the feel of his skin, so smooth and warm, giving off a visceral heat. Her fingers slid down over the curve of one shoulder to test the long, sinuous line of muscle in his arm, so solid and hard. How gloriously, wonderfully different he was from her!

Then her eyes met his in the dark, and she stopped, unsure of herself, embarrassed at her boldness. Her stomach fluttered. She had not a clue as to what to do next.

"I've dreamed of you," she whispered, not realizing until the words were out that she had uttered them aloud.

He cupped her jaw in one hand and kissed her mouth. "I've dreamed of you, too." Then he guided her hand down to touch him there where he was hot and hard and . . . *huge.* Gwin's fingers curled around him, more out of sheer astonishment than anything else. It was, she thought, quite thrilling and magnificent, but how on earth had the good Lord ever intended for *that* to fit into . . . ?

"Oh, Gwin, yes," he groaned as his hand closed over her fingers, patiently instructing her.

Gwin felt a secret thrill as he seemed to grow harder still beneath her grasp. It wasn't long before he tensed and pulled away. "Not yet," he said, and before she had time to consider what he meant, he kissed her again, thrusting his tongue into her mouth, ravishing.

In her dreams, his kisses had been chaste and gentle, his caresses soft and leisurely, but this was not a dream. His kisses were fevered, his breath hot on her skin as he feasted first on her neck, then her breasts.

Gwin forgot to think as her body responded to his touch. It responded immediately, shamelessly, and unconsciously. Cole said words to her, incoherent murmurings most of them, but she was beyond hearing. She could only feel, her mind seeming to separate and drift a thousand miles from her rapturous body.

When she opened her eyes, he was already positioning himself above her. His weight, for just one brief second, as he moved over her, was heavy and oh-so-warm. Then he was supporting himself on his forearms, bending his head once again to sweep her open mouth with his tongue, pushing her legs far apart with his knees.

Gwin had never felt so vulnerable in all her life. *Trust him,* she thought, fighting a sudden wild urge to panic. Then she felt the first pressure of him entering her, and, despite her resolve not to, she instinctively stiffened.

He stopped abruptly, whispering between clenched teeth as realization hit him, "Ah, Gwin . . . damn it."

Sensing that he might pull back, Gwin hugged him tight. She knew that to end it now would be all wrong. "It's all right."

His breath was ragged, agonized. "I didn't know."

But he didn't pull back. Instead, he reached down, palming one hip to brace her. Then she felt a brief pain assuaged by the utterly indescribable sensation of him filling her as he penetrated.

Gwin gulped in a rush of air when he stopped, Cole's breath coming hot and fast against her neck. She hugged him tight with her thighs as the pain started to ebb.

He kissed her and asked breathlessly, "Are you . . . ?"

Gwin squeezed her eyes shut. "Oh, yes."

"I hurt you."

"A little. It's all right now."

After a moment, he kissed her again, gently this time. Gwin opened her eyes to meet that familiar, steady gaze. At that moment, she felt as if he was seeing straight through her, straight through to her confused mind and bewildered heart.

He reached up to take one of her hands from around his neck. He kissed her palm, then intertwined his fingers with hers. It was a comforting, intimate, totally unexpected gesture. Then he started moving inside of her in slow, sensual strokes.

It hurt a little, but it also felt wonderful. Once again, Gwin let her mind drift. He murmured something, her name, she thought, but she couldn't bring herself to answer. She pulled him to her, falling mindlessly into his ageless rhythm, straining with him and against him toward something, something elusive she couldn't quite understand.

But Cole understood. With each thrust, he took her with him, a little higher, a little brighter, a little closer. Desire built inside of her and then rapidly unfurled. In a sudden, spiraling rush of heat, Gwin gasped out one word, *"Yes!"*, as her consciousness shot skyward, like a bullet, where the light of a thousand stars seemed to burst and shimmer behind her eyes.

She did not fall back to earth; she floated, like a single solitary snowflake on a quiet winter afternoon breeze. *No one ever warned me of this,* she thought, her heart dancing in her chest.

He too had stopped moving, the length of his body now tensing against her as he let out a low groan next to her ear.

Still weak and tingling with delight, Gwin clutched at him as she felt him release, again and again and again, very deep inside of her.

He collapsed part of his weight onto her, burying his face in the pillow behind her head. Gwin accepted him gladly, imagining that she could actually feel his heart beating next to hers. For a long time, there was no sound save that of their mingled breaths, harsh, exhausted, sated.

Finally, he raised his head. "Gwin?"

"Hmmmmm?"

"We're pretty much done. You can take your fingernails out of my back now."

Her eyes flew open. "Oh!" She let go of him, mortified. "Are you all right?"

"All right," he said, his head dropping again, muffling his voice into the pillow. "*More* than all right. *God*, yes."

"I'm sorry. I just never realized it could be so . . ."

"So . . . yes. I never realized it either. So . . . *so.*"

"I can't think of a word for it," Gwin murmured.

"If one occurs to me, I'll let you know."

"Does your shoulder hurt?"

"What shoulder?"

They were both quiet. Gwin heard faint strains of piano music coming from a dance hall across the street. It reminded her of a drafty flat in Kansas City. A long, long time ago.

He raised up then, shifting his weight. She was sorry to feel him withdraw from her, making them two again. He rolled off of her onto his back, carefully rearranging the sheets to cover them, then slipping one arm beneath her to encircle her shoulder.

Gwin had read in one of her mother's books once that the heart must be free, that it cannot be ordained whom one shall love. *Love.* The full realization came surprisingly easy, like a single sheet of paper bearing a simple message slipped beneath a locked door. *I love you, Cole Shepherd.* It might have started out as a dream, but it was real, as real as the feel of his fingers now combing absently through her hair, as real as the lingering, most precious ache between her legs where he had just claimed her innocence. And there was nothing she could do now to change it.

He squeezed her shoulder gently. "Gwin? Are you . . . ? I mean, was it . . . ?" He sounded apologetic.

"It was wonderful," Gwin said, turning on her side away from him, fearing she might actually burst into tears from the sheer, irrepressible joy of it.

"I'm sorry if I hurt you."

Gwin sighed, knowing that if he forced her to say much more now, she would inevitably reveal too much. "Don't talk, Shepherd," she whispered. "Just keep your hands on me."

His free arm slid around her waist, pulling her tight up against him, his body turning to envelop her from behind in its comforting masculine heat. After a moment, he whispered in her ear, his breath warm and tickling and intimate. "Like this?"

"Hmmmmm. Yes. Like that," she murmured, content now to drift on gossamer wings of sleep, to push aside the questions tomorrow would bring. "Just exactly like that."

Unmindful of his naked state, Cole crossed the room, nudged back the corner of one lacy curtain, and peered out onto the street below. The sun had risen over the mountains. A few early risers strolled of the boardwalk. Across the street, a ...er in apron and rolled shirtsleeves stepped out in front of his store, broom in hand.

A train's whistle blared in the distance, and Cole let the curtain fall back into place. He turned around to see Gwin in the massive canopy bed, her face peaceful and unlined in slumber. She lay on her side, snuggling with her feather pillow as if it were a lover. That magnificent red hair was spread out all over, snaking down over pale, ivory shoulders and trailing out onto the bed behind her like curling flames. Her face, so guileless in repose, was almost angelic. Entangled in the top sheet, her body was only partially hidden from his gaze. Cole's eyes slid appreciatively over one slim flank, the tiny curvature of her waist, and the swell of one plump breast. *Face of an angel, body of a temptress,* he thought wryly. No wonder he'd lost all self-control.

He found it hard to believe he had just met this girl less than a week ago. Somehow she had managed to work her way into his life, into his blood, into his every waking thought, and *that,* he noticed, hadn't stopped with the consummation of their physical attraction, either.

The memory of their lovemaking—both last night's and this morning's—was still warm and achingly vivid in his mind. It was clear to him now that he had been wrong about her from the very beginning. He had prejudged her and he had wronged her, and, by rights, last night shouldn't have happened. But he still couldn't quite bring himself to regret it.

Cole watched as Gwin sighed fetchingly in her

sleep, then curled up even tighter with her pillow-lover. Indeed, how could he bring himself to regret what had happened between them if at this moment all he wanted was to *be* that pillow she was hugging so tightly to those tempting breasts?

He crossed the room and bent to retrieve his clothes from the floor. He tried to picture himself explaining this situation to Fritz back at the Chicago office: *Well, you see, Fritz, it happened like this.* No, no, no, that was no way to start. *Well, Fritz, one thing just led to another.* Cole winced and straightened, absently clutching his trousers in one hand. He wasn't sure there was any satisfactory way to explain deflowering his first assignment. It could very well be a first in the history of the Agency.

"Hmmmmmmmmmm."

Cole looked up to see her stirring awake, arching her neck and stretching one sleek, bare leg out in a startlingly erotic pose. *Damn,* Cole thought, turning his eyes away to save himself from further torture.

"Oh, dear. What time is it?"

Cole looked back to see her sitting up groggily, still hugging that pillow to her chest like a misplaced papoose. "Early," he replied.

She blinked at him through a tangle of curls, struggling to focus. "Early?"

Then her eyes suddenly widened, her gaze sweeping over him like a painter's brush, from head to toe, before her mouth dropped open and she abruptly averted her face. "Oh."

It took Cole a minute to realize what had caused her reaction. He was probably the first unclothed man she had ever seen in her life. He tried to force back a stupid grin. *Penny for your thoughts, my lady.*

"You'd better look your fill," he said aloud, not able to resist teasing her just a little. "I certainly have been."

She turned around to look at him, her cheeks burning scarlet. "What time did you say it was?"

"The clock on the dresser reads six-thirty."

"Are you always such an early riser?"

"Always," he replied, bending again to retrieve the rest of his clothing from the floor.

Her corset, he discovered, had somehow gotten all tangled up with his shirt. He rose again to full height, hanging it up by one finger as he eyed it over thoughtfully.

"If you wouldn't mind, sir."

He glanced up to see her giving him a pointed look. "Corsets," he said, approaching, tossing it to the bed. "I hate these things. I thought you didn't wear them."

"I don't usually, but with a dress like that—" Gwin stopped and narrowed her eyes at him suspiciously. "Wait a minute. How would you know what I usually wear under my clothes?"

Cole tried to look innocent. "Well, uh, I'm a detective, remember?"

The corners of her lips twitched, fighting a smile. "They teach you that kind of thing at detective school?"

"Not really. Some things just come naturally."

"Oh, I'll just bet they do," she said, wrinkling her nose at him before changing the subject. "So, are you going to continue to just stand there like that?"

"Like what?"

"Naked as a peeled potato."

Cole dropped his clothes to the floor and spread his arms wide, grinning like a fool. "Why? Do you have something against potatoes?"

"No, not at all. Actually, I'm quite fond of potatoes. But, while we're on the subject, do you think you could throw some of my clothes over here, please?"

Cole pretended to mull this over. "Hmmmm, I don't think so. I think I prefer you like this." He sat on the corner of the bed and playfully tugged at the pillow she still clutched to her chest. "As a matter of fact, the more potatolike, the better."

Blushing furiously, she hugged the pillow tighter, earnestly fighting him for it. "Cole Shepherd! I thought you were a gentleman!"

He laughed. "Why, Guinevere Pierce! I never imagined you were so shy!" And with that, he gave a hard pull, yanking the protective pillow away, baring her to his appreciative eyes. But he didn't have much time to enjoy it.

She squealed and made a grab for the bed sheet, yanking it up to cover herself. In her panic, she exposed the bottom sheet. And there it was, *blood*. Not much of it, but enough to catch her eye and his. They both stared at it for a moment before raising their heads to look at each other.

"Why didn't you tell me?" Cole asked.

She blinked at him, still clutching the sheet to her chest. "You didn't ask."

Cole opened his mouth to answer, then closed it again. Well, she had him there. He cleared his throat and hastened to smooth things over. "I guess I assumed that maybe, somewhere along the way, you and Clell Martin had . . ."

Gwin sighed and lay down. "He asked me to marry him once, but I just never felt that way about him. He was like a brother. You don't go marrying your brother."

Cole watched her face, experiencing an undeniable sense of relief that he had misread her feelings for Clell Martin. "No, I suppose not," he said finally, nudging her over a bit to lie down next to her. He turned onto his side and rested his head on one hand. "Still, if I'd known—"

"Would it have ended up any differently?"

"Maybe." He paused, then, "I don't know."

She didn't answer. She just continued to look at him with those incredibly pale blue eyes, waiting, apparently, for a better answer.

He thought back to what had passed between them the night before. He had never experienced anything quite like it, not even with Cynthia. And he had fancied himself in love with Cynthia.

He sighed then, giving in to the truth. "In the long run, I suppose probably not." He reached out to touch her hair. "I heard what you said, you know."

She looked at him, puzzled. "What?"

"On the train. Right before you tried to leave me. You said, 'Oh, my love, I am all yours.' Just like that."

She rolled her eyes and grumbled, "Oh, I did not."

"Oh, yes, you did."

"I didn't."

"Yes. You did."

She pushed his hand away. "You misunderstood."

"I didn't misunderstand anything," he persisted,

sneaking his hand beneath the sheet to caress her hip.

"You heard wrong."

Her skin was bed-warm and soft and very female. "I'm a trained investigator, Miss Pierce. I do not hear wrong."

"Well, you heard wrong this time." She sniffed indignantly, but she didn't try to move away from him.

Cole leaned forward to kiss her neck. She still smelled faintly of lilacs. It clung to her hair. "I don't think so. What did you mean?"

"It was just a poem, if you must know. I was thinking about a poem, and I guess I must have said some lines out loud. It certainly had nothing to do with you, so you can get that thought right out of your big fat conceited head right this minute."

Cole let his open palm slide over her flat stomach, then back down over a hip to her outer thigh as he snuggled closer. He was getting aroused. Again. "Hmmm. What poem?" he asked, nipping at her earlobe.

She jumped a little, and Cole felt her hand on his shoulder, bracing him gently. "Well, it wasn't a poem exactly, it was just this stupid story my mother read to me. I don't remember the name of it."

Cole raised his head to look into her eyes, eyes that were *lying*. "What was this stupid story about?"

"None of your business."

"A mite touchy on the subject, aren't you, your ladyship?"

She raised an eyebrow at him. "You're a fine one to talk about being touchy."

He ran his hand back up along the curving line of her waist to cup a breast, grinning. "I can't help it. You're here and you're beautiful and—"

She let out a sigh and closed her eyes as Cole played his thumb over the stiffening crest. She wasn't going to push him away. He knew that by the way she was gripping his shoulder, her fingernails starting to sink into his skin. He could feel his own body reacting to their closeness as he bent his head again to bury his face in a mass of fragrant, fire-red curls.

"And what?" she prodded after a moment of silence.

Cole raised his head reluctantly and finished. "And when a beautiful young lady tells me she loves me, well . . ."

She frowned then, her eyes fluttering open. "I didn't say any such thing."

"I don't believe you."

"It's the truth."

His retort stuck in his throat and died there. Her denial belied what was laid bare in her eyes. For a girl who made her living at it, she sure didn't lie very well. Not very well at all.

He kissed her then, parting her lips, touching her tongue with his own, then moving down to nuzzle her neck again. It was good. He felt her fingers slipping through his hair, lazily massaging, as he moved down still lower to taste one breast.

She let out a little sound, something between a sigh and a squeak, and that was all it took. That little sound. He knew he wanted to make love to her again, for the third time in a matter of hours, and he should have been ashamed of himself. But he wasn't.

He shifted position, pushing away the sheet that covered her and sliding down lower in the bed so that he could rain a column of kisses down her stomach. He started to move over her, palming her hips, holding her still as he played with his tongue across her navel.

He heard her catch her breath. "Oh my. What are you doing? Where are you *going*?"

"I told you, Miss Pierce. I'm a trained investigator. I am driven to investigate."

She laughed. "It tickles!"

Cole raised his head and squinted up at her, feigning insult. "Tickles? This is *not* supposed to tickle, Miss Pierce. This is supposed to—"

They were both jolted by an urgent pounding on the door, and Gwin shot up like a spring. Before he knew it, Cole found himself unceremoniously shoved out of bed. He thwacked his head on the edge of the night table on his way to the floor. "Ouch! Holy hell, Gwin!"

She didn't seem to hear him as she scrambled to cover herself. "Oh my God! Who in the world?"

Another knock. "Gwinnie? Gwinnie? Are you awake?"

Her face paled. "No! It's Arthur!"

"Gwinnie! Wake up! Are you in there?"

Cole sat up and rubbed the back of his head where he suspected a new lump would be forming on top of the old lump he'd gotten from jumping the train. "For heaven's sake, Gwin, answer him."

Gwin stared at Cole as if he had just spoken in Latin, and he suddenly realized that she wasn't just uncomfortable or embarrassed at the idea of Arthur discovering them together, she was actually terrified of it.

She finally called out in a tremulous voice. "I'm here! What do you want?"

"Let me in, Gwinnie! Something's happened!"

"I can't! I'm not dressed! What's wrong?"

"Cole's gone, Gwinnie! He's gone!"

Gwin's mouth opened but nothing came out. She was immobilized.

Cole fed her a line. "Say I told you I had to go out this morning to pick up our things at the Prices."

Gwin opened her mouth. "I told you—"

Cole's hand shot up to grab her arm. "No! *He* told *me!*"

Gwin's eyelids fluttered and she cleared her throat. "I mean, *he* told *me* he was going out early to pick up our things at the Prices!"

Arthur sounded puzzled. "But his bed is still made! It looks like he never came back last night!"

There was a silence. Gwin turned back to Cole, at a loss.

Cole rolled his eyes and coached, "Tell him I always make my bed in the morning."

"He always makes his bed in the morning!"

Arthur piped back. "He does? How do you know?"

Gwin frowned at Cole. Cole shrugged. She thought for a moment, then raised her voice again. "Well, he's a Pinkerton man, Arthur! What else would you expect?"

There was a short silence while Arthur apparently thought this over. "Oh. I guess you're right."

Cole whispered, "Tell him to go back to his room."

"Go on back to your room, Arthur! I'll be right over as soon as I'm dressed, all right?"

Another moment of silence. Then, "Well, all right. But as soon as Cole comes back, can we go for some breakfast?"

"Sure we can! You go on back to your room now, all right?"

"Okay." Arthur's feet padded back down the hall. At the sound of his door closing, Gwin rested a hand over her heart and let out an audible sigh of relief.

Well, hell just froze over, Cole thought. *Now I lie better than she does. Life is just full of surprises.*

Gwin looked down at him anxiously. "That was close."

"You don't want him to know?"

"He wouldn't understand."

"You may be right," Cole agreed after a moment. Then he had an interesting thought and promptly offered her his hand. "Give me some help up, will you?"

She looked puzzled. "What?"

"It's the least you can do after kicking me out of bed, isn't it?"

She weighed this for a moment before finally reaching out to take his hand. Cole yanked, and she tumbled, with a thump and a squeal, onto the floor with him. Before she could get her bearings, he already had her flipped onto her back, his knee between her legs, his hands gripping her small wrists and pinning them to the floor over her head.

"Cole!" She was buck naked, sputtering indignantly, and Cole had the fleeting, lascivious thought that this was definitely how he liked her best.

"What are you doing?" she demanded. "Arthur's going to wonder—"

"He'll wait," Cole interrupted her.

"We don't have time for this!"

"We have time to get one thing straight, Gwin. Last night, you said you'd think about going to San Francisco with me, and now I want an answer."

"Are you going to let me up if I say no?"

"Absolutely not. Granted, they'll eventually have to slip crackers under the door to keep us from starving."

Gwin gritted her teeth. "This isn't funny, Cole."

"I know."

"My first responsibility is to Arthur."

"So is mine."

A frown creased her brow. "You really mean that, don't you?"

"I won't let anything happen to either of you. I promise you that. Just give me a week."

She bit her lip tentatively. "A week?"

"One week. If we don't come up with any leads by then, I'll buy your tickets and put you on a train myself."

She studied his face soberly. "Do you know something that I don't?"

"All I have are a few hunches, but those aren't going to lead anywhere unless we work together."

Neither of them moved, and she didn't say anything for a long time. Then, "All right. One week. Now, can I get up?"

Cole smiled and ran his eyes down the length of

her captive figure. "Well, since time is of the essence, I suppose I'll have to say yes. This time."

He released her, and she sat up, crossing her arms across the luscious swell of her breasts. "Honestly, Shepherd, this all does take some getting used to, you know."

He had to agree with her. It did take getting used to. He doubted, however, that they would have much time for that. One week. Not much time at all.

18

San Francisco

Jasper Barnes jumped down from the California Street cable car with an agility that belied his rotund physique. In the wake of his billowing Inverness cape, the closemouthed Mr. Ringo followed dutifully at his heels.

"Just like him, isn't it?" Jasper demanded as he puffed the rest of the way across the cobblestone street and stepped up onto the curb. "To run off without informing a soul! What could he be thinking of?"

Jasper wasn't smiling this morning. He was, in fact, glowering as he chomped on the soggy end of his Havana cigar. "Charging like a flaming fool right into a veritable hornet's nest!" he exclaimed as he turned and chugged determinedly down Kearney Street.

"He's been acting unusual," Ringo concurred in his

deep bass rumble, echoing Jasper's thoughts to a T as the morning fog, which was only now beginning to dissipate, swirled around them.

"Unusual indeed. Not good at all," Jasper muttered to himself as they continued on past a line of retail shops. Jasper was moving at his quickest pace, but it undoubtedly still took a conscious effort on the part of his towering companion to keep from overtaking him on the sidewalk. Jasper rarely gave much thought to this gesture of respect anymore. It had been this way between them for years now.

Jasper puffed and wheezed like an overtaxed steam engine as they crossed the busy Market Street thoroughfare and continued on their path south to Third Street. When they turned onto Mission, they soon spotted a crowd ahead. It was just as the spying butler, Frederick, had warned. In lieu of a soapbox, Sidney had chosen the steps of the new Saint Patrick's Church. Thus situated, it was not surprising that he had already attracted a large crowd, mostly a collection of unemployed Irish laborers, judging by the many thick brogues that now reached Jasper's ears. Here stood the heart and soul of the anti-Chinese Workingman's Party, the political phenomenon that, a few years ago, had swept San Francisco like a fever. Due largely to disorganization, the party itself was starting to break down, but its candidate for mayor, a wild-eyed, firebrand minister, still remained Sidney's most formidable opponent in the upcoming election.

This morning, Sidney wore no coat, just a simple black vest and a white shirt, unbuttoned at the collar.

Gone too was the ascot tie and his customary silk top hat. In place of the hat, an old derby perched far back on the crown of his head as he addressed the crowd. "It's simple to point our fingers at the Chinese and claim that there lies our problem! Too simple! It's simplistic, it's naive, and it's self-defeating!"

Standing on the outer fringes of the group, Jasper mused under his breath to Mr. Ringo. "Hard to believe that just last night he was addressing a banquet hall full of stuffy nabobs, isn't it?"

A voice from the crowd arose to challenge the speechmaker. "Oh, yeah? Whatta you know about hard times? Sitting up there on the hill in your big fancy castle?"

Sensing trouble, Jasper plucked the smoking nub of his cigar from his mouth, "Uh oh, here it comes, Mr. Ringo. Here it comes."

But Sidney seemed unperturbed as he squinted at the anonymous man in the audience. A sly smile played about the corners of his mouth. "What do I know, you ask? Do you think I was born with a silver spoon in my mouth, sir?"

"Well, we don't know much about that!" another voice quipped. "But we figure by now you got enough silver spoons to feed an army!"

An appreciative titter rippled through the crowd.

Sidney grinned. "You're right about that, my friend! I've earned myself enough silver spoons to line the Central Pacific track from here to Utah!"

Another laugh from the group, this one at the heckler's expense.

Sidney continued, "But it wasn't always that way!

My father worked the coal mines in Pennsylvania! I followed in his footsteps when I was thirteen! There were twelve mouths to feed in our family, and the wages the mine owners paid didn't amount to a hill of beans!"

"The coal mines of Pennsylvania?" Jasper echoed in a low voice. "Quite an inspired piece of autobiographical fiction, is it not?" He raised a bushy eyebrow at Mr. Ringo.

"And impossible for those muckraking newspapermen to disprove," Ringo added.

Jasper nodded thoughtfully, raising the cigar stub to his mouth once again. Mr. Ringo was much more intelligent than people gave him credit for. He didn't speak often, or say very much when he did. It was a fact that most people tended to mistake reticence for stupidity. Jasper had never been one of them.

The restive crowd started to settle down as Sidney continued. "It wasn't until much later that I struck out on my own, determined to make a better life for myself! It was in Virginia City that . . ."

Jasper listened as Sidney recounted a rags-to-riches story that bore only the faintest resemblance to the actual truth. The men in the audience, many of whom had been scowling only moments ago when Jasper had first arrived, were cocking their heads to one side, muttering to their companions thoughtfully.

Jasper puffed on his cigar, his analytical ear tuned to the persuasive undercurrent of Sidney's words. It was incredible. It was utterly, unbelievably fantastic, but it appeared that he was actually beginning to win this crowd over.

Jasper dropped his cigar, absently grinding it to shreds beneath his bootheel. "It's a gift, Mr. Ringo, the ability to sway a crowd, even an innately hostile crowd such as this one. If I wasn't seeing it with my own eyes, I wouldn't believe it. A Nob Hill millionaire appealing to the disgruntled masses. Oh, we do indeed have a gem on our hands. Even I never realized the true potential of his talents."

Oh, but Jasper had recognized Sidney as a diamond in the rough from the beginning. Casting himself in the role of lapidary, he had done all the necessary cutting and polishing over the years, and now, it seemed, they were about to harvest the fruits of all this labor. Sidney was sparkling brighter than even the most brilliant of South African gemstones.

Kingmaker, Jasper thought, his thick lips crooking into an avaricious grin. *They'll call me the kingmaker.* He was picturing at this moment not just San Francisco City Hall—a plum tree of graft just ripe for the picking—but the United States Senate, perhaps even the presidency. Jasper, of course, would be the *real* power behind the throne.

It was uncharacteristic of Mr. Ringo to express an unsolicited observation, but he did so now, rudely shattering Jasper's burgeoning fantasy. "He's going to make a break."

Jasper's grin abruptly faded. His eyes clouded. "What?" He craned his neck to look up at Ringo sharply. "He's *what?*"

Ringo turned his head very slowly to focus on Jasper. "He's been acting unusual ever since his brother came to town. He's going to make a break."

A TOUCH OF CAMELOT 267

Jasper frowned up into flat, gray eyes before returning his attention to Sidney's gesturing figure. "Yes, ever since—"

And just that suddenly, it was all very clear. And irrefutable. Jasper wasn't even sure whether Sidney himself knew it yet, but what Mr. Ringo had just said was true.

"Blackmailers are an unscrupulous lot," Jasper mused aloud, tapping his walking cane slowly, rhythmically, on the sidewalk. "They inevitably keep coming back for more."

Ringo grunted assent, and Jasper continued. "There were bad feelings there, you know. Over a woman. Terrible thing, bad feelings between brothers. Why, Silas was likely to bleed his brother dry, then turn right around and expose his past just for the sheer joy of it. Yes, yes. Unscrupulous lot, blackmailers. I should know. I've dabbled in it once or twice myself."

Jasper's chubby fingers curled and tightened around the silver handle of his cane as he watched Sidney Pierce reel in the disbelievers. It was true that Sidney had been acting unusual of late. He was acting like a man with a conscience.

Jasper's black eyes narrowed as he spoke. "Conscience, Mr. Ringo. Pity the man who suffers from it. Imagine being dogged day in and day out until finally you snap. Not a pretty thought, is it?"

Jasper looked up at Ringo. Ringo looked down at Jasper, and Jasper continued. "Reflecting back now, I suppose we should have waited to dispose of Mr. Silas Pierce. Once out of town, it's doubtful his demise would have made the papers. Sidney would have been none the wiser."

"It's done," Ringo said coldly.

"Ah, well." Jasper donned his customary smile. "Foresight always lacks the wisdom of hindsight, does it not?"

Ringo didn't answer.

Jasper adjusted his cloak, turning to leave. "Perhaps it's come time for Sidney to employ a round-the-clock bodyguard. After all, with so many hooligans about these days, one can never be too careful. You remember, of course, what happened to President Lincoln?"

"Tragic," Ringo grumbled.

"I can think of no one more suitable for the job than you yourself, Mr. Ringo. You must watch out for our Sidney. You must not leave his side for a minute." Jasper slid him a cunning side glance. "You must keep your eyes peeled for trouble. Do you understand?"

"I understand."

"And in the unlikely event that trouble should rear its ugly head," Jasper added as they strolled back up Mission Street, "I have every confidence that you will know how to deal with it."

Despite her anxiety over returning to San Francisco, Gwin actually enjoyed most of the train trip from Reno to Oakland. The scenery, once they traveled into the Sierra Nevada, was breathtaking, and some of it, especially as they crossed bridges that spanned treacherous canyons, was downright hair-raising. They passed through Sacramento at the end of their first day, and by midafternoon of the following day, found themselves disembarking on the Oakland side of San Francisco Bay.

They had taken a ferry across the sparkling blue bay to land in San Francisco proper. A horsecar took them up Market Street, where they ate dinner at a small café. Afterward, they set out on foot to find accommodations. Locating a lodging house with two vacancies that also fit into Cole's stringent budget had proven to be a challenge. It was well past dusk when Gwin finally dropped her valise onto the bed in her new room.

She turned a slow pirouette, eyeing up the peeling floral wallpaper of the tiny room. The furnishings consisted of one sagging brass bed, one cane chair, and a washstand with an empty tin basin and pitcher. There wasn't even a closet, just a pair of wooden pegs on which to hang her clothes. The sign over the front door of this humble residential establishment read, *Rooms For Rent. 50 Cents And 75 Cents.* This was one of the seventy-five cent rooms. Gwin shuddered to think what one of the fifty-cent rooms must look like.

Cole stood just inside the open doorway, examining the bolt lock. The rusty piece of hardware was missing two screws and looked to be hanging by little more than spit and a prayer. "We'll have to get this fixed," he muttered. He had been thrilled to find two vacancies in this monolithic brick building on Kearney Street, but she couldn't help noticing that he didn't look quite so thrilled at the moment.

Arthur's head looped in from the hallway to survey the room. "Holy crow!" he exclaimed brightly. "What a dump!"

A look of mild irritation flitted across Cole's features. "I wouldn't exactly call it a dump."

Gwin slid him an amused side glance. "We've lived in a lot of dumps in our time, Cole. Suffice it to say, we know one when we see one."

"Don't you think you're exaggerating a bit?"

"Modest accommodations, you said. Why didn't we do it right and just pitch a tent?"

Cole threw up his hands. "I don't believe you two! You've got a roof over your heads and running water right down the hall."

"Yes, and did you see that tub?" Gwin said. "I swear the last time it saw a scrub brush was during the gold rush!"

"Well, it's nothing that a little soap and elbow grease won't fix. Besides, no one's going to think to look for you here."

Gwin laughed. "You're probably right about that!"

"Oh, come on," Cole urged, his expression brightening as he crossed the room to sit on the rickety brass bed. "The landlady said she does laundry every day!" He slapped the mattress firmly. "Why, the linens are clean as a whistle! No bedbugs!"

Gwin wrinkled her nose. "No bedspread either."

"Well, excuse me, Queen Guinevere."

Gwin blinked at him, startled. He had never called her that before.

His tone softened. "You know we have to watch our expenses. Tomorrow, I'll have to send a telegram to

Fritz at the Agency. After paying for dinner and this room, we've just about run out of money."

Gwin smiled. "You worry too much. We can always get money."

"Oh, we can, can we?"

"Certainly. In a town like San Francisco, there are dozens of opportunities."

Cole gave her a doubtful look. "Opportunities."

"That's right. Opportunities."

"If you're talking about gambling again, Gwin, you can just forget it."

Gwin waved him away with one hand. "Oh, pshaw! Not gambling! You obviously have no imagination at all!"

"And you *do*, I suppose?"

"Absolutely! Why, I'll bet even young Arthur here could come up with a few interesting ideas of his own."

Her brother, who had donned his favorite overalls before Gwin had had a chance to catch him this morning, beamed up at her now from beneath the brim of his cap. "Sure! We know how to get money! Anytime! Anywhere! Right, Gwinnie?"

Gwin felt her juices begin to flow. "You bet! How about that old game, the Pigeon Drop?"

Arthur jumped up and down. "Yeah! Yeah! You mean the one where Silas used to pretend to find some money and then—"

Gwin snapped her fingers as another idea occurred to her. "Oh! I know! We could—"

"All right! Stop it! Hold it right there, you two!"

Gwin and Arthur both froze at the indignant tone

in Cole's voice. They turned to see that he had risen to his feet, wearing the look of a man who had just discovered a fly in his soup.

Arthur spoke first, a trifle insulted. "Jeesh, Cole, you don't have to yell. If you have an idea, just say so."

Now that Cole had their undivided attention, he raised a finger. "I just want to know one thing."

Gwin eyed him cautiously. "And what's that?"

"Has it ever occurred to either of you to just get a job?"

Gwin and Arthur looked at each other. Gwin wrinkled her nose. Arthur grimaced. They spoke in perfect unison. *"A job?"*

"That's what I thought. We'll wire the Agency."

Gwin gave him a teasing smile. "Suit yourself, Shepherd. Just trying to help."

"That kind of help I can do without. We're liable to end up in the county jail."

"At least you wouldn't be able to complain about the rent."

A slight smile tugged at his lips. "You have an answer for everything, don't you, Miss Pierce?"

"Not everything," she replied. "As a matter of fact, I have a question for you."

"Yes?"

"When do we get started?"

Cole's eyes narrowed slightly. "Started what?"

"When do we get started on our case?"

Cole raised an eyebrow. "Our case?"

"Yes. Now that you've dragged us back to San Francisco, what's next, Mr. Pinkerton Detective?"

"First thing tomorrow, I get to work on this case."

"You? I thought we were working together on this. You *do* remember saying that, don't you?"

"Not out in the open we're not. You two might be recognized, and until we know who our enemies are—"

Gwin cut in, snapping her fingers. "I know!" She started to pace back and forth excitedly as her mind set to work. "We could disguise ourselves!"

"Oh, I don't think so."

Arthur hopped up and down. "Yeah! Yeah! We could disguise ourselves!"

Gwin stopped pacing and threw both hands up. "It's not like you're dealing with two amateurs! As a matter of fact—"

Cole broke in, "As a matter of fact, you're both out of your minds if you think—"

"Look, look," Gwin insisted hurriedly, turning to Arthur to demonstrate her theory. "Anybody who knows us will be looking for a woman and a boy, but would they ever think to be on the lookout for two boys?"

She snatched the engineer's cap from Arthur's head and promptly set it down on her own, pulling the brim down low and stuffing her loose curls beneath it to make her point. "See? Put me in a pair of pants and a coat, and . . . see?"

Cole stared at her, his head cocking to one side slightly. A look of distinct puzzlement crept over his face.

Taking his speechlessness for approval, Gwin prodded again. "Pretty good, huh?"

The look of befuddlement passed quickly and he

glowered. "*Not* pretty good!" He snatched the cap from her head and slapped it back against Arthur's middle.

"But I'll be wearing pants and a big coat and—"

Cole waved her protestations aside. "Come on, Gwin! No right-thinking person would ever mistake you for a boy!"

"B-but—"

"No buts! The subject is closed!"

"B-but—"

Cole closed the distance between them, catching her up by the shoulders, his voice lowering. "I am telling you, Miss Pierce, that no matter how you try to disguise yourself, no red-blooded man worth his salt is going to mistake you for a boy." His gaze dipped meaningfully to her full bosom before rising again to her face.

Gwin felt a flood of color rise to her cheeks. "Not even a *really* big coat?"

"Not even."

Gwin opened her mouth again to protest, but could not, for the life of her, think of a word to say. There followed a silence, a long, lingering silence, during which time they both seemed to become aware of how close he held her. Gwin felt her knees start to weaken as she sensed Cole's thoughts beginning to turn in an entirely different direction.

Arthur piped up. "So, are you two done arguing now?"

Gwin couldn't seem to tear her eyes from Cole's. "Oh, I think so. Why don't you go wash up before bed?"

"What? Again?" Arthur sounded horrified.

"Just do it."

"Holy crow! Cole, do I have to?"

"Go on, Arthur. We'll wait for you here."

"Jeeeeez! Wash up! Wash up! All I ever do is wash up! It isn't healthy! I'm gonna end up getting sick from it! You just watch and see if I don't!" But his voice was fading. It faded down the hall, where a door slammed with righteous indignation.

Cole bent his head so that his lips hovered tantalizingly over Gwin's. "Is it my imagination, or is this the first time we've been left alone since yesterday morning?"

She closed her eyes. "Not your imagination."

He kissed her then, one hand dropping to her waist, his other hand slipping behind her neck, massaging her nape. Just about the time Gwin thought she might swoon, he pulled back. "Last night, on the train, I couldn't sleep. I kept thinking about—"

"I know," Gwin said, wondering at how so simple a kiss could scramble her insides worse than a morning egg.

He kissed her again, harder this time. When he pulled away, she had to catch her breath. "Tonight," he said, "after Arthur's asleep."

"Yes," she agreed. Too quickly, too easily, she knew. But she couldn't seem to help herself. Succumbing to temptation once, it seemed, had not quelled her desire for him. If anything, it had only fanned the flames. She had spent the better half of last night lying awake, thinking of him in the next berth, dreaming of the previous night they had spent together. Was she being a fool? She didn't know.

They heard the door down the hall squeak on its hinges, and Cole pulled away from her with a reluctant sigh. "That had to be all of ten seconds to ourselves," he muttered. "I have to wonder if that kid actually uses soap."

Gwin tried to force a smile. A moment later, her brother was back in the room, and, by then, it was too late to change her mind.

19

Cole lay on his back in one of two narrow camp cots, listening morosely to the songs of drunken revelers as they passed on the street one story below. They had probably come from one of the many noisy gambling parlors or saloons just up the street near Portsmouth Square. San Francisco, it seemed, did not suffer from a lack of nightlife.

"Cole? Are you awake?"

"What do you want, Arthur?"

"Can I go along with you tomorrow?"

This was not the first time he had posed a question seemingly out of the blue. It would be just about the time Cole dared to think that maybe the boy had drifted off to sleep that his child's voice would spike the dark to cruelly dash all hopes.

"Absolutely not," Cole answered, trying his best not to sound as impatient as he felt.

"Why not?"

"Well, first, I'm going to the police station, and then I'm going to the jail to visit our friend, Mr. Cortez."

"He's the man they said did it."

"Yes."

"But he didn't."

"That's what we're going to try to prove."

"I could help you."

"No, Arthur."

"Why not?"

"Because no one's supposed to know you're here, remember?"

There was a short, thinking silence.

"I could wait outside and hide. I'm good at hiding."

Cole smiled despite himself. "I have no doubt that you are, but the answer's still no. Now, go to sleep."

"Jeeez."

Cole rolled over onto his side and stared into the dark. It wasn't long before he began to picture Gwin in the next room, her hair loose and wild, her eyes closed, her lips parted enticingly, and stark naked, of course, just waiting for him. Waiting and waiting and waiting.

"Cole?"

Cole gritted his teeth. "What?"

"Do you think we could ride the cable car?"

"We aren't here to ride the cable cars, Arthur."

"But it only costs five cents."

"The five cents has nothing to do with it. Go to sleep."

"Jeeez."

Cole listened as the tower bell of Old Saint Mary's Church tolled the hour. One. Two. Three. All the way to eleven before its melancholy echoes finally fell silent.

They lay quietly for another few minutes before Arthur spoke again. This time Cole heard something different, something distinctly troubling, in the boy's voice. "I hope we get him."

Cole didn't have to ask who he was talking about. "We're sure going to try."

"Then maybe I can stop seeing his face."

Cole frowned. "Stop seeing his face?"

There was a short span of silence before the boy answered. "In my dreams. That giant, big as Goliath he was, I swear. After we get him, maybe I'll finally stop seeing his face."

Cole thought about this soberly before replying. "We'll get him, Arthur. And you *will* stop seeing his face."

"You promise?"

Cole hesitated, knowing full well that it was pure foolishness to promise the boy anything. In reality, Cole figured his chances of tracking down Silas Pierce's murderer were pretty slim. He still sometimes wondered to himself why he had talked Gwin into coming back to San Francisco. And those were times when he also had to wonder if there wasn't some truth to her accusations about his job being more important to him than their welfare.

There was only one thing he knew for sure, and that was that he had to try. If he returned to Chicago without at least trying to uncover the truth behind Silas's murder, it would be to admit defeat. He would have to admit that he really didn't have what it took to be in this profession. And that fact would disillusion more than just his superiors at the Agency.

Cole steeled himself. "I promise, Arthur. Now, I want you to try to get some rest, all right?"

"All right. Good night, Cole."

"Sleep well, Arthur."

Gwin had left her door unlocked for him. Cole pushed the flimsy bolt lock back into place, reminding himself to speak to the landlord in the morning about getting it fixed. Light from a street lamp filtered through the sheer curtain in the window, illuminating Gwin's figure in the bed.

"Gwin?"

There was no answer. She lay unmoving beneath the sheets. He crossed the room and undressed before climbing into the bed, sidling up next to her, and burying his face in a mass of luxuriant curls. "Gwin?" he whispered, reaching with one arm to encircle a tiny waist that he discovered, with great delight, was naked to the touch.

She sighed languidly and rolled over to face him, nestling in his arms as if she had been made to fit there. She was warm and fragrant from her bath, and Cole snuggled up against her, knowing that his wait had been well worth it.

"I thought you weren't coming," she whispered.

"It took a while for Arthur to fall asleep," Cole answered, content for the moment just to lie here, holding her in his arms.

"Sometimes I think he's afraid to fall asleep," Gwin said pensively. "He has nightmares, you know. He tries not to let on, but that night was a nightmare in itself. I doubt he'll ever get over it."

"Maybe in time."

Gwin lifted her head to look at Cole in the dimness. "He hasn't had any bad dreams, not since we've been with you. He trusts you. He feels safe with you, but now that we're back in San Francisco, I'm a little worried about him."

"We'll just have to make sure he's safe."

"Yes."

"And what about you?" Cole asked.

"What about me what?"

"Do *you* trust me?"

She paused. "I'm here, aren't I?"

"I'm not sure that answers the question."

"Trust has never come easy for me."

Cole pictured her then as she had looked on the train pulling out of Topeka, idly shuffling her cards and eyeing him askance. *"What's your game, Shepherd? Everybody has a game."*

"I reckon it doesn't come easy for you," he said. "But there's always a first time, isn't there?"

He felt her arms slip around his neck, her breasts pressing enticingly against his chest, and his body inevitably started to respond. "Yes," she whispered, "perhaps there is."

They made love as if they had all the time in the world, each reveling at leisure in explorations still tender and new. Cole had been alone for so long that he had come to take it as life's most natural state, but this, he thought as their fingers interlaced and he entered her body, was life's most natural state—a man and a woman, their bodies matched and mated, naked flesh to naked flesh, moving in that unspoken concerted rhythm that spun the senses.

Later, he opened his eyes to see her straddled above him, her head thrown back, her hair wild and tumbling down her back, as she rode his slow and sensual strokes, and the sight inflamed his heart. He grasped her hips and drove into her, again and again until she finally gasped and shuddered above him, climaxing mere seconds before he felt that elastic shock shoot through him to spill deep inside her.

When it was over, they lay for a long time, their dampened limbs entangled as their hearts and breathing slowed. There were whispers and caresses in the dark, and when she finally fell asleep in his arms, Cole was reluctant to leave. He held her and listened to the church bell of Old Saint Mary's toll midnight as he closed his own eyes, content. He soon fell into a shallow, restless sleep, a sleep riddled with confused, overlapping dreams.

He dreamed of Gwin and Arthur and Fritz Landis. He dreamed of the blonde on board the Union Pacific Express, except in the dream, she didn't just look like Cynthia, she *was* Cynthia, and she was traveling with the Oriental assassin, who wasn't dead after all. None of the dreams made much sense, least of all the last one. The last one, however, would be the one he would always remember.

In the dream, he stood at the foot of Market Street directly in front of the ferry depot building. He was standing in the same spot where they had boarded a horsecar earlier this afternoon, but there was no horsecar now. As a matter of fact, there were no horsecars anywhere. Likewise, there were no vans or drays or passenger conveyances, which probably wasn't so surprising considering there were also no people. The depot was an empty shell. And outside, where he stood, where just this afternoon there had been throngs of busy-footed travelers moving from pillar to post, there was no sign of life.

All was quiet. The sun was bright. A soft, noiseless sea breeze wafted through his hair. Signs were strung out above the many arches that lined the length of the sprawling Ferry Building, points of destination: *Yuma, Portland OR, St. Louis, San Jose, Sacramento, Los Angeles, Chicago . . .*

Chicago, he thought, *that must be why I'm here. I'm going back to Chicago.* He turned around to face Market Street. It too was deserted.

Then he heard it: "Ladies and gents, are you bothered by the rheumatism? Consumption? Night sweats? Cold feet? Are you haunted by headaches? Back pains? A sick and nervous stomach? I have in my hand the answer to your prayers!"

Cole whirled around. Directly behind him, where only a moment ago there had been no one, there stood upon a makeshift stage a gentleman dressed all in white. His hair, as white as his suit, was almost shoulder-length and swept back into a pompadour. He stood in relief against the broad side of a tall wagon upon which was painted in bright red calligraphic letters: *Professor Throckmorton's Restorative Cordial and Blood Renovator*.

"Not only does this miraculous elixir offer a cure for all these afflictions, it's been known, and proven, ladies and gents, *proven,* to do more, much, much more! But don't—"

"Excuse me!" Cole raised a hand to attract the showman's attention. "Sir? Excuse me?"

The man onstage fell silent and raised one hand to shield his eyes from the sun. His gaze moved counterclockwise, as if scanning through an audience to spot a heckler, but when that gaze finally settled upon Cole, he broke into a broad grin. "Are you speaking to me, young man? Will that be one bottle or two?"

"Who else would I be talking to? There's nobody else here!"

The man seemed to ponder this for a moment before nodding his head. "Point well taken, young man. Now, tell me, what is it I can do for you today?"

Cole approached the stage. "Where is everybody?"

"Where?" The man scratched his head. "Well, I'm not so sure that I know, but I would expect they'd be wherever it is that you last left them."

Cole stopped at the edge of the raised wooden platform. "I didn't *leave* them anywhere! They were gone when I arrived!"

"Ah, yes! Well, it doesn't really matter where you left them, does it? Sooner or later, they all develop an annoying tendency to start moving around. You can put them here and you can put them there, but they pretty much end up wherever it is they want to be, anyway."

Cole narrowed his eyes. "We've met before, haven't we?"

The man chuckled and approached the edge of the stage, where he hunkered down, crooking his finger to urge Cole closer. "I can see that you know how to drive a hard bargain, son, so let me tell you what I'm going to do."

Cole interrupted. "I'm not buying any of your tonic, mister. It's a fraud. Just like you."

The man gasped and drew back as if hurt. "A fraud? How can you pass judgment on something if you haven't even tried it?"

Cole started to answer, then stopped. The man had a valid point. He thought for a moment, then took another tack. "What you're selling is nothing but dreams."

"Dreams!" The single word reverberated across the deserted depot. "Dreams, most certainly! And entertainment, young man! Entertainment! Wherever you go in this world, the people want a show!" The man winked conspiratorially. "And that's just what I give them!"

Cole's jaw unhinged, and he stumbled back from the stage. "Oh my God! You're Silas! You're Silas Pierce!"

The man in white rose to full height and clapped his hands enthusiastically. "Eureka! A round of applause if you please! No wonder he works for a famous detective agency!"

"But—but you're dead!"

Silas stopped applauding and emitted a long, regretful sigh. "Ah, yes. Unfortunate but true."

Cole's initial shock at realizing he was conversing with a dead man began to dissolve as he realized that this was an opportunity to learn the truth about the murders. He forced himself to speak. "Do you know who killed you? Do you know why?"

Silas clasped his hands behind his back and peered up at the cloudless blue sky. "You know, that's a very good question. If only I could remember."

"You've got to remember!"

Silas paced the stage, muttering to himself. Then he turned to Cole, squatting down at the edge of the stage and motioning for him to come closer.

Cole complied without a trace of hesitation. "Who killed you, Silas? Why?"

Silas didn't answer at first. He held out one big hand, empty palm up, then he closed it.

"Why were you killed, Silas?"

Silas winked, then flicked his wrist and uncurled his fingers. Upon his open palm, where there had been nothing before, rested a fat brown cigar. "Care for a stogie?" he offered, his pale blue eyes sparkling devilishly.

Cole frowned. "How'd you do that?"

"One of the few advantages of being dead, my dear boy."

"You smoke up in heaven?" Cole asked doubtfully.

"In heaven?" Silas echoed, lighting up, sending puffs of cigar smoke swirling into the air. "Only after a banquet! Now, in hell, I hear they *smoke* quite a lot, don't you know."

"Now I know where Gwin gets her sense of humor."

Silas rose to full height. "Take care of Gwinnie and

Arthur for me, Shepherd. They're your responsibility now."

"I know that, but it would help if you could answer my questions."

He waved his cigar hand through the air. "I'd dearly love to, but I can't right now! I'm in the middle of a show!"

"But there's nobody here!"

"Of course they're here! The crowds! The crowds!" Silas raised both arms majestically, his stage voice booming. "Look around you, Shepherd! Look around!"

And he was right. Suddenly there were people. People everywhere. The horsecars were back. The air was full of sounds—sounds of bells clanging, of conductors calling, and of hooves clopping against cobblestones.

"Oh, my!" A pudgy, bearded gentleman bumped into Cole, searching through his vest and coat pockets. "What time is it? Where is my watch?"

Just over the man's shoulder, Cole glimpsed a boy. He wore a black duster over baggy denims. The brim of a navy blue engineer's cap was pulled low over his forehead, hiding the telltale color of his hair, but Cole would recognize that cap anywhere. The kid weaved his way in and out through the dense, bustling crowd, clearly in a hurry to make the ferry.

"Arthur!" Cole pushed by the gentleman who had misplaced his watch.

At the sound of his name, Arthur threw a hurried glance over his shoulder. When he spotted Cole, his eyes widened in alarm. Then he broke into a run.

"Arthur! Stop!"

The boy kept up a good pace, zigzagging his way through milling adults and moving vehicles. Cole was aware that he was earning quite a few stares as he jostled past disgruntled bystanders, but it didn't matter. He was determined not to lose sight of Arthur.

The boy burst through the edges of the crowd and disappeared around the far corner of the Ferry Building. Cole followed, soon emerging on the other side of the building, and where logic dictated there should be boats and docks and the San Francisco Bay, there were, instead, cattle yards—dozens of them, all empty. And beyond that, for as far as the eye could see, vast, flat, barren plains. Cole recognized where he was immediately. It was the prairie. It was Kansas. Home.

He didn't take time to consider this abrupt change in locale. He was too busy concentrating on Arthur, who was now scaling one of the fences. The navy blue engineer's cap vanished as he dropped down on the other side.

Cole reached the fence and pulled himself up over the top slat. The boy was streaking across the empty stockyard, nearing the fence at the far end. Cole landed on his feet and took off, rapidly closing the distance between them. Arthur reached the opposite fence and started to scramble up over it just as Cole caught up to him. "Arthur! Give it up!" He reached out and snagged the boy's pant leg.

Arthur didn't give it up. Instead, he back-kicked with his free foot, narrowly missing Cole's face. *"Give it up now and it'll go easier on you!"* Cole yelled, yanking hard on Arthur's pant leg, bringing the boy down on top of him. They collapsed together onto the ground, Cole landing on his back, hugging the boy's middle.

Arthur struggled mightily, but Cole held fast, rolling them both over until the kid was securely pinned down beneath him. "Arthur! Settle down! Listen to me! Arth—"

The name died on Cole's tongue. Incredulous, he stared down at the face that now looked up at him. The kid's hat had fallen off in the scuffle, freeing a flood of fire-red curls. A pair of long-lashed, pale blue eyes were blinking up at him in shock. It wasn't Arthur.

"Gwin!"

Cole sat bolt upright in bed. He could still see her face, the face of a woman-child, different in many ways from the way she looked now, but close enough to make recognition, once realized, inescapable. "Holy hell!" Cole exclaimed. "It was Gwin!"

The dam had broken. The memory flooded back, vivid and complete. Could it be true? It had been how long ago? Eight years? Nine? He thought maybe he was about sixteen the summer his father had taken him to visit his uncle in Abilene.

Gwin stirred awake next to him, her warm hand settling on his forearm. "What's the matter? Cole?"

Cole scrambled up onto his knees, grasped both of her wrists, and straddled her hips, peering down at her face, trying to convince himself it wasn't true.

Light from the streetlamp outside revealed the lines and shadows of her exquisite features. "Hey! What's going on?"

"It was you!"

Gwin struggled to free her wrists. "What are you talking about? Have you gone mad?"

"I remember! It was you, Gwin!"

"Stop talking nonsense, and let me go!"

Cole spat out the word. "Abilene!"

Gwin stopped fighting. Her eyes rounded and her mouth dropped open.

"You knew!" Cole accused, reading her expression. If he had needed any more proof that he was correct, it was right there, written all over her guilty, guilty, guilty face!

She closed her eyes and mumbled, "Oh, no."

"You sneaky little thief!"

These words seemed to stir her to battle. "Well, you crazy do-gooding lunatic!"

"My head ached for days!"

"Served you right, you lecher!"

Cole gaped down at her, aghast. "Lecher?"

Gwin tried to wrest herself free from his hold, wriggling ineffectually beneath him. Under different circumstances, Cole might have found this quite stimulating. At the moment, however, he was too distracted by a maelstrom of conflicting emotions. What had she just called him? "Lecher?" he repeated again.

Gwin stopped wriggling. "That's right! Lecher! You know what I'm talking about!"

Then, all at once, he *did* realize what she was talking about. "Sweet mercy," he muttered to himself. "You were my first . . ."

Still stupefied by this new recollection, Cole's gaze dropped to her chest where the bed sheet barely hid the heaving swell of her breasts. "No wonder I didn't recognize you. You've . . . *grown*."

Gwin screwed up her face and resumed her struggle against him. "Ooooh! Let go of me!"

Cole tore his eyes from her chest and forced himself to focus on her face. "You knew, Gwin, and you didn't tell me! Why didn't you tell me?"

"Well, I didn't know right away, and when I finally figured it out, I didn't tell you because I knew you'd be mad!"

"Mad?"

"Yes!"

Cole released her and rolled onto his back beside her, covering his face with one hand. "When I first saw you in Caldwell, I had the feeling I'd met you somewhere before. I thought it was my imagination."

"Well, I'm surprised you didn't remember right away," Gwin said. "Unless, of course, you so enjoy chasing terrified children through the streets that you make a habit of it."

Cole's hand slid from his face, and he turned his head to look at her. "Terrified child? I think your memory is a little faulty, Gwin. You picked that man's pocket. I saw you."

"It wasn't even your watch! What did you care?"

"I was doing my civic duty!"

Gwin snorted, regathering the sheet to pull it all the way up to her neck, a defensive maneuver if there ever was one. "Civic duty? You were crazy! You're *still* crazy!"

"Oh, so you think it's acceptable to stand by and watch a crime being committed?"

"That's not the point!"

"That *is* the point! Suppose some old lady is knocked down in the street and—"

"He wasn't an old lady! He was some filthy rich cattle broker!"

Cole fixed his eyes on the ceiling. "You're incorrigible, you know that? Your type will try to rationalize their way out of anything!"

Gwin bolted upright, still clutching the sheet. "And you! With you, everything's black or white, right or wrong, isn't it?"

She sounded, incredibly, on the verge of tears. Cole resisted the urge to look at her. Instead, he set his mouth stubbornly and climbed out of bed to retrieve his clothes from the floor. "Not everything, Gwin, but some things are. Some things just *are*."

"And me! My type! If that's how you feel, what are you doing with *me*, Shepherd?"

Cole took a deep breath. Good question. What *was* he doing with her? "I don't know." He climbed into his trousers. "I really don't know."

It was then that they heard it, a cry from the hallway, muffled footsteps, and a frantic banging on the door. "Gwinnie! I saw his face! I dreamed of that man again! Gwinnie!"

Before either of them could react, the shoddy lock tore loose, the door burst open, and there was Arthur in his nightshirt, standing immobile in the archway, his face streaked with tears and contorting into an expression of shock. "Gwinnie! Cole! What . . . ? What . . . ?"

Cole could only imagine the incriminating picture

the boy was confronted with. His sister, naked except for a bed sheet, Cole, bare-chested with his trousers half undone, and both of them looking guilty as hell. Arthur might have been a child, but he was a wizard at arithmetic. He could certainly add two and two.

Time froze. None of them moved or said a word for what seemed forever, then Arthur bolted, leaving the door hanging wide open, the archway accusingly empty.

20

Gwin was not in good spirits. One full day and night had passed since that awful scene in her room, and, still, Arthur was barely speaking to her. Yesterday, they'd had an awful argument, after which Arthur had spent the rest of the day skulking around the neighborhood alleyways, shooting at rats and tin cans with his slingshot. Cole had been gone most of that time, launching his investigation into Silas's death. This had left Gwin with a lot of time to ponder the truth of Cole's feelings toward her.

His sudden remembrance of their first meeting in Abilene had only served to underscore the insurmountable differences between them. She knew now what it was he saw when he looked at her. A thief. It was true that he was attracted to her, and perhaps he had even grown somewhat fond of her during their time together, but love her? How could he ever love a woman whose whole life stood for everything he despised? No. Even if Gwin could turn her life around right this minute, it wouldn't matter. There would always be her past. And there was nothing she could ever do about that.

The three of them were seated in a small basement eatery on Kearney Street known as Coffee Dan's, consuming their breakfast in awkward silence. It was like walking on eggshells.

Cole cleared his throat. "Could someone pass the bread?"

Arthur didn't even look up, and so Gwin took it upon herself to pass the small basket. "I was just thinking," she ventured cautiously. "If Sidney Pierce is still in San Francisco, and we can find him . . ."

Cole tore off a chunk of warm French bread. "Yes?"

"Maybe he'd be able to help."

"I thought Silas and Sidney parted on bad terms."

"Well, yes, but that was years ago."

"If that's the case, don't you think that if he was still in San Francisco, he would have come forward when his brother was killed?"

"Maybe he doesn't know," Gwin offered.

"Maybe."

Gwin sighed in disgust. "Maybe he's not even here."

"And maybe you're looking for excuses to find him. You'd like to meet him, wouldn't you?"

"Well, I suppose that I would. Can you blame me?"

"No."

Neither said anything for a long moment, so Gwin broached another subject. "What are your plans for today?"

"I'm going to pay another visit to the police. There are a few more questions I'd like answered. And I'm interested in seeing whether the same detective decides to try to follow me when I leave."

Gwin almost choked on her scrambled eggs. "Follow you? You didn't say anything about that! What detective? Did he follow you to our boardinghouse? What's going on?"

Cole held up one hand to ward her off. "First of all, no, he didn't follow me back to the boardinghouse. And second, it was the same detective who headed up the investigation into Silas's death."

"You mean that detective who questioned us? Detective . . . oh, what was his name?"

"O'Connell."

"Yes, O'Connell. That's the one. He's the one who tried to get Arthur to change his story."

"I believe it," Cole said.

"You do?"

"Oh, I knew there was something dirty about that guy even before he followed me out of the building. I could practically smell it."

Gwin sat back in her chair. "I'm surprised to hear that."

"Why?"

"I don't know. I guess I wasn't sure you'd be able to believe that some policemen are crooked."

"I worked for the New York City Police Department for almost a year, Gwin. Believe me, I saw enough corruption there to last me a lifetime."

"Is that why you left? New York, I mean?"

"That was part of it."

Part of it? Something turned over in her stomach. She wasn't sure whether it was the tone of his voice or the way he was avoiding her eye, but she was suddenly very sure that the *other* part of it had something to do with a woman.

Gwin looked down at her plate, trying to digest this new realization along with the beginnings of a breakfast that she had suddenly lost all appetite for. Why should this bother her so much? Surely she had realized before this that there had been other women in his life.

But he was in love with this one. That was the difference. He had loved her and something had happened to tear them apart. Had she died in a tragic accident? Was she a rich girl betrothed to another man? Or perhaps she had been a schoolteacher? A shopkeeper's daughter? Did it matter? Whatever she had been, she had been a nice girl, a respectable girl, the kind of girl that an honorable, upstanding young man like Cole Shepherd would have considered marrying.

"What's the matter?"

Gwin jerked her head up to meet Cole's inquisitive gaze. "What?"

"You're not eating. Something wrong with your food?"

"No, no, it's fine. Nothing's wrong." Gwin stabbed a piece of ham from her plate and took it off her fork, chewing with relish to prove her point. It tasted like dirt.

"So, tell me, what makes you think Sidney could still be in San Francisco?" Cole asked.

Gwin was glad for the change in subject. She tried to compose herself before looking up. "According to Silas, he always talked about California, and a week before the revival—" She turned to her brother. "Arthur, wasn't it about then that he saw something in the newspaper that reminded him of Sidney?"

Her brother, who had been picking at his food, looked up, scowling. "What?"

Gwin ignored his hostility. "I was talking about the week before you came to San Francisco with Silas and the others. You told me Silas had been reading one of the local papers when he said something to you about Sidney."

Cole interrupted. "Wait a minute. This was the week before he was *killed?*"

Gwin urged her brother. "Tell him, Arthur. You do remember, don't you?"

This seemed to get his goat. "Of course I remember!"

Gwin turned back to Cole, explaining. "Silas and the rest of the group camped about twenty miles south of San Francisco the week before they came to town. Silas always liked to get ahold of some local newspapers before a revival just to make sure we wouldn't be playing against any competition."

Cole raised an eyebrow at her. "Competition? How many faith-healing preachers are there, anyway?"

"Not that kind of competition. I'm talking about a circus or some other event that would discourage attendance."

Arthur cut in, perhaps forgetting for a moment that he was still angry with both of them. "We played the same day a circus came to town once, and it was a disaster. Hardly anyone showed."

"Anyway," Gwin continued, "Silas was going through some San Francisco newspapers when he—" She turned to her brother. "You tell him, Arthur."

Arthur still wore a sullen expression, but he relented on his vow of silence long enough to explain. "He seemed real interested in one of those papers. After he finally put it down, he turned to me and said, 'I do believe our ship has come in.' I asked what he meant, and he answered, 'Your long-lost Uncle Sidney has struck gold!' I still didn't understand what he was talking about, but he wouldn't say any more."

Cole frowned. "Did you get a look at that newspaper?"

"Sure," Arthur answered. "After he left the wagon, I picked it up, thinking maybe there would be an article about someone striking gold, but there wasn't. I went through the whole paper. There was one article about gold prices but not one on new strikes."

"Isn't that strange?" Cole muttered, setting down his mug. "Do you remember which newspaper it was?"

"The *Chronicle*."

"Would you recognize that issue if you saw it again?"

Arthur wrinkled his nose obnoxiously. "Do skunks stink? You want me to quote the front page for you?"

Cole ignored the boy's sarcasm and gave Gwin a significant look. "This could be important."

Gwin felt a stab of hope. "You think so?"

"It's worth checking into. Maybe Sidney is here. Maybe he knows someone who could help us."

Gwin sat forward, forgetting the food left on her plate. "But how will we find him?"

Cole thought for a moment, then turned to Arthur. "How about we go find a copy of that newspaper Silas was reading?"

Arthur glowered. "I told you there was nothing in it! No gold! No Uncle Sidney!"

"I know, but something caught Silas's eye that day, didn't it?" Cole looked at Gwin. "Maybe, knowing what we know now, we'll come up with something Arthur missed."

Arthur sounded petulant. "I never miss anything!"

"But where are we going to a get a copy of that paper?" Gwin asked.

"We'll go right to the horse's mouth."

"What?"

"The *Chronicle* office." Cole glanced at Arthur. "You willing to go?"

"Do I have to?"

"Yes."

"Well, I'm ready." Gwin moved to pick up her napkin.

"You're not going," Cole said.

"What are you talking about? Of course I'm going! It was my idea!"

"I need Arthur along with me because he saw the paper, but you're not going anywhere. By showing up at the police station yesterday, I very well may have rattled some cages. Until we find out what shakes loose, the less we're all seen together, the better. We'll meet you back at the room."

Gwin opened her mouth to argue but couldn't

think of any words convincing enough to utter. She sat with her arms folded in annoyed silence as Cole counted out sixty cents and a tip to pay their bill. He pushed back from the table and motioned to Arthur.

He was right, of course. The detective who had followed him yesterday would report Cole's presence in San Francisco to whoever it was he was working for. Now they had to be more careful than ever. Still, as Gwin watched Cole and her brother leave the restaurant, it galled her to be staying behind. She had a feeling they were on to something. If Sidney were here, he would certainly be able to help them. She felt it in her bones.

Cole and Arthur emerged from Coffee Dan's, squinting in the bright morning sunlight, a stark contrast to the basement eatery. The morning fog was long gone and the sun was already beginning to bake the pavements beneath their feet as they turned south on Kearney toward the Market Street intersection.

Although he had grown up in a small town, Cole had already lived in more than his share of large cities. He acclimated easily to urban surroundings, and San Francisco was no different. He had obtained a city map yesterday morning before setting out for the county jail, but since then, he had only glanced at it a few times. He remembered city landmarks as he passed them, and the *Chronicle* building was a hard one to miss. On the corner of Kearney and Market, it stood, like many in this thriving metropolis, as a multistoried monument to modern architecture.

Cole tried his best to make conversation but Arthur wasn't biting. By the time they crossed Sutter Street, Cole had already surrendered to the boy's balky silence.

Cole's thoughts turned, instead, to his investigation. His first stop yesterday had been the county jail to interview Ricardo Cortez, the man accused of murdering Silas and the others. Before he had exchanged even one word with the dark-haired bandit, Cole had known there was something dreadfully amiss with the police investigation that had brought him up on charges of murder. Young Arthur Pierce, the only true eyewitness to the killings, had described the perpetrator as a Goliath. The man that had faced Cole from behind those bars barely topped five feet six. Naming Arthur as a key witness for the prosecution of this case was obviously a farce. Whoever was pulling the strings in this puppet show had no intentions of allowing that child anywhere near a witness stand.

Cole had started out this morning with a plan. That plan had been to return to the police station to do a little shadowing of his own. He figured maybe Detective O'Connell might lead him to whoever was padding his salary. Would that benefactor be the civic-minded Mr. Phineas Taylor, the man who had hired the Pinkerton Agency to bring Arthur and Gwin back to San Francisco? Cole would have to wait to find out. His plans had changed. They had changed the moment Gwin had brought up Silas's comment about his brother, Sidney. Cole's inner alarms had gone off. Things were starting to come together. They were starting to come together so rapidly, Cole was having a hard time containing his excitement. His instincts were buzzing.

Gwin had told him that Silas had disappeared into town on business the day he was killed. What business? Silas had never been to San Francisco before in his life. Gwin had told him that Silas's estranged brother had probably settled here in California. Could he still be here? Could the business Silas had traveled into town for be unfinished business? Unfinished business between embittered brothers? Of course, it was entirely possible that Sidney Pierce's presence in San Francisco, the city where his brother had been brutally murdered, was just a coincidence.

The trouble was, Cole didn't much believe in coincidences. It was a fact that true coincidences did occasionally occur in everyday life, but when they occurred in the course of an investigation, they were the yellow flags that inevitably snagged any detective's attention. One supposedly coincidental event was usually tied to another. The trick, of course, was in finding the elusive thread that bound them together. Cole was beginning to think he was getting close to that thread. Very, very close.

Cole glanced down casually to see that Arthur was gone. He stopped, trying to swallow an immediate urge to panic. He hadn't really thought about how easy it would be to lose a child in a city this size, especially a child that might want to be lost. When he turned around, however, a wave of relief swept over him. There was Arthur, in plain sight, standing like a statue back at the last street corner.

Cole hurried back. "Why are you stopping? The *Chronicle* office is right up here."

Arthur's arms were folded stiffly, his eyes glued to a line of retail shops across the street. "I'm not going."

"Not going?"

"That's right! I'm not going anywhere with *you!*"

Cole stiffened. Whatever trust Arthur had placed in him was gone. Maybe Cole hadn't realized until now just how much he had come to value that trust. "Look, Arthur, the sooner we get this over with, the sooner you can get away from me. Now, come on."

"I don't have to listen to you. You're not my father. You're not my brother. You're not even my friend."

Cole grew aware that they were garnering curious glances from pedestrians. "Well, I *am* your friend, Arthur, whether you choose to believe that or not."

"A friend wouldn't have . . . " He faltered, his ears starting to turn pink. "A friend wouldn't do what you did!"

"You may be a little young to understand this, but no one's perfect, no matter how much you want them to be. I'm sorry if I let you down. Maybe when you're older, you'll look back and be able to understand a little better."

"I am *not* too young to understand! I understand better than you think!"

The sun was already hot and seemed to grow hotter by the second. They were now earning more than a few curious stares. Cole reckoned that if Arthur grew much more belligerent, they might even begin attracting a crowd. And a crowd inevitably attracted a policeman.

Cole lowered his voice. "Look, if you've got a bone to pick with me, we'll have it out in private later. Now, either stop acting childish and walk with me to the newspaper office, or I'm going to drag you there."

"No." Arthur folded his arms and tilted his chin arrogantly. Cole was intimately familiar with this expression. It was an exaggerated version of his sister's "try-me" look.

Frustrated, Cole reached out to wrest one of Arthur's arms. "All right, if that's the way you want it!"

Neatly dodging Cole's hand, Arthur ran to lock both arms around a nearby lamppost, hugging it to his chest. "No! No! No!"

"Damn it, Arthur! People are staring!"

Cole wasn't exaggerating. Already, a woman bedecked in a fashionable day dress and ostrich-plumed hat was slowing her stride. Judging by the expression on her face, Cole suspected she was debating on whether to club him over the head with her parasol or start screaming for the police.

"Let them stare! I hate you!"

Cole's patience snapped. "That's it!"

As he snatched one of Arthur's arms, the boy suddenly uncoiled and sprang out at him, fists flying. Cole's naturally quick reflexes permitted him to sidestep almost instantaneously, but not in time to fully avoid being clipped in the jaw by a solid punch. Cole's teeth clapped together, barely missing his tongue. Otherwise, he was uninjured by a blinding right cross that would someday pack a hell of a wallop.

The boy's cap flew off as he swung again. Cole threw up an arm, blocked this second punch, and snagged one of Arthur's elbows. Yanking the boy off balance, he dragged him in close enough to pin his other arm. Furious at being so easily contained, Arthur kicked Cole in the shin.

"Ouch! You little brat! Stop it!" Cole wrapped both arms around him to hold him still.

Arthur soon gave up struggling and craned his neck to glare at Cole. "You may be bigger than me, but I'm not scared of you!"

"I noticed. Now, are you going to calm down and act like a man, or am I going to have to drag you back to the room?"

"If I were a man, you'd be laid out on that sidewalk."

Sensing that all of the fight had left him, at least for the moment, Cole released him. "You're probably right about that."

A moment of tense silence crept by. Many of the passersby who had stopped to gawk lost interest and moved on.

"I think we need to talk about this." Cole bent to scoop up the boy's cap and steered him toward the corner of a nearby millinery shop. Cole waited, giving them both a chance to calm down before handing Arthur his cap. "You pack a heck of a punch for a kid."

Arthur set the cap down on his head. "You deserved it. You disgraced my sister."

"It really wasn't like that, Arthur."

"Am I going to be an uncle?"

"I don't know."

"You don't *know?* How can you not know?"

"It's not exactly something you can tell right away."

Arthur's fists clenched, and Cole had to wonder briefly if the kid was going to attack again. He sputtered, "B-but you said that—" Finally, he spit it out. "Didn't you have a watch?"

Cole was flummoxed. "A watch? What are you talking about?"

"You told me it had to do with timing, didn't you?"

Cole remembered their birds and bees conversation on the train. Timing. The boy had taken him literally. "Arthur, that's *not* the kind of timing I was talking about."

"Ah, jeeeeez!" Arthur dropped his head and shoved his fists deep into his pockets. "What's she gonna do?"

"Listen, Arthur, if it comes to that, I promise I'll stand by her. You know me well enough to know I wouldn't go back on a promise, don't you?"

"But do you love her?"

This question caught Cole by surprise, but it forced him to think. He tried to picture Gwin's face, and the first image that sprang to mind was that of her sitting at that candlelit dinner table in Virginia City. God, she had looked beautiful that night. The remembrance brought a little smile to his face.

Maybe he *was* falling in love with her. And, if so, why should he be surprised? She was beautiful, she was smart, and, although she did her darnedest to hide it, she had a good heart. He imagined for a moment that his father was alive and what it might be like to take Gwin home to meet him. *Well, Pa, it's true, she's a cardsharp, a horse thief, and a thimblerigger, but, other than that, I really think you're going to like her.* By now, Cole was starting to grin like a buffoon.

"What's so funny?" Arthur demanded, shattering Cole's daydream.

Funny? It was funny, all right. It was downright ludicrous! Guinevere Pierce. Guinevere Shepherd. He liked the sound of that. He liked the idea of having her around to talk to and laugh with and, yes, even to argue with. He liked still better the idea of not having to return to an empty apartment when he came home at the end of a long assignment.

"Hey! I asked you a question!"

Cole forced himself to focus on Arthur's upturned face. Maybe he *was* falling in love with Gwin, but he couldn't quite bring himself to say it. Not yet. The revelation, the very possibility, was still too new, too fragile to utter aloud. He needed to ponder it, to savor it, to keep it to himself for a while longer.

"Never mind," he replied, taking Arthur by the elbow. "We can have this out later. Right now, we've got work to do."

21

The bespectacled clerk in the business office of the San Francisco *Chronicle*, a callow youth in rolled-up shirtsleeves and vest, seemed friendly enough. Arthur stood with Cole as the clerk arose from behind a rolltop desk and strode forward to shake hands.

"Pinkerton Detective Agency, you say? Hey, I've heard of you fellows. I've even got a couple of Mr. Pinkerton's books. Say, you don't happen to know him personally, do you?"

Cole smiled politely. "Well, actually, yes. I work out of the Chicago office."

"So, what brings you all the way to San Francisco? Working on a big case?"

"Well, not exactly, Mr., uh . . ."

"Oh! Sorry!" The sandy-haired clerk pushed absently at spectacles that had slid down his nose and grinned again. "Warren Besecker's my name. So, what is it I can help you with, Mr. Shepherd?"

"Are you a reporter, Mr. Besecker?"

"Well, no, not yet, but I sure will be one of these days!"

"I'm glad to hear it, Mr. Besecker. Maybe you can help me with something."

"Call me Warren, please."

Arthur shoved his hands into his pockets, no longer paying attention to their small talk. Deep in one pocket, he felt a handful of walnut-sized rocks, leftovers from the day before when he had spent the afternoon target-shooting with his slingshot. He had killed three rats, each in one shot, right between the eyes, but even that hadn't helped to dispel the anger and resentment eating away inside him.

Now, he wasn't feeling so mad anymore, but he still felt pretty miserable. He had said some mean things to Gwinnie. Cole's recriminating words now haunted him: *"No one's perfect, no matter how much you want them to be."* It was true. Silas hadn't been perfect. Even his beautiful, talented mother hadn't been perfect. Why did he expect so much more of Gwinnie? Because she was all that he had left? Maybe, deep down inside, he was afraid she would leave him, too.

Cole interrupted Arthur's gloomy musings. "Arthur, do you have any idea of the date of the issue we're looking for?"

Arthur wasn't quite ready to forgive him. Not just yet. His reply was deliberately frosty. "I didn't read the date."

Arthur was glad to see an expression of mild irritation flit across Cole's face. "Do you think it was early June?"

"Perhaps," Arthur answered coolly.

Cole turned back to the clerk. "Warren, do you think you could let us have a look at the first two weeks in June?"

"Certainly! Won't take but a minute! Wait right there!"

Warren disappeared behind a door in the back, leaving Arthur and Cole to stand in awkward silence. Cole folded his arms and turned around to stare at the print of a clipper ship that hung on one wall. Arthur could tell by the look on his face that he was already a million miles away. That suited Arthur just fine. He didn't have much to say to Cole right now, anyway.

Warren soon appeared with a collection of newspapers tucked under one arm. "Well, here you go. I hope this helps."

Cole walked over to the desk as Warren flopped down the newspapers. "Come here a minute, Arthur."

Reluctantly, Arthur moved to Cole's side as he began to thumb through each edition. "Which one was it?"

Arthur shook his head at each one as it passed. "No, no, no, no, no, . . . wait." He tapped one. A column heading had caught his eye: *Taylor Likely Draft for Mayoral Race*. "That's it."

He remembered that heading. Heck, he remembered practically every article on that front page. This particular one had begun, "As keynote speaker,

Phineas Taylor once again enthralled members of the Pacific Club last evening with his new ideas on . . ."

Cole slipped the paper from the stack, unfolded it, and began to scan it with interest.

Warren spoke up. "Find what you're looking for?"

Cole didn't look up. "Maybe I have."

Arthur frowned. What was he talking about? There hadn't been anything in that paper about Sidney Pierce. He had read it over twice and found nothing. Bored, Arthur turned to Warren Besecker. "Mark Twain ever work here?"

The young man frowned. "Mark Twain? Uh, no, I don't think so. He reported a while for the *Morning Call*, I think."

Cole spoke up. "Warren, how much do you know about this Phineas Taylor?"

"He's running for mayor. What do you want to know?"

"I've heard he's quite wealthy, is that right?"

Warren snorted. "Wealthy? That's an understatement. He lives up on the hill with the railroad and silver tycoons!"

"Got a pretty fair chance at winning, you think?"

Warren nudged his spectacles and adopted a scholarly tone. "Well, I think he's got a good shot at it. There's a lot of money behind him, and he's even been gaining some popularity with the working folks."

Cole folded up the paper and handed it back to Warren. "Where did you say he lives?"

"Washington Street. Up near the top of the hill."

Arthur observed Cole as he listened very closely to the newspaperman's street directions. Cole wasn't just acting interested, he *was* interested. Cole was on to something. Arthur frowned, beginning to think that maybe he *had* missed something important in that newspaper, after all.

Warren strolled with Cole to the door. "Just take Kearney up to Washington, then catch a cable car up to..."

Arthur glanced down at the folded issue of the *Chronicle. Taylor Likely Draft for Mayoral Race.* He still didn't see what this Taylor fellow had to do with anything. Nevertheless, he threw a hurried glance in Cole and Warren's direction to make sure their backs were still turned before snatching the paper. He turned his back, folding it and sliding it neatly behind the front bib of his overalls. When he turned back to face them, he wore a studiously innocent expression.

Cole motioned. "Come on, Arthur. Let's go."

Arthur moved to Cole's side as Warren Besecker shook Cole's hand for the second time. "Say, you wouldn't be working on a case that has something to do with Mr. Taylor, would you? Now, that could be big news."

Cole laughed good-naturedly. "Sorry, Warren."

"Well, if you stumble onto anything interesting, you just remember good old Warren at the *Chronicle*, all right?"

Cole winked as he rested a hand on Arthur's shoulder, urging him toward the door. "You've got yourself a deal."

* * *

At the sound of their footsteps approaching in the hallway, Gwin jumped up from her bed and fairly flew to the door, remembering only at the last second to throw back the bolt on the lock Cole had insisted the landlord fix only the day before.

She caught sight of them in the hallway, and just by the look on Cole's face, she knew right away that he had found something. She accosted him before he could even reach the doorway. "What did you find?"

Cole motioned for her to quiet as he ushered both Arthur and her ahead of him into the room. "Shut the door."

Gwin wasn't in the least bit daunted as she followed his instructions, even throwing the bolt for good measure. "All right, Shepherd, spill it!"

"Spill what?"

Gwin wasn't amused. "Is Sidney in San Francisco?"

"I don't know. There's one more thing I have to do."

Gwin was losing all patience. "Is Sidney here or isn't he?"

Cole closed the distance between them and took her gently by the shoulders. "I'll explain everything tonight. Over dinner."

"I can't wait that long!"

He wore an indecipherable smile. "If this pans out, I'm taking you and Arthur to Delmonico's."

Gwin frowned suspiciously. Delmonico's was one of the most expensive restaurants in San Francisco. Why, he had come up with something, and he was deliberately holding it back from her! Before she had time to protest, he bent down and pecked her on the lips.

Gwin's mouth fell open in shock as, taking her full into his arms, he kissed her again, much more thoroughly this time. Despite herself, Gwin melted against him, reveling in the feel of his arms around her, of his lips moving warm and persuasively over hers. Being in his arms felt like coming home again, and this to a girl who had once thought she would never know what a real home felt like.

When he finally pulled away, he was grinning down at her. "Now, I want you to shut up and stay put," he commanded, putting her away from him firmly and turning to leave.

Gwin stammered, struggling with an annoying combination of giddy elation and righteous indignation at the same time. "Shut up and . . . stay . . . stay put?"

Cole threw the bolt before glancing back at her. "Trust me, Gwin. I've got to check something out. When I get back, I'll explain everything. Promise you'll stay put?" He opened the door and hesitated. "Promise me, Gwin?"

Gwin was barely able to recover her voice, much less her thinking faculties. "I promise."

Cole winked and then he was gone.

"He kissed you." Arthur's voice, flat and indignant, reached her ears from across the room.

"He kissed me," Gwin echoed.

"Right smack on the mouth! If he doesn't quit that kind of stuff, I'm gonna have to punch him again!"

Punch him again? Gwin managed to recover from her shock long enough to notice that her brother's tone, while distinctly annoyed, no longer seemed to hold the unmitigated hostility it had earlier this morning. He was finally thawing.

"Arthur," she ventured cautiously, "you didn't . . . ?"

"I sure as heck did!"

Gwin fought to control a sudden swell of affection for her young brother. *What I wouldn't have given to have been there when those two . . .* She shook off the thought and turned to stare once again at that closed door. "I sure would give just about anything to have a look at that newspaper."

Arthur cleared his throat, prompting her to look at him. She was surprised to see that for the first time in almost two days, he was wearing just the hint of his familiar bright smile. "Anything?" he drawled slyly.

And it was then that her little brother, bless his sneaky heart, pulled a folded copy of the San Francisco *Chronicle* from beneath his faded overalls.

Cole stood on the front porch steps of the boardinghouse, taking a moment to gather his thoughts. He had one stop to make before visiting his Agency's mysterious client, Phineas Taylor. That stop was the telegraph office. It was time to bring Fritz Landis up to date.

The moment Cole had spotted Phineas Taylor's name on the front page of the *Chronicle*, another yellow flag had risen in his mind. Arthur was correct that Sidney Pierce's name didn't appear anywhere on that front page, and Cole had no doubt Arthur was also correct when he insisted it didn't appear anywhere else in that day's edition. But that didn't matter. What, after all, was in a name? Silas Pierce had assumed a number of aliases during his colorful career. Why expect his brother to be any different? Especially if he had a public reputation to maintain, a reputation that depended upon his checkered past remaining a secret.

Cole intended to pay a visit to Mr. Taylor, and, in so doing, he was aware that he might be walking directly into the lion's den. The problem was, he couldn't very well solicit any help from the San Francisco authorities. He didn't have any evidence yet, and, more importantly, he wasn't sure who he could trust. That was why it was important to wire the Agency first. While he doubted that Taylor would actually do him bodily harm in the middle of the day in his own residence, it was better to be safe than sorry. If something *were* to happen to him, it would be better if Fritz knew all the facts. There would be somebody left to pick up the thread.

With that grim thought in mind, Cole descended the front steps of the boardinghouse and headed south on Kearney toward the telegraph office.

Arthur handed the newspaper to Gwinnie, secretly pleased that he had been able to satisfy her curiosity. In a way, it made him feel better about some of the awful things he had said to her the day before.

Gwin sat on the corner of her bed as she read over the front-page article. "And you're sure *this* is the one Cole seemed so interested in? The one about this Taylor fellow?"

"That's the one, all right. He even asked the newspaperman for directions to the guy's house."

Gwin shook her head, seemingly perplexed, as she spread the paper on the bed, turning the pages slowly, scanning the columns. "It doesn't make any sense," she mumbled to herself after a few minutes. "I mean, who *is* this guy that Cole should be so interested in—" She stopped and her eyes widened. "Arthur . . . oh, Arthur," she said.

"What?" Arthur felt a stab of alarm. Gwinnie's face was ashen. "What? What?"

Gwin folded the paper in half, then held it up for him to see. "Look at it, Arthur."

With one finger, she tapped a thumbnail sketch no bigger than an advertisement, a political cartoon featuring two main characters, a bug-eyed minister and a man in a black top hat, positioned as snarling opponents in a boxing ring. He strained to read the caption, something about that politician named Taylor. "What?" Arthur asked again, confused.

"The picture, Arthur! Look at the picture!"

And he did. Edging closer, he squinted at the newspaper artist's crude caricatures. "I don't understand."

"Who does he look like?"

"Which one? The one with the big eyes or the one with—" Arthur began, and then he started to see it. He began to see what it was that she saw, and his stomach clenched up.

Gwin prodded him. "He looks like . . ."

Arthur blinked hard, his vision suddenly misting over. "Silas!" he blurted. And it was true. How had he not seen it before? The artist's rendering was unflatteringly exaggerated, but the square line of his jaw, the shape of his eyes, and that tilted, "dare-you" smile were utterly unmistakable. "It looks like Silas!"

Gwin rose to her feet. "He looks like Silas because he's Silas's brother," she stated. "It's Sidney, Arthur. Sidney Pierce is Phineas Taylor."

22

Gwin had no trouble locating Phineas Taylor's home. The elaborate residence and its grounds, set far back from the municipal sidewalk and encircled by a tall, wrought-iron fence, stood over three stories tall. Its painted wooden exterior simulated marbled stone to such an extent that it was impossible to tell the difference until one actually crossed onto the property itself. The house was surrounded by a manicured lawn and garden.

Gwin hesitated at the end of a flagstone walk to observe a pair of ornamented turrets. They reminded her of a castle, a castle that might have once nestled in the mythological land of Camelot.

Gwin climbed the stone steps to the entrance of the imposing residence, passing an Oriental gardener, who busily tended a cluster of blooming rosebushes.

She raised her hand to a brass knocker, letting it

fall twice before retreating a few steps. As she looked up to behold an elaborate stained-glass mosaic above the wide archway, she half-hoped there would be no answer to her summons.

The monstrous door creaked open to reveal a lanky butler. He sported a narrow mustache and thinning dark hair slicked back from his forehead. "May I help you, madam?"

"I'm here to see Mr. Taylor."

The man inspected her unfashionably dressed figure, disdainfully noting the tiny blue silk reticule that clashed with her daytime attire. "May I tell him who is calling, madam?"

Gwin squared her shoulders. "Miss Pierce."

The butler stepped aside and opened the door wider for her to pass. "Very good, Miss Pierce. Won't you come in?"

Gwin found herself standing in a huge foyer, peering cautiously around the expressionless butler's shoulder at a majestic marble staircase. It was warm outside, but now, as the heavy wooden door swung shut behind her, echoing in the vast stillness that surrounded them, it suddenly seemed very cold.

"Make yourself comfortable, Miss Pierce. I'll inform Mr. Taylor that you're here." The butler turned crisply on his heels and headed for the staircase.

Gwin watched the man ascend until he finally disappeared around the corner of a second-floor landing, then she turned cautiously to take in her surroundings. She jumped and gasped upon spying what at first appeared to be a human figure standing not ten feet away from her on the other side of the staircase.

Upon second examination, she realized that it was nothing but an empty suit of armor. And it was not unique. Here and there, interspersed at various points throughout the wide entrance hall that bisected the first floor, she saw a number of similar figures posted by closed-off doorways. These served to complement an impressive collection of ancient weaponry and lush Renaissance-era paintings that hung on the walls. Apparently, Gwin's initial impression of this place as a medieval castle was precisely what the owner intended.

As she began to move, the soft click of her heels against the gleaming marble floor followed her in the form of a hollow, all-surrounding echo. She observed rich gallery paneling on the walls and thick marble columns before tilting her head back to survey the unstained roof timbers two stories overhead.

Oh, Mother, she thought to herself, *this might have been your Camelot.* Gwin shook her head sadly. But it could never be hers. She had discovered just a touch of her own Camelot this morning, and that had been in Cole Shepherd's arms. Perhaps neither of them, mother nor daughter, were ever fated to attain the full measure of their dreams.

Gwin passed beneath a set of sparkling chandeliers to examine more closely the armored figure she had first mistaken for a live person lurking by the curved banister of the staircase. A deep, masculine voice boomed behind and above her.

"A full suit of field armor. It was crafted in Germany sometime during the first quarter of the sixteenth century."

Gwin turned to behold on the staircase a figure whose broad-shouldered stance and distinctive countenance brought a flood of memories crashing back to her. She was seeing a ghost. *Silas.* But *not* Silas. This man was younger, perhaps a trifle more handsome in the classic sense of the word. His forehead was lower and his thick hair was a darker shade of blond than Silas's natural color. *My father,* she thought, more than a little awed by the sight of him, *this is my father.*

"That other one," the Silas-figure continued, pointing as he descended the stairs, "the one to your left, was known as parade armor. Notice the rich decoration, the elaborate scroll design, and the gilt ornamentation. It was probably made in Antwerp in the seventeenth century."

"They must be very expensive," Gwin said.

"Very. So are the weapons," he replied as he reached the bottom step, waving his arm to indicate the whole of the collection that lined the paneled walls.

Gwin's eyes swept over swords, daggers, shields, maces, war hammers, partisans—some of them silver, some gilt in gold, some set with precious stones. All of them, Gwin noted, were very old, and all of them were no doubt worth a small fortune in a collector's market.

Gwin frowned. "Quite an arsenal. You don't happen to have a dungeon down below to go with all of this, do you?"

"Sorry. It seems the architect was deficient in that aspect of medieval design."

Gwin turned away to amble across the entrance

hall to a sitting area by an imposing marble fireplace. Furnished with two cushioned settees, bentwood end tables, and a marble-topped center table, Gwin thought this was probably where a guest was to make himself comfortable while awaiting an audience with the lord of the manor. As for herself, she was not feeling very comfortable at all.

Gwin kept her back to him as she spoke. "Do you know who I am?"

"Yes," he replied calmly. "You're Gwendolyn. You look quite a lot like your mother."

"That's 'Guinevere.'"

"Guinevere?" For the first time, he seemed slightly nonplussed, and Gwin felt a queer sense of gratification. "I suppose I just assumed—"

"Everyone assumes. Call me Gwin if you like." She looked up at a monstrous, gilt-framed painting over the mantel. It depicted a violent battle scene featuring muscular half-man, half-equestrian creatures, many of them sweeping partially clad screaming women off their feet.

"*Rape of the Lapith Daughters*," he said. "An episode from the Hercules legends."

"How charming," Gwin commented flatly.

"You don't care for the decor?"

"Well, it's certainly replete with history."

"Replete with myth, my dear, not history. Myth is an entirely different matter altogether."

"Dreams, you mean."

"Perhaps," he said. "Dreams must manifest themselves in some way, I suppose, even among the most practical of souls."

"You deem yourself practical, then?" Gwin asked, turning back to him.

"Eminently, my dear. Practical to a fault. As I suspect you may be, too."

Practical to a fault. Who was he to be analyzing her character? He might have fathered her, but he certainly hadn't been around to raise her.

"As I said before, you look very much like your mother. *Are* you very much like her?"

"I certainly hope not."

Sidney seemed to find this amusing. "Didn't you love your mother?"

"Sometimes," Gwin answered defensively. "Did you?"

His lips curved into a sly smile. "Sometimes."

"I adored her when I was a child, but as I grew older—"

"Ah, yes." Sidney bowed his head, still wearing that small, privately amused smile. "As you grew older, you realized that real life is not a fairy tale and that things are not always as they appear to be."

"Yes. Or as they should be."

"Yes."

They stood, each appraising the other, before Gwin spoke. "She's dead, you know."

The smile faded. "I know."

Gwin continued cautiously. "And Silas—"

"It was in the papers."

"You knew."

"Yes, I knew."

Gwin tried to fight down a surge of hostility. "Well then, why didn't you . . . ?"

Sidney spread both hands, palms up. "What would you expect me to do?"

Gwin opened her mouth to reply but came up short when she spotted a tiny web of skin at the juncture of his left ring finger and little finger, a familial deformity Silas had told her she had inherited from a grandfather she had never met. This really was her father. It was true. If she'd had even one last shred of doubt concerning her mother's veracity on the subject, it dissolved in that moment.

It took her a few seconds to recover from her shock and find her voice. "But he was your brother."

"Yes, but that all ended years ago. Did he tell you about it?"

Gwin nodded.

Sidney smiled, but there was little mirth in the expression. "We had nothing in common anymore. We were strangers, really."

"You had one thing in common," Gwin said.

"And what was that?"

"Emmaline."

His pale blue eyes clouded. "For a short while, perhaps, but Silas and I parted ways a long time ago. I was sorry to read of his death, but there was nothing I could do after the fact."

Despite the impassive expression on his face, Gwin sensed something cracking behind this man's facade, and she hazarded to press further. "But perhaps there *is* something you can do."

Sidney started to move away from her. "If that's the reason you've sought me out, I'm afraid I'll have to disappoint you. It would be my heartfelt suggestion that you take your leave of San Francisco and never look back."

Gwin tried to control the disgust and anger that roiled in the pit of her stomach. There was, however, about as much hope of controlling it as there was of controlling the eruption of a rumbling volcano. She lashed out. "You're a heartless bastard! He was your brother!"

Sidney stopped in his tracks, but he didn't turn around. He clasped his hands behind his back and looked down at the floor. "I can understand your feelings, Gwin. He was your father, and naturally—"

"*You* are my father!"

Her exclamation echoed throughout the empty foyer, reverberating off marble columns and wooden beams, haunting them both until silence descended to blanket them like a shroud once again.

Finally, he turned around to face her. "That's impossible."

This last outburst had spent Gwin of her inner rage for the moment. She was able to answer him in a normal tone of voice. "Impossible?"

"Where did you hear such a thing?"

"Emmaline."

Another mirthless smile crossed his face. "Well, that explains it then, doesn't it? I don't have to tell you that your mother was often given to prevarication."

"This was no lie."

"And what makes you think so?"

Gwin took a deep breath, digging in her heels. "She was already with child when she married Silas."

"Easily explained, my dear. Your mother was no

saint, I'm afraid. She and Silas were sleeping together long before they married, you see."

"No."

"But I saw them."

"No." Gwin felt strangely calm and suddenly very sure of herself. She was gaining a foothold. He, she sensed, was beginning to lose his. Something had flickered in those pale blue eyes. Doubt? Gwin pressed on. "You saw what she wanted you to see. It was her way of getting your attention. She knew she was pregnant."

The smile was gone from his face. "I saw them together."

"If you think about it, it was just like her, wasn't it? She tried to make you jealous, to trick you into marrying her."

Sidney didn't seem to hear her. His gaze had turned inward, focusing on his own memories of that time long ago. He started to pace, and, for the first time since meeting the man, Gwin got the feeling she was beginning to catch a glimpse of what might really lie behind the mask. "You don't understand!" he insisted. "I saw them! I saw them together!"

"You *are* my father. She wasn't lying this time."

"No. That's not how it was."

Gwin dropped her reticule on an end table and held up her left hand, spreading her fingers, displaying the tiny deformity she had inherited from him. She didn't need to say anything more. He stopped pacing and stared. "Oh, God damn that woman."

"No one else in the family has it, do they?" Gwin demanded, driving home her point. "No one but you and me."

"Why didn't she tell me?"

Gwin lowered her hand. "As a last resort, I suppose she would have, but you were already gone. Remember?"

Sidney pondered this for a moment before an odd expression crossed his face. His head lifted, ever so slightly, like a deer picking up the scent of a hidden predator. Then he looked around, his newly alert gaze settling on the empty staircase before he turned back to Gwin, his voice hushed. "We mustn't talk here. Come into my study."

Gwin was surprised at this unexpected change in manner, but she followed him as he led her to one of the doors leading off from the foyer. He motioned for her to precede him into the room, closing the door firmly after he had entered behind her.

Gwin's eyes swept the room, taking in the rich mahogany furnishings, a tall window with red velvet tie-back draperies, and another marble fireplace. Over the mantel, Gwin beheld an elaborate oil painting that caused her mouth to drop open in shock. "Good heavens," she said.

Sidney's voice, self-deprecating and ironic, reached her ears. "Yes. I commissioned it during one of my weaker moments, and I've never been quite able to bring myself to part with it."

The painting was an artist's interpretation of the final parting of Guinevere and Lancelot. What was clearly not a product of that artist's imagination, however, was the face of Guinevere. It was Gwin's own mother, looking not much older in the painting than Gwin was now herself.

"It's beautiful," she said, still mesmerized.

"She was a unique woman, and we were well suited to each other. I must admit, I've never met anyone else quite like her."

"I believe you," Gwin said. "She used to tell me stories."

He chuckled. "Ah, yes, stories. She was a splendid storyteller. Most dreamers are, and your mother was a dreamer. So was Silas. I, on the other hand, was a doer."

"Yes, otherwise I wouldn't be here, isn't that right?"

"I'll be damned, but you are her daughter, aren't you?"

"And yours." Gwin realized now for perhaps the first time the real reason she had come here. She had come so she could meet him, yes, but she had also come so he could meet her, so he would know of her existence.

He appraised her for a moment, then, as if reading her thoughts, he asked, "Why did you really come here, Gwin?"

"Because I thought you might be able to help us."

"And?"

"And because I wanted to see you."

He nodded as if he had expected as much. "And you've seen."

"Yes."

"And what do you think?"

"I don't know what to think."

"I suppose that's understandable."

"And you," Gwin said, challenging him, "what do *you* think?"

He sighed. "Part of me is glad that you came.

Another part is saddened. Perhaps it would have been better not to know I have a daughter."

"Why?"

He turned his back to gaze out the window. "I let go of family a long time ago."

"And so what has one visit changed?"

"Somehow it's easier to let go of the notion of traitorous brothers and faceless nieces and nephews than it is to let go of the notion of one's own offspring. I never thought—"

He turned to face her. "You've got a good head on your shoulders, Gwin. You'll do quite well on your own, but if you ever need help—financial help, I mean—you may contact me by telegram or letter. I would suggest, however, that you use a different name in your correspondence. You see, my dear, the walls have ears."

Gwin shook her head, confused. "I don't understand. I didn't come here for money."

"I know that. Nevertheless, the offer stands. You must never again come to see me in person, however. That would be dangerous. I daresay we may have dallied too long as it is."

"You're not making sense."

"Gwin," he said firmly, "you must get out of this house. You must get away from me. You must know that there are people who would like to see you and your brother dead."

"What?" Gwin gasped, shocked. "How did you—"

"My dear, I'm afraid that what you've done, quite unwittingly, is stumble upon a nest of vipers."

* * *

Alphonse Ringo stepped out of the shadows of the second-floor landing, his colorless eyes fixed on the door of Sidney's study. He was a large man, but he had long ago mastered the art of melting into his surroundings. He could be as silent and unmoving as a chameleon when occasion called for it, and, in his particular occupation, occasion often called for it.

He had overheard every word that had just passed between Sidney and his long-lost daughter. He thought it had been a very touching exchange; or rather, it would have been if he were a man inclined to be emotionally touched by much of anything, which he wasn't.

He turned his head now toward the third-floor landing and motioned for Frederick to descend. When the butler finally reached his side, he spoke in a low voice. "You're sure she came alone?"

"Oh, yes! And she wasn't shy about giving her name, either. Rather odd, don't you think?"

Ringo didn't bother to answer. He was, by nature, a meticulously efficient man. Never, in all the years he had worked for Jasper Barnes, had he ever left a witness behind. Not until now. And it had been eating at him from the inside out for weeks. It galled him to think that because of his own sloppiness, there existed the possibility that he could be brought down by a mere child and a woman!

"How many servants are on the grounds?"

"Well, there's the cook and the housekeeper. Oh, and the gardener and the groom, I believe. That's all."

"Get rid of them."

Frederick's eyelids fluttered. "Get rid of them? But

how will I explain it? They'll naturally think it a bit unusual to let them go so early in the day, and—"

"Do it."

At catching the look on Ringo's face, Frederick's ruddy complexion paled. "I . . . well, of course," he stammered. "I . . . I'll certainly think of s-something!"

Ringo watched dispassionately as Frederick cleared the stairs in record time and disappeared out the front door. Jasper Barnes was due to arrive any minute. Jasper would know what to do. In the meantime, Ringo's job was to make sure that the girl did not leave this house.

It was a fact that Arthur was a healthy young boy; nevertheless, he was struggling for breath by the time he reached the high point of Washington Street. He had left the room at the boardinghouse in a hurry, on impulse, even after Gwinnie had told him to stay behind, and he had not thought far enough ahead to filch himself a nickel for a cable car ride.

Eager to reach his destination as soon as possible, he had not spared his pace any as he had climbed the steep inclines. By the time he had finally located his Uncle Sidney's mansion, the muscles in his sinewy young legs had begun to ache in protest.

He hunkered down behind a set of prickly bushes beneath a window on the east side of the house. Although the grounds had been deserted when he had arrived, it was by sheer luck that he had rounded the corner of the massive structure and was just barely out of sight before he had heard the approach of another visitor.

Arthur peered out from behind the shrubbery to see that the little fat man in the top hat had climbed the front steps. Arthur had no desire to be caught trespassing. He had no idea what to expect of his Uncle Sidney. None of the stories he had ever heard about him had been particularly flattering. For all Arthur knew, his Uncle Sidney could be some grouchy old money-grubbing stuffed shirt who would just as soon see his nephew sitting in jail as sitting at his dinner table.

Arthur thought it better that this first visit remain as clandestine as possible. All he really cared about, after all, was that Gwinnie stayed safe. Arthur was still annoyed with Cole, but that didn't change the fact that Cole had been dead right to tell Gwinnie to stay put until he got back. It had been stupid and careless of her to go out all by herself. After what had happened to Silas and Clell, Arthur was not about to let his sister out of his sight for a minute.

Arthur listened hard, picking up only faint snatches of a clipped conversation after the front door opened to admit the visitor. It was only when he heard the heavy door swing shut that he dared to straighten up, flexing his aching legs and grimacing.

He examined the window just over his head. It was closed and shuttered, but this was a fine, sunny day. He doubted that all of the first-floor windows would be closed against the sunlight and fresh air. Surely, if he continued to explore, he would find one open.

His hunch soon proved correct as he crept stealthily toward the rear of the house. Crouching below an open window, he first threw a quick glance around to be sure he was unobserved, then he stood and reached up to grip the lower sill. With a hoist and grunt, he was up, both feet dangling off the ground as he peered into a deserted room holding the longest dining room table he had ever seen in his life. He grinned, immensely pleased with his own detective work, as he threw first one leg, then the other over the sill to drop down, silent as a cat, onto the carpeted floor inside.

23

"Where's Frederick?" Jasper inquired curtly, doffing his top hat and flipping it to Ringo, who moved to hang it neatly on a nearby hat rack.

"He's busy," Ringo said.

"You shouldn't be answering the door. That Pinkerton man, he hasn't shown up here, has he?"

Ringo shook his head.

Jasper hardly seemed relieved as he transferred his walking cane from one hand to the other, searching the pockets of his coat. "Well, it's just a matter of time. He's been nosing around all over town. Unfortunately, that fool, O'Connell, lost him yesterday and hasn't been able to locate him since."

Ringo spoke. "The girl is—"

Jasper pulled out a cigar and fumbled to strike a match. "The girl and the boy are with him. Why else would he have come all this way?"

Ringo spoke again. "The girl is here."

Jasper stopped, the match flame hovering over the tip of his cigar. "The girl is . . . *what?*"

"The girl is here."

"Here? Where?"

"With Sidney. In his study."

"And the boy?"

Ringo shook his head.

Jasper pondered this new revelation. "It doesn't make any sense that she would show up here alone." He shook his head, then finished lighting his cigar. "All right," he said, accepting the situation and addressing it. "We must tread carefully, Mr. Ringo. We must keep the girl here. The boy will undoubtedly follow, as will the Pinkerton operative."

"And then?"

"I don't think it would be wise to hurt her. Not for the moment, at least, and definitely not in front of Sidney."

Ringo bristled at this. She was a witness. She must be disposed of. Wasn't that what all of this was about? Cleaning up the mess? Mr. Barnes was wrong.

Jasper seemed to sense Ringo's inner rebellion. "Do you understand, Mr. Ringo?"

"She cannot live."

Jasper smiled. "No, of course not, but we must be very careful concerning Sidney's sensibilities on the subject. He's indispensable to us right now."

Ringo's fists tightened convulsively at his sides. "He's no longer loyal. If he's no longer loyal, he's of no use to us."

"But he can be persuaded, Mr. Ringo. Once they're

taken care of, he will have nothing left to fight for. Things will return to normal. We will win the election." He repeated his question. "Do you understand, Mr. Ringo?"

Ringo wasn't stupid. He understood Jasper's convoluted reasoning, and he resented the fact that Jasper questioned him as if he were some witless idiot. The problem was not that Ringo did not understand. The problem was that Ringo did not agree. Sidney Pierce had become rich and powerful enough in his own right to make a clean break from the Round Table. Maybe not here in San Francisco, but somewhere else, somewhere far away—New York City, Europe, or even South America. If Jasper wasn't able to see that, he was a fool. He was confusing his own dreams and aspirations with Sidney's, and that was a grave mistake. Sidney Pierce was turning, and, once turned, a man stayed turned. He was of no use. He had to be eliminated. Coddling the girl and the boy in order to pacify him only added insult to injury. They were witnesses. They needed to be eliminated. They *would* be eliminated.

"Yes," Ringo answered after a moment of tense silence. "I understand."

Jasper nodded as if satisfied, then plunked the cigar back into his mouth. "How many servants are on the grounds?"

"Frederick is dismissing them now."

Jasper gave Ringo an admiring side glance. "I should have known you'd take care of that. You never were one to leave witnesses behind, were you, Mr. Ringo?"

Ringo didn't see that this question required an answer.

"You are armed, I take it?"

Ringo grunted his assent.

Jasper held out one hand expectantly, and Ringo complied with the unspoken request by pulling a Schofield revolver from an inside coat pocket. He placed it in Jasper's pudgy hand with slight misgivings. It wasn't that Ringo was inherently fond of his gun. In fact, he rarely used it, preferring instead a more hands-on approach to dispatching his victims. It was simply a matter of practicality that he knew how to handle just about every firearm available. Jasper, on the other hand, had never shown much of an interest in becoming proficient in their use. Ringo just hoped that his esteemed employer didn't end up shooting himself in the foot.

Jasper slid the revolver into his coat pocket. "I'll be joining them in the study," he said. "I want you to keep an eye on things out here. If the boy shows up, hold him."

"And the Pinkerton man?"

Jasper smiled. "In recognition of your formidable patience in this matter, I think it's only fair that you may have him. When you're through, you may dispose of him somewhere down near Deadman's Alley. It will be unfortunate for his reputation when he's discovered in such an unsavory neighborhood, but . . ." Jasper threw up a careless hand as he started across the vast foyer to the study. His mood, Ringo noticed, had improved considerably since he had arrived. He tapped the marble floor merrily with his walking cane as he moved. "Those are, as they say, the stakes of the game."

* * *

Gwin stood in the middle of the study, her feet rooted to the floor. "How could you know? How could you possibly know about the attempts on our lives?"

Sidney's head was bowed. He hadn't moved from behind his desk. "On the day Silas arrived in San Francisco, he came to me. He threatened to expose my past. He knew that I was running for mayor and that his exposure would ruin me. He wanted money."

"You were part of it!"

"I would have paid him, Gwin. I would have paid him anything he wanted just to get him out of my life, but when my business colleagues learned of the situation they took matters into their own hands. They have a lot at stake in this election."

Gwin shook her head, squeezing her eyes shut, hoping that this was just some terrible dream. Surely, she would awaken soon to find herself back at the boardinghouse still waiting for Cole and Arthur to return from the *Chronicle* office.

Sidney continued, "There was nothing I could do. By the time I learned what had happened, it was too late."

"And when you found out they intended to see me and my brother dead, was it too late then, too?"

Sidney's expression was leaden, unreadable. "It's too late to turn back the clock. What matters now is getting you and your brother out of San Francisco as soon as possible." He pulled open the top drawer of his desk and withdrew a black velvet bag. He loosened the drawstring and unceremoniously dumped its contents, a collection of gold double eagles, out onto the desk blotter. "It's all I have on hand at the moment, but it should be enough to get you out of town and well away from here."

Enough? More than enough! Gwin thought that they could probably travel to Kansas City and back ten times on what was casually spilled out across the desk top. She looked up. "I don't want your money."

Sidney appraised the lovely young woman before him. His daughter. The reality of it had not yet truly penetrated his consciousness. It was incomprehensible to him that the woman he had loved and deserted all those years ago had actually borne him a daughter. It was perhaps even more ironic that the child they had accidentally created had turned out to be made of much sterner stuff than either of her sorry parents.

At this point, there was nothing Sidney could do to change his own life. He was who he was, and that would never change, no matter how many regrets he might harbor over his blemished past. The truth was, he had fought to get where he was, and he was who he wanted to be. But he'd be damned if he was going to stand by any longer and allow this young woman to be sacrificed for it.

He leaned over the desk toward her. "What you *want* isn't important. What you *need* is to keep you and your brother alive."

This, the blunt truth, seemed to stir a reaction from her. She frowned, then turned to gaze up at the portrait of her mother.

Sidney also looked up at Emmaline's face, seeing clearly for perhaps the first time that she wasn't really there. Perhaps she had never really been there, the

Emmaline he had grown over the years to cherish in his secret heart. Perhaps, in his own anguished mind, he had recreated her into something she had never been. Was it any wonder that no other woman had ever seemed to measure up?

"Before you go, there's something I think you should have." Sidney pulled open a drawer of his desk. There, lying next to his old Calvary Colt revolver, was the daguerreotype of Emmaline, forever young and smiling, forever beautiful. He stared at the faded picture for a long moment, fighting an overwhelming wave of nostalgia for a time in his life that was long since past. He nudged aside the revolver and picked it up.

"Perhaps it'll help you remember your mother in a more favorable light," he said. "Back in those days, she really was something."

Gwin reached for the picture. She looked at it for a few seconds before raising her lovely round blue eyes to Sidney's face. Her next words came as a surprise. "I'll just bet she was."

Sidney nodded, feeling suddenly more right with the world than he had in a very long time. "Enough of this," he said, clearing his throat and squaring his shoulders. "You'll have to leave quickly, through the service entrance, if—"

The door to the study swung open. Gwin turned, still clutching her mother's picture.

Jasper filled the doorway from one side to the other. He grinned at them from around a plump Havana cigar. "I apologize for so rudely interrupting, Sidney, but I must beg to differ with you." He pulled out a revolver. "No one is going anywhere."

24

Cole was unimpressed by the grandeur of Phineas Taylor's mansion. He doubted he would ever earn a fortune in his lifetime, certainly not in his line of work, but if he ever did, he would never throw it away on such a gaudy showpiece as this.

He climbed the front steps to the door and lifted the heavy brass knocker.

A butler soon answered his summons. "Sir?"

"My name is Cole Shepherd. I'm here to see Mr. Taylor."

To Cole, the butler appeared to have the sharp-beaked, heavy-lidded countenance of a sated vulture. "Is Mr. Taylor expecting you, sir?"

"No, but I'm from the Pinkerton Detective Agency in Chicago. Mr. Taylor is one of our clients."

The butler opened the door wider. "Do come in. I'll see if Mr. Taylor is available."

Cole stepped over the threshold, taking in his opulent surroundings with one sweeping glance. As the door swung closed behind him, the thought crossed his mind that the place reminded him of an ancient castle. Why anyone would want to surround himself with such a vulgar display of wealth was beyond him.

"Your hat, sir?"

Cole removed his derby and handed it to him.

"Very good." The butler hung it next to a silk top hat on a rack by the door. "I'll be but a moment, sir."

Cole watched as the butler continued past him toward one of the doors off to the side of the wide entrance foyer. The butler rapped once, then, at a muffled response from within, promptly vanished into the closed-off room.

Shortly after his unorthodox entry, Arthur had recognized himself to be in one of two adjoining dining rooms. As he passed by an elaborately carved mahogany sideboard, he was unable to resist running his fingers over a solid silver tea service and matching candlesticks. He thought his Uncle Sidney must be richer than Midas.

He passed stealthily into another room, which featured an ornate billiard table, gleaming silver cuspidors, and towering bookshelves. From there, still without running into another soul, he had passed through a kitchen, a scullery, a morning room, and a library.

It had been while browsing through some books in the library that he heard voices out in the hallway, the

A TOUCH OF CAMELOT

first indications of a human presence in the house since his arrival. One of those voices sounded familiar.

He skittered silently across the room to the door, opening it just a crack to peer out. Sure enough, there was Cole, standing by what must be the front door, handing his hat to some starchy-looking butler. The butler started down the hallway toward the library. Startled, Arthur jumped back from the door and flattened himself against the wall behind it, holding his breath.

He heard a knock, then an unintelligible response. A door across the hall opened and closed. Arthur let out his breath. Holy crow! That had been close! Now that Cole was here, he didn't have to worry about Gwinnie anymore. Now his biggest problem was getting out of here without being caught.

Cole strolled past two sets of armor figures to examine an array of ancient weapons that hung on one wall. They looked quite authentic and quite deadly. He was already beginning to form a mental composite of Mr. Phineas Taylor: rich, charismatic, vain, and—judging by the collectibility of the art and artifacts that hung in his entrance hall—quite a shrewd investor.

Cole turned away from the weapons collection, and that's when he saw it. He tried to convince himself that his mind was playing tricks on him. He moved forward a few steps to refocus on the object lying so carelessly, so innocently, atop one of the end tables. It wasn't his imagination. It was Gwin's blue silk reticule, the one she had purchased in Virginia City.

Before this fact and its full ramifications could even register, Cole was reaching for the gun holstered at his hip. Instantaneously, he sensed a presence behind him, a distinctly human presence and not one just simulated by an empty set of armor. He whirled around, the Colt cocked and ready, to behold a towering man standing near the bottom of the staircase. It was surprising; no, it was nigh on inconceivable to Cole that such a large man had apparently been able to move down those stairs without making a sound.

The door where the butler had disappeared only moments ago opened, and an unfamiliar, chuckling voice assaulted his ears. "You should be proud of yourself, Mr. Shepherd! You have crossed the finish line! You have won the prize!"

Without shifting his aim from the motionless figure on the staircase, Cole turned his head slightly to behold a short, very round, bearded man. His spirits sank dismally when he saw Gwin standing mutely before him. The man held a gun on her.

That cocksure, cackling voice fell on Cole's ears again, taking on the echoing unreality of a dream. "What is it that our Mr. Shepherd has won, Mr. Ringo?"

The giant on the staircase, seemingly oblivious to the fact that Cole's revolver was still aimed dead-center at his broad chest, finished descending the stairs.

"Oh, you can put the gun down, Mr. Shepherd. I wouldn't want to have to hurt the lady."

Cole looked down at the revolver in his hand, useless as a feather duster. The man was holding a gun on Gwin. He had the power to kill her at any moment, and there wasn't a damned thing Cole could think of to do about it.

The man's playful tone of voice took on a sharper edge. "Put the gun down, Mr. Shepherd."

Cole laid the gun down on the table next to Gwin's reticule. The little man spoke again. "Frederick, please confiscate Mr. Shepherd's weapon."

"You're not quite what I expected, Mr. Taylor," Cole said as the butler took the revolver and transferred it to the waiting hand of his rotund commander.

The man puffed on his cigar and chuckled. "The name is Barnes. Mr. Taylor seems to be dallying." He glanced back at the door, which still hung ajar. "Sidney? Are you there?"

A well-dressed, distinguished-looking man, tall and blond with pale blue eyes, appeared in the open archway. Cole knew then that his hunch was correct. Phineas Taylor and Sidney Pierce were the same man. Sidney's voice was dour. "I'm sorry, Mr. Shepherd, that it has come to this."

An earsplitting clatter caused Cole to turn. Mr. Ringo had apparently been busy. Cole looked down to see that an ancient double-edged sword had been flung at his feet. Incredulous, he raised his eyes to meet Ringo's waiting gaze. In one powerful hand, he wielded a long-handled partisan. Its wickedly sharp, curved edge put Cole in mind of an elaborate hatchet. Even though the big man had not said a word, the implication was clear enough. Cole was being challenged to some kind of duel.

"It seems Mr. Ringo has decided to give you a chance to fight for your life, Mr. Shepherd!"

Cole glanced back at the little man. "That's ridiculous! I'm not going to—" But he caught a movement out of the corner of his eye and turned to see the partisan completing a horizontal backswing. He ducked, hearing the sleek blade cut the air, feeling it actually lift the hairs on the top of his head.

"Whoa! Damn!" Cole scrambled to grab up the sword. Jumping back to his feet, he thrust the sword up two-handed just in time to deflect another blow. The shock of it shot down his left arm, jarring the healing bullet wound in that shoulder.

He heard Gwin call out behind him, but he dared not look back. The man called Ringo had not disengaged. He continued to apply ever-increasing pressure, the head of his weapon bearing down against the uplifted broadside of Cole's sword. One slip and the gleaming blade of that partisan would bury itself in Cole's skull.

The man was built like a grizzly and quite possibly as strong. It took every ounce of Cole's strength, fueled by a healthy dose of raw fear, to stave him off. Finally, after five or more agonizing seconds of stalemate, Cole knew he couldn't hold out much longer. He lunged to the left, angling his sword blade down and to the right at the same time. With a nerve-racking scraping of metal on metal, the partisan's blade turned harmlessly aside on the downswing.

Ringo merely smiled as he moved to his right, clearly intending to angle in for another deadly swipe. Cole sidestepped to his left, mirroring his adversary's movements. They circled warily, Cole sweating, struggling to gain a surer hold on his weapon.

The giant swung again, and Cole raised his sword to meet the descending blow with a loud clang. This time his adversary immediately disengaged, drawing his blade back. They circled, Cole concentrating, watching for an opening. When he saw one, he surged forward, slicing the air neatly but missing his target as the big man sidestepped and retaliated, swinging in from the left.

Cole just managed to block that blow, then another, then another, each more brutal than the last. This contest was likely to boil down to the man with the most staying power, and if that proved to be true, Cole, with his injured shoulder and disadvantage in size and strength, was going to be the loser.

Forced into retreat, Cole backed up a few more steps. He was losing ground, drawing nearer to the opposite wall, and that was bad. Once his back was to the wall, there would be nowhere else to go.

Gwin was horrified by the barbaric spectacle taking place before her. Forgetting the gun Barnes had trained on her, she moved forward. "What's he doing? Stop this!" she cried, just as she felt Sidney's hands grasp both of her arms from behind.

Panicked, Gwin twisted around to look up at Sidney's grim face. "Tell him to stop!"

"He doesn't take his orders from me."

Gwin turned back to the lopsided confrontation and was glad to see that Cole had at least gained a solid footing, enabling him to strike back at Mr. Ringo.

She strained against Sidney's hold, not knowing or

caring what she could actually do to help if she managed to break away. "What do you want? I'll do anything! Just get him to stop!"

She heard Sidney address Barnes from behind her. "This has gone far enough, Jasper. Put an end to it."

"I'm afraid it's out of my hands, Sidney. I've seen Mr. Ringo like this before. He won't stop until he's finished."

Gwin looked over at Barnes, full of rage. He could stop the big man if he wanted to, if he even cared to try, which it was evident that he did not. He was chomping on that infernal cigar, grinning, still holding the revolver trained on her even as he kept one avid eye on the brutal contest playing out in the foyer before them. He was enjoying himself!

Gwin looked around, trying to quell her rising hysteria, forcing herself to think. The butler appeared essentially harmless. He was moving slowly, steadily back toward the door of the study, looking nervous as a spooked cat. It appeared to Gwin that he might actually bolt at any moment. No, it was Barnes that was the problem; Barnes and that cursed gun.

Her gaze slid over to the fireplace, where a set of polished brass utensils gleamed: a brush, a dustpan, a sharp-ended poker, and a pair of andirons. The poker or the andirons would do if only Barnes's attention could be diverted. She had no option now but to wait for an opportunity.

At the first sounds of weapons colliding, Arthur had not been able to resist cracking open the door to the library to peer out into the entrance foyer. What he saw caused his stomach to clench into a knot of pure horror. It was the giant—the face of the man in his nightmares, the face of the man who had killed Silas and Clell and the others. The vivid terror of that night—much of which his mind had mercifully repressed until now—swept over him. For a moment, he couldn't hear anything but shotgun blasts and screams, *see* anything but that hard-angled, cruel, cold face. The grating, metallic clash of weapons jarred his senses, snapping him back to the present.

His vision cleared. He looked down at his hands to discover they were trembling. *Do something this time!* his thinking brain screamed. *Do something!* He struggled to swallow his fear, and slowly, soundlessly, he inched the library door open just a little bit wider, just enough for him to slip through sideways and out into the hallway. None of the others noticed as he dropped into a crouch and began to move forward.

The wall was at Cole's back. Desperate, he thrust with the sword, but Ringo parried easily. Cole's heart sank as his blade snapped in two against the sharp edge of the partisan.

Time stopped. The two combatants stared at each other. Then the big man smiled. Cole dropped the useless haft of his sword and ducked sideways on the partisan's upswing. The blade came whistling down, cutting the air to bury its gleaming silver head in the wall paneling next to Cole's ear.

With a blaring curse of frustration, Ringo yanked it

back and forth savagely, trying to free it. Cole took advantage of this diversion to dash toward the perpendicular staircase wall. Weaponless, he had no chance of surviving. A jeweled dagger hung just within reach.

Gwin let out a horrified scream as Cole missed certain death by mere inches. Despite her best efforts, she was losing control. She strained against Sidney's renewed hold on her. He was squeezing her shoulders so hard, there would be bruises. "Make him stop! I'll do anything! Please! Just end this!"

Sidney jerked her around to face him, his voice sharp and imperative. "Gwin! Get ahold of yourself! *Now!*" And his final word—*now!*—ground out between clenched teeth, finally caught her attention. She stopped struggling and gaped up at him.

He was right. Becoming hysterical wasn't going to help her or Cole out of this. She tried to calm herself. Maybe then Sidney would release her and Barnes would stop watching her so closely. Maybe then she could try to go for the poker. It was her only hope.

Seeming to read her mind, Sidney set her back away from him and let go of her. "Stay calm," he said pointedly. Then he reached up to swipe at his chin with the knuckles of his right hand before stepping back and folding his arms stiffly across his chest.

Gwin questioned her own eyesight. In her highly agitated state of mind, had she imagined it or had he just signaled her? Barnes still watched them both, and so Gwin couldn't even hope for any repetition or clarification. Did Sidney mean to help them, after all? And would he be able to act in time to save Cole's life?

One more second and he would have had it.

Cole actually reached the haft of the jeweled dagger but hadn't yet gotten a good grip on it before he was propelled face-first into the wall by a bone-jarring force from behind.

One massive hand was at his back, pushing him into the wall; the other was tightening around his arm just above his elbow. Ringo yanked downward, causing Cole's limp fingers to slip from the haft of the dagger. The weapon was sent soaring, end over end, through the air.

Arthur crouched down low beside one of the suits of armor. He watched, tears of frustration and white-hot rage stinging his eyes. Cole was losing. But what could Arthur do? He had no gun, and he knew the weapons on the wall above him were hopelessly out of reach.

He gritted his teeth, tears now spilling down his cheeks. He had to do something. Even if it came down to running out there and throwing himself at that giant. Because this time he wasn't going to stand by and just watch it happen. He thought he would rather die than do that.

Arthur's hands clenched into white-knuckled fists as he watched that giant beating down on Cole . . . that giant as big as Goliath himself. And that's when he thought of it.

* * *

Desperate, Gwin glanced at the fireplace, preparing to move when she heard Arthur. For a split second, she froze, thinking she couldn't have heard right. Her brother wasn't even here. He couldn't be here! But when she turned her head, she saw him stepping out boldly from behind an armored figure in the hallway. He planted both feet and raised his slingshot.

"You son of a bitch! You killed Silas!"

Gwin's mouth dropped open in shock, but otherwise, she had no time to react. The sling snapped, and now, as always, Arthur didn't miss. Ringo jerked and abruptly released his hold on Cole. One hand shot up to the back of his head. Gwin thought Arthur's missile hadn't only surprised him but had also taken a nice-sized chunk of scalp along with it.

Cole, she saw with palpable relief, was still on his feet—not moving much—but on his feet. Alive!

It was only natural for Ringo to turn his head in the direction of this new attack. Only natural, but it was a mistake. Arthur had wasted no time in reloading. He was already stretching the sling back as the big man turned his head. His timing was perfect. When he let it fly this time, Gwin knew even before he released where he was aiming.

Ringo let out an animal-like howl as both hands flew up too late to protect his eyes. He staggered back into the banister of the staircase, which collapsed like a row of toothpicks beneath him. Blood from his ruined eye soaked his hands as he moaned amid the wreckage.

Barnes raised his revolver, aiming for Arthur's stalwart little figure across the great hall.

Gwin screamed, *"NO!"*

A shot rang out, echoing off the walls. Gwin whirled, expecting to see Arthur down and bleeding, but he still stood on two feet, his tousled head turned in their direction, his mouth dropped open in an expression of surprise. *But he was all right!*

Gwin looked back at Barnes, who stood frozen as Lot's wife, his pudgy arm still extended, the gun still cocked, *unfired.* His eyes were wide and bulbous in their sockets. And it was only then that she realized why. His cigar, the one he had been clenching in his teeth, looked as if it had literally exploded. A thin, dying curl of smoke rose from its tattered remains.

Except for the moaning Ringo, all movement in the cavernous foyer had come to a dead standstill. Sidney's voice broke the silence. "I think, Jasper, that things have gone far enough."

Gwin turned to see that her father had a long-barreled Colt revolver trained quite calmly on his shocked colleague.

He raised an eyebrow at her. "Don't look so surprised, my dear. Who did you think taught your mother that trick?"

25

Justice was swift, once the wheels got turning. Alphonse Ringo's trial was over, and the prosecution was in the process of concluding its damning case against Jasper Barnes. Gwin had already testified, Arthur was in there now, and Cole was scheduled to appear next.

Gwin and Cole sat alone in the empty hallway just outside the sequestered courtroom. Thanks to the judge's order limiting public seating and stipulating that only one reporter from each newspaper be allowed access to this section of the Hall of Justice, it was quiet and deserted out here while court was in session.

Ever since Phineas Taylor's name had hit the papers, the trials of his cohorts had turned into a public circus. Ringo and Barnes had not been the only ones to fall. Thanks to Sidney Pierce's decision to cooperate with the authorities, four members of the police department were scheduled to come to trial for their parts in concocting the false charges against Ricardo Cortez. In addition, there were rumors to the effect that a few of San Francisco's most influential citizens would be criminally implicated by Sidney's testimony. One well-known socialite, a wealthy banker, had already disappeared mysteriously in the night. The most popular theory was that he had packed his carpetbags and stolen off to South America. Whatever the truth of the matter was, it was clear that the secret group known as the Round Table was in the process of disintegrating.

Cole shifted his position on the hard wooden bench and glanced over at Gwin, breaking the silence that had fallen over them. "Glad it's almost over?"

Gwin let out a weary sigh. "Yes. Ohhhhh, yes."

Cole stole a look at the closed double doors of the courtroom. "I hope Arthur's doing all right in there."

"If he got through Ringo's trial, he can get through anything. He's a tough kid."

"That he is." Cole winced visibly as he changed position on the uncomfortable bench. His right arm—splinted and bandaged—was confined by a sling. He had also suffered a cracked rib and a fractured nose from his near-fatal confrontation with Alphonse Ringo. He had spent a few days recuperating in the hospital, and, though Gwin would have given anything for him not to have suffered those injuries, her time spent visiting with him in the hospital had been the most precious hours they'd had together since all of this had happened.

They had talked a lot; she about her childhood, he about his. She had learned about his late father, a peace officer in a small Kansas town. She had learned about his mother—what little he knew of her—the woman who had died giving birth to him. This story had brought tears to Gwin's eyes. How tragic that his mother had not lived to see what a fine young man her son had grown to become. How tragic that, after his father's death, Cole should now be left alone in the world.

It had not escaped Gwin that most of their talk had been of the past, not of the future. This was because they had no real future, had they? Not together, anyway. This thought never failed to bring an unbearable heaviness to Gwin's heart.

Only once during his hospital stay had Cole delicately steered the conversation onto the subject of their relationship. "Uh, about what's happened between us, Gwin. There could be certain consequences."

Gwin, who was seated on a chair by his bed, raised her head cautiously. "Consequences?" she echoed, although she knew very well what he was getting at. He was worried that she might be carrying his child. The ensuing silence within that tiny hospital room soon grew stifling.

"Are you pregnant?" He tried his best to look her in the eye even as she was doing her best to avoid him.

"I . . . I don't know," she stammered, her eyes glued to the hospital floor. And she hadn't known. Not then.

"You'd tell me, wouldn't you, Gwin? You wouldn't try to—" He cleared his throat awkwardly. "Promise you'll tell me if—"

"Yes. Of course," she answered abruptly, wanting only to end the conversation. And she had gotten her wish. At that moment, one of the nurses, a cheerful, middle-aged nun, had swept into the room brandishing a gleaming metal lunch tray.

For the last few days, Gwin had felt the familiar stirrings of her body's monthly cycle, and this morning, she had learned for certain that Cole had not given her a child. Part of her knew that this was for the best. If she had been pregnant, she knew that Cole would have offered to marry her.

It wasn't that she didn't want marriage. She was hopelessly in love with Cole Shepherd. This was a fact she could no longer ignore or rationalize away. She didn't regret for one moment the decision she had made in that hotel room in Virginia City, and she would have given almost anything to spend the rest of her life in his arms at night. *Almost* anything. She wouldn't sacrifice her self-respect. Neither would she expect Cole to sacrifice a chance for real happiness with a woman he could truly love. No. If he had offered to marry her, Gwin knew that it would have been done out of his deeply ingrained sense of honor, not out of love. And Gwin knew from bitter experience—Silas and Emmaline's—that it took more than just one person's love to make a true marriage.

She tried to ignore these depressing thoughts as she cast an anxious glance at the courtroom doors. "I hope that defense lawyer isn't giving Arthur a hard time."

"Oh, I rather think it's the other way around," Cole replied. "You said it yourself. He's a tough kid. I sure wouldn't want to tangle with him. Especially if he's still got Excalibur in his pocket."

"He *always* has Excalibur in his pocket," Gwin answered as her gaze shifted to linger on Cole's handsome face. The swelling of his broken nose had gone down, but there were still some bruises to testify to the punishment he had suffered. It was rather amazing that not even a broken nose could detract much from his wholesome good looks.

The door to the courtroom swung open and Arthur emerged under the arm of a burly bailiff. After testifying at Ringo's trial, Arthur had come out looking pale and shaken, and perhaps that was what Gwin was expecting to see this time as she jumped to her feet. This time, however, he was standing tall and proud in his brand-new suit of clothes. His hair was still combed back neatly from his forehead, and there was a certain glint in his eye, a glint of confidence. He looked older to her in that moment than he ever had before, and she caught just a fleeting glimpse of what Arthur would look like as a young man. She suddenly realized that her little brother wasn't so little anymore.

"Mr. Shepherd?" The bailiff motioned for Cole to enter the courtroom, and Cole complied by rising to his feet. He had removed his coat earlier due to the summer heat, and he reached down now to snatch it up from the arm of the bench.

Gwin held it for him as he carefully slipped his left arm into the sleeve. She draped the other sleeve over his right shoulder. "There," she said, forcing herself to smile up at him encouragingly.

"Thanks, Nurse Pierce." He winked and turned to the waiting bailiff. "This shouldn't take long, but if you want to go on back to the hotel awhile, I can meet you later."

"All right," Gwin said, shifting her attention to Arthur, who now stood by her side.

"Good luck, Cole," Arthur offered before the courtroom door closed again. He looked up at Gwin. "Easy as pie," he said, apparently reading the concern on her face.

Gwin patted his shoulder, relieved and proud that he was trying to take all of this in stride. He *was* a tough kid. "Well," she sighed, "why don't we take Cole's advice and head back to the hotel?" She stopped, her eye catching on a piece of paper at their feet. "What's this?"

She bent to retrieve it and glimpsed the words *Western Union Telegraph Company* printed across the top. "Oh," she mumbled, frowning. "It must have fallen out of Cole's pocket." Then something else caught her eye. Without even meaning to, she had glanced at the scrawled words on the message, and there, jumping out at her like a jack-in-the-box, was her own name.

"What is it?" Arthur tried to squint at the paper.

Gwin jerked her hand up, snatching the communication away from Arthur's inquisitive eyes. "It's nothing! Just a telegram. It must have fallen from Cole's coat pocket. Why don't you go on ahead outside and wait for me? I'll be there in a minute."

"What does it say?"

"I don't know what it says, and it's none of our business anyway! Now, go wait for me outside, will you?"

"You're going to read that telegram, aren't you?"

"No, I am *not* going to read the telegram! I am going to visit the convenience room, if you must know."

Arthur rolled his eyes. "The convenience room? How *conveeeenient!*"

"Oh, go on!" Gwin made a shooshing motion with one hand.

Arthur moved away from her reluctantly, throwing a suspicious glance over his shoulder before he finally pulled open the heavy door at the end of the hall, disappearing into the stairwell.

Gwin stood immobile for a moment, her eyes glued to the spot where her brother had vanished. She half-expected his head to come popping back out again, but, after a few seconds, she convinced herself he was really gone.

She fingered the crumpled telegram. It really *was* none of her business. But her name was there, and she hadn't really meant to see it.

Gwin wrestled with herself. A month ago she wouldn't have thought anything of it—sneaking a peek at private correspondence. She wouldn't have felt this nagging, admonishing voice whispering in the back of her head. *Fold it up, put it away. It's none of your business.*

But she had seen her name.

Hurriedly, Gwin unfolded the telegram and scanned the scrawled message.

Cole,
   Under the circumstances, I am happy to grant your request for an advance in salary. Also, the

other arrangements you requested have been made. I have personally contacted the marshal in Garden City, and he will be awaiting your arrival with Miss Pierce. You may take great pride in a job well done. We look forward to your return to the home office.

A. Pinkerton

Her hands were trembling. She stared at the words, reading them over and over again, her mind at first refusing to grasp their meaning. *The arrangements you requested . . . the marshal in Garden City . . . awaiting your arrival with Miss Pierce.*

But there was no room for misunderstanding. Cole had requested that arrangements be made for her return to Garden City, the town where she was still wanted on a horse-stealing charge. But why? Why would he betray her like this?

Cole's own words now came spilling back into her mind, echoing, jeering, until she thought she could no longer bear it. *"What I do, Miss Pierce, is my job. I do my job, that's all."* And part of that job was turning in lawbreakers, wasn't it? It was unbelievable, but there it was, in black and white.

Tears welled in her eyes, causing the words on the telegram to blur into an unintelligible mass of squiggles. What had she expected? Hadn't she been telling herself for days now, *weeks* now, that she and Cole Shepherd had no future together? Hadn't she learned to accept that? Why did this come as such a heart-wrenching surprise? Why did it hurt so much?

"I've been such a fool," she whispered, still staring at the quivering paper in her hands. "Such a fool."

But, in her mind's eye, she saw Cole's face, his heart-melting smile. She remembered the way he had touched her when they made love and the way they had opened their souls to one another in that hospital room. There was still a part of her that couldn't fathom what she was seeing with her own eyes. There was still a part of her that couldn't believe Cole could be so unfeeling, so hardhearted, but she was not inclined to recognize that part of herself anymore. No. Never, never again.

At the sound of approaching footsteps, she hurriedly turned her back to the newcomers, stuffing the telegram down deep into her skirt pocket.

When she turned around again, she saw who was approaching. It was Sidney, followed closely by a uniformed policeman. His handsome face broke into a genuine smile upon seeing her. Gwin moved to smooth her hair and adjust her hat, empty movements designed more to clear her head and gather her composure than to neaten her appearance.

She had declined his initial offer to stay at his home, mostly because she was afraid Arthur might suffer nightmares after the horrible scene that had taken place in the entrance foyer. Sidney had then insisted upon putting them up at the luxurious Palace Hotel, and, upon seeing Arthur's face light up at the suggestion, Gwin had not had the heart to say no.

Gwin hadn't seen much of Sidney this past week. She had been too tied up with her own role in the trials that were taking place, but now she knew she would be leaving town. Very, very soon. And this might be her last chance to speak with him.

Sidney and the uniformed officer approached at a casual pace, their footfalls echoing on the hardwood floors of the deserted hall. "You look like you've had a trying day, my dear," Sidney commented when he reached her side.

Gwin noticed that his hands were clasped behind his back. As he turned to look back at the youthful policeman who accompanied him, she realized, with a sudden jolt, the reason for this. "Now that we've arrived, do you think we could dispense with these infernal contraptions?" he asked, motioning downward with an inclination of his head.

Gwin watched, confused, as the officer removed the handcuffs that confined Sidney's wrists.

Sidney stretched his arms and flexed his wrists. "Much better! Much better!"

"They've arrested you?" Gwin asked, shocked.

"Well, it seems there have been some irregularities discovered in my business accounts, and—"

"But I thought they'd agreed not to press any charges against you in exchange for your testimony!"

"Well, I won't bore you with the details. Suffice it to say, there are some people in high places who have seen to it I won't walk away a free man. I've now been offered the guarantee of a lighter sentence in exchange for my testimony. It's a deal I'm hard-pressed to decline at the moment."

"I don't understand. People in high places?"

Sidney addressed the officer. "Would you mind

giving me and my daughter a moment of privacy, Officer O'Brien?"

"Well, I'm not really supposed to leave you out of my sight, Mr. Taylor."

"Oh, of course not! Wouldn't expect you to! But they never said anything about out of *earshot*, did they, Jim?" Sidney stopped and rested one hand on the youthful officer's shoulder. "May I call you Jim? I feel that we've come to know each other rather well since this morning."

"Well, I, uh, suppose."

"Is it too much to ask, Jim? A moment alone with my lovely daughter? I'm a doomed man, and we both know it. Is it too much to ask?"

"Well, I guess it's all right, just for a minute or two," Officer O'Brien said grudgingly. "But I'll be right over here."

"Bless you, my good man!" Sidney beamed as the young officer moved to stand by the courtroom door with his arms folded.

Gwin pressed on as if they had never been interrupted. "What are you talking about? People in high places? I thought your testimony was to bring these people down for good!"

"Even my knowledge of the men who constituted the Round Table was limited. I knew of their activities, but I only met a small portion of the group."

"You mean, there are still some of them out there? *Free*?"

"No doubt."

Incredulous, Gwin studied Sidney Pierce's impassive expression. "Wait a minute. You knew all along that there were more of them, and you still agreed to testify against the others?"

Sidney shrugged. "Perhaps it's just my way of stirring up the pot."

"Just what kind of prison sentence can you expect for stirring up this pot?"

Sidney chuckled at his newfound daughter's indignant tone. "Three years in San Quentin, or so they tell me."

"But it won't be safe for you there! Those men you testified against will—"

"No doubt try to have me killed," Sidney finished quite matter-of-factly. "I would imagine there's quite a long line forming by now."

"But, it's not fair," she said.

"Fair? Life is never fair, is it? But we make our own odds. Didn't Silas ever teach you that?"

Gwin could only shake her head. "It must have been so hard for you to give it up, all that power, all that wealth. It must have taken you years to climb that ladder." Gwin narrowed her eyes. "Even if it *was* a slightly crooked ladder, as I suspect."

"Ah, well, there are ladders and then there are ladders," Sidney said, flicking a piece of lint from the lapel of his suit coat. "I haven't given up all that much, really."

"I will never understand you," Gwin said. "Not for as long as I live."

"And I hope that will be for a very very long time." He smiled graciously. "You will be leaving soon, I gather?"

"Yes. Very soon."

"Where will you be going?"

She thought about this. Where would she go? She hadn't had time to think about that yet. "I'm not sure," she answered hesitantly, "Kansas City, maybe."

"I rather hoped that would be your choice. Kansas City, I mean. When you return to your hotel, you will find an envelope waiting for you at the front desk."

"An envelope?"

"In it you will find the name of a bank in Kansas City, the number of an account, and a safety deposit box key. They have been changed over to your name."

"Why?"

"Because, Gwin, I happen to have an account in Kansas City, and I truly doubt I'll be needing it where I'm going. Perhaps you can find some use for it."

Gwin placed a hand on one hip. "Now, why would you have a bank account in Kansas City?"

"If he's smart, a trapeze artist never practices without a net. A bank robber will always make sure he has his horse saddled and ready, and our kind—"

"Always keeps one foot close to the door," Gwin finished flatly.

Sidney lowered his voice. "Precisely, my dear. I always thought it prudent to have accounts in a variety of places: Philadelphia, New York, London, Honduras, or . . ." He slipped her a secret smile. "Well, you get the idea."

"Yes, but it's not going to help you now, is it?"

He cocked his head to one side. "Well, one never knows what the future holds, does one?"

Oh, how true, Gwin thought. "Perhaps you should keep your money."

"Don't worry about me. I'll hardly be destitute."

"Well, I don't know."

"Is there a problem?"

Gwin shook her head. "I just . . . I never wanted your money, and I . . ."

"Speak. We haven't much time."

Gwin let out a frustrated breath and blurted, "Well, I can't help wondering how you got it."

"Got what?" Sidney asked, perplexed.

"All that money!" she snapped, growing irritated without even quite knowing why. "I mean, I don't want any part of dirty money or anything like that, and—"

"Dirty money?" Sidney echoed, appearing genuinely baffled. "Why, I don't believe I've ever heard the expression. Could this be the rumblings of a conscience?"

Insulted, Gwin opened her mouth to retort, then promptly closed it again. So, what was so bad about having a conscience?

"Interesting," Sidney said, "a conscience. I wonder wherever in the world you acquired such a thing?"

Gwin studied his face. He was her father, this man. She was beginning to feel a certain sort of affection for him, but perhaps that was because of gestures and expressions that reminded her of Silas. What she had told Sidney was true. She didn't understand him, and she was fairly sure she never would, but she did know one thing: In the end, he had chosen, at great cost to himself, to save their lives.

Officer O'Brien cleared his throat. "I think that's enough time, Mr. Taylor."

"Please. Call me Sidney."

Gwin offered Sidney her right hand. "Well, goodbye, then."

He reached out, but instead of shaking her hand, he swept it up in his own and bent to kiss it. When he straightened, he gave her a dastardly wink. "Nothing worse than some gifted stock speculation, my dear. Some people *would* call that dirty money."

Then, without another word, he turned and smiled at his uniformed guardian. "Shall we go join the party?"

Officer O'Brien grimaced at the gallows humor. "This way, Mr., uh, Sidney."

Gwin watched her father disappear into the courtroom. As the doors swung closed behind him, her throat tightened, and she found herself blinking back a swell of tears. This was because, in her heart, she knew she would never see him again.

26

Cole awoke the next morning, early as usual. He stretched and turned over, acutely aware that he was sleeping single in a roomy double bed. He was growing tired of sleeping alone; of *being* alone. Funny, he hadn't ever thought much about that until lately.

He had received an answer to his last telegram yesterday from Allan Pinkerton himself. In it, Mr. Pinkerton had beckoned him back to Chicago, intimating that a plum assignment would be waiting. Cole should have been ecstatic at the thought of returning home to resume his career, a career that now seemed to hold all the promise he had ever dreamed of, but upon actually reading the words, he had felt curiously unmoved.

As he climbed out of bed, careful not to jostle his healing arm, he squinted at the clock on the dresser.

Six-thirty. He didn't have to meet Gwin and Arthur for breakfast until eight. Nevertheless, he knew it would be useless for him to try to go back to sleep. He crossed the plush hotel room to a washstand, poured some clean water in the basin, and absently gathered together his toothbrush and a straight-edge razor.

He thought about his time in the hospital. Gwin had visited every day. In fact, she had spent about as much time there as the nurses and doctors had permitted.

As Cole applied the shaving soap to his face, he recalled a particularly revealing conversation having to do with Arthur's future. Gwin had jumped from her seat to pace the small room. "I want to settle down and live in one place. I want Arthur to go to school and learn about all the things Silas and I could never teach him. I want him to go to college and hold the world in the palm of his hand."

"And you," Cole interjected gently, unable to take his eyes from her glowing face. "What is it you want for yourself?"

"Myself?"

"If you could have anything in the world, Gwin, what would it be?"

"Well, I don't know." She smiled wistfully and turned her back to look out the window. "Well, I guess I wish that I could wipe the slate clean and start all over, but . . ."

"But what?"

"Well, that's impossible, isn't it?" she asked in a subdued voice. "Undoing the past? Starting over?"

"I don't know," he answered thoughtfully.

A TOUCH OF CAMELOT 373

Later that night, in the darkened hospital room, he had remained awake for a long time thinking. Maybe it wasn't impossible to undo the past. Maybe it wasn't impossible to wipe the slate clean.

The next morning, he had enlisted the aid of one of the nurses to get a telegram off to Fritz in Chicago. The Pinkerton Agency wasn't all-powerful, but its formidable reputation was influential in many circles of law enforcement—especially in the Midwest.

Cole had received an encouraging reply from Fritz, who had been at work on his request. And in yesterday's telegram, Mr. Pinkerton himself had assured Cole that everything was taken care of. All that was left to do was to sit Gwin down and tell her the good news, and he had intended to do just that, but last night had not been the right time.

She had seemed distracted by something all through dinner. He supposed it was natural for her to be feeling a little let down now that it was all over. The trials had passed quickly, but not without exacting an emotional toll on both Gwin and Arthur.

No, last night had not been the time to bring up the subject. Perhaps this morning would prove different. Cole cursed as he finished shaving, nicking himself repeatedly in the process. He was learning to become proficient with his left hand at a number of tasks. Unfortunately, shaving wasn't one of them.

He made short work of dressing and took the elevator down to the hotel lobby. Normally, the Palace Hotel would have been outside of his budget, but it was Sidney Pierce who footed the bill for all this extravagance. Cole still wasn't sure what to make of the man. His natural inclination was to classify him with the rest of the villains he had chosen to associate with, but there was something different about Sidney, something Cole couldn't quite pin down. One thing he knew for sure, though; he wouldn't be alive today if Sidney hadn't made the decision to draw his gun when he did. That decision, belated as it might have been, was a hard detail to overlook. And if there was one thing Cole had learned from his association with Gwin, it was that you couldn't judge a book by its cover.

Cole crossed the expansive lobby to the front desk, noting the time on a grandfather clock in passing. Seven. He still had an hour until he had to meet Gwin and Arthur for breakfast. He had been turning over in his mind the problem of just how to bring up the subject of Garden City with Gwin, and now he thought maybe he had an idea.

"Excuse me?" he motioned for one of the clerks.

"Yes, Mr. Shepherd?" A balding, middle-aged man with a thin black mustache approached him from behind the desk.

"You wouldn't happen to know where I could get some fresh flowers at this time of the morning, would you?"

The clerk gave him a knowing look. "Would you be speaking of a fresh bouquet for a certain young lady, perhaps?"

"Is it that obvious?"

The clerk smiled. "I would suggest you try one of the pushcart vendors along Kearney Street. There's one in particular, a man named Mr. Winfrey, who sells the most delightful summer bouquets."

"That sounds perfect." Cole turned to leave, then stopped. "Oh, maybe I should leave a message for Miss Pierce in case I'm late getting back."

"A message? For Miss Pierce?"

Cole read something in the man's expression that caused his soaring spirits to fall. "Is something wrong?"

"That's Miss Guinevere Pierce, correct? The pretty one with the young brother?"

"Yes, that's the one. Is there something the matter?"

"Well, she's gone, sir."

Cole was stunned. "Gone?"

"Yes. She and her brother checked out this morning."

"They checked out?" Cole repeated, his voice rising. "They couldn't have checked out! I was supposed to meet them here for breakfast in another hour!"

"I'm sorry, Mr. Shepherd, but I'm quite certain they're gone. They both had their bags, and I accepted their keys myself. Over an hour ago now, I would think."

Cole felt like he had just been sucker-punched in the gut. "D-did she leave any message?" he managed, swallowing hard.

"No message. I am *sorry*, Mr. Shepherd."

Jilted. Twice now, Cole reminded himself morosely. But why? Why would she pack up and leave without saying a word? Why, after all they had been through together, would she leave him like this? Why run? Why *now?*

"Mr. Shepherd?"

Cole looked up miserably. "Yes?"

"She did say one thing."

"What was that?"

"She asked when the first ferry was scheduled to depart for Oakland."

The Oakland train station was bustling. Gwin and Arthur stood in line to board behind a robust, ruddy-faced gentleman with muttonchop whiskers. Going home, Gwin thought. Home. Kansas City for starters. Then? It was hard to think about where she wanted to go when all she could think about was what she was leaving behind.

Gwin and Arthur boarded, soon locating an empty compartment near the back of one of the Silver Palace sleeping cars. Gwin slid their bags beneath the table separating their seats and settled in with a tired sigh. She was trying her best to remain cheerful for Arthur's sake, but it wasn't easy. At least he had finally stopped asking her about Cole, about why they hadn't waited to tell him goodbye. Gwin didn't yet feel up to disillusioning him with the ugly truth.

Arthur wore a new set of clothes, a clean white linen shirt with brown trousers. He had even combed his hair this morning. Gwin was impressed by the fact that he had done all this without her having to nag him about it.

"Hey, Gwinnie! Look!"

Gwin turned her head and immediately saw what had caught her brother's eye. The gentleman seated with his back to her was reading the paper. Over his shoulder, she could easily make out a double column heading on this morning's *Chronicle*.

Gwin's mouth dropped open in astonishment. She could hardly believe her eyes. *Slick Sidney Slips the Knot!* And there, beneath it, was a lengthy article.

The gentleman, obviously sensing a lingering presence directly over his shoulder, lowered the newspaper and craned his neck around, glowering. "Is there something I can help you with, young lady?"

"No."

"Harumph!" The man turned back around, snapped the paper huffily, and raised it again to pick up where he'd left off.

Not in the least bit discouraged, Gwin continued to read: "Only hours after delivering incriminating testimony . . ."

The man whipped his head around. His voice was stinging. "Am I inconveniencing you, madam?"

"No, not at all," Gwin returned politely, although she thought she *was* starting to get a crick in her neck.

"Is there something of particular interest to you, madam?"

"Well, actually . . ."

He held up the paper, offering it to her. "Perhaps you would like to peruse it at your leisure so that I could then read my newspaper in peace?"

Gwin snatched it up, flashing him her most charming smile. "Why, aren't you kind? Much obliged, sir!"

Before the man could change his mind, Gwin turned around in her seat and spread the newspaper out on the table between her and Arthur. Her nose was already buried in the article. "I can't believe it. I can't believe it," she mumbled.

Only hours after delivering incriminating testimony against ex-business partner Jasper Barnes, as well as a number of well-known San Francisco businessmen and members of the city police department, Sidney Pierce, better known as City Hall hopeful Phineas Taylor, escaped the custody of a none-too-alert police department yesterday evening when . . .

"Gee whillikins, Gwinnie," Arthur exclaimed, awestruck. "He got away."

"I'll be damned." Gwin shook her head.

"Attaboy, Sidney!" Arthur cheered, pounding the table. "They can't keep us Pierces down, can they?"

"I have a feeling he's gone for good this time, Arthur. I don't think we'll be hearing from him again."

"But at least he got away."

Gwin couldn't repress a smile. "He sure did, didn't he?"

She returned the paper to the grumbling gentleman behind her. It appeared that somehow—*how* even she couldn't imagine—Sidney had convinced the authorities that he needed to return to his home to retrieve evidence that was still hidden in one of his safes.

Escorted by three police officers, Sidney had arrived at his home only to be greeted in the foyer by a teary-eyed woman. After a heartrending homecoming scene, Gwin imagined Sidney might have taken the three officers aside. *"We're all men here, aren't we? I can speak frankly? Pete? Carl? Jim?"*

Yes, it could have gone like that. Sidney would have gestured in the heartbroken woman's direction.

"I'm a doomed man and we all know it. Can you blame me for wanting just one last precious hour alone with my lady love? Is it too much to ask?"

Yes, yes, they were all men. They would have understood. But they wouldn't have been stupid about it. One man would have been posted outside the bedchamber door while another watched the windows and the balcony from the courtyard below.

It had been well over an hour later that they had finally broken down the locked bedchamber door only to find the room deserted. Sidney and his mysterious lady love—now suspected to have been an infamous courtesan by the name of Jasmine Devereaux—had inexplicably vanished.

The police had practically torn the place apart in their search, soon discovering that the design of Sidney's house resembled a medieval castle in more than just outward appearance. The mansion was riddled with secret doors and winding passageways. *Safety nets and saddled horses.*

Gwin smiled to herself. She had to give Sidney credit. He was *good.*

Arthur was now separating the slats of the venetian blinds with two fingers, peering out the window at the observation deck that sided their sleeping coach. "Hey, no one's out there. Let's go out so we can feel the wind when the train starts up."

Gwin started to decline, then thought better of it. Why not? They were going to be cooped up on this train for four days. "All right, just as long as you let me catch some shut-eye later. Promise?"

"You bet! I'll be quiet as a mouse!"

That'll be the day, Gwin thought to herself as she followed her brother. She was dead on her feet after getting precious little sleep the night before. The words in that telegram had continued to play over and over in her mind. She wondered how long it would be until she was able to put the painful memory of Cole Shepherd behind her.

Once outside, Gwin was glad that her brother had suggested the move. The morning sun was warm and bright in the cloudless blue sky, and there was a cooling breeze coming in from the bay. She gripped the iron railing and leaned forward, closing her eyes and tilting her head up to let the sun bathe her face.

She thought about Sidney's bank account in Kansas City. She had no idea how much money was in it, but she had already decided to leave it untouched for now. It would be their nest egg, their *safety net,* available for an emergency should they need it. Otherwise, it seemed to Gwin that a sum of money like that should be saved for something important, something like Arthur's education.

She heard the outer door to the observation deck open behind her and felt a twinge of annoyance at the thought of some chatty passenger intruding on her solitude.

Arthur's awestruck voice. "Cole! Holy crow! What are you doing here?"

"A better question might be, what are you doing here? Just where in hell did you two think you were going?"

Gwin stiffened. Her breath caught and jammed in her throat. She thought she was through having to face him. Now, here he was, expecting what? To apologize? To take her into custody?

Gwin turned to face him. He looked as tall and gallant and princely as ever, but his expression was somber and there was a hint of anger smoldering behind those intelligent brown eyes.

"You should have known I'd catch up with you, Miss Pierce. I always do."

Gwin didn't answer.

They appraised each other, intimate strangers, neither of them moving or saying anything for a long moment. Cole broke the impasse. "Could you leave us alone for a minute, Arthur? I want to talk to your sister."

Arthur looked from one to the other like a saloon cowboy expecting two gamblers to push back from the table and fast-draw at any minute. "Well, uh, okay." He moved for the door. "I'll, uh, keep your seat warm, all right, Gwinnie?"

"Fine. This won't take long."

As soon as Arthur was gone, Cole spoke. "What the hell's the matter with you?"

"What's the matter with *me?*" Gwin asked, flabbergasted that he had the audacity to even ask her that question. All of her hurt and rage suddenly erupted like a boiling geyser. "Garden City! *That's* what's the matter with me!"

Cole shook his head, seemingly confused. "What's Garden City got to do with . . . ?" Then, a sudden understanding sparked in his eyes. "How did you even know about that?"

Gwin turned away, finding and grasping the railing

with trembling fingers. "It doesn't matter how I found out! What matters is that you were planning on turning me in!"

"Where did you get a stupid idea like that?"

Gwin tried to steady herself, furiously blinking back tears. "Well, you can just give it up, Cole Shepherd! I'm not going anywhere with you! Not now! Not ever! Maybe it's true I stole that broken-down old horse, but we were desperate! We'd run out of money, and the nearest town was miles away, and—"

"Gwin!"

She swung around to face him, forgetting her tears. "How could you do that to me? After . . . after we . . . ?"

Cole closed the distance between them in two strides, grabbing her arm at the wrist and holding it rigid between them. "If you'll just shut up a minute, I can explain!"

Gwin yanked back with all her might, but Cole didn't release her. Even with one arm in a sling, it was still no contest. "Oooooh! Let go of me!"

"Not until you've heard my side of it! Now, do you want to know the real reason I wanted to take you back to Garden City or would you prefer to go on believing I'm some kind of heartless monster?"

They both stood tense as two finely tuned piano strings, their eyes locked. Gwin didn't like him touching her, standing so close, so overpowering. It wasn't fair. It unsettled and frazzled emotions that weren't setting on such firm foundations to begin with.

Her voice turned coldly sarcastic. "So, what are you going to do with me this time, Cole? Wrestle me to the deck? Handcuff me to the rail? Shackle me to the cowcatcher?"

"None of those suggestions strike me as bad ideas at the moment."

"Fine. Say your piece."

"Do you remember telling me that if you could have one wish in the world, it would be to wipe the slate clean and start all over? You remember that, Gwin?"

"What are you talking about?"

"In the hospital. You told me you'd give just about anything to be able to wipe the slate clean."

Gwin tried to recall the conversation he was referring to.

"Well, I took you at your word," Cole continued. "I sent a telegram to Fritz at the Agency asking him to look into the charges that were still pending against you in Garden City."

"The horse-stealing charges?"

Cole shook her wrist fiercely, then flung it down, disgusted. "Yes! The horse-stealing charges! What else? And do you know what he found?"

Gwin massaged her wrist, starting to get the feeling that perhaps she had jumped to a hasty conclusion. "No, what did he find?"

"He found out that the fellow you stole that old roan from was a horse trader by the name of Simpson."

Gwin wrinkled her nose. "No wonder he had so many horses tethered to the back of his wagon."

"I always knew you were a smart girl."

"But I still don't understand what that has to do with—"

"Have you ever met an honest horse trader?"

"Well, no."

"Simpson is no exception. Turns out half the county can't stand the man, including the marshal. As far as he's concerned, if you show up to face charges and agree to pay restitution to smooth out this Simpson fellow's ruffled feathers, he's willing to drop the charges."

"Oh." Gwin focused on the brown lapels of Cole's alpaca coat. She felt drained, utterly totally drained. And stupid. Oh, so very stupid. "I don't know what to say."

His tone was dry. "Well, I certainly hope someone's keeping track of this momentous event for the history books."

She looked up at Cole. He wasn't angry anymore, but she read something in his eyes that made her feel even worse—wounded accusation.

"I'm sorry," she mumbled. "I guess I'm going to Garden City."

"I guess you are."

"I'll get a job, and—"

"You don't need to get a job. I have the money."

"What money?"

Cole patted his coat pocket. "Two weeks' advance salary. Right here. That should about cover it, I think."

"But what are you going to live on?"

"I've got some saved. Enough to get by."

"No, no, I can't let you do that."

"Yes, you can."

"No, I can get a job, and—"

Cole let out an exasperated sigh. "No job."

Gwin stared up at him, feeling tears starting to well up again. She wondered when it was she had turned into such a weeping ninny. She thought it had been about the time that Cole Shepherd had entered her life. "But why?" she asked. "Why are you doing this?"

"You haven't figured that out by now?"

"Why do you want to do this for me when all I've ever done is make you miserable?"

"Because I . . . Ah, damn it!" Cole reached out with his good hand and wrapped it around the back of her neck, pulling her to him roughly as his mouth descended to take hers.

What began as a startled cry rapidly dissolved to a fading whimper of contentment as Gwin inevitably melted into his kiss. Her hands slid up over the lapels of his coat to encircle his neck. Gwin knew then that even if she could manage to run to all four corners of the earth and back again, she would never be able to stop loving this wonderful young man.

When he abruptly ended the kiss, Gwin was breathless, her heart pounding in her breast, her knees weak. She opened her eyes to find that he had pulled back only far enough to study her face. He still had not let go of her, and she felt his long fingers spread to idly massage her nape. "Come to Chicago with me."

Gwin's heart leapt. She wanted to cry out *yes!* She wanted to jump up and down with joy. She wanted to hug him tight and never let go. But something held her back.

It took her a moment to gather up the mettle to say it. "Is it because you're worried I might be expecting?"

He paused, seeming to try to read something in her eyes. "No. Unless . . ." He paused, his hand sliding from the back of her neck, releasing her only to rest one forefinger beneath her chin. "Are you?"

Gwin continued to look up at him, no longer caring that her eyes were probably red and puffy. "No," she whispered.

"Oh." Then an unexpected smile lit his face. "Well, that's okay. I reckon we'll get it right sooner or later."

Gwin blinked at him, taken aback by the sudden change in his demeanor. "W-what?"

Cole held her face in one hand, his thumb rubbing gently over the curve of her dampened cheek. "I'm tired of being alone."

Gwin gazed up into those familiar tawny brown eyes for a long moment, feeling herself falling for him—all over again. He let go of her, and she stepped back self-consciously, trying to collect herself as she raised a slightly unsteady hand to dry her cheeks. "So, you're tired of being alone. Does that mean you need a housekeeper?"

Cole reached into his pocket, pulled out a clean handkerchief and handed it to her with a sigh. "I already have a housekeeper, Miss Pierce."

"You need someone to wash your socks?"

"She already washes my socks."

"Does she cook for you, too?" Gwin asked, squaring her shoulders to meet his amused, sparkling gaze.

"Well, actually, I cook pretty well for myself."

"Hmmmmm," Gwin said. "Would it be your bed, then, that's empty, Mr. Shepherd? Don't tell me she warms your bed for you?"

"No, she doesn't. And now that you mention it—"

"Well, perhaps we can arrange something,"

Gwin interjected, "but I have just one question for you."

"What's that?"

She tucked the handkerchief into her skirt pocket. "Why did you really come after me? If it wasn't out of some misplaced sense of honor, and if you already have a housekeeper and—well, let's face it, I assume there's no shortage of women in Chicago who would be willing to, uh, wash your socks—why me? You said it yourself, Shepherd. I'm a horse thief, a cardsharp, a—"

"It's very simple." Cole reached up to smooth a curl from her temple. "It's because I'm in love with you, Miss Pierce. I have been for quite some time now."

Gwin's heart swelled. Oh, how she had dreamed of him saying those words! Unable to contain herself, she slipped her arms around his waist beneath his coat, hugging him, feeling giddy. "Oh, for *days* now, I'll bet."

"Weeks," Cole corrected, reaching with his good arm to encircle her shoulders. "I think I was a goner from the moment you barreled into me on the street in Caldwell, Miss Pierce. As a matter of fact, if Clell Martin hadn't knocked me out in that cow pen in Abilene, I can't help wondering if—"

"It never stopped me, Shepherd." Gwin lifted her head to gaze up at him rapturously. "I've been dreaming of loving you for a very long time."

Cole cocked his dark head to one side, wearing a puzzled smile. "What?"

"Never mind," she replied. "Maybe I'll tell you about it someday."

The train's whistle cut the air, announcing the last call for their imminent departure.

Gwin rested her head back against his chest with a sigh. She felt as light as a sprig of dandelion fluff on a breezy summer day. "Chicago, hmmmm? You know, I read somewhere that your Agency employs lady detectives."

"Now, don't go getting any harebrained ideas."

"Why, we could even work as a team."

"You're going to give me nightmares, Gwin."

"But we *do* make a good team," she pressed.

"Yes, but I had *other* activities in mind."

Gwin sighed, willing to drop the subject. For *now*. "You asked me a question once, Shepherd, and I think I want you to ask me again."

"What question was that?"

Gwin closed her eyes, listening to the steady beat of his heart. It was a sound she wanted to listen to for a very, very long time. "You asked me if I believed in fairy tales. You asked me if I believed in once upon a time and princesses in tall towers and knights in shining armor and living happily ever after."

Cole laughed. "I remember. You said no."

"Well, I want to change my answer."

As the Central Pacific Express began to pull out of the Oakland station, Gwin smiled to herself. They were headed east, headed *home*. She had a feeling she was going to love Chicago.

AVAILABLE NOW

CIRCLE IN THE WATER by Susan Wiggs
When a beautiful gypsy thief crossed the path of King Henry VIII, the king saw a way to exact revenge against his enemy, Stephen de Lacey, by forcing the insolvent nobleman to marry the girl. Stephen wanted nothing to do with his gypsy bride, even when he realized Juliana was a princess from a far-off land. But when Juliana's past returned to threaten her, he realized he would risk everything to protect his wife. "Susan Wiggs creates fresh, unique and exciting tales that will win her a legion of fans."—Jayne Ann Krentz

DESTINED TO LOVE by Suzanne Elizabeth
In the tradition of her first time travel romance, *When Destiny Calls*, comes another humorous adventure. Josie Reed was a smart, gutsy, twentieth-century doctor who was tired of the futile quest for a husband before she reached thirty. Then she went on the strangest blind date of all—back to the Wild West of 1881 with a fearless, half-Apache, outlaw.

A TOUCH OF CAMELOT by Donna Grove
The winner of the 1993 Golden Heart Award for best historical romance. Guinevere Pierce had always dreamed that one day her own Sir Lancelot would rescue her from a life of medicine shows and phony tent revivals. But she never thought he would come in the guise of Cole Shepherd.

SUNFLOWER SKY by Samantha Harte
A poignant historical romance between an innocent small town girl and a wounded man bent on vengeance. Sunny Summerlin had no idea what she was getting into when she rented a room to an ill stranger named Bar Landry. But as she nursed him back to health, she discovered that he was a bounty hunter with an unquenchable thirst for justice, and also the man with whom she was falling in love.

TOO MANY COOKS by Joanne Pence
Somebody is spoiling the broth in this second delightful adventure featuring the spicy romantic duo from *Something's Cooking*. Homicide detective Paavo Smith must find who is killing the owners of popular San Francisco restaurants and, at the same time, come to terms with his feelings for Angelina Amalfi, the gorgeous but infuriating woman who loves to dabble in sleuthing.

JUST ONE OF THOSE THINGS by Leigh Riker
Sara Reid, having left her race car driver husband and their glamorous but stormy marriage, returns to Rhode Island in the hope of protecting her five-year-old daughter from further emotional harm. Then Colin McAllister arrives—bringing with him the shameful memory of their one night together six years ago and a life-shattering secret.

COMING NEXT MONTH

COMANCHE MAGIC by Catherine Anderson

The latest addition to the bestselling Comanche series. When Chase Wolf first met Fanny Graham, he was immediately attracted to her, despite her unsavory reputation. Long ago Fanny had lost her belief in miracles, but when Chase Wolf came into her life he taught her that the greatest miracle of all was true love.

SEPARATING by Susan Bowden

The triumphant story of a woman's comeback from a shattering divorce to a fulfilling, newfound love. After twenty-five years of marriage, Riona Jarvin's husband leaves her for a younger woman. Riona is in shock—until she meets a new man and finds that life indeed has something wonderful to offer her.

HEARTS OF GOLD by Martha Longshore

A sizzling romantic adventure set in 1860s Sacramento. For years Kora Hunter had worked for the family newspaper, but now everyone around her was insisting that she give it up for marriage to a long-time suitor and family friend. Meanwhile, Mason Fielding had come to Sacramento to escape from the demons in his past. Neither he nor Kora expected a romantic entanglement, considering the odds stacked against them.

IN MY DREAMS by Susan Sizemore

Award-winning author Susan Sizemore returns to time travel in this witty, romantic romp. In ninth-century Ireland, during the time of the Viking raids, a beautiful young druid named Brianna inadvertently cast a spell that brought a rebel from 20th-century Los Angeles roaring back through time on his Harley-Davidson. Sammy Bergen was so handsome that at first she mistook him for a god—but he was all too real.

SURRENDER THE NIGHT by Susan P. Teklits

Lovely Vanessa Davis had lent her talents to the patriotic cause by seducing British soldiers to learn their battle secrets. She had never allowed herself to actually give up her virtue to any man until she met Gabriel St. Claire, a fellow Rebel spy and passionate lover.

SUNRISE by Chassie West

Sunrise, North Carolina, is such a small town that everyone knows everyone else's business—or so they think. After a long absence, Leigh Ann Warren, a burned out Washington, D.C., police officer, returns home to Sunrise. Once there, she begins to investigate crimes both old and new. Only after a dangerous search for the truth can Leigh help lay the town's ghosts to rest and start her own life anew with the one man meant for her.

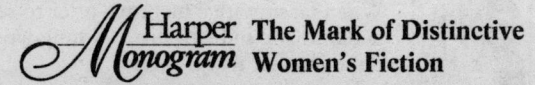

Harper Monogram The Mark of Distinctive Women's Fiction

Harper Monogram By Mail

Looking For Love?
Try HarperMonogram's Bestselling Romances

TAPESTRY
by Maura Seger
An aristocratic Saxon woman loses her heart to the Norman man who rules her conquered people.

DREAM TIME
by Parris Afton Bonds
In the distant outback of Australia, a mother and daughter are ready to sacrifice everything for their dreams of love.

RAIN LILY
by Candace Camp
In the aftermath of the Civil War in Arkansas, a farmer's wife struggles between duty and passion.

COMING UP ROSES
by Catherine Anderson
Only buried secrets could stop the love of a young widow and her new beau from bloomimg.

ONE GOOD MAN
by Terri Herrington
When faced with a lucrative offer to seduce a billionaire industrialist, a young woman discovers her true desires.

LORD OF THE NIGHT
by Susan Wiggs
A Venetian lord dedicated to justice suspects a lucious beauty of being involved in a scandalous plot.

ORCHIDS IN MOONLIGHT
by Patricia Hagan
Caught in a web of intrigue in the dangerous West, a man and a woman fight to regain their overpowering dream of love.

A SEASON OF ANGELS
by Debbie Macomber
Three willing but wacky angels must teach their charges a lesson before granting a Christmas wish.
National Bestseller

For Fastest Service
—
Visa & MasterCard Holders Call
1-800-331-3761

MAIL TO: HarperCollins Publishers
P. O. Box 588 Dunmore, PA 18512-0588
OR CALL: (800) 331-3761 (Visa/MasterCard)

Yes, please send me the books I have checked:

☐ TAPESTRY (0-06-108018-7)	$5.50
☐ DREAM TIME (0-06-108026-8)	$5.50
☐ RAIN LILY (0-06-108028-4)	$5.50
☐ COMING UP ROSES (0-06-108060-8)	$5.50
☐ ONE GOOD MAN (0-06-108021-7)	$4.99
☐ LORD OF THE NIGHT (0-06-108052-7)	$5.50
☐ ORCHIDS IN MOONLIGHT (0-06-108038-1)	$5.50
☐ A SEASON OF ANGELS (0-06-108184-1)	$4.99

SUBTOTAL ....$_____
POSTAGE AND HANDLING ....$ 2.00
SALES TAX (Add applicable sales tax) ....$_____
TOTAL: $_____

*(ORDER 4 OR MORE TITLES AND POSTAGE & HANDLING IS FREE! Orders of less than 4 books, please include $2.00 p/h. Remit in US funds, do not send cash.)

Name _____

Address _____

City _____

State _____ Zip _____   Allow up to 6 weeks delivery.
(Valid only in US & Canada)   Prices subject to change.
HO 751

ATTENTION: ORGANIZATIONS AND CORPORATIONS

Most HarperPaperbacks are available at special quantity discounts for bulk purchases for sales promotions, premiums, or fund-raising. For information, please call or write:
Special Markets Department, HarperCollins Publishers, 10 East 53rd Street, New York, N.Y. 10022.
Telephone: (212) 207-7528. Fax: (212) 207-7222.